THE WINGS OF DRAGONS

Book One of The Dragoon Saga

Josh VanBrakle

 Arboreal Press

This book is a work of fiction. All characters and events in this book are fictitious. Any resemblance to persons living or dead or actual events is a coincidence.

Arboreal Press
Sidney, NY 13838
www.arborealpress.com

Library of Congress Preassigned Control Number: 2013907674
ISBN-13: 978-0-9891957-0-6
First Edition: 2013
10 9 8 7 6 5 4 3 2 1
Cover design and typesetting by Heather Hilson

Find out more about the author and upcoming books at
www.joshvanbrakle.com

ACKNOWLEDGMENTS

Writing my first novel has been both the most laborious and the most rewarding undertaking of my life. It is also something that never could have happened without the support of some truly incredible people. First and foremost, I want to thank Shannon Delany, author of the *13 to Life* series and the *Weather Witch* series, whose writing workshops literally changed my life and convinced me to pursue my dream. Shannon, without your advice, I would never have completed this novel.

I also owe a great deal to those who reviewed drafts of this manuscript and whose comments and copy-edits helped me refine my work. Tom Foulkrod, Jim Hilson, Gretchen Smith, and my dear wife Christine, I truly appreciate your willingness to stick with me through the numerous revisions and support me as I begin my writing journey.

Finally, I especially want to thank Heather Hilson, who turned my manuscript into an actual book. Heather designed my cover as well as handling the typesetting and formatting for both the paperback and e-book versions.

If this book is any good, it is only because of these wonderful people.

TABLE OF CONTENTS

PROLOGUE

Bitter cold engulfed the young woman as she realized the truth. She would not live to see the dawn.

"Stay in the house!" her husband had cried to her. Less than an hour ago, that's where she'd been: curled up next to the fire and falling asleep with her head against his arm. Now she stood in the middle of a pasture, clutching a tiny package to her chest with all her strength. Tears cascaded from her cheeks at the sight of the two figures before her. Mere yards away, they clashed in the night, sparks flying each time their blades met. In spite of her husband's warning, she'd followed him. She wouldn't cower inside while he fought for his life and those of his family! As long as she breathed, she would never abandon him, nor would she relinquish her cherished bundle that the pair of them, against all common sense, had created together.

The fiercest spark yet lit up the pasture, and a moment later a sword arced through the air toward her, landing on the ground not a foot away. Frantically, she stared into the darkness, and she just barely made out the silhouette of a disarmed man on his knees, pleading. His triumphant opponent paid no heed and stabbed deep into the defeated man's chest.

With a single glance at the sword before her, the woman knew which fighter had fallen. She wailed in the night at the death of her husband.

At the sound, the murderer turned and walked slowly toward her. The woman froze, so filled with fear she couldn't think. She gazed upon the villain's foul blade, still dripping with her husband's blood. Tracing with her eyes up the killer's arm, she beheld the face of her death. The murderer hesitated briefly and then, fist clenching around the hilt as though steeling for what would come next, swung.

The woman felt surprisingly little as the blade sliced through her neck, and shock, more than pain, caused her to drop to the ground. As she fell, her tightly guarded bundle came loose from her arms and rolled a short distance, coming to a stop next to her fallen husband's sword. The cloths protecting it fell away, revealing a tiny infant boy, the tip of his shoulder resting gently on the blade's hilt.

As the attacker readied the third death blow of the night, the dying mother beheld her son open his eyes, his piercing sky blue eyes. She flashed back to earlier that night, when those same eyes, this time belonging to her husband, stared at her with worry. "He will be hated," he'd told her, "just as I am hated."

"He will be loved," she'd declared without the slightest doubt, "just as you are loved."

He'd smiled at her, the same sad smile that made her fall in love with him, the one that hid nothing of his grief. Just once, she wished she could have seen him smile at her genuinely, from the other side of that pain.

Instead, the last image the woman saw was the downward thrust of the murderer's blade toward her son.

CHAPTER ONE
Left in the Tower

Toah. Toah. Toah.

Iren Saitosan's eyes snapped open at the sound of something he almost never heard, yet instantly recognized: the echoes of footsteps on the stone tower stairs leading to his chamber.

Toah. Toah. Toah.

He threw off his tattered blankets and leapt out of the hard bed. Almost no one came up here. Every so often, children would dare each other to see who could climb the farthest up the steps without getting frightened. They considered scaling the tower all the way to the top and knocking on the Left's door the ultimate sign of bravery.

Toah. Toah.

These steps didn't belong to children though. They were too heavy, and there was no associated chatter. Those not making the climb always teased the challenger, alternating between goading them on and threatening them with what the evil Left might do to them if they dared to continue. No, these steps came from an adult.

Toah. Toah.

Iren tensed. Since the day King Azuluu had decreed that he must live up here away from "normal people," no adult had ever climbed the tower.

Toah.

That was odd. Iren furrowed his brow. The steps were slowing down, as though whoever made them were hesitating. It was probably just some gawker, no different from the children, coming to see the freak, the Left.

The sound of nervous breathing made Iren focus on his chamber door.

Whoever had come had made it all the way to the top and now stood just outside. The door was already slightly ajar, just as Iren had left it. He grinned. This was his favorite part. He couldn't help but glance above the door at the wooden bucket resting precariously against the top of the door and the wall. His little trick always worked on the kids; he wondered if an adult would be stupid enough to fall for it too. Folding his arms, he leaned against the windowsill and waited.

After a moment a loud grunt came from the steps, and then the door flung open as the intruder shoved his way in with a shoulder charge.

"Ow!"

The bucket slammed into the man's head, dumped its load, and then rolled away, rumbling on the stone floor. Its former contents, a full load of water, now soaked the intruder. Across the room, Iren cocked his head sideways and smiled innocently, saying, "Should have knocked."

The intruder put a hand to his head, feeling for a bruise. "Captain Angustion warned me you might pull a stunt like this." He started to say more, but some of the water snuck inside his mouth, making him gag.

"That's smart, Balear, spitting it out," Iren said lightly. "Do you know how many times I've washed my clothes in that?"

Balear's face paled, then just as quickly reddened as he shouted, "You left-handed demon-child!"

Iren didn't react to Balear's outburst. He'd been called worse in his tenure at Haldessa Castle. Instead, he did his best to look unintimidated, even though Balear carried a broadsword on his belt. "Why don't you head to the baths and wash off?" he suggested. "Also, I hate to tell you, but you should really consider drying your uniform. That's a very unbecoming look for an officer in the Castle Guard."

Balear seethed, sending drops of water cascading off him.

"Something the matter, Balear?" Iren could barely restrain his laughter. Balear was perhaps the most stuck-up of all Haldessa's residents. His short-cropped blonde hair and black uniform were always immaculate. It must be killing him to have a Left get the better of him, especially one wearing discarded jester's motley and with unkempt tan hair that hung loosely around his shoulders. "Here," Iren offered with mock sincerity, "let me help you back down the stairs."

He stepped forward and reached out his left hand, but Balear recoiled as though from a poisonous snake. "Stay away from me!" Wild-eyed, the sergeant located a small rock sitting atop Iren's nearby dresser. He threw it, and Iren winced as it struck the floor just short of his foot.

When the stone clattered to a stop, Iren's grin was gone. Numbly, he picked up and dusted off the pebble, cradling it like an infant. Setting it gently on the windowsill behind him, he turned his back on Balear and said no more.

He'd hoped it would be enough for the thick-headed sergeant to get his meaning, but apparently Balear was too stupid for that. Behind him, the soldier barked, "Hurry and make yourself decent, or as decent as a freak like you can get. That order comes from Captain Angustion himself. The king's ordered a celebration tonight to honor the captain's successes against the Quodivar. All castle residents must attend, and while I can't begin to understand why, the captain says that includes you. Make sure you come."

Iren scoffed, responding without turning around, "Why would I do that? All Amroth wants to do is prance around and recount his, no doubt, single-handed victory."

Balear stiffened. "How dare you insult Captain Angustion! Our gracious captain extends you a personal invitation, something you cannot possibly deserve, yet you haven't the slightest humility at his offering. You foul, disgusting, Left cur!"

With that, Balear stormed from the room, slamming the door behind him. Its harsh ring, and the harsher ring of "cur," echoed mockingly off the stone walls for what felt like an eternity afterward. Iren folded his arms on the windowsill. It was bad enough King Azuluu forced him to live up here without straw-haired bigots bothering him. With a deep breath, he vainly attempted to wipe the encounter from his mind.

The scenery admittedly helped. Haldessa Castle and its surrounding city were built on a bluff overlooking the ocean, and Iren never tired of the salty smell or the way the sun sparkled on the water. He wished he could swim in it, just once, but he wasn't permitted outside the castle walls.

With a sigh, Iren pulled himself back into his room. He considered his unparalleled view atop the Tower of Divinion one of his life's few pleasures, but today it just depressed him. His tiny chamber felt increasingly like a cage. He could see the incredible landscape of Lodia, the rolling farm fields dotted with villages and wooded thickets, but he couldn't touch it.

More than anyone else, Balear always reminded him of that fact. Iren clenched his fists. In so many ways, they were the same. They were almost the same height, just under six feet, and had similar muscled builds.

"Even in age," he muttered. At twenty, Balear had just two years on

Iren.

Despite their outward similarities, however, he and the sergeant differed in one way, the one that mattered most. Because of that difference, the right-handed Balear had achieved everything Iren desired and yet would never accomplish. Balear had joined the Castle Guard at fourteen. He'd battled the Quodivar and killed dozens of them without ever suffering more than minor injuries. Everyone who served under him enjoyed his command. Despite his young age, rumors already circulated that Balear would replace Captain Angustion someday. Iren believed them. Even Amroth openly considered the young man his protégé.

By contrast, Iren had never once fought in a battle, a tournament, or indeed done anything noteworthy at all. When he'd asked Amroth to join the Castle Guard at fourteen, the captain had just laughed and told him to go away.

Seeking a distraction, Iren grabbed his stolen mop from a corner and began cleaning up the water spilled by Balear's intrusion. As he swept, shouting from the window caught his attention. He recognized the voice immediately. One of the Castle Guard drill instructors was holding a practice session.

Iren's grip tightened on the wooden handle. Facing the window, he held the mop before him like a sword. As the officer bellowed commands, Iren followed through with each of them, swinging the mop with increasing speed and power. Beads of sweat formed on his temples, but he ignored them. While he practiced, he didn't have to think. He didn't have to think about the soldiers in the courtyard below developing a lifelong camaraderie that would never include him. He didn't have to recall the angry eyes of every man in the company the first and only time he'd tried to join them for practice. He could forget their jeers as the instructor chased him away at the point of a sword.

When the session ended, however, all those thoughts came flooding to him at once. Slamming the mop on the floor, Iren shouted, "It's not fair! Everyone else in the whole kingdom is right-handed. Why am I the only Left?" Grasping the rock Balear had thrown at him, Iren whipped around and launched it, not bothering to aim or even care what he hit.

In truth, he could damage little. His chamber had little adornment: a hard bed with three discarded blankets and a dresser with the few outfits he'd fished from the trash. The only object of merit was a large painting hung on the wall beside the dresser. As if guided by fate, the rock struck its frame, and the artwork clattered to the floor.

The harsh sound yanked Iren from his temper. He knelt and retrieved both the stone and the fallen painting. They were his finest treasures. The stone, little more than a black pebble, had come from the ocean. The surf had tossed it until it had worn perfectly smooth. Years ago, one of the castle children had brought it home, but his mother had commanded him to get rid of it. Iren swiped it that night, his only possession that had ever touched the sea.

As for the painting, while he couldn't truly claim to own it, he still considered it his. It had hung in this tower since long before he arrived, yet it apparently held such low value that no one bothered to remove it when he took up residence. Still, he couldn't help feeling a deep attachment to it, the only thing in his room he hadn't stolen or pulled from the garbage.

Iren surveyed it closely. "No harm done," he whispered with relief.

Returning the painting to the wall, Iren stepped back and took in its splendid image: a serpentine dragon. Though unsigned, the painting's remarkable realism made the great beast almost come alive. Blue streaks and hairs off its spine accentuated its gleaming white body. Its wings stretched beyond the painting's borders, so that they appeared to extend forever to the heavens. Though its mouth opened wide in a silent roar, its expression invoked not terror but majesty.

The painting's frame held a small plaque that read, "Divinion, the Holy Dragon." Iren smiled, proud of his unshared knowledge. It gave him a small satisfaction, knowing something the vast majority of the populace did not. Though everyone called Haldessa's tallest spire the Tower of Divinion, few understood the name's origin. Growing up, Iren overheard mothers tell their children that long ago, the tower served as a temple to worship dragons, sacred creatures that brought balance to the world.

Of course, no one used it for that purpose now. Nobody believed in the dragons anymore. Most had forgotten that they even had names, let alone what those names were.

As Iren looked at the dragon's face in the artwork, though, for a moment he saw more than a painting. The creature stared out at the room with sky blue eyes, eyes that eerily matched Iren's. Their gaze bored through his body, and a sudden hopelessness washed over him. Barely conscious of his actions, Iren backed away from the painting and collapsed on his bed, burying his head in his hands.

CHAPTER TWO
Amroth's Speech

What exactly made Iren get off his bed an hour later, wipe his face, and attend Amroth's feast after all, even he didn't know. Perhaps he longed to escape the dragon's probing look. Or perhaps he simply realized that, should he not attend, he likely wouldn't eat until at least the following morning. Reluctantly, he left his room and plodded down the steps of the Tower of Divinion, emerging into the long shadows of the castle courtyard.

Much to his pleasure, Iren found the area mostly deserted. Pairs of guards still lined each doorway except, Iren noted with distaste, the one to the Tower of Divinion. A group of five young women, dressed in gowns for the evening's festivities, chatted and giggled excitedly. Iren rolled his eyes at the noise; no doubt each girl hoped that her dolled-up looks would impress the great Amroth, well known as Lodia's most eligible bachelor.

The moment Iren began walking across the courtyard, the girls stopped talking and stared at him with cold, empty eyes. Most everyone in the castle looked at him that way, with eyes that saw past him, a thing so contemptuous the senses rejected it.

Doing his best to ignore the women, Iren headed for an archway at the northern end of the courtyard. The guards there glared at him, but they said nothing as he approached. Their lack of response barely fazed him; few people ever opened their mouths around him. Passing them without a second glance, Iren walked down a long stone corridor lined with torches. Gradually, he began smelling the sweet odors of fresh water, perfumes, and soaps, signaling that he'd almost arrived at his destination.

At last the passage split in two, with a pair of guards blocking the left path. For a moment Iren stood at the intersection, debating. He could hear vociferous calls from both directions. Initially he turned to the left, but when the soldiers drew their swords, he backed down and went to the right.

"The one place in this stupid castle they'll actually stop me from entering," he grumbled.

After a short walk, the new passage opened up, revealing one of Haldessa Castle's most spectacular features: its baths. At over a hundred feet square and thirty feet high, only the grand hall surpassed them in size. Thick stone columns supported the ceiling, and seafoam green Tacumsahen tiles covered every surface. The light reflecting off them from the numerous torches gave the space a warm, ethereal glow.

Iren followed the outer border of the room. It was an open space wide enough for two men to walk abreast with the chamber wall on one side and an interconnected series of seven-foot high wooden changing closets on the other. To Iren's delight, most had their doors shut, indicating they were in use. Better still, he could hear splashing in the pool. Evidently, he wasn't the only one planning a bath before the feast.

After walking nearly halfway around the room, he found an unoccupied changing station and stepped inside. The closet had just enough space for one person, but it had a door on two sides. One, which Iren had entered, faced the chamber's outer wall, while the other faced inward toward the pool. A stout wooden shelf about two feet off the ground provided a place to sit, as well as a spot to house a stack of white linens.

Undressing, Iren stifled a chuckle. He never tired of what came next. Grabbing a towel and washcloth from the pile, he slammed open the door facing the pool and paraded forward, grinning broadly. At the noise, several faces turned and initially disregarded him as just another bather, albeit a noisy one. A few seconds later, their heads snapped in a double take as they realized that bather's identity. Shouts filled the bath, and the furious splashing of water as everyone rushed for the edge only added to the din. In less than five minutes, the uproar ceased. The chamber had emptied completely.

Sliding into the water, Iren laughed. "How lucky I am!" he shouted, a little louder than he'd intended. "Nobody else gets to bathe in private!"

Iren neither knew nor cared how long he bathed. As long as he stayed, nobody else would dare enter the chamber. Whenever he came here, he typically stayed for hours, gleefully noting that all the while he forced dozens of other boys and men in the castle to go on smelling awfully.

As he relaxed, he couldn't help but admit a grudging admiration for the people who'd constructed the baths. To heat the water, the engineers had excavated a basement chamber that passed beneath both this bath and the women's adjacent to it. Inside that room, fires burned constantly. The basement's location as a heat source proved ideal. Not only did it make for tepid water, but it also gave the tile floor a warm touch. Even on the coldest winter nights, one could always thaw out here.

At the pool's far end, just below the water line, Iren spied the chamber's water source: a heavy metal gate, linked by thick chains to pulley systems on either side of the room. The gate separated the pool from a long canal that connected to the clear waters of the Ute River, which flowed past the northern side of the castle and cascaded in a magnificent waterfall to the sea. A second gate linked the pool to another canal that allowed used water to exit. When the baths needed changing, castle workers opened the second gate to drain the pool, then closed it and opened the first, letting fresh water flow in. The staff obeyed a rigorous schedule in replacing the water, changing it daily precisely when the sun reached its highest point.

Iren closed his eyes and dozed, as close to content as he ever came. When he awoke, he reluctantly pulled himself from the water, dried off, dressed, and made for the passageway back to the courtyard.

As he reached the doorway out of the men's bath, though, a shadow passed the corner of his eye. Reflexively, he turned, watching intently, but the only movement came from torchlight playing off the pool's surface and the shiny tiles.

Shaking his head at his own paranoia, Iren returned to the courtyard. By now, the sun had set, plunging the open area into darkness. As his eyes adjusted, Iren noted that the guards had all gone, and even the crowing maidens had vanished.

"The feast must have started already," Iren said to the empty quad, rubbing his hands together. This was great. He could sneak in without anyone noticing, all the better for pilfering a bite or pulling someone's chair out from under them.

He crossed the courtyard, went through another archway, and traveled down a hallway until he came upon a massive set of wide open, thick cherry doors. Festive carvings adorned the behemoths, alerting all that the room beyond was a place for celebration.

And indeed it was. Haldessa Castle's grand hall had no other purposes besides opulence and revelry, and tonight it was in full form. More than twice the size of both the men's and women's bathhouses combined, its high vaulted ceilings precluded the need for support columns and made the room appear to stretch on almost infinitely. Eight gargantuan chandeliers, each glimmering with gold plating, lit the hall, their thousands of crystals spreading the light from hundreds of candles. The room contained enough tables and chairs to seat every man, woman, and child in the castle. Upon those tables the kitchen staff had piled inordinate amounts of food: whole roast chickens and pigs, trays of each of the eight Lodian cheese styles as well as two goat's milk varieties imported from the Tengu mountain men of Eregos, mounds of fruits and vegetables procured from local farms, fresh breads and cakes direct from the castle bakery, and of course, more wine, beer, and spirits than the entire population of Haldessa could consume in a week, let alone an evening.

Near the room's far end sat a circular wooden platform raised two feet above the floor. Upon it, three troupes of musicians armed with trumpets, drums, flutes, and raucous singers belted out the king's favorite songs. Two court jesters and no less than a dozen dancing girls in billowing skirts paraded around the stage's edge, swaying in time with the music. It came as no surprise that many of the older men in the crowd had chosen their seats as close to the platform as possible.

The instant Iren entered the hall, he grimaced. Why did parties always have to include so much noise? It didn't help that the feast had apparently started some time ago, and already the assembly had become thoroughly drunk.

Iren nicked some food off the tray of a passing servant and took up a standing position along the back wall, searching for easy victims to prank. The ideal candidate, of course, had to be King Azuluu. Seated at the front of the dining hall on a golden throne, the obese king laughed and carried on so loudly that even from over a hundred yards away, Iren could clearly discern his bass voice. Wine and grease spilled down his fine purple robes as he plowed through yet another turkey leg in one hand and a goblet the size of Iren's head in the other.

In the place of honor immediately to the king's right sat the man of the hour: Captain Amroth Angustion, leader of the Castle Guard. Though in his early forties, his broad shoulders and toned body indicated age hadn't decreased his physical prowess in the slightest. He wore the same black military uniform as Balear, except the captain's had gold trim and, Iren wryly noted, wasn't soaked in old laundry water. Amroth laughed heartily, slapping his knee at the king's raunchy jokes. The five young women Iren had passed in the courtyard encircled the captain, playing with his auburn hair and offering to help him eat and drink.

Of course, it wasn't all fun for the captain. Iren smiled thinly. As loud as Azuluu sounded from the back of the room, Iren couldn't imagine how Amroth's left ear felt at the moment.

No one else sat at the front table with Azuluu and Amroth. The king had no family, though he had a well-deserved reputation for debauchery. New claims of illegitimate children cropped up almost monthly. He had no advisors either; he had no need for them. With the exception of occasional Quodivar raids, Lodia had been peaceful for nearly two hundred years.

Finally Azuluu stumbled to his feet, nearly falling on his face before Amroth reached out and steadied the fat king. Stretching his arms to either side, Azuluu called in his booming voice for silence. The volume in the hall continued unabated. Azuluu shouted again, and this time Amroth rose beside him. The room fell silent at once, and all the dancing girls and musicians cleared the dais to make space for the captain. As they did, Amroth, looking mildly embarrassed at upstaging Azuluu, sunk back into his chair.

Clearly unaware of what had just happened, the king stepped around his table to the platform. He raised a meaty hand and, still clenching his goblet, shouted, "Cheer with me, friends, for the great hero of our time has returned to us!"

Everyone in the hall save Iren cried, "Hail, hail!"

As the cheers subsided, Azuluu continued, "Long under my reign, and that of my fathers, has Lodia prospered. To what do we owe our thanks for this wealth? Naturally, much of the praise must be lavished upon myself. Without a strong leader, no nation can survive."

The audience responded with more than a few chuckles, but Azuluu ignored them as he prattled on, "However, some matters no king can resolve alone. We face one such challenge even now. As many of you know, a bandit gang calling themselves the Quodivar has been attacking our merchant convoys. I cannot stop them by myself, but fortunately a champion has emerged who will combat the Quodivar and keep our caravans safe. His name is Amroth!"

Cheers of, "Hail Amroth!" and, "Hail the captain!" filled the hall.

"Amroth," the king continued, "I know of no mightier warrior in all of Lodia, and your talents extend off the battlefield as well. I cannot in good conscience allow you to remain merely a captain. No, for the first time since taking the throne, I will formally offer to someone the position of king's chief advisor. I offer it to you, Captain Amroth Angustion. Do you accept?"

The entire crowd, Iren included, became silent. The king had no heir; illegitimate children were ineligible. In Lodian governance, if a king had no direct male descendent, rule passed to his chief advisor. Naming Amroth to that position virtually proclaimed him the next king of Lodia.

Amroth froze for a pair of seconds at the king's words. Quickly, however, he regained his composure and answered Azuluu, "My liege, you honor me beyond words. If this is how I may best serve this great nation, then I cannot decline. I humbly accept the position of chief advisor. I hope to bring glory to the station as well as you in all my actions henceforth."

The audience erupted in applause at Amroth's acceptance, and now cries of "Hail the king!" accompanied the cheers of Amroth's name. Iren folded his arms and scowled at all the useless flattery.

Content with his speech, the king took his seat and downed his glass in a single gulp before nodding to Amroth. The meaning was unmistakable. Amroth couldn't possibly get away without a speech after becoming heir to Lodia's throne. After only a brief hesitation, Amroth rose with much ceremony and took the platform. He addressed the crowd, "Fellow lords and ladies! I welcome your cheers, but I do not deserve them. Without the gallantry of my fine companies, I surely could not have achieved my victories these past days. These thieves, these hoodlums, these Quodivar, have arms that rival our own and viciousness far surpassing mere bandits. I believe their ambitions lie beyond simply raiding our traders. In fact it would not surprise me if they seek no less than the utter domination of Lodia itself!"

Gasps filled the room. Only when the clamor began to die itself down did Amroth press on, "Take a look around this grand ballroom. Gaze upon its walls, lined with tapestries and paintings passed down through generations of Lodians. I myself am fortunate enough to have six of my own works on display here. It humbles me to have my paintings in such company. In between missions I have labored hard on my art, so that future generations may remember me for more than just bloodshed. Into each, including my favorite," he pointed at a portrait of Azuluu seated at his throne, "I have striven to include the deepest detail, the utmost intricacy, and the fullness of every brushstroke. Into these paintings I have poured my soul, and I will fight long and hard to protect them from brutes like the Quodivar. But know that I would sacrifice all these paintings to the fire if, in so doing, it brought peace to Lodia. The security of this nation means everything to me. This country is truly great. Its people are truly great. And I shall never, while breath is in me, allow Lodia to fall!"

Iren yawned. Although Amroth's words enamored the rest of the audience, Iren just found the exaggerated rhetoric annoying. It was all a bunch of nonsense; the captain didn't deserve the attention he was getting for it. What this party needed wasn't more boring speeches but something truly spectacular, something the attendees would never forget. He glanced around, seeking inspiration. There were any number of pies and gravy boats that he could toss into the crowd, but those wouldn't have nearly enough effect.

Then he spied it. One of the chandeliers hung directly above the platform on which Amroth stood. Tracing with his eye, Iren found the single heavy rope that held the chandelier in place. To light its candles, the fixture needed to be lowered to the floor, so the rope connected from the chandelier via a pulley system to a metal hook on the wall. Ordinarily, a dozen strong men or more would work together to lower the light and then raise it again. Snagging a carving knife off the nearest table, Iren stealthily made his way across the room.

If Amroth noticed Iren's actions, he didn't show it. He dropped his volume and adopted a more somber tone, drawing in the audience with his tension. "Much like our great king," he gestured to Azuluu, who smiled stupidly, "I cannot win this fight alone. Our latest battle with the Quodivar taught me much. I rode out not a fortnight past with a company of two hundred men to squelch these vermin. The Quodivar, however, do not fight like soldiers. Indeed, they do not fight like men at all. They enter battle only when they know they can catch their opponents unawares, and if the situation turns against them, they flee like cockroaches. Many fine men who rode with me did not reenter these castle gates. We cannot fight this enemy as soldiers. However, I have a plan that will rid us of these vile cowards once and for all!"

Everyone in the room leaned forward, desperate to hear Amroth's strategy. The Quodivar were the greatest threat to Lodia's economy in more than a century, and the vast majority of the nobles gathered here had strong ownership in at least one merchant company. Amroth provided hope not only for peace, but for fat wallets as well.

"My plan requires great risk, but it is the only hope we have. Large armies do not work against the Quodivar. My last mission proved this. Instead, I will assemble a small team, an elite force of Haldessa's finest. With this team we shall seek out the Quodivar and battle them the way they battle us: with stealth and cunning. I come here tonight to name the two men with whom I intend to enter battle. I will trust these two with my life, and with the fate of Lodia itself."

A young boy near the front cried excitedly, "Who? Who will save us along with you, Captain Angustion?"

Amroth smiled kindly at the child, apparently not begrudging the interruption at all. "The first is a man whom you all know as a fine swordsman, a capable leader, and a loyal companion: Sergeant Balear Platarch!"

The crowd cheered heartily, and Balear, seated about midway between Amroth and the back of the room, stood and waved his hand with an embarrassed gesture. He bore the vacant expression of someone who had clearly drunk too much. Amroth motioned for him to come to the platform and stand beside him. Balear tripped more than once, but in the end he reached his beloved commander.

Across the room, Iren arrived at the chandelier's cord. He spun the knife in his hand expectantly. He would time it just as Amroth finished his speech. The moment they stepped off the stage, he would cut cord and drop the chandelier. It would crash horrendously behind them, everyone would gasp, and he would have the pleasure of watching both Amroth and Balear pick themselves off the floor.

When the cheers calmed, Amroth became contemplative as he said, "The second person I have chosen you all know well, and yet, I would guess, also do not know at all. I have thought long and hard on this choice. I do not make it lightly. I make it for the sake of Lodia, for we must have the best to succeed in this endeavor. For the final of my group I have chosen Iren Saitosan!"

The shouts of praise died in the crowd's throats. Iren whipped his head up, utterly shocked, and then it happened. As his body jerked to face the captain, his hand swung downward. The sharpened carving knife sliced through the chandelier's rope without pause.

Only Amroth's quick reactions saved him from death. When he'd called Iren's name, he had turned to face the lad, revealing that he'd known all along where Iren was. Reaching out, the captain grabbed Balear by the sleeve and tugged hard. The pair spilled over the dais just as the chandelier smashed down, splintering the stage, the light fixture, and all the musical instruments into countless pieces. Shards rained over the audience, but fortunately, no one was seriously injured.

As the crowd slowly recovered, all eyes turned to Iren. He gulped at their faces. Some looked at him with fear, others with loathing, and still more with blank stares pretending he didn't exist at all.

King Azuluu slammed his meaty hands on either side of his throne. "Seize him!" he roared. "Bring him forward to meet the justice of Lodia!"

Two Castle Guard members approached Iren. Though they looked like touching him was the last thing they wanted to do, they grabbed him roughly and shoved him on his knees before the king, Amroth, and Balear.

"Too long have we suffered your antics! Now you've nearly killed the heir to the throne!" The king swung his fat fist. "I took you in when any other man would have let you die, filthy Left orphan dog. This is the thanks I get for my kindness. Well, it ends here. Justice! Execution!"

The crowd cheered, their faces gleaming with sadistic glee. The denizens of Haldessa enjoyed nothing more than a public beheading.

Iren scowled at the unfairness of it all. He hadn't meant to hurt anyone; it was just a mistake of timing. The oaf only wanted an excuse to get rid of him.

"My liege, please do not do that."

Iren's eyes leapt to the speaker: none other than Captain Amroth Angustion himself. He had spoken quietly, so that only Balear, Azuluu, Iren, and the guards grasping him could hear. Even so, the crowd fell silent just seeing Amroth's lips move.

"What is the meaning of this?" the king asked curtly. "Explain yourself, Amroth!"

The captain gestured at Iren. "If he dies, my mission cannot succeed. I can't defeat the Quodivar without him. Choose between your vengeance and your desire for security in Lodia."

The king looked like he might detonate. "Just a minute!" he cried, his face purple. "How can you think you can rely on Ir...Ir..." he seemed unable to bring himself to utter Iren's name, "that thing for this mission of yours? This plan risks not only your life, but the hopes and dreams of all Lodians. With such stakes, you would put your trust in a Left?"

Amroth's expression leveled, and his voice matched his even look. He raised his volume so the crowd could hear, "No soldier in Lodia can match Iren's strength. You've read the stories. He is a weapon. We should use him as such."

Iren couldn't decide whether Amroth's words made him happy or upset. True, the captain was sticking up for him as no one had ever done before, but getting referred to as an object wasn't exactly uplifting.

An old woman near the front of the crowd stood. Iren recognized her as Haldessa's librarian. "Captain Angustion, please think of what you're saying! I have read all the great texts of Lodia. I know of these Lefts; the oldest histories speak of them. None mention a name, but they all agree on two points. The Lefts spawn from darkness, and they bring death and destruction to all in their path! Just look at that chandelier!" She turned slightly, revealing a thin cut on her shoulder where a piece of glass from the shattered fixture had sliced into her. "That monster wounded many tonight, including myself. Worse, he almost crushed you and Sergeant Platarch to death, simply for his own amusement! He may look like a child, but he is a devil!"

"Indeed," Amroth spoke as though the librarian had proven his point. "Not many can claim to have nearly killed Amroth Angustion. Instead of wasting such destructive talent, why not point him in the direction of the Quodivar?"

The crowd had nothing to say to that, but Iren could see them all fuming, particularly the Castle Guard members. Probably they felt cheated, believing Iren had stolen their spot on Amroth's team.

Looking ill at ease, the king raised his hands. "We've all had a lot to drink tonight. Let's retire. Level heads will prevail in the morning. Guards, take the boy to the Tower of Divinion and ensure he stays there."

While no one had any desire to leave, the king had given his order. Slowly, the crowd headed out the back door. Several of those nearest Iren spat on him as they passed. Once everyone else departed, the two men clutching Iren dragged him to his tower chamber, tossed him inside, and slammed the door shut.

Iren pressed his ear to the door. From just outside he could hear the two men's tense breathing. He couldn't escape. Hopelessly, he walked to his room's window, staring into the starlit night. It was the first full moon of spring, and despite the crisp air, Iren found it clean and refreshing. If he had to pick a last night alive, this one would just about do it.

Why wait? Azuluu wouldn't change his mind on something like this, not even for Amroth. The castle residents would riot if the king denied them their spectacle. Iren clenched his teeth. Azuluu wouldn't let him die quickly. He would be tortured, publicly humiliated, and then executed in as grotesque a manner as Azuluu could devise. He would suffer immensely, just to put on a good show.

He slapped both palms on the windowsill. "Absolutely not!" If he had to die, he certainly wouldn't let them have fun with it. Sticking his head out the window, he noted the dark courtyard a dizzying distance below him. If he fell from this height, there was no way he could survive.

He had one foot on the sill when he heard a muffled scuffling on the other side of his door. Curious, he retreated from the brink and faced the tower steps. All fell silent for a moment, and then his door creaked open. Iren's eyes widened.

Standing there, the two guards unconscious at his feet, was Captain Amroth Angustion.

CHAPTER THREE
A Night of Three Murders

Iren stood frozen until Amroth hissed, "Quit stalling and give me a hand with these two." They dragged the soldiers into the room. Amroth swiftly shut the door behind him, leaning against it with his full weight so that no one could open it from the other side.

Finding his voice at last, Iren asked belligerently, "What on Raa do you think you're doing?"

In the wan moonlight, Amroth's mysterious countenance frightened Iren a little. "You pulled quite the stunt tonight. Thanks to you, I have to accelerate my plans."

The young man's ears grew hot. Unspoken between them was the fact that if Amroth hadn't stood up for him, Iren might well be dead now. Still, Amroth's actions made Iren suspicious. "What plans?"

"You've no doubt made the same determination I have about Azuluu. Tomorrow, he'll order me to choose a replacement and then execute you. He's left us no other choice. We'll leave immediately. Do you know the stables just inside the castle gate?"

Iren nodded, and Amroth continued, "Meet me there an hour before dawn. Make sure no one sees you. You shouldn't have any issues. Everyone's too drunk to pay much attention. You, Balear, and I will sneak out while everyone else is sleeping or fighting their hangovers."

With a skeptical look Iren asked, "You'll directly defy the king? Why? For that matter, why did you stand up for me, or want me on this mission in the first place? I can't fight!"

Amroth averted his face and remained silent for a long time. When he at last looked at Iren again, the smug, almost arrogant expression he had worn during much of the feast had disappeared. A forlorn look replaced it, one that gazed upon Iren in a way the boy had never seen before. It was not fear, or hate, or even a desire for him to go away.

It was pity.

"I'm sorry," Amroth struggled to say.

"For what?"

"I've made your life a nightmare."

Iren scowled. "You and everyone else in this castle."

Amroth shook his head. "No, you don't understand. They all treat you poorly, but I caused them to do so. With this mission, I'll atone for that mistake."

"What do you mean?"

Working his mouth, Amroth asked, "Do you know how you came to Haldessa Castle?"

"No. I've lived here my whole life."

"As I thought. You were only an infant when I brought you here."

Raising a disbelieving eyebrow, Iren asked, "You brought me here?"

The captain nodded. "Just over seventeen years ago."

Iren's head spun. He had, of course, wondered about his past for many years. He longed to know who the Lefts were, why people hated them so much, and why he was the only one. He could never get answers on his own, and nobody would ever talk to him about it. "Please, Captain," he pleaded, "tell me."

"Are you sure?" Amroth asked darkly. "Sometimes, ignorance is better than the truth."

Iren's voice hardened. "Yes. You can't expect me to say otherwise when you've already said what you have."

Amroth sighed and motioned to the bed. "You'd better sit down for this." Iren obeyed, and the captain began, "Seventeen years ago, I was a lieutenant in the Castle Guard. Because of my skill, Captain Tret Ortromp, a bull of a man and the Captain of the Guard before me, chose me to accompany him on an investigation. We'd heard rumors from farmers in Tropos Village that a Left man lived nearby. The villagers claimed he committed all sorts of terrible crimes. Officially, our mission was to verify their claims and, if true, arrest the Left. However, Captain Ortromp had other plans. He believed the legends about the Lefts and concluded that we couldn't capture one alive. Instead, after he learned the location of the farm where the Left supposedly lived, he decided we would go just after midnight and kill the man in his sleep."

Iren felt sick. He didn't like where Amroth's story was heading at all.

"The night we arrived at the farmhouse," the captain continued, "we found it deserted. At first we were surprised, but then we heard, off in the distance, the ringing of steel against steel. We crept toward the sounds, and we were shocked to come upon two human shapes clashing in the fields, their weapons sparking on impact. A third person huddled away from the combatants, clutching a package. I didn't know which of these people, if indeed any of them, was the Left we sought, but I sat transfixed as the battle unfolded.

"I can't say how long the pair fought, but it ended in an instant. One fighter lost his sword, the weapon landing but a few feet from the kneeling person. His enemy slew him with one stroke. Then, to my horror, the winner walked over to the helpless crouching person and sliced out their throat. I reached for my sword, but my captain stopped me. The murderer then hesitated, and I feared he'd noticed us. After what felt an eternity, though, he vanished into the night. Once he departed, Ortromp and I inspected the battlefield. The dead combatant was our Left; his sheath hung on his right hip. The kneeling person was a woman, and she too had departed this world. Whether or not she was a Left, I don't know. When we examined the bundle she guarded with her life, the contents shocked us both: an infant boy."

Iren barely managed to whisper a single word, "Me."

Amroth nodded. "I can only conclude that the two slain people on the field that night were your parents. I don't know why, but their killer must have chosen to spare you at the last moment."

Sitting on his bed, Iren's vision grayed. In all his years, he'd never once suspected that someone had murdered his parents. He couldn't believe it. A thousand questions filled his mind, but two took the fore. Who? Why?

Then a new question popped into his head, and struggling to regain his composure, he said, "Wait. If Ortromp hated Lefts enough to kill a defenseless man in his sleep, wouldn't he also want to slay a Left baby as well?"

Amroth began shaking, as though something terrible inside him were finally bubbling to the surface. At length he said, "I am that reason, Iren. Ortromp did want you dead. He ordered me to kill you, but I couldn't do it. Left or not, you were just an infant."

"I doubt Ortromp liked your decision."

Amroth collapsed beside the door, his head in his hands. "No, he didn't. He told me that while you might look like an innocent baby, if we let you grow, you would become a demon just like your father. Then he shoved me aside and said if I lacked the resolve to do what was necessary, he would. Sword drawn, he came for you."

Iren's heart thumped in his chest. Even though he knew he couldn't have died that night, Amroth's tone and the haunting moonlight filled him with dread.

"I didn't think twice," the captain cried. "You didn't choose to have a Left father. We didn't even know if you were left-handed. I couldn't accept Ortromp killing you, so I…I…"

All at once the captain, the great Captain Amroth Angustion, newly appointed heir to the throne, started shrieking in a panic, "I killed him, Iren! I attacked Ortromp from behind and stabbed him. My body shook when I realized what I had done. It still keeps me awake. He was my commander! I, who have risen to become head of Lodia's military, slew a Lodian officer!"

Iren's breathing came so rapidly he feared he would hyperventilate, but he couldn't stop himself. Amroth had murdered a superior officer on his behalf, a crime punishable by death.

"I knew I should take my own life," Amroth clutched his knees with both hands, pressing so tightly Iren thought the captain might break them, "but I couldn't do it. If I did, I would doom you as well. You would catch hypothermia and die in a day, making Ortromp's murder pointless. So instead of committing suicide, I buried your parents and my slain captain and set off for Haldessa Castle with you in my arms. Day and night I traveled, not pausing even to rest, until I returned to the castle late at night. I banged on the front gate, but no one came. At last, when I thought I would have to sleep outside, an old woman happened by and offered me shelter. I didn't know her, but she was tiny and appeared unable to cause any harm. She took me to her home, a hovel in the dirtiest section of Haldessa. She told me her name, Rondel Thara, and offered me what little food she had. Finally, she inquired about the bundle in my hands. When I showed you to her, she named you 'Iren Saitosan.'

"I suppose I could have left you with her, but she couldn't have supported you. Instead, the next morning I took you to King Azuluu. I lied to him, to my own king, that the Left had killed Ortromp, and that you were a normal orphan boy whose parents the Left had also slain. He should have executed me, but not knowing the truth, he promoted me to Captain of the Guard. He also took you in, for a time raising you as his own."

Iren nodded. "I vaguely remember. He taught me to speak, as well as how to read and write. At least until he realized I preferred holding my pen in my left hand."

"When Azuluu discovered your left-handedness, he wanted to toss you from the castle immediately. I convinced him to let you stay in the Tower of Divinion. I couldn't bear to put you on the streets of Haldessa so young, but neither could I adopt you. That is my greatest regret. In my desire for success, I chose my well-being over yours. I allowed you to suffer, alone and hated, when I could have served as your friend and mentor. I could have let you join the Castle Guard, but instead I kept up appearances and shunned you. For that, I am truly sorry."

Iren didn't know whether to thank Amroth or punch him. On the one hand, the captain had sacrificed dramatically to keep Iren alive. On the other, to preserve his reputation, he had allowed everyone to treat Iren like a monster.

Amroth began again, but now a twinkle sparkled in his eye. "On my last mission, though, I finally figured out the way to atone for my mistakes toward you."

Iren's brow furrowed skeptically.

"I want to defeat the Quodivar, as you know. The mission I proposed at the feast can do that. However, I have two ulterior motives. First, by bringing you on this mission, I give you the chance to prove yourself to Lodia. If the Quodivar fall because of your aid, you may earn some respect among the people. Second, and far more important, it will give you a chance to avenge your parents."

"Avenge them? How?"

Looking Iren dead in the eye, Amroth replied, "The night your parents died, the darkness prevented me from determining their killer's identity. However, the sparks from the clashing weapons and my own battle experience taught me much of his fighting style. I have never forgotten it, for the image of your parents' murders remains burned into my heart. How surprised I was, then, on my latest mission, when I fought no less than the leader of the Quodivar himself! When I clashed swords with him, I knew. His technique perfectly matches what I saw seventeen years ago. I can't say for certain, but I suspect that the Quodivar leader killed your parents."

Iren felt like Amroth had struck him with a hammer. The man who murdered his parents still lived! "Did you kill him?" Iren asked, torn between hope and fear at how Amroth might respond.

"Unfortunately, no. His strength overwhelmed me, and I barely escaped. But I believe you can defeat him. In fact, I believe you are the only person who can succeed where both your father and I failed."

Iren hugged himself, slowly absorbing Amroth's words and what the captain hoped Iren would accomplish. He couldn't do it. He couldn't fight. He had never even held a weapon. After hearing Amroth's tale, though, he already knew his answer. Firmly, he replied, "I'll see you at the stables an hour before dawn."

Amroth gave the slightest incline of his head, then rose and opened the door a crack, listening for any sign of movement. Satisfied no one was in the tower, the captain vanished down the steps.

As Iren sat on his bed, taking in the poor trappings of his life, a sense of direction he'd never experienced came to him. For seventeen years, no one had wanted him. He'd been unnecessary. Thanks to Amroth, all those feelings of doubt and insecurity fled before a new resolve. What did he want from life? For years he'd asked himself that question, never having an answer. Now, for the first time, he did.

Revenge.

CHAPTER FOUR
Stupid Old Hag!

Sergeant Balear Platarch woke quickly, helped by some horridly loud banging that turned his almost-a-headache into a migraine in about three seconds. Initially, he thought the sound came from the minstrels' drums at the feast, but then he slowly remembered that the festival had ended. Also, the musicians' instruments lay tattered beneath the remains of the chandelier that Left demon had nearly dropped on his head. No, this revolting noise came from something else: an incessant pounding on the door to his quarters.

After a minute with no sign that the banging would cease, Balear sighed and opened his eyes, promptly shutting them again as he realized it wasn't even dawn yet. He swore. Who would have the gall to make such a racket at this time of night?

He got his answer as the familiar voice of Captain Angustion bellowed on the other side of the door, "Balear! Hop to! Get out of bed and open up at once!"

Balear swore again, but this time only mentally. With a great effort, he shoved himself into a sitting position on his bed, swooning with dizziness as he did so. Stumbling to the door, he unlocked it, opened it a fraction, and answered groggily, "Captain? What are you—"

He didn't get a chance to finish, because as soon as he cracked the door, Captain Angustion shoved it open all the way, knocking Balear back as he forced his way in. Once inside, he shut the door behind him and blocked it with his body.

"Hurry and get dressed," the captain growled, "and not in your Castle

Guard uniform. Wear civilian clothes, something that will travel well. Bring a weapon, but not military issue. Maybe a bow. Come to the stables in an hour. That's an order. Iren and I will meet you there."

He waited until Balear gave a confused affirmative, and then the captain whisked back through the door, leaving the recovering sergeant standing like an idiot in the middle of his room. He remained that way for a long time, trying to process what had just happened, and why Captain Angustion would give him such odd commands. At last, through the fog of his hangover, he started to remember. He recalled, barely, his superior's speech, the one about a mission, a mission that involved the captain, Balear…and Iren Saitosan.

Balear groaned. Today was going to be a very bad day.

* * *

Captain Amroth Angustion, heir to the throne of Lodia, marched swiftly down the corridor, grinning subtly to himself. He'd given Balear quite the rude awakening. He had no doubt, though, that Balear would arrive at the stables on time. Balear's loyalty, more than his fighting prowess, had won him his position on Amroth's team. If Amroth gave an order, Balear would follow it, even with a hangover.

The captain entered the castle courtyard, still deserted in the predawn hour. Again Amroth smiled, noting the ease with which his plan was proceeding. Avoiding drinking at the feast to stay focused had proven a smart decision. He'd suspected something like this would happen. Even if Iren hadn't played his little prank, Amroth doubted Azuluu would ever have agreed to let the boy come. The captain couldn't allow that. Everything hinged on Iren.

Reaching the stables, he glanced around, confirming no one had followed him. When he'd gone to the Tower of Divinion earlier, he'd sensed that someone was stalking him through the corridors, even though everyone in the castle should have been asleep. He'd checked repeatedly but never seen anyone. He must have imagined it.

Inside the stable, Amroth found the packages he'd brought there after meeting with Iren. While the castle snored, he'd spent the entire night rushing from one end of the fortress to the other, gathering supplies, sneaking leftover food from the kitchens, preparing changes of clothes, and readying three of the Castle Guard's finest horses. Now they could begin.

* * *

Iren Saitosan arrived at the stables twenty minutes early, his whole body bristling with excitement. Amroth smiled at the boy, but his grin quickly faded.

"I appreciate your enthusiasm," the captain said flatly, "but we'll need stealth to accomplish this mission."

"What do you mean?" Iren asked, confused.

Amroth pointed at him. "You won't sneak up on many Quodivar dressed like that."

Iren looked down at his flamboyantly orange and purple motley and shrugged. "I don't have anything else."

Shaking his head, Amroth knelt beside a pile of supplies. "Take these. I packed them for myself, but I think they'll fit you well enough." He handed Iren black leather boots, belt, and vest, along with thick, gray woolen pants, shirt, and cloak. Iren stepped into one of the empty stalls and changed. Though a size too big, he beamed as he donned them. Since the castle had learned of his Left heritage, no one had ever given him a gift, certainly not clothes like these that lacked tears and moth holes.

Giving Iren a once over, Amroth crossed his arms and said, "You'll also need a weapon."

"What do you suggest?" Iren asked.

Amroth smirked. "Actually, I think I have the perfect blade for you. What do you suppose happened to your father's sword after he died?"

Iren started. "You didn't."

"I did. When I saw it, I couldn't bear to leave it out in that field to rust. I carried it back, sheath included, along with you. I've kept it all this time, waiting for the right moment to give it to you. I believe that time has finally come."

Amroth bent down and pushed aside a pile of straw, revealing a sheathed sword about three feet long. Reverently picking it up, he passed the blade to Iren, who stared at it, spellbound.

"No other sword like it exists in all of Lodia, I assure you," Amroth said.

Iren could tell that just by the sheath. It was curved and white with sky blue streaks. The whole thing gleamed in the moonlight. The sheath felt metallic, but it looked like no metal Iren had ever seen. It weighed far less than its size suggested, and despite Amroth's account of the weapon's age, it showed no sign of wear or dirt whatsoever. In fact, it looked perfectly new.

The blade's hilt was even more impressive. Forged of the same strange metal as the sheath, the swordsmith had crafted the hilt into the winding shape of a serpentine white dragon. The hilt was white, save for two tiny sapphires that formed the beast's eyes. Iren touched the gems delicately, yet with a sense of familiarity. The creature reminded him of Divinion, the dragon in his tower painting.

Three concentric rings of symbols encircled the hilt, and they were so far removed from Lodian writing that Iren couldn't begin to decipher them. "What do these—"

"I don't know," Amroth interrupted. "I can't read them, nor can anyone I've taken the sword to. Come; let's see you draw it. I must admit I tried to use it when I first came upon it, but that dragon-shaped hilt always felt uncomfortable."

Iren grasped the sword tightly with his left hand. He didn't want to disagree with as experienced a swordsman as the captain, but he didn't find the grip uncomfortable at all. The flowing dragon's body admittedly made for an unorthodox handhold, but not a bothersome one. As Iren drew the blade, it came free from its sheath easily, as though it had waited all this time for him to claim it.

The young man marveled at his father's sword. Amroth hadn't lied; no other weapon in Lodia looked like it. It had a slight curve, with an edge only on one side. As he took a few practice swings, he noticed that the weapon felt almost weightless in his hand.

"Amazing," he whispered. The blade itself was forged from the same white metal as the hilt and sheath, though it lacked the sheath's blue streaks. Looking closer, Iren realized that the blade and hilt were actually a single piece. That surprised him, as he'd seen blades getting constructed at Haldessa Castle's forge, at least until he got chased out at the end of a hammer. Normally, the swordsmith made the blade and attached the hilt later.

"In all my travels across Lodia, the Eregos Mountains, and even the Tacumsah Islands, I've never seen another sword like this one," Amroth said. "It may be a sword model unique to the Lefts."

After that, the captain left Iren to practice. With each swing, the blade grew on him. He had never held a sword before, yet this one felt natural, even organic, in his left hand. He couldn't explain it, but he had the odd sensation that he and the weapon were made for each other.

Meanwhile, Amroth continued readying supplies and loading up three horses. Balear arrived precisely on time, dressed in traveling clothes and bearing a longbow and quiver in addition to a short sword. Despite his impressive attire, the sergeant looked bleary-eyed, and when he saw Iren armed, he grimaced. Amroth immediately set Balear to work checking that their stores of food would support them on a trip lasting several days.

At last Amroth called Iren over and announced they were ready to go. As the captain began mounting his horse, however, a light, airy voice called out, "Ready to go? Go where?"

Iren and Balear simply looked around in confusion, but Amroth became suddenly tense. He stared in the direction of the voice. It had come from inside one of the horse stalls. Iren heard shifting straw, and then the stall door opened from within. Exactly who or what Iren expected to emerge, he couldn't say. What did appear, though, wasn't it.

An old woman with long, flowing hair of pale silver stumbled drunkenly through the doorway, her face adorned with glazed-over emerald eyes and a wide, almost stupid-looking grin. Five feet tall at most, the diminutive crone had a frame so light Iren thought he could probably knock her over if he so much as tapped her.

Balear scoffed, probably at the old woman's clothing, which, if at all possible, was worse than Iren's former outfit. Her shoes looked like she'd fished them from a trash heap. Multiple holes made her tan woolen shirt and pants look little better than rags, and they were so oversized they billowed around her. She was armed, though only with a dagger with a round wooden handle that hung from a moldy rope tied around her waist. Poking out of her right sleeve, which was so long it obscured her hand, was a bottle of what looked like red wine.

While Iren continued staring dumbfounded at the odd, drunken elder, Amroth recovered from his momentary shock. Regarding her, he noted dryly, "The stables are an odd place to take a nap."

The old woman shrugged nonchalantly. She kept her expression in the same broad grin, and when she spoke, her words slurred. "I had a lot to drink last night. I knew I'd made a smart move, coming into the castle yesterday. Azuluu always holds a feast when you return from a mission. That means free food and booze for me." She paused and tapped her bottle knowingly. "Guess I did overstay my welcome a bit though. When did they start barring the gate?" She hiccupped and took a swig.

Amroth cocked an eyebrow.

"Anyway," she continued, "since I'm here, I might as well go with you." She stretched her arms above her head.

A loud crack filled the stable, and the woman fell backwards on the straw. "Ow, my back!"

Sighing, Amroth said, "You can't come with us. Where we're going is dangerous."

In what seemed too fast for a drunken crone who had just popped her spine out of alignment, the woman climbed to her feet. "I know; that's why you'll need my help to rout those nasty Quodivar! Balear there looks too hung-over to stay on his horse, and what you ever saw in that young Left is quite beyond me."

The crone didn't as much as glance at Iren while she spoke those words. In fact, she hadn't looked at Iren once since coming out of her stall. He clenched his fists. This drunken bird was just like all the others. "Stupid old hag," he growled under his breath.

The woman didn't miss a beat. As if by instinct, she retorted, still without looking at him, "Monstrous brat."

Infuriated, Iren opened his mouth to shout at her, to call her any of a half-dozen names he'd already thought of for her, but Amroth's next words silenced their exchange cold.

"You don't need to pretend, Rondel. I told him everything."

Recognition flashed through Iren. This was Rondel Thara, the old woman who'd helped Amroth seventeen years ago. She didn't look like someone who would welcome strangers with babies into her home. In fact, she didn't look like someone who even had a home. She looked like a bum.

As Amroth spoke, Rondel's smile faded. "He knows about seventeen years ago?"

The captain nodded. "Yes, and that's why he's coming with me. No one else can kill the Quodivar leader."

For the first time, the woman's eyes fell on Iren. It seemed to require a great deal of effort for her to focus on him, and even then, she wouldn't look him in the face. Instead, her gaze settled upon the now sheathed sword sitting at his right hip. "You gave him the...I mean, his father's sword?"

Iren perked up at that. The? The what? Did this stumbling bat know something about his father's sword?

Amroth didn't respond verbally; he just gave her a smirk and then turned away to face Iren and Balear. "Let's go. Rondel, we don't have the supplies to take you with us, even if you wouldn't be a liability against the Quodivar."

The crone's grin returned and got, if possible, even bigger. "Well then, good thing I happen to have everything I need for travel right here! What a coincidence!" She ducked back into her stall and began making an awful racket. "By sheer luck, I happen to always have my things ready to depart at a moment's notice!"

Something about the way she said it made Iren seriously doubt that luck had anything to do with it.

Rondel emerged moments later heavily burdened with a pack and bedroll. On each step, her bundle clinked with the sound of numerous glass objects rubbing against each other. "So can I come?" the old woman asked innocently. She kept on smiling, but a subtle edge crept into her voice as she went on, "You'd best let me. Imagine what might happen if you left me here to tell the king about how you snuck out of the castle in the middle of the night, taking a criminal sentenced to death with you."

Amroth had already opened his mouth to rebuke her, but he stopped short. The old hag might be a homeless bum, Iren thought, but at least this time, she'd outsmarted the great captain. With the subtlest of nods and an audibly irritated, "Humph," he leapt onto his horse and rode from the stables. Balear followed, glaring at both Iren and Rondel.

Iren approached the nearest horse, but it shied away from him. Tentatively, he reached a hand out, but the ornery creature simply snorted and turned away. "What's the matter?" Rondel asked, looking incredulous. "Don't you speak horse?" Iren shot her a withering stare.

The crone ignored him. Throwing a saddle on the mare nearest her, she whispered, "*Kuylet, trempiot.*" Iren's brow furrowed. If those were words in the Lodian tongue, he'd never heard them. The mare apparently understood, though, because she bowed her head and allowed Rondel to climb onto her – backwards.

"Onward!" the hag cried, and then the horse bucked and ran out of the stables, Rondel swearing as she bounced around in the saddle.

Iren couldn't decide if Rondel was a fool or not. All the same, he now stood alone in the stable, and his horse had decidedly no interest in allowing Iren to ride him. With nothing to lose, Iren shrugged and tried what he'd heard Rondel say, "*Kuylet, trempiot.*"

At first he felt idiotic, falling for Rondel's stunt. The annoying witch had probably made up the ridiculous phrase. "Speak horse, I bet," Iren muttered. A few seconds later, however, the stallion lowered his head and whickered. This time, he allowed Iren to get in the saddle with no trouble at all.

Iren was just thinking how amazing it was that Rondel's trick had actually worked when the stallion's nostrils flared, and he shot out of the stables. The energetic horse bolted right past the others, all the while Iren shouting, "Stop! Stop please!"

As his horse cavorted around the courtyard, and the drunken bat Rondel sat backwards on her steed, Iren couldn't help but wonder how this absurd group would ever defeat the most skilled bandit force Lodia had ever seen.

CHAPTER FIVE
Departure

"All right," Amroth began once Iren's horse calmed down. "Before we leave, there's one last thing I need each of you to do." The captain held up several pieces of parchment, ink wells, and pens. "This mission is different from any other. I cannot order any of you to participate. If you come, you do so of your own free will. Under Lodian law, if you died on such a mission, I, as your commander, would become responsible for paying restitution to your survivors. I have neither the means nor desire to do this, so you will each have to write a waiver noting that you understand the risks involved."

Iren found the concept rather silly. He had no survivors in any case.

"What do we need to write, Captain?" Balear asked, chirping like a bird.

Amroth pulled out another sheet, which had a flowing, elegant script written on it. "I've already completed my waiver, so you can just copy what I've put down." He motioned to a table near the entrance to the stables. "When you're finished, sign and date your waiver and bring it to me. I'll leave them with the king's legal assistant. He'll understand well enough."

The last thing Iren wanted to do was dismount his horse; getting on it once had given him enough trouble. Amroth would not relent though, so he reluctantly got down and joined the others at the table.

Legal nonsense, Iren decided of the waiver. "I, Iren Saitosan, do here absolve Amroth Angustion, my Great King and Leader Azuluu, and all agents of the government of the Nation of Lodia and City of Haldessa of any responsibility should I perish on this dangerous mission. I recognize the task's extreme peril and small window for success, but my desire to bring justice to the Sneaky and Monstrous Enemy of Lodia, the Quodivar, is unquestionable."

Balear completed his first, signing his name and handing the waiver to Amroth. Iren finished next, but when he handed his over, Amroth frowned. "Really?" He turned the parchment around, revealing numerous smudges that made many of the letters hard to read. Iren glanced at his left hand. Black ink smeared the pinky side of it.

"I hate writing," he declared, stalking away.

Rondel finished last. She took a painfully long time, her right hand shaking from the exertion. "Old age sure has caught up with me," she said, smiling. "This gets harder and harder each time I do it." At last she handed over her waiver, composed of basic, blocky lettering. Amroth nodded his approval and said, "Good. Wait here while I take these to the legal office." He exited through a doorway on the far side of the courtyard.

From under her sleeve, Rondel whipped out the bottle of wine she'd been drinking from earlier. She went to take a swig from it, but then eyed it with disdain. "Empty," she whined, seemingly to herself. "It's always empty." Turning to Iren and Balear, she grinned broadly and said, "I'll be right back. Make sure Amroth waits for me if he returns before I do."

"Doubtful," Balear muttered as she disappeared through another doorway, the one that led to the kitchens. Iren nodded; for once he agreed with Balear.

Fifteen minutes later, Amroth emerged from the same doorway he'd entered and said they could depart. A few seconds later, Rondel appeared as well, carrying a bottle of some vile liquid. A quarter of it had already vanished, and Iren felt pretty confident he knew where it had gone.

Getting back on the horses, fortunately, was less of an adventure than the first time, though Rondel rode unsteadily and nearly fell off her mount twice before they'd even made it to the castle gate. Amroth roused the guard to the point where he could open the gate, and the fool was hung over enough that he didn't seem particularly concerned.

The first whispers of dawn crept over the horizon, and still the sleepy castle and surrounding city rested. Upon reaching the city bounds, Amroth directed them up a trail that led northwest. The crisp morning air chilled Iren, but he also felt the promise of warmth in it. It was still early spring, and while the snows had melted for the year, winter still clung stubbornly to the nights as best it could. Even so, it was gradually losing the fight. The grass had already begun to grow again, and in the distance, Iren could see the first buds on a clump of trees sheltered by a south-facing hillside.

As they rode, Amroth explained their task. They would head to Veliaf, a village in Lodia's northeast, posing as a family of traders hoping to obtain some of the durable minerals harvested from the village's mines.

"What's Veliaf like?" Iren asked, barely able to contain his excitement, which grew with each hard click of the horses' hooves on the cobble road. He couldn't believe he was finally beyond the castle.

"A hardy village, with a population to match," Amroth explained. "They have to be, both to work in the mines and to keep themselves safe, what with Akaku on their doorstep."

"Akaku?" Iren questioned. "What's that?"

Balear sneered, "You really don't know anything, do you? What a brainless idiot! Akaku is the boreal forest that forms the northern border of Lodia. Isn't that correct, Captain?"

Amroth gave the sergeant a sharp look. "Let me make two things quite plain, Balear. First, as we're posing as civilians, you should under no circumstances call me 'Captain.' Furthermore, you will address Iren only by name, and not refer to him as 'brainless' or any other derogatory term. Understood?"

Balear looked stung, and Iren could guess why. The sergeant surely didn't expect Amroth, leader of Lodia's Castle Guard, to favor a Left like Iren Saitosan over a loyal soldier like himself.

"All the same," Rondel piped up from the back of the line, shaking her now half-empty bottle, "I think I'll just go on calling the brat whatever I feel like."

Amroth turned in the saddle and glowered at Rondel. "As for you, I would prefer if you didn't speak at all."

Iren shifted his gaze from Amroth to Rondel and back again. Try though he might, he couldn't understand their relationship. Rondel had helped Amroth seventeen years ago, but as the day wore on, the two showed no signs of stopping their griping at each other. Iren wondered what could have happened between them.

Maybe it simply meant that Rondel wore on Amroth's nerves. She seemed to have that effect on people.

Deciding he was probably better off just ignoring the homeless bat, Iren refocused on the earlier conversation about their destination. "Amroth, why do the residents of Veliaf need to keep themselves safe from Akaku? Is the forest dangerous?"

"Few who enter Akaku return alive," Amroth responded. "The lives of those in Veliaf are steeped in eternal caution of it. A thick stone wall surrounds the village, including the mine entrance, and sentries stand upon it at all times." Vehemently, he concluded, "The rest of Lodia could learn a few things from them."

Iren thought about his life inside Haldessa Castle. For the first time, he felt grateful for it. The people treated him poorly, to be sure, but until his accident with the chandelier, he'd at least always felt safe there. Veliaf, by contrast, lived under constant threat, and that dread shaped every moment of their lives.

"Why go to Veliaf at all, Capta…Amroth?" Balear shifted uncomfortably as he spoke. Iren laughed quietly at him; evidently the sergeant had a hard time not acting like a soldier. He sat bolt upright in his saddle, carrying himself regally as though participating in a grand parade. Iren intentionally rode closer to Balear to make the proper young man that much more ill at ease.

"Over many missions," Amroth replied, ignoring Balear's discomfiture, "I sought to end the Quodivar, but they do not fight like a military. Their commanders hide in the shadows, issuing orders in secret and sending their grunts to conduct the actual raids. To defeat the Quodivar, we must find their leadership and destroy it. On my last mission, we traveled this road, heading for Veliaf. The Quodivar ambushed us, and many fine Castle Guard members no longer walk among us because of it. In the end, though, we rallied and pushed them back, forcing them to flee to the northwest. I wanted to know where they went, so I and five other men tracked them. After three days, they entered Akaku a few miles west of Veliaf. I think their base lies somewhere in the forest."

Rondel shouted from the back, "Blind speculation, and you know it! You'd better not have dragged us out here for nothing!"

Amroth scowled. "Last I checked, I didn't drag you out here; you invited yourself."

"And I wouldn't miss it for anything," Rondel replied, her grin as wide as ever.

Throwing up his hands, Amroth pressed on, "Anyway, I dared not enter Akaku with only a handful of men. We started back to Haldessa when I saw him at the edge of the forest: the man who, I have no doubt, leads the Quodivar."

Iren tensed at the mention of his parents' killer. "What was he like?" he asked.

"I've never met a larger person," Amroth replied. "He easily stood over seven feet and must have weighed at least three hundred pounds. He had the dark complexion and black hair of a Tacumsah islander, and on his back, he carried a single sword, more massive than any I have ever seen. As we lacked the manpower to attack him, I gave the order to withdraw. Then the worst happened; the enemy spotted us and attacked. My comrades all perished, and I had to flee in order to live."

"You ran from battle?" Balear sounded even more hurt than when Amroth had rebuked him for calling Iren "brainless."

"What choice did I have? Had I stayed, I would have died, and I needed to pass on the Quodivar's whereabouts."

"Then you really are leading us on a pointless mission," Rondel called. "If they saw you escape, they'll abandon their hideout now that you know their location."

Amroth nodded. "That's why I wanted to get underway so quickly. Even without Iren's stunt yesterday, I would have opted for a rapid departure. It's also why I made Veliaf our first stop. If the Quodivar did vacate, the residents might have some idea where they went."

The day wore on as they talked and continued their journey. When afternoon gave way to evening, Amroth motioned for them to leave the road. Continuing in the dark would only get them noticed by Quodivar roaming the trail, and setting up camp near the road would be just as bad. The captain led them to the top of a small rise about half a mile west of the path, where they could easily see the lay of the land around them. There were no trees or thickets nearby, so they did without a fire and ate their dinner cold. Rondel whined bitterly as she downed her third bottle since leaving Haldessa. Iren, however, could find no reason to complain. Cold or not, he'd consumed few meals in the castle that matched this one. If nothing else, at least he hadn't needed to steal it.

With their bedrolls prepared, Amroth volunteered to take the first watch. Iren tried to sleep, but he couldn't even doze. He stared at the sky, losing himself among the stars.

After about an hour, he heard the captain whisper, "Wait for me, Nadav; it's almost time."

Iren heaved himself into a sitting position. "Amroth?"

The captain didn't turn to face him. "I thought you were asleep."

Crawling from his bedroll, Iren took a seat beside Amroth. "I can't."

Looking impressed, the captain replied, "All day in the saddle and you aren't tired at all? Lefts really are something."

Iren shook his head. "No, honestly, I do feel exhausted, but this is my first time outside the castle. I don't want to miss anything."

Amroth half-smiled. "We'll need four days to reach Veliaf. You'll have to rest at some point, no matter how excited you are."

"I guess, but not tonight."

The pair sat in silence, staring together across Lodia's darkened landscape. Working up his courage, Iren asked, "So who's Nadav?"

For a long time Amroth didn't reply. His face became nostalgic, and Iren sensed that Amroth relived some old memory. When the captain spoke again, he did so quietly and humbly, "Before I came to Haldessa, I served in Caardit's militia. Nadav was my commander."

"Caardit has a militia? I thought the Castle Guard was Lodia's military."

Amroth snorted. "As do most people, including Azuluu. They think the Castle Guard can protect them from anything. And why shouldn't they? On the surface, Lodia is a peaceful and prosperous nation. We trade extensively with both the Tengu of Eregos and the humans of Tacumsah. Our farms produce most of the food and raw materials for clothing used throughout northern Raa. You saw our opulence on display at the feast. That is the Azuluu family's legacy."

Iren didn't consider all that food and drink a bad legacy at all, but he could see in Amroth's face an indignant look, one of righteous contempt.

"It is a fool's legacy," the captain spat. "The fat oaf squanders our wealth on trinkets while our people suffer and die at the hands of the Quodivar."

"The Quodivar," Iren repeated, "who are they, really? What makes them such a threat?"

Amroth's eyes narrowed dangerously. "Hooligans and thugs, or at least that's all they should be. You see, the Quodivar are merely a symptom of a greater problem. Azuluu doesn't want to admit that Lodia is in crisis. He views military spending as wasteful. He is blind and stretches the Castle Guard too thin. Since we don't have the strength to restrain them, the Quodivar have transformed from minor thugs into practically an army."

"So Caardit formed its militia to protect itself from the Quodivar?"

Amroth nodded. "Caardit is the most remote town in Lodia. It's in the northwest corner of the country and contributes little to Lodia's economy, so the Azuluu family never saw a reason to devote much to it. Nadav rescued us. He taught us strength, that we could only have peace if we had power greater than our enemies. He taught me everything I know about fighting and life." He sighed. "I wish he were still alive."

"He died?"

"In battle, sacrificing himself trying to save me and his other subordinates. That day, I swore revenge on those who had slain my great commander. Everything I've done in my life since then has been for that purpose. Now, with your help, I may achieve that dream."

Iren saw Amroth with new eyes. The captain had lost everything when the Quodivar killed Nadav. "Just like me," he muttered. "We're the same."

Amroth must have heard him, because he smiled warmly. "You and I both owe a debt to those who've made us suffer. Together, we can pay them back." The captain paused, gazing at the moon. "Well, you may not be able to sleep, but I'm bushed. Shall I leave you to handle the watch?"

Iren grinned and saluted. Anything for Amroth.

CHAPTER SIX
First Blood

Iren watched as Amroth collapsed onto his bedroll. Within a few minutes the captain started snoring.

Filled with new passion, Iren seated himself in the center of camp, trying to examine every detail of the surrounding countryside. With the moon nearly full and the skies cloudless, he could see a considerable distance. Amroth had chosen a good spot that allowed whoever took the watch to spot enemies approaching from any direction.

While he kept watch, Iren reached into his pants pocket and withdrew his small, black sea stone. He didn't know what had made him bring it. As his only childhood memento, though, he couldn't bear to leave it behind. Palming it gently, he derived a strange sense of calm as he caressed its smooth contours.

The hours passed uneventfully. Although the hilltop provided excellent visibility, it also left him exposed. In the windy night air, Iren's hands quickly numbed. The stone only robbed them of warmth faster, so he placed it back in his pocket.

As he did, his hand brushed against the hilt of his sword. He still couldn't quite get used to the fact that it belonged to him. He'd never used a sword in his life, and he'd never even seen one of this quality. He wondered if perhaps the weapon had a name. Back in the stables, Rondel had started to call it something. He felt certain of that.

There was also the issue of Rondel herself. Iren peered at the old hag, who was snoring louder than he thought possible. He found it hard to believe that she'd just so happened to have all those supplies ready to go, even if it was almost all alcohol. Nor did he consider it likely that she'd accidentally gotten lost after the feast and wound up sleeping in the stables. Whatever she might say to the contrary, she hadn't come on this mission by mistake.

Iren made up his mind, his curiosity getting the better of him. Giving a quick pass over the countryside to confirm no one was around, he abandoned his post and hunched over Rondel, trying hard not to breathe or make any sound whatsoever. He sat there for what felt like hours, studying her and trying to figure her out. Eventually, when his legs started falling asleep, he backed away.

As he did, his numb limbs made him lose his balance. Reaching out to catch himself, he placed a hand on Rondel's shoulder. A violent shock ripped through him. Rondel's eyes snapped open, and to Iren's amazement, blue sparks filled them. Iren collapsed on his back in surprise. Not a second later, Rondel crashed on top of him, throttling him with an expression of utmost hatred on her face. Despite her miniscule frame and tiny hands, her grip held firm against his best efforts to dislodge her.

"Rondel, it's Iren!" he whispered hoarsely, as much from fear as from an inability to breathe.

For a moment Rondel appeared not to hear him, but gradually her hold relaxed, and the bizarre lightning leaping across her irises disappeared, if indeed it had ever existed. Iren already doubted himself. Surely it was just the panic of the moment.

Dusting herself off, Rondel snapped, "What on Raa do you think you're doing?"

Iren started to reply, but the aggravating crone clamped her hand over his mouth. Without looking at him, she hissed, "Wake the others quietly. Enemies have us surrounded."

Rondel's abrupt shift in demeanor terrified him. Her smile had vanished, and her high-pitched voice that reveled in making light of everything and everybody had deepened into a deadly seriousness.

The old woman released him, and Iren turned his head in circles, surveying the landscape. He could see no one.

"I get it," he finally deduced. "You're angry that I startled you, so this is all an act. You want to get me in trouble by having me sound a false alarm and wake the others unnecessarily."

The crone glared at his chest with such venom that he feared she might throttle him again. Something about that expression made Iren pretty sure she wasn't joking. So, still half convinced Balear and possibly Amroth too would hound him mercilessly for it, he did as instructed. He woke the captain gently and then, just for the sake of revenge at getting called "brainless" earlier in the day, raised Balear by giving him a hard kick in the ribs.

The sergeant swore, but Iren covered the knight's mouth. "Shut up. Enemies."

Balear looked like he might vomit. Iren couldn't tell if it was nerves about an impending attack or the fact that Iren had touched his face.

The four regrouped around Rondel. "I'd say twenty of them," she whispered. "They're clever. They ripped up patches of sod and covered themselves, then crawled to the base of the hill. They have us surrounded."

Rondel's altered demeanor still stunned Iren, and judging from Balear's reaction, the sergeant felt the same way. If the change fazed Amroth, though, he didn't show it. He responded firmly, "We'll charge their line. By the time those on the other side of the hill reach us, we'll have dealt with the first few."

"No," Rondel countered. "If we do that, it means abandoning our campsite. While we're busy fighting on one side of the hill, our foes on the other side will simply loot our gear, steal our horses, and leave. We'd survive, but we'd have to go back to Haldessa to resupply."

The captain's strained expression indicated that going back to Haldessa didn't sit well with him at all. "What do you suggest, then?" he asked.

Iren shook his head, sure he wasn't hearing right. Amroth was taking orders from Rondel?

"Fan out to the edge of the campsite and form a perimeter," Rondel commanded. "We'll each have to fight five of them. Not great odds, but all of us have faced worse. Except the child."

Iren gulped at her reference to him. The cold way Rondel put it drove home what he had avoided thinking about until now. Everyone else, likely including their enemies, had battled before. Apparently, even the doddering windbag had seen combat. He alone would enter this fight a total novice.

"I have faith in him," Amroth said. "Iren's no child, and he won't die as easily as this."

Cursing repeatedly under his breath, Iren tried for the captain's sake at least to look brave. Following Rondel's instructions, they spread out.

The old woman stood to Iren's right, and Amroth positioned himself to the left. Balear took the opposite side of the hill. Iren, meanwhile, felt paralyzed. His hands grew so sweaty he feared he might drop his father's sword the moment he tried to swing it.

As the four took their positions, their enemies suddenly threw the sod off their backs and charged the hill at full speed. The steel of their weapons glinted in the moonlight. Iren tried hard not to think about what would happen if he screwed up. At the same time, a perverse kind of curiosity took him, wondering what it would feel like to have a sword cut him in two.

He was pretty sure he didn't want to find out.

Then he had no more time for thought, because the first attacker reached him, lunging forward with a long, narrow sword. Panicking, Iren leapt back, avoiding the blow but leaving him far out of range to counter-attack. His breath came in gasps, not from exhaustion but terror. He knew he would die. There was a huge difference between swinging a mop at imaginary opponents inside the Tower of Divinion and wielding a sword against a real person trying to kill you. He didn't stand a chance.

Then again, maybe he did. He kept dodging, weaving, and retreating. He blocked only when absolutely necessary. With his foe's greater reach, Iren couldn't get close enough to attack, but even so, his opponent hadn't landed a strike yet either. Indeed, after the time spent under the sod, the charge up the hill, and the first series of strikes, the bandit looked exhausted. He was sweating profusely and breathing hard, even though they'd only been fighting for a few seconds.

Iren no longer panted; his breath came as steadily as on a gentle stroll. Soon his initial panic evaporated, and the fight became almost like a dance in Haldessa Castle's grand hall. Conscious thought faded away, and his body reacted on its own, shifting in time to music only he could hear. When the second opponent reached him, he just adjusted the tempo to match his pace to that of his two foes. Iren couldn't understand it. These enemies obviously knew how to fight, yet he found their techniques absurdly predictable. The instant one of them committed to an attack, Iren's block was already waiting for it.

Then the rhythm faltered. The first bandit's stance shifted. It was a momentary lapse, but Iren recognized it as a weakness in his enemy's left leg. For the first time, Iren attacked. He swung his sword from the outside, intentionally aiming for the thief's blade. Metal crashed against metal, and the force jerked his foe's sword hard to the left. The man's weakened knee gave under the strain, and when it did, Iren quickly flicked his blade and struck him in the side, just above the right hip.

Blood spattered the hill, and the man screamed as he dropped to the ground. Without hesitation, Iren followed through on his attack, striking down on the fallen thief's throat.

The screaming stopped.

Iren's second opponent paused briefly at the loss of his comrade, but he quickly redoubled his efforts. There was no time for Iren to contemplate that he had just killed a man, had just ended someone's life the same way the Quodivar leader had ended his parents'. The dance of battle prevented such thoughts. Soon two more bandits joined in, forcing Iren to face three enemies at once. His eyes glazed over. It was like viewing someone else fight for his life. He watched passively, as from a great distance, while he slew his three assailants without getting so much as a scratch.

When his foes lay dead around him, he took a moment to recover and observe the battlefield. He couldn't see Balear, but he heard clashes from over the hill. Rondel and Amroth both still struggled against their foes as well. Iren was amazed. Somehow, without any fighting experience, he had defeated his foes more quickly than Lodia's finest warriors.

A rustle downhill distracted him. He whipped around, looking for an enemy, but he saw only grass.

Sharp pain filled his lower left leg, and he collapsed. His mistake came to him immediately. Rondel said there were five opponents for each of them, but he'd only killed four. The fifth man, whom he'd completely forgotten, had remained hidden. Once Iren was distracted, the thief had used a long knife to slit Iren's hamstring.

Iren howled as his blood leached over the hill. The bandit stood over him, triumphant. Iren tried to swing his sword, but the thief quickly threw his knife down and pierced Iren's arm, pinning it to the ground and forcing him to drop the blade. Blinding agony overwhelmed him, and he thought he would black out. Through dim vision, he saw his enemy draw a second knife and stab it toward Iren's head.

Instead of his own dying screams, however, Iren heard a strange gurgling noise. A thin steel point protruded from the thief's chest. It withdrew a second later, and the man's hot blood cascaded onto Iren's prone form.

Iren panted. He couldn't believe he had survived, though as he felt the burning pain in his left arm and leg, he knew he was severely, perhaps mortally, wounded. Then, despite his injuries, he noticed something that made all thoughts of death vanish from his mind.

The thief's limp body dropped, revealing Iren's savior. Rondel stood over him, holding her dagger with its triangular, double-sided blade that ended in a lethal point. It was not the weapon itself that shocked Iren, however, but the way Rondel held it: in her left hand.

He had no time to ask her about it. Without speaking, Rondel sheathed her dagger and knelt to examine Iren's wounds. After a quick once-over she retrieved his father's sword and pressed its hilt into his left hand, wrapping his fingers around it. "Keep hold of that, no matter how much it hurts," she said.

She sounded calm, but her words made Iren despair. Everyone knew a warrior died with his weapon. Even dying of old age, a Lodian Castle Guard member always wanted a blade in his hands at the time of his passing.

If Rondel was the least bit concerned about him, though, she hid it well. In fact, considering twenty bandits had just ambushed them, she looked remarkably at ease. She breathed normally, and she didn't have a bead of sweat on her. Without the slightest hint of doubt, she called to Amroth and Balear, who had finished dealing with their opponents. Balear had received a small wound to his right arm but nothing threatening. Amroth, as expected, remained unhurt.

The captain ran over, eyes wild. "What happened to him?" he cried.

Rondel shrugged nonchalantly, and Iren noticed that her grin had returned. "You brought along quite the bumbler in this one."

From his spot on the ground, Iren growled, "How can you joke at a time like this? Don't you realize I'm about to die here?"

The irritating hag kept right on smirking. "What do you mean, whiner? You don't have any injuries."

He glared at her, confused and furious. She'd seen his wounds. She'd handed him his sword, a sure sign he would perish. How dare she pretend he had no injuries while he lay here in searing pain!

Then it hit him. He'd gotten so angry at Rondel that he'd forgotten the pain. Now he remembered. That was the right word for it, too, because he no longer felt any. Gingerly, he reached down with his right hand and felt where he knew the knife had cut him.

There was no wound.

He uttered a cry and leapt to his feet, which amazed him all the more.

He couldn't explain it. All too clearly, he recalled the intense agony of both strikes. He could feel blood on the back of his leg, and on his left arm too. He could see tears in his pants and shirt where the knife had sliced through them. The injuries themselves, though, no longer existed.

Iren stared at Rondel, open-mouthed. "I know the thief cut me. I should have died. How could I heal just like that?"

The hag folded her arms. "As if I would know, you Left freak." She spat the last two words to emphasize them, but even so, he noticed that she didn't look at him as she did.

"Devil magic, if you ask me," Balear offered. Amroth, Iren, and even Rondel shot him dirty looks. "What? It's as good an explanation as any."

Shaking her head, Rondel replied defensively, "You all should listen to your elders more. I told you, didn't I? He didn't have any injuries."

Iren eyed her shrewdly. "You're lying," he said. "You know I got injured, and you know how I recovered. What's more, you've been lying to us from the start. I saw which hand you used to finish off that bandit. Rondel, you're a Left!"

CHAPTER SEVEN
Ryokaiten

Nobody got any more sleep that night. Rondel stormed off, refusing to speak to anyone. Amroth busied himself surveying their fallen assailants and concluding that they were, in all likelihood, Quodivar. Balear made himself useful by shouting at Iren about what an idiot he was.

"Well of course she walked away!" he bellowed. "Luckily for you, she didn't do anything else. If you accused me of being a Left, I'd probably kill you. Also, what a useless fighter you turned out to be! Honestly, if you can't take this mission seriously, you should just turn around and go back to Haldessa."

"Enough, Balear," Amroth's sharp retort carried over the hill. "Hurry and get the horses loaded. I can't stand the smell of this carnage. Dark or not, we're leaving."

Everyone hurried to follow his command. Iren felt Balear's hard gaze on him, but he only had eyes for Rondel. The cantankerous bat was decidedly avoiding him.

The four set off wordlessly, though more for safety than anything else. They had killed a large group of Quodivar, but they couldn't relax. If anything, it meant more bandits could easily have hidden themselves nearby.

Fortunately, they encountered no resistance the rest of the night. As day dawned and they returned to the road, Balear at last broke the silence. He said, "Capta...Amroth, you seriously don't intend to let Iren continue traveling with us, do you? Aside from the fact that he's a devil-child, he's clearly worthless in a fight."

Not bothering to turn around, Amroth countered, "The first time you held a sword, could you have slain four enemies in a row?"

Balear had already opened his mouth to speak but promptly shut it.

Continuing, Amroth said, "Iren performed excellently last night, and having experienced his first battle, he'll be all the more prepared the next time. Right?" He turned and gave Iren a warm expression.

Truthfully, Iren didn't want to think about last night, and he really didn't want to think about having to fight again. The feeling of cutting down another person, the look on their face as they realized they were going to die and never see anyone they cared about ever again...it was too much. Back at the castle, he had never thought twice about teasing people. Even at his worst, though, he had never wanted to kill any of them.

He tried to justify it. Those Quodivar would have murdered him. If he hadn't defended himself, he'd be dead. That didn't make him feel any better. Quite the contrary, it made him realize that to survive this mission, he'd likely have to kill again. It sickened him. Even the thought of slaying the Quodivar leader bothered him. Up until last night, he had looked forward to exacting revenge on the man who had killed his parents. Now he doubted himself. If and when he finally confronted his enemy, he didn't know if he could bring himself to attack.

But Amroth's look was so kind that Iren couldn't stand to let the captain down, so he simply replied, "Yes, I'll be ready."

Amroth nodded, apparently deciding the matter resolved. Balear didn't seem happy about it, but he followed Amroth's lead and fell silent once again.

Iren next turned to Rondel, who brought up the rear and looked rather less chipper than on the previous day. A stoic glare replaced her earlier smile. One thing about her hadn't changed, though. She was still drinking, this time from a large bottle of Tacumsahen rum.

"So will you tell me the truth?" Iren asked.

Rondel finished taking a long gulp before replying sharply, "The truth?"

"You used your left hand to kill that bandit."

The old woman rolled her eyes. In her high, airy voice she countered, "If you want to live, I suggest you learn how to fight with both hands. Also, you should learn more respect and social graces. Otherwise, you're bound to upset someone."

Iren found it ironic that someone like Rondel would chastise him for lacking manners, but he supposed she had a point. That said, she still hadn't answered his question. He asked her again, but she refused to speak. After pestering her for over an hour, he finally gave up the matter.

That night they camped just inside a small thicket. Rondel's dour mood had lifted a bit, and her usual dumb smirk had returned. When Amroth asked her to gather firewood, she responded, "Oh, sure, send a frail old woman like me. I'll break a hip hauling logs around. Make one of these strapping young lads do it."

Amroth glared, but Iren was simply glad things had returned to normal. As annoying as he found the sarcastic, drunken Rondel, the cold, serious Rondel that could make even Amroth follow her orders just plain scared him. He'd take the clown any day.

"Fine, fine," she grumbled, "but don't blame me if I have a heart attack off in the woods. You'd be in a sore spot then."

Sighing, Amroth relented. "All right, but I won't let you get out of it. Take Iren with you." Amroth leaned close so only Iren could hear. "And while you're out there, for all our sakes, apologize!"

Iren didn't feel like fetching wood. He was already so tired from the battle and two days of riding that he could barely move. He also had no desire whatsoever to apologize to Rondel, especially when she called, "Well hurry up, you Left whippersnapper! The firewood won't gather itself. Honestly, kids these days!"

"Slave-driving witch," he grumbled as he forced himself to his feet and followed her into the thicket.

Other travelers had picked the area around their campsite clean, so Rondel and Iren had to venture far to find any downed wood. Soon they passed well out of view and earshot of the others. All the while, Rondel drank from her latest bottle, a hip flask she'd concealed under her baggy clothes. After hiking for about twenty minutes, Rondel stopped abruptly and whipped around. Her grin was gone. "We've come far enough." Her voice dropped in pitch to the same cold level as last night during the attack.

Her sudden change unnerved Iren; she was almost two different people. Her breath still smelled like alcohol though. "Far enough for what?" he asked.

"I meant what I said earlier. You should learn proper manners. For instance, did you ever think that I might not want to answer your questions with those two around?" She pointed back in the direction of camp.

Iren stopped. In truth, no, he hadn't thought that at all. He just had a question and wanted it answered.

Pressing her thumb and forefinger into her temple, Rondel said, "I guess subtlety isn't your strength, is it? All right. Yes, I'm a Left, but humans made up that horrid term. The real name for us is Maantecs. We're a different species."

Iren scrunched up his face. Maantec…finally, he had a name for what he was.

Rondel continued, "You already know the discerning feature. Every human, whether from Lodia or Tacumsah, is right-handed. In the same way, all Maantecs are left-handed. If you want to hide your Maantec heritage, you'd better learn how to use your right hand."

Iren sat on a fallen log, staring blankly at the ferns on the forest floor. After a long pause he said, "I thought I was the only Left in the world. How many of us are there?"

At this, Rondel sighed, took a swig from her flask, and raised her gaze to the treetops. "No idea. I've wandered over most of Raa, but I've hardly ever seen another Maantec in all my journeys. A thousand years ago, though, no race surpassed our might, or at least, so we believed. Maantecs have speed, strength, and reaction times beyond humans. That's why you easily defeated those Quodivar despite your total lack of experience. However, our skills made us arrogant. We began a war to subdue all the other species, but they rose against us. At the end of that war, the few Maantecs who remained were defeated and scattered. Our species has slowly declined ever since."

"How?" Iren asked. "If we get wounded, our bodies heal the injury almost instantly."

Rondel shook her head. "No, only your body will do that, and only because of that sword."

Iren pulled his father's blade from its sheath. "You made me hold this last night after I got injured. Why?"

Drawing her dagger, Rondel held it before Iren. "Let's try an experiment. Sheathe your sword, then slide your finger along the edge of my dagger."

Though nervous about the idea of intentionally wounding himself, Iren did as instructed. The pain was swift and surprisingly light; the sharp blade carved easily through flesh. He held up his finger, watching for the healing power to take effect. A minute passed, but he continued to bleed.

"You're vulnerable, just as I am," Rondel explained. "That healing ability has nothing to do with you. To finish our experiment, touch the hilt of your sword."

Iren obeyed, and a few seconds later, his wound closed. Staring in astonishment first at his healed finger and then at his weapon, he stammered, "The sword healed me? How?"

Rondel smiled. "You possess perhaps the most powerful weapon on the continent of Raa. That sword is a katana, a weapon style unique to Maantecs. Beyond that though, it bears a name. Maantecs call it the Muryozaki, literally translated as 'Holy Dragon Sword.'"

"Holy Dragon Sword?" Iren raised an eyebrow. He had a hard time believing his father's blade was some kind of divine weapon.

"What do you know about dragons, Iren?"

The young man shook his head. "Dragons don't exist; they're fairy tales."

"Partially correct. True, no physical dragons roam Raa. However, somewhere on this continent live eight dragons."

Iren's brow furrowed. Despite her drinking, he'd found Rondel remarkably lucid up to this point. Now, he wondered if everything she had said merely amounted to alcohol-induced ramblings. "You crazy bird, there can't be 'no dragons' and 'eight dragons' at the same time!"

She smacked him on the back of the head. "Watch your mouth, brat, and listen when people talk to you! I said no physical dragons roam Raa, but it does have eight dragons. They simply no longer have a physical form." She sighed. "I'd best start at the beginning. Otherwise, a dunce like you will never understand. You know that, centuries ago, people worshipped the dragons as gods. However, they're more like forces of nature, made by the Creator, Juusa, to maintain balance in the world. He intended for them to live in peace, but instead, the dragons warred among themselves over which had the most power. Ultimately, ten thousand years ago, their squabbling sank an entire continent, Teneb, or so Maantec history says."

Iren shuddered at the thought of creatures so powerful they could sink continents, but he didn't see how the legend could be true. Skeptically, he asked, "What does all that have to do with my sword?"

Rondel's sharp reply came immediately, "It has everything to do with your sword! After Teneb sank, instead of realizing their folly, the dragons merely shifted their war to the sole remaining continent on our world: Raa. Two hundred of the finest sorcerers gathered to address the problem. They couldn't convince the dragons to stop feuding, and they couldn't kill the dragons without upsetting the balance of nature. Instead, they combined their might and cast a spell that sealed the dragons into gemstones, one for each. Though alive, the dragons could no longer war among themselves. Forever locked in their gems, the dragons cannot influence the outside world. But the story doesn't end there, although it should have."

Iren gulped as Rondel's tone darkened.

"The sealing spell required so much magic that it killed all two hundred casters. As time passed, foolish Maantecs forgot why their ancestors willingly died to seal away the dragons. They began to desire the dragons' magic for their own. Five thousand years ago, they developed an enchantment that, if placed around a dragon's gem, allowed anyone who touched it to draw upon that dragon's power. They inscribed the sequence on eight weapons, turning them into Ryokaiten, or 'Dragon Weapons.'" Rondel motioned at the Muryozaki. "Your sword is one of them. See the three concentric rings of symbols on its hilt? Those markings are kanji, the Maantec form of writing. At their center, just beneath the surface, rests the Holy Diamond, containing the spirit and magic of the Holy Dragon, Divinion."

Iren stared at his sword with new fascination. Divinion, the dragon in the painting, the creature whose name adorned the tower in which he'd lived most of his life, resided in his father's katana. He could hardly believe a simple farmer would own a weapon that contained one of the mightiest beasts ever to live on Raa.

Rondel seemed to sense Iren's thoughts. After a quick sip from her hip flask, she continued, "Over time, nearly all of the Ryokaiten have disappeared. Few Maantecs even know about them anymore; your father probably didn't understand what he had. I can say this much for certain though. Throughout history, those who desire power have coveted the Ryokaiten. It could explain why someone would murder your parents."

Two unspoken follow-up questions came unbidden to Iren's mind. If the Quodivar leader had killed Iren's parents to obtain the Muryozaki, why hadn't he retrieved it at that point in time? And second, what would he do once he found out that Iren had it?

"You must understand both the might and the danger inherent in that sword," Rondel noted firmly. "It can grant you great power, but it can also destroy you. Evil will seek you, wanting to claim the Holy Dragon Sword's power for its own. No magic surpasses that of a Dragon Knight."

Iren grimaced. "A Dragon Knight?"

"To put it bluntly, a Dragon Knight is someone who wields a Ryokaiten. The fact that the Muryozaki healed you proves you're a Dragon Knight. You drew on Divinion's power to do that."

"Does that mean Amroth is a Dragon Knight too?" Iren asked. "He gave me this sword, and he's had it in his possession for seventeen years."

Rondel shook her head. "That isn't how it works. The sword chooses one owner and one owner only. That person becomes the Dragon Knight, and once the bond is made, only the knight's death can sever it. As long as you live, neither Amroth, nor anyone else, can become the Holy Dragon Knight."

Iren held up the Muryozaki, trembling. "Why me?" he asked, mostly to himself. "Why would a dragon, especially the Holy Dragon, want to bond with me? Or for that matter, any person at all?"

"One question at a time!" the old woman called out, laughing momentarily before turning serious again. "Let's start with the last one. Imagine for a moment that you're a dragon. Originally, you were a creature of nearly limitless power. Now you spend eternity locked inside the tiniest space, in utter darkness, unable to move, unable to control what happens in the world, yet you still feel the flow of time. Sealing the dragons may have preserved Raa, but it sentenced them to the most fiendish prisons possible. Bonding with a Dragon Knight, however, gains them a window to the outside world.

"As for why Divinion chose you specifically, I can only say this much. The dragons don't choose randomly. When a knight dies, the dragon finds its next partner by testing any non-Dragon Knight who touches its Ryokaiten. If the person passes the ordeal, they become the knight, but if they fail, they die. That means that if you aren't already a Dragon Knight, touching a Ryokaiten whose owner has died is extremely dangerous. You might gain incredible power, but you could just as easily perish. Each dragon administers a different test. In Divinion's case, Maantec lore says that he judges based on purity of heart. When I helped Amroth seventeen years ago, he gave me his account of your finding. I suspect that when your mother died, she dropped you. As you fell, you rubbed against your father's blade. As an innocent infant, you easily passed Divinion's test. You've been the Holy Dragon Knight almost all your life."

"But I never healed myself until last night."

"Of course. Holy Dragon Knight or not, Divinion's power remains locked within the Holy Diamond and the Muryozaki. That's why your finger didn't heal until you touched your sword. Specifically, it didn't heal until you touched the symbols on the hilt. Those kanji spell out the enchantment that connects you to Divinion. Unless some part of your skin touches them, you cannot use his magic."

Iren's head spun with all he had learned, but he nevertheless jumped to his feet. "Come on!" he cried. "Let's hurry and tell Amroth! With Divinion, we can defeat the Quodivar easily."

Rondel downed the last drops from her flask. "Don't you listen to anything I say? Do you not realize that I could have told you all of this at any time while we rode? Amroth can't know about Divinion."

"Why not? We're all in this mission together."

The old hag said derisively, "You really think so? Take care, little boy. That man you admire so much means to send you to your death."

"Amroth saved me from execution, you drunken windbag! He gave me my chance for revenge! He's only acted kindly to me, unlike you."

"Acting is indeed the right word for it," Rondel countered. When Iren folded his arms and scowled, she waved her hand dismissively. "Fine, fine, don't listen to me. But whether you trust Amroth or not, know this. There's more to this mission than simply defeating the Quodivar. Far more."

CHAPTER EIGHT
Okthora's Law

On the fourth day since departing Haldessa, the village of Veliaf finally came into view. All day, Iren and the others had watched as the boreal forest Akaku grew on the horizon, spreading from east to west in a blanket of conifer spires. Iren had considered the tiny wood where Rondel told him about the dragons impressive, but Akaku put that to shame. Its giant trees must have been at least twice the size of any in that thicket, and they grew so close together that almost no light could penetrate them. Iren could understand why Lodians feared it so strongly.

Veliaf didn't look much more welcoming. A high stone wall encircled it, so as they approached, Iren could see nothing of the village itself. The only entrance appeared to be a solid metal gate, which faced the road.

"When we reach the gate, let me handle it. Don't say anything." Amroth turned in his saddle and glowered at Rondel. "Especially you."

Iren gave the captain a sideways glance. Even if he didn't believe her, Rondel's warning about Amroth unsettled him.

Then again, considering the way Rondel could change her personality on a whim, she seemed the more likely actress. Immediately after reentering camp the other day, she had assumed her typical idiotic self and proceeded to grate on everyone's nerves, Iren's included, all the way to Veliaf. At the moment, she was complaining about the road conditions and how her horse kept stepping in every pothole. The useless beast of burden, she whined, would surely cause her to fall and break her arm. She waved an empty bottle in the air as she bellowed, having finished the last of her alcohol an hour ago.

The crone gave an impressive performance; Iren had to give her that. She didn't look like someone who could speak seriously about Maantecs, dragons, and events that happened thousands of years ago. Nor did she look like the kind of person who could kill six Quodivar without breaking a sweat. If anyone in their group was disguising their true motives, Iren considered Rondel the most likely suspect.

Maybe instead of Amroth, he really needed to watch out for her.

"Amroth!" Rondel piped up, "My eyes have withered with age and no longer see what you young folk easily spot. From back here, I don't see any watchmen on the wall. Can you?"

The captain fixed his gaze on the fortification, as did Iren. The annoying hag was right. Coming from this direction, they should easily see Veliaf's guards silhouetted against the clear blue sky.

Amroth suddenly snapped, "Weapons ready, all of you."

The group approached warily. Arriving at the gate, they found it nearly torn from its hinges. As they passed through it and entered Veliaf, Iren glanced around with disgust. Admittedly, he'd only ever known the manicured grounds and passages of Haldessa Castle, but surely villages should not look like this. Not a soul walked the cobble streets, even though it was barely midafternoon. All of the windows in every building were smashed, and many of the structures lacked doors as well.

Iren shuddered. Even in pristine condition, he would have considered the town intimidating. He couldn't spot a single tree or blade of grass. Instead of individual houses, identical stone two-story row homes lined both sides of the roads. As a cold wind howled through the narrow corridor of the street, Iren felt claustrophobic. He clutched his arms around his chest.

Amroth's eyes narrowed as he swiveled his head to take in the village from as many angles as possible. "Veliaf thrived when I came here on my last mission. What could have happened in such a short time?"

Dismounting, the group searched nearly a dozen houses and shops near the village entrance but found nothing of consequence. The town was devoid of life.

"I don't even see any bodies," Balear said when they reconvened back at their horses. "If someone attacked the village, shouldn't we see corpses, at the very least?"

"I didn't notice any valuables while examining the houses either," Amroth added. "Someone has completely looted this place."

"Quodivar?" Balear suggested, but while Amroth nodded curtly, Rondel did something unexpected. Adopting a broad grin, she started heading down a side street away from the others.

"This is all much too depressing," she said innocently when Amroth asked where she was heading. "I'm going to find a drink."

The captain raised a hand in warning, but she disappeared around a corner before he could say anything. He sighed. "I guess we'd better go after her before she gets herself killed. Leave the horses here; that alley's too narrow for them anyway."

After tying up their mounts, the trio pursued Rondel. The narrow lane twisted and turned several times before reaching the open ground of the village square. Arriving there, they found not only Rondel but a terrible sight.

The bodies of men, twenty or thirty of them, lay heaped and rotting in the square's center. Dried blood caked nearly all of the square's cobblestones. Four pikes surrounded the corpse pile, each topped with a decapitated head.

Iren and Balear both vomited at the smell; the people had died days ago. Even Amroth had a hard time keeping his composure. Rondel, however, appeared oblivious to the sensory overload. She stared lividly at the square, her body vibrating.

As Iren wiped his mouth, he realized he had overlooked a crucial element of the scene. He'd found the stacked carcasses so overpowering that he had missed a group of a dozen men about two hundred feet away on the far side of the square. The men jeered and kicked at something they surrounded. Through their taunts, Iren could barely discern muffled cries. Someone remained alive in the center of all that violence, though likely not for long. For the moment, the men contented themselves with just kicking the person, but each of them carried arms fit for war. All had bows and well-stocked quivers, as well as either a sword, axe, or spear. With an involuntary glance at his leg, Iren guessed that they likely had more than a few knives and daggers hidden away too.

Amroth gestured to Iren and Balear to take shelter in a nearby building. With Balear's bow their only long-distance weapon, they had no chance of stopping those brutes. They would all be shot long before they could get within sword range. The captain tapped Rondel on the shoulder to get her to come also, but she refused. Giving up on her, Amroth joined Iren and Balear.

Rondel marched slowly into the square. As she did, Iren got a brief look at her face. He gasped. Sparks jumped in a crisscrossing pattern that filled her irises. Three nights ago, Iren had felt confident he'd only imagined the odd bolts in the hag's eyes. Now those malicious sparks cowed him with fear.

Because this time, he knew they were no illusion.

"Excuse me!" Rondel barked, her voice low and with an edge keener than any blade's. "What are you all doing there?"

The men stopped their kicking and faced her. One of the brutes, bigger than the rest, stepped to the front and said, "What's it to ya, ya decrepit buzzard?"

In spite of the situation, Iren couldn't help but smirk. Decrepit buzzard…he'd have to remember that one if they lived through this.

Rondel, however, ignored the man's question. She gestured with her chin to the pile of bodies. "Who killed those people?"

The brute sneered, "They dared to resist the Quodivar and Lord Zuberi."

"In other words, you did it as a warning."

"All who defy Lord Zuberi must die."

Rondel's cold voice sounded almost sadistic as she replied, "You know, I haven't been in a great mood these past few days. Killing you all would help that tremendously."

The big Quodivar spat at the threat. Before his spittle reached the ground, the man next to him drew his bow and fired an arrow straight at Rondel's face. Iren cried out in grief. Maantec or not, the crone couldn't dodge a speeding arrow. He buried his head in his hands as he saw the projectile sail past, cleanly through her head.

Amroth forced Iren to look back into the square. Rondel still stood, apparently unchanged. Iren paled, knowing that in a few seconds he would have to watch Rondel's limp body fall gracelessly to the ground. He clenched his eyes shut, unwilling to view the dreaded moment.

"How rude of you; I wasn't finished speaking."

Iren's eyes snapped open. Rondel still stood there uninjured. Somehow she'd dodged the arrow.

"If I were a kind woman, I might tell you to lay down your weapons and surrender if you don't want to die." Iren had thought Rondel's voice couldn't get colder or more frightening, but he'd been wrong. "However, I am not a kind woman." She drew her dagger with her left hand. Sparks jumped over the blade just as they did on her eyes. "I follow Okthora's Law: evil must be annihilated."

The bandits all drew their bows and began firing rapidly. Rondel had nowhere to run, trapped between the tall townhouses lining either side of the street at the edge of the square. Iren cried out again, but this time, determined to see the tragedy through, he kept watching as arrows bombarded her location. At first he didn't follow what was happening. Then his jaw dropped.

Rondel was dodging the arrows, her body blurring as she did so. The arrows aimed for all parts of her, yet she easily avoided every one. Her ancient body swayed with precision and balance so fluid, she made King Azuluu's finest dancers look clumsy by comparison. Iren couldn't believe it. Rondel had said that Maantecs' speed and strength surpassed those of humans, but surely not by this much. He considered it highly unlikely that he could dodge all those shots if he and Rondel traded places. He could barely see most of them, and he had an even harder time tracking Rondel's movements.

The barrage kept up until every bandit fired every last arrow he possessed. When they saw that Rondel remained unharmed, three of the Quodivar threw down their weapons and fled. As soon as they did, Rondel dropped into a run, her body blurring across the distance. She crossed the square in under a second. Her dagger flashed, dropping all three thieves at the same time. The other bandits, probably hoping to catch her off-guard, drew their close-range weapons and charged as one. The hag simply looked up, her eyes still sparking, and ran forward to meet them at a blinding pace. Several flashes ensued as Rondel's blade danced, and then she emerged uninjured on the far side of the Quodivar. All but one of her enemies collapsed. The lone survivor, the man who had jeered at her so confidently mere moments ago, knelt before her with panicked tears in his eyes.

"Wait!" he called out. "I didn't mean it! Zuberi said he would kill me if I didn't take over Veliaf! I had no choice. Please, you believe in mercy, right?"

Rondel's sparking eyes stared unfeelingly down at him. "No."

The dagger swung hard and fast.

As the thief hit the ground, Rondel stepped around him without looking back. She wiped her blade clean and sheathed it. With a deep breath, she closed her eyes. When they opened again, they had returned to their normal green. The sparks had vanished without a trace.

Amroth, Iren, and Balear all stared into the village square, stupefied. When they recovered their wits enough to move from their hiding place, they ran to Rondel. Iren and Balear immediately bombarded her with questions. The old hag remained silent, her gaze fixed on Amroth. The captain calmly walked from bandit to bandit, checking each one's pulse. When he finished, he faced Rondel with a passive expression. In a calm, level voice, he said, "I had no idea Lefts were so capable in battle."

Rondel's stupid grin sprouted on her face, but now Iren perceived what he had previously missed. A deep cunning hid in the narrow eyes behind the smile. "So you think I'm a Left too, just like Iren," she replied, shaking her head and acting exasperated. "Always underestimating old people. You both really should learn to respect your elders."

Amroth was not dissuaded. "I do respect my elders, and I know that no human, of any age, can move like that."

The crone sighed but didn't drop her grin. "I guess you have me. You really should stop calling us 'Lefts,' though. As I explained to Iren, the proper name for our species is 'Maantecs.'"

Balear turned red. "So, so Rondel is one of them too? Great, Captain, just great." He loosed a long string of curses.

Amroth shrugged. "Frankly, Balear, I can't imagine a better situation. With two companions who can fight like that, we should have no trouble defeating the Quodivar. If we can find them, that is. I'd counted on getting information here, but Veliaf is deserted."

Iren turned his gaze to the crumpled person the Quodivar had been beating before Rondel intervened. Kneeling down, he felt for a pulse. The man was still alive. "Maybe this guy knows."

The captain leapt to Iren's side, clapping him on the back. "You may be right, Iren! If he survives all these wounds." Amroth gingerly ran his fingers over the man's body. The captain's expression grew grimmer with each passing inch. The man, who looked about the same age as Amroth, had bruises covering every exposed patch of skin, and blood matted his black hair. His tattered clothes bore testament to his beating. At last Amroth said, "He has multiple broken ribs, and his right arm and leg are shattered. The gash on his head goes clear to the bone. More than likely, he's bleeding internally. If we move him, he'll die immediately. If we leave him here, he'll perhaps last another hour. Either way, he's lost consciousness and will never wake up again. We won't get any information from him unless, by some miracle, we can heal him."

As he spoke those last four words, Amroth met Iren's eyes, and the young Maantec guessed the captain's thoughts. Amroth hadn't accepted Rondel's claim that Iren had avoided injury during the battle on the hill. He'd guessed that Iren had somehow reversed his own fatal wounds. The boy gulped, knowing that Amroth expected him to cure this man the same way. He didn't know how he would do it though. Thanks to Rondel, he knew that he was the "Holy Dragon Knight," but he had no clue what that even meant. All he knew for sure about it was that holding the Muryozaki caused his injuries to heal.

That gave him an idea. He had to try it. If he did nothing, the man would die anyway. Iren drew his father's katana. Balear reached for his own sword, calling Iren a demon and arguing that killing the man was not proper. A withering glare from Amroth made the sergeant fall silent.

Iren placed the Muryozaki's hilt in the wounded man's palm. He watched and waited for the weapon's healing power to take effect. Seconds, then minutes, passed.

Nothing.

"Why?" Iren shouted, becoming horribly frustrated. "Why doesn't it work? Why can't I save him?" He clutched the man's hand along with the katana's hilt, his eyes winced shut as he pleaded, "Please, Muryozaki, or Divinion, or whatever you are, I don't know anything about you, or Maantecs, or dragons, but whatever you did for me, do it for this man too! He doesn't deserve to die like this!"

It made no sense to him why he cared so much for this guy. He'd never known the man before today. In all likelihood, even if he had, the man would simply have hated him. He probably would have stared at Iren with the same empty eyes as everyone in Haldessa. Iren would have teased him, or carried out some awful prank in retaliation on the jerk. He certainly wouldn't have helped him. And yet, kneeling over the dying man, Iren felt compelled to act. Maybe it was the injustice of the situation. Maybe it was watching Rondel avenge the fallen villagers. Or maybe it was just that, for the first time in his life, someone had regarded him as something other than a monster.

Whatever the reason, he couldn't just sit here and let this poor man die!

A moment later, Balear, Amroth, and Rondel all gasped. Opening his eyes, Iren saw the Muryozaki glow a brilliant white. Its light spread over the man's body, bathing the entire area in its glow. It did not blind or cause pain. On the contrary, it left Iren with a warm, calming sensation. Even Balear smiled when it washed over him.

Slowly, the light faded away. The wounded villager still lay on the ground, unmoving. Amroth felt over the man's body as he had the first time, but now his morose expression shifted. After a breathless pause, he looked at Iren and beamed.

Iren, meanwhile, had gone deaf. He could see Amroth's mouth move and his arms gesture excitedly, but no sound came from him. The injured man stirred and fluttered his eyes. As he did, gray rings formed around Iren's field of vision. He just barely saw the villager sit up before his world went black.

CHAPTER NINE

Encounter with the Almighty

He was flying.

No, that didn't make sense, because Iren could feel solid ground beneath his feet. Darkness surrounded him; he fluttered his hand in front of his face but couldn't see it at all. The floor, if one existed, felt like flat stone. He took a few steps. The hollow ring of each footfall unnerved him. With trepidation he called, "Hello?" but only his nervous breathing replied. He reached for the Muryozaki, but it had disappeared from his hip. Fear took hold. Somehow, he had become lost in an infinite void without even a weapon to protect him.

Just as his desperation grew too great, a faint light appeared in the distance. At first Iren took it for a star, but it grew bigger the longer he stared. It soon took the form of a great undulating serpent with majestic wings, bursts of light erupting in every direction with each wingbeat. The vast majority of the dragon, for it could be nothing else, was of the purest white, with a few sky blue streaks accentuating the lines of its massive yet elegant body. Most impressive of all, however, were its eyes. Even from far away, they shone with a blue that bore through the blackness.

As the dragon flew closer, its light swallowed the shadows so that Iren nearly forgot they had ever engulfed him in the first place. The creature's glow did not act like a beacon in the night, guiding ships to shore like the lighthouse at Ceere. Rather, it simply made the darkness go away, so that there was no need for such a lantern.

Iren gulped as the beast's size truly came into perspective. Its eyes alone measured over five feet in diameter. The dragon's teeth offered no comfort; each was longer than Iren was tall and had an edge that made the Muryozaki look like a worn butter knife.

The creature landed on four legs, each with three claws longer and sharper still than its fangs, and came into striking range. Iren expected it to devour him, but instead the dragon lowered its head in a deep bow of respect. The gesture so astonished Iren that he could do nothing but stare and take in the strange beauty of the awe-inspiring reptile. Long blue hair grew all along its spine, and two gigantic blue whiskers, each as thick as Iren's thigh, adorned its face.

At last the dragon rose and, giving Iren a curious expression, loosed a low grumble, which sounded more like a sigh than anything threatening. Then, with a booming voice that shook the very fabric of the universe, the creature said, "So you are my knight. You are Iren Saitosan."

Iren tried stammering a few syllables but couldn't. It was like meeting Juusa the Creator face to face.

The dragon watched him with its huge eyes, and Iren knew it could see past him into his mind and heart. He didn't have to say anything, because the dragon already knew everything about him.

When Iren remained silent, the dragon blinked slowly, and then its whole body began shaking. Light streamed off of it, and as Iren watched, the mighty beast shrunk. It grew smaller and smaller, disappearing at such a pace that Iren thought it would vanish. He didn't know whether to feel relief or despair at the possibility. As it neared his height, however, the shrinking slowed. Gradually, the dragon changed. Its wings disappeared into its back, and it stood up on its hind legs. As its scales melted into smooth skin, it took the form of an old man with long, pure white hair. An equally white moustache adorned his face. The man wore white robes, flecked with blue, and matching sandals. The transformation amazed Iren. He never would have guessed this man could be a dragon in disguise. The only clue lay in his eyes; they retained their original piercing blue. Though he looked like an ordinary old man, Iren knew he still couldn't hide anything from him.

The transformed dragon gave Iren a genuinely warmhearted smile, then said, "Well, Iren. I believe you already have some idea of who I am." His words sounded soft and kindly, not at all like the booming voice the dragon had spoken with earlier.

Though still nervous, the creature's transformation set Iren marginally more at ease. "You…you're Divinion," he managed, "the Holy Dragon."

Divinion nodded his approval. "Until now, the Holy Diamond has trapped my will inside it, keeping me hidden from you. However, today you released enough magic to breach that barrier."

Iren's face grew hot. He felt he'd made a terrible error. According to Rondel, the dragons were so dangerous they'd wiped out a continent.

If Divinion had any such plans in mind, however, they didn't show on the old man's face. Instead, he put an arm around Iren's shoulder and said, "This is the first time you and I have had a chance to speak. I first met you over seventeen years ago, and I've waited desperately to see you again, to see how you had grown. I know you walk a difficult path, and you have walked it well."

Iren didn't know what he had expected the dragon to say, but that definitely wasn't it. The people of Lodia always berated him, calling him "Left" or "freak" or any number of other derogatory terms. To hear such praise from the Holy Dragon himself was something he never believed possible.

The old man looked to the heavens, cocking his head as though studying something far beyond Iren's sight. A warm but sad smile filled his face. Forlornly, he said, "It seems our time together has run its course. The part of my will that entered you when you cast that spell is dissipating back into the Holy Diamond. Soon you'll return to the physical world, and I'll return to my gemstone prison."

Divinion once more took the form of the serpentine dragon, and as he took flight, he called with a hint of dry humor, "Until next we meet. Perhaps you'll have more to say then?" With a shower of light, Divinion vanished, but the glow he had created lingered, illuminating that strange world for a few more brief seconds before it became dark once again.

CHAPTER TEN
Lightning Sight

Iren awoke with a start, heart pounding as he questioned what he'd seen. He wondered if he'd really met Divinion, or if it had just happened in his head. It felt so real.

Taking in his surroundings, Iren found himself in a small bedroom. The only illumination came from moonlight through the single broken window, remnants of shattered glass untended around it. He lay on a bed, though he considered the term generous. It was little more than a flap of canvas stretched between four boards. The Muryozaki leaned against the bed. An involuntary sigh of relief exited him. After his encounter with Divinion, he'd feared he might never see the sword again.

His weapon's presence was the only thing comforting about the room. The rest of it looked like a storm had blown through. All the furniture was strewn about, and much of it was broken. Dresser drawers lay smashed on the floor. Someone had thoroughly rooted through everything in here.

The only other person in the room sat in a plain, hard wooden chair not three feet from him. Despite the darkness, Iren had traveled with this man long enough to recognize his profile and white blonde hair that almost glowed in the dark.

"Bedside vigil, Balear?" Iren asked.

Balear rose and walked to a door on the far side of the bedroom. Placing a hand on the latch, he replied curtly, "It was my turn." He opened the door a crack, hesitated a moment, then looked back at Iren. To the young Maantec's shock, the soldier wore a tiny grin. "By the way," Balear said, "I still don't understand who or what you are. I can't explain how you can do the things you do. Maybe you do have devil magic. All the same, what you did today was impressive." Then the sergeant departed, leaving Iren more confused than when he'd first awoken.

As he sat on the stretched-canvas bed, he noticed Balear had left a small plate on his chair with half a loaf of bread and a small cup of water. It was far from appetizing, yet the moment Iren saw it, a strong hunger attacked him. He hadn't eaten since before they'd arrived in Veliaf. Grabbing the bread with both hands, he plowed into it. It was hard, stale, and tasteless, but his stomach didn't mind.

He'd only taken a few bites when Balear returned, this time with Rondel, Amroth, and another man. Rondel tripped in the darkness, cursing in her high-pitched whine. The bottom of a glass bottle stuck out from her right sleeve. Iren shook his head. Leave it to the old hag to find alcohol even in a village overrun by bandits.

"I still don't get why we can't light a candle," Rondel prattled on. "I'm likely to fall and snap my wrist, or worse."

A sharp, low hiss came from the unknown man, "I've explained it perfectly well before, but if you're so senile you've forgotten already, then just go to bed and stop bothering us."

"Really, is that any way to treat your rescuer?" Rondel teased.

"Knock it off, both of you," Amroth sounded tense. He turned to Iren. "From what Dirio's told us, the Quodivar have issued a curfew for the village. Any lights on after dark, and the house becomes a target."

His mouth full of bread, Iren asked, "Diwwio?"

The unknown man stepped forward. "Ah, yes, that would be me. I'm the lucky soul you and your comrades rescued this afternoon. I owe all of you my life, but it seems I owe you more than any of them."

"What about me?" Rondel asked with mock hurt.

Amroth ignored her, saying to Dirio, "Perhaps in gratitude, you could tell us what happened to Veliaf."

The black-haired man walked to the smashed window, a grieving look on his face as his gaze swept over the remnants of his once proud village. "All this damage has happened in the past week. As you probably know, Veliaf prospers thanks to its mine. The durable stone we extract gives us wealth beyond our size. You've seen its quality in the wall that surrounds the town, as well as our buildings and streets. I myself work in the mines as a foreman, or rather, I did until last week. You see, we were working in the mine when one of my employees reported that the walls in the northwest section sounded different when struck. I told the men to stop, fearing a possible cave-in, but the idiotic manager above me overrode my decision and ordered them to continue. Later that day, we discovered why the wall sounded different. The miners broke through it, revealing a natural cavern on the other side.

"We sent teams to investigate whether the cave had any exits. You can understand our fear. We have always been careful to limit the ways outsiders can reach us, what with Akaku on our doorstep. Breaching the cavern jeopardized our safety. If it had an exit outside the village wall, enemies could reach us through the mines."

Dirio paused a moment, his hands clutching the wooden window frame so tightly that even in the dark Iren saw drops of blood slide down the wall. At length the foreman continued, "The teams sent to explore the cavern never returned. Barely an hour after we sent them, we heard screams within the mine. I had returned to the surface at that point, so I ran to the mine entrance to see what was happening. Then I beheld the worst sight of my life: Yokai pouring from the mine, the blood of my workers slick on their blades."

Balear opened his mouth wide, and Rondel's eyes narrowed dangerously. Her grin became a furious scowl, her bottle utterly forgotten. Amroth, however, simply leaned against the wall nearest the door, arms crossed, and nodded as though he had expected this.

Iren had finished his meager meal by now, and he set his plate on the floor beside him. He gave everyone a quizzical look. "Yokai?"

Balear smacked himself on the head. "Surely you at least know about Yokai!"

When Iren's blank stare conveyed that he, in fact, knew nothing about Yokai, Rondel interjected, "It doesn't shock me that you don't know. In Haldessa, only Castle Guard members are told of their existence. Azuluu's predecessors ordered all books on Yokai burned centuries ago."

"What are Yokai then," Iren asked, "and why keep their existence secret?"

"They're a sentient race," Rondel answered, "though they do the word a disservice. Thousands of years ago, they dwelt in the Eregos Mountains on Lodia's southern border. The Tengu pushed them out in a great war, and the Yokai tribes, quarreling over who to blame for their defeat, separated. Most went south and disappeared into lands beyond the knowledge of humans. But one tribe settled in Akaku, hoping to take advantage of

Lodia's northern settlements. Over the centuries, places like Veliaf have had no choice but to defend themselves, hence Veliaf's wall. Caardit, in northwest Lodia, has a similar construction."

"Besides Veliaf and Caardit, no Lodian settlements lie within sight of Akaku," Balear added. "Once those towns built walls, the Yokai lost their easy prey and went into hiding in the forest. King Azuluu's ancestors didn't want the public panicking over the fact that Yokai dwelt on Lodia's borders, so they decreed the subject forbidden. They hoped that, as generations passed, the Yokai would fade from memory, and so they have."

Amroth spoke for the first time in quite a while. "So Yokai killed all those men in the square? Yokai looted your homes?"

Dirio shook his head. "No, the Yokai swarmed our village, killing many, but our militia rallied and pushed the beasts back into the mines. We then dragged a heavy stone over the mine's entrance and sealed it shut. Doing so cut off our source of livelihood, but what option did we have? With the mine compromised, we had to seal it for the good of the village. We took the dead outside the walls and buried them the next day, as is our custom."

"But your troubles had only just begun, correct?" Amroth fixed his gaze on Dirio. With each question, the captain looked more and more like a cat stalking a mouse.

The foreman nodded. "Two nights later, the gatekeeper on duty was slain and the gate opened. Quodivar poured into Veliaf. Our militia engaged them, but the Quodivar butchered them all and stacked their remains in the square. The village has since decayed into what you saw today. Those devils took nearly all the remaining residents as slaves. As one of the few people left uncaptured, I tried to sneak out and flee to Haldessa to alert the Castle Guard. Unfortunately, the Quodivar noticed me. I thought they would beat me to death." The poor man shuddered.

Amroth ignored Dirio's pained gesture. "Where did the Quodivar take the villagers they captured?"

The question set the foreman in a panic. He covered his head in his hands and slid down the wall, howling in despair, "Into the mines! Those fools opened up the sealed mine and went in, taking the villagers with them!"

Again Amroth didn't react to Dirio's outburst. Instead, he replied evenly, "I'm sure the Yokai came back into the village at that point, killing Quodivar and residents alike."

Dirio looked up from the floor, wiping his face on his sleeve. "No, that's the strange part," he admitted. "The Yokai have left us alone ever since the Quodivar reopened the mine. I don't know if the Quodivar killed them or merely pushed them from the cavern, but I haven't seen a single Yokai since the bandits arrived."

Amroth nodded, clearly unsurprised that Dirio disagreed with him. "I expected as much. The Quodivar have always had better weapons and armor than mere thieves should own. I knew they couldn't be acting alone; they needed some other force arming them. The Yokai provide the only logical possibility."

Dirio gave him a shocked look. "So the Quodivar didn't drive the Yokai from the cave?"

"Quite the contrary. The Yokai must permit the Quodivar to use the cave as their base. I would venture that on the day the Yokai came swarming through the mine, one or two Quodivar snuck in with them. They hid in the village until they could open the gate from the inside. Because you were so preoccupied with the Yokai, you failed to notice the human enemy in your midst."

Iren cocked an eyebrow. "But why would the Yokai help the Quodivar?"

"Because the Quodivar and Yokai have the same desire: the complete overthrow of Lodia," Amroth replied. "But neither group can manage it alone. The Yokai don't have the numbers to conquer even a small town like Veliaf, and without the Yokai supplying them with armor and weapons, the Quodivar are little more than thugs. Joined together, however, they could conquer even Haldessa."

"Surely they couldn't become that powerful!" Balear cried. "We must go back immediately and warn the king!"

Amroth shook his head. "No, we have neither the time nor the manpower to do that. Rondel gave us a narrow opening today, and we'll need everyone here to take advantage of it."

Balear nervously asked, "What do we do?"

To everyone's surprise, Amroth smirked. "Simple. I suspected the Quodivar had their base in Akaku, but I couldn't figure out how to reach it. Aimlessly wandering that forest would kill us for sure. Now, thanks to Rondel, we have a clear line of attack. Both the Yokai and Quodivar believe the men Rondel killed today guard Veliaf's mine. If we strike before they realize those men have died, we can catch them by surprise. We'll sneak into their base from the one direction they consider themselves invulnerable: below." The captain turned to Dirio. "You'll have to come too. You know the mines better than any of us."

The foreman initially looked ill at Amroth's request, but then his expression hardened. "If it frees my fellow citizens, I'll do as you say."

Amroth nodded. "All right, we'll leave at dawn. Let's get what sleep we can. We'll need it."

Everyone except Iren rose and headed to the door. As they did, Iren said, "Wait, Rondel. Can I talk to you alone for a minute?"

The others exited the room, Amroth last of all. He gave Rondel an interrogative look, but the old hag simply smiled innocently, shut the door in his face, and took a seat in the chair beside Iren's bed. Apparently remembering her bottle for the first time since they'd started speaking about the Yokai, she raised it to her lips and took a long draught.

Iren didn't wait for her to finish. "Why did I pass out today?" he asked.

Rondel kept drinking until she drained the bottle. Wiping her mouth, she replied, "First of all, while I commend you for healing Dirio, you need to understand the severity of your actions. Remember how I told you that you drew on Divinion's power to heal yourself? You did that today too. However, you can't draw on his magic without also drawing some of his spirit, his will, out of the gemstone prison and into your body. Using magic is essentially a contest of wills between dragon and knight. If you draw small amounts of magic, little of the dragon's will comes with it, and you easily triumph. But the more spells you cast, the more the dragon's will seeps into you. If you draw more power from Divinion than you yourself possess, his spirit will break yours."

"What does that mean? What would happen to me?"

Rondel shivered. "In Maantec history, a few arrogant Dragon Knights attempted to use too much of their dragon's power with disastrous results. They foolishly believed their minds strong enough to win the contest of wills, no matter how much magic they used. None succeeded. In every case, the knight's body transformed into that of a dragon, losing control and going on a rampage."

Iren became ashen at the thought of turning into a dragon. "Maybe I shouldn't use magic at all," he mumbled.

"Not if you can help it," Rondel agreed. "Fortunately, a dragon's will can only exist outside its gem for a limited time. Even though you pushed your magic to the brink today, you can use it during the battle tomorrow."

Iren gulped. He didn't want to think about tomorrow. If Amroth had guessed correctly about the cavern being the Quodivar's base, they could very well end up meeting the bandits' leader, his parents' murderer, down there.

Trying to distract himself from that possibility, he changed the subject and asked, "Rondel, you used magic to kill those thieves today, didn't you? You also know a lot about the dragons. Are you a Dragon Knight?"

She smiled and drew her dagger, holding it up for Iren's inspection. The hilt, hand guard, and pommel were all perfectly round and made of dark wood. Staring closely at the hilt, Iren looked for what he knew should be there: three concentric rings of kanji symbols identical to those on his own blade.

After a moment, he snorted. The hilt looked perfectly smooth. "Guess not."

Rondel rolled her eyes. "You really are hopeless, aren't you? That close and you still couldn't notice?"

"Notice what, you dried up crone?"

"Ignorant child! I'm trying to teach you here."

"Oh, is that what you call this?"

The two turned away from each other a moment before Rondel, shaking her head and sighing, said, "I learned long ago that advertising yourself as a Dragon Knight is a good way to die. Fools challenge you constantly, wanting the dragon for themselves. Sooner or later, one of them will succeed. Better to hide your power and never let anyone know your true abilities. After today, though, I can't hide anymore." She pointed directly at the center of the hilt, and at last Iren saw it, barely visible. The wood had been stained a beautiful red, but on top of that someone had applied a second stain with a thin brush, just a hair darker. With it, they had penned the ring sequence, all but invisibly.

"This is the Liryometa, the Storm Dragon Dagger, and in its hilt rests Okthora. Like you, I can use magic, although I must admit, mine looks a little flashier. Thanks to Okthora, I can manipulate lightning."

"Whoa," Iren couldn't help saying. He imagined Rondel summoning bolts of lightning from the sky, obliterating all in her path.

Rondel must have detected Iren's worry, because she laughed and said, "Don't expect me to call up a thunderstorm any time soon. Remember how you passed out healing Dirio? You used too much magic. The same can happen to me. Instead, I prefer a simpler tactic. Rather than use the lightning outside, I rely on the lightning within myself."

Iren scoffed. Rondel had told him a lot of crazy things in the past few days, but he was pretty sure people didn't have lightning inside them. At least, he hoped not.

Unflustered by Iren's disbelieving retort, Rondel explained, "When you want to flex your arm, do you know how your brain tells your muscles to move? It uses an electrical signal. The muscles also generate signals when they contract. Each signal has only the most miniscule charge, so controlling them requires little magic. But even small changes to them can have fascinating results. For example, by increasing the amount of voltage flowing to my muscles, I can move extremely rapidly."

"That's how you crossed the square so quickly," Iren realized. "What about your eyes, though? They had sparks in them!"

Rondel beamed with pride. She closed her eyes briefly. When she opened them again, blue bolts were dancing across her irises. "This is my best magical invention, a technique I'm proud to say no other Maantec can do. I call it Lightning Sight."

"Lightning Sight?" Iren asked, mystified.

"You see, not only does the brain use electrical charges to communicate to your muscles, but the senses use them to signal what they encounter to the brain. Increasing those signals boosts my senses. In the case of Lightning Sight, the enhanced vision lets me pinpoint every detail of a scene, observe an object over long distances, and even see in total darkness."

Iren thought about his previous experiences with Rondel. Lightning Sight explained how she easily dodged all the Quodivar's arrows. She could perceive the tiny motions of the thieves' bodies and use them to predict what they were going to do. Also, once they fired their arrows, she could track the projectiles' flights with perfect detail. Lightning Sight effectively gave the crone an instantaneous reaction time, and when combined with her increased speed, hitting her would become almost impossible.

Rondel stretched, stood, and headed for the door. "Well, if that's all, both of us should get some rest."

Iren almost let her leave when he felt a strange urge, and he burst out, "Rondel, have you ever met your dragon, Okthora?"

The aged Maantec had a hand on the door. She stood silently for a long time before responding carefully, "Why do you ask?"

"When I passed out, I saw Divinion. He talked to me."

Rondel turned in the darkness, her expression inscrutable. "No, I haven't," she replied, "and if you want my advice, you'll refrain from ever speaking with yours again." With that, she exited the room.

For a long time Iren lay awake, pondering Rondel's words. At last, exhausted from the events of the day and the promise of battle tomorrow, he fell into a deep and, thankfully, dreamless sleep.

CHAPTER ELEVEN
Descent into Darkness

After a hasty breakfast at dawn, Balear and the others headed to the entrance to Veliaf's mine. Hardly an elegant structure, the mine's opening was nothing more than a large hole in the ground covered with a pair of hinged wooden doors that swung to either side. Next to the doors sat a gargantuan chunk of blue stone with heavy ropes and pulleys wrapped around it. Dirio explained that it had come from a slag pile near the mine's entrance. Balear wondered how many villagers it had taken to haul the boulder over the entrance.

Captain Angustion motioned for Dirio to take the lead alongside him. Rondel came next, still grinning in that way that made Balear want to punch her in the face. The Castle Guard's code forbade him to strike a woman, in particular an old woman, but Rondel really, really pushed him. After her display yesterday, though, Balear was in no mood to challenge her.

The captain had ordered Balear and Iren to serve as rear guard. They hadn't seen any more Quodivar in the village, but that didn't necessarily mean they weren't there. Moreover, even if the bandits Rondel had killed yesterday were the only Quodivar left in Veliaf, the spiderweb of mine passages could hide any number of them.

Balear cast a surreptitious glance at Iren. Admittedly, his opinion of the Left had changed a little in the past twenty-four hours. Healing Dirio, even though Balear didn't understand how on Raa that could happen, had at least proved Iren capable of good deeds. For this particular assignment, however, Iren still made him deeply uncomfortable. The Left had barely survived his first skirmish. The heart of the Quodivar and Yokai's territory wasn't the place for basic training, whatever devil magic Iren might have. Making matters worse, Captain Angustion kept heaping praise on the boy. He never made such glowing remarks to other soldiers.

All the same, Balear knew his superior must have his reasons. If Captain Angustion considered Iren's talents acceptable, Balear would just have to keep his own feelings in check and obey.

The group slipped into the dank mine, shadows enveloping them the moment they crossed the threshold. Leaning down, Dirio located a large box just inside the mine entrance. A shower of sparks erupted, and a torch flared to life in Dirio's hand.

Putting away his striker, Dirio retrieved enough torches from the box and gave one to each of them. The light did little more than cast a pale glow on their path, but even so, Balear took in the mine with awe. The tunnels had square cross sections large enough to allow even the tallest workers to walk around comfortably. Sturdy wooden cants, some so thick Balear doubted he could have wrapped his arms around them, supported the ceiling. Dirio tapped one and turned to the group. "Spruce timbers from Akaku," he whispered. "Nowhere else around grows them this big."

Balear marveled not only at the mine itself, but also at the incredible work that had gone into making it. Aside from the constant threat of death by cave-in, he knew the workers had risked their lives by entering Akaku to cut trees. The flat walls bore the occasional divot signifying where crews had carved their way through the solid earth, deeper and deeper until finally reaching the stone they wanted.

With each step, Balear's muscles tightened. Thus far, no one had approached them, whether from the front or from behind, but the mine's emptiness only set him more on edge. It was full of blind corners, and every turn could reveal an enemy. Worse, while their torches helped light their path, they also gave away their approach to anyone lurking around a bend.

Eventually, Dirio called them to a halt with a silent wave. Balear looked ahead and beheld the breach in the mine that led into the cavern beyond. Peering into the opening, he saw that the cave's walls curved up and away from him, far higher than the mine's ceiling.

Captain Angustion doused his torch, and the others quickly did the same. They'd needed the torches so Dirio could navigate them to the cavern, but they couldn't risk using them any longer. Now they had truly entered Quodivar territory, and stealth could make the difference between victory and death.

For a moment Balear fumbled in the total darkness, unable to see even an inch in front of his face. Cold mist from the cavern swirled around him, dampening his clothes as well as his spirits. Gulping, he stretched out a hand and grasped the shoulder of the person in front of him. The height told him it belonged to Iren. He instinctively recoiled, but focusing on the mission, he reluctantly took hold and let the freak guide him.

They walked in a line, each person with a hand on the one in front of them. Rondel led the way. Balear could barely perceive the faintest glow coming from around her head. She must be doing that crazy thing with her eyes again. More devil magic, he knew. Still, she managed to weave her way through the black tunnel without difficulty, and Balear doubted an approaching Quodivar would consider the tiny light her eyes created anything out of the ordinary.

More likely, they would notice the noise the group made. Deprived of his sight, every sound felt magnified a dozen times over. Every crunch of his boots on the gravel floor, every drop of water from the ceiling, every hissed breath became more deafening than Haldessa's great hall during an evening meal.

Rondel led them on for an indeterminate amount of time, the floor gradually sloping downward as they hiked. The only problem with the Left leading the way was her height. She seemed to forget, or maybe she just didn't care, that the men following her all measured at least a head taller than her. While she could easily avoid low ceilings, more than once Balear collided into one that jutted out of nowhere. In the total darkness, he never received the slightest warning. He quickly lost track of how many bruises had already started forming on his head.

Suddenly, there was a loud crash right in front of him. Iren's shoulder disappeared from his grip, and Balear was left alone in the dark. He reached for his sword, terrified that the enemy had ambushed them and begun slaughtering them one by one. Before he could draw his weapon, however, he pitched forward, tripping over a mound that came almost to his waist. The pile was fortunately soft, and the moment he hit it, the series of muffled "Oofs!" and a high-pitched cry of "My back!" told him what had happened.

Rondel had stopped for some reason, but in the blackness no one could tell. Balear disentangled himself from the inglorious heap, and the others did the same. Next to him, Balear heard a series of popping noises, and then Rondel said, "Well, I guess it's fine after all."

Although he couldn't see her, Balear knew the old Left was smiling.

"Why did you stop?" Iren whispered, but he needn't have asked. Just ahead, around a bend in the passageway, a dull light shone. Captain Angustion poked his head around the corner and gestured that it was safe to proceed.

With the captain leading the way, they slowly advanced. The tunnel narrowed until Balear felt rock scraping against both of his arms. It made him fear for Captain Angustion. In the cramped space, his superior would have no support. Balear couldn't fire his bow here, and he doubted the captain could even draw his long hand-and-a-half sword.

To Balear's great relief, the tunnel ultimately opened into a much larger room, though just how big he couldn't tell. Dozens of torches lined the chamber walls, but their light faded before reaching the ceiling. Balear judged the distance to the torches on the far wall at well over a hundred feet. In the middle of the room, the Quodivar had mounted a series of pedestals bearing even more torches.

What those torches revealed made Balear's breath catch in his throat. Gold and silver coins, fine textiles, exquisite jewelry, and masterful paintings covered most of the room's floor.

The Quodivar's plunder, however, had not made Balear react. No, his concern stemmed from the wooden table in the room's center. Six crude chairs fashioned from logs surrounded it, and upon each sat a man. They appeared distracted with a dice game, but each of them had a dagger at his belt and a sword just behind him within easy reach. Balear pursed his lips. He and his companions were in shadow here, just beyond the edge of the room, but as soon as they entered, the men would notice them.

Amroth apparently made the same calculation, because he looked back, gave the faintest of nods, and then charged into the room at full speed, sword drawn. At first, Balear didn't understand the gesture, but when Iren nearly bowled him over to join the fray, at last the young soldier understood. Since they couldn't sneak up on the enemy, they might as well just get noticed and take them out as quickly as possible.

By the time Balear drew his bow, the battle had nearly ended. Iren and Captain Angustion had each slain two men already, and as Balear nocked his first arrow, Rondel stabbed another from behind. The sixth fighter, however, the one farthest from where they had entered the room, had fled the moment the attack started. The captain raced after him, disappearing into a passageway that led further down.

For a moment the others stared in shock at the empty canyon entrance. Rondel recovered first. "Let's go," she said. "The fool's going to get himself killed."

They dashed for the far passage, Balear taking the lead. He had to reach his captain. He had to protect him. Captain Angustion couldn't die! Balear crossed the threshold into the canyon, and then the explosion knocked him flat.

The bone-crushing shower of stone missed him by inches. Coughing amid the dust, Balear regained his feet. A wall of debris blocked the passageway. He cursed and smashed his fist against it.

"A trap," Dirio suggested, "meant to crush anyone who crosses into the canyon."

Rondel looked doubtful. "Then why didn't Amroth trigger it? Or that Quodivar?"

"Who cares?" Balear shouted. He wrapped both arms around one of the larger stones, trying and failing to heave it aside. "We've got to reach Captain Angustion!"

They all rushed to help, but with each rock Balear removed, his thoughts drifted, unbidden, to Rondel. He highly doubted that the collapse had occurred naturally, but surely no manmade effort could have caused it. The explosion that preceded the cave-in and the horrible timing of it stunk of devil magic.

After entirely too long, they cleared enough of the rock fall for Balear to squeeze through. Once past the debris, he bounded down the tunnel at a full sprint. He knew he was opening himself up to an ambush, but he didn't care. He would run until he found his captain, dead or alive.

As he charged through the gloom, he was dimly aware that this latest passage looked nothing at all like the previous ones. Those had rough, jagged walls that stuck out at odd angles and changed direction at random. This tunnel, by contrast, was wide, round, smooth, and perfectly straight. Just like the cave-in, he had the odd feeling that nature hadn't created it, yet neither did it resemble a human effort like Veliaf's mine. The walls looked poured, not excavated, and everything had an eerie sheen that made it look like glass, except black.

The bizarre tube finally ended, and Balear ran into another open room, this one looking natural. Though barely fifteen feet at its widest, its ceiling, like the previous room, rose so high he couldn't begin to discern it. Reaching the room's center, Balear tensed. Something about this place made him uneasy.

A hand grasped Balear's shoulder, and he jumped in panic even as Rondel whispered, "Stop." Balear turned and saw Rondel's stressed, even worried face. Considering her impressive display yesterday, that look unsettled him more than anything he'd seen in years.

The old Left methodically surveyed the room, those crazy sparks in her eyes again. At first Balear thought Rondel had satisfied herself, because she took a few steps toward the room's far end. The young sergeant stared at her back, wondering what passed through her head.

Without warning Rondel spun around and drew her dagger. "Get ready," she spat, her terse voice low and acidic. "There are ten of them."

Iren and Dirio finally came into the room, the foreman huffing and puffing after all the effort. "Ten of what?" he breathed, his hands on his knees.

Rondel didn't get a chance to answer. As soon as Dirio spoke, a hideous cackling filled the room, and a mass of grotesque shapes cascaded from the ceiling. The dim cavern torches cast odd shadows off their five-foot frames, reverse jointed legs, and lanky arms that nearly reached the ground. Their angular faces sported glowing yellow eyes and a pair of three-inch horns sticking out above them. Worst of all, though, the beasts had bright red hair, which reflected the torches perfectly and made their ghastly heads appear aflame. Each monster carried a pair of two-foot long swords, one in each hand, the blades adorned with barbs and a tip that curved backward. Balear trembled. Those swords weren't designed to slice cleanly, but rather to torture and inflict maximum pain on their victims as they were slowly cut to ribbons. Only one race would craft such swords and take so much delight in using them.

Yokai.

CHAPTER TWELVE
Ambushed!

Iren grimaced, all he had time for as the Yokai attacked without mercy. They moved completely unlike the Quodivar he had battled on the hill, using their muscular reverse-jointed legs and light bodies to bound over the floor and walls. With each leap, they flipped in midair and whipped their swords in tight arcs. Iren dismayed. He couldn't get a strike through those spinning blades. Even if he did, each Yokai wore a crude steel breastplate, increasing its protection that much more.

Bone-jarring impacts replaced Iren's doubts as he clashed with his first enemy. The Yokai's strength was unreal, far beyond what the creature's small frame suggested it should be. When a second beast joined in, Iren felt himself getting pushed steadily back against the cavern wall. Between the two Yokai and four swords he faced, he barely blocked deathblow after deathblow.

He prayed for the others to help him, knowing they could not. Dirio had vanished behind a screen of Yokai and probably already died. Meanwhile, Balear fought three opponents at once. Despite the sergeant's experience, the Yokai's inhuman capabilities easily overwhelmed him. Like Iren, he had his back to the cavern wall as his enemies pressed him. That wall offered little protection, however, because the Yokai had the uncanny ability to jump and stick themselves to it, finding the imperfections in the cavern and climbing around it like spiders. Balear soon faced two opponents on the ground and one from above.

As for Rondel, Iren couldn't see her at all, even though the old hag should have been just past Balear. He desperately hoped the Yokai hadn't killed her in their initial ambush. Of any of them, she stood the best chance against these monsters.

Iren kept up his furious battle, but each time the Yokai swung their swords, their attacks got a little closer. A barely-dodged slash aimed at his head cut off several of his hairs. Two more close calls left him with shallow wounds on both legs. His breathing became labored, but he ignored the pain, trusting in the Muryozaki to heal his injuries.

With each passing second, Iren hated the Yokai more. He despised their swords and the way they swung them constantly like fans. The motion acted as both offense and defense. While one blade effectively blocked all of his attacks, he still had to contend with three that could strike him. He tried everything he could think of to get inside their guard, but the swords simply moved too fast.

Then the answer hit him. With a great effort he jumped several feet to one side, outside the range of his two enemies' short blades. The move bought him only a second as the Yokai leapt to face him, but it made the difference. Though too far away to land a lethal blow, his sword, longer and narrower than theirs, thrust forward and landed on a Yokai's wrist, severing the hand. The beast howled and stepped backward, clutching its stump with its other hand. Iren beheaded it without a second thought.

He cried out, "Everyone, aim for their hands!" Frantically, he glanced around, hoping the others had heard his message. He still couldn't locate Dirio or Rondel, but Balear at least must have caught Iren's words. A few seconds later, the struggling sergeant managed to stab one of his opponents in the hand and ultimately slay the creature.

The Yokai's lack of camaraderie astounded Iren. When one became injured, the others made no effort whatsoever to protect it. Through the haze of combat, he wondered if in Yokai culture, someone who couldn't fight was considered dead.

Although Balear had managed to kill one of his foes, the taxing battle had left him spent. The sergeant's sword drooped. With two Yokai still on him, Balear would die in less than a minute. Already he had numerous cuts, and one or two looked serious.

Iren wanted to help, but he couldn't disarm his second opponent. Wizened to its foe's new strategy, the monster kept dancing beyond his reach. Each time Iren struck, it jumped away. It moved almost lazily, as though it had all the time on Raa.

Then Iren realized the creature's cunning. The Yokai had seen what

Iren had seen, and it too knew Balear would die soon. With Dirio and Rondel nowhere in sight, once Balear fell, Iren would stand alone. All the remaining Yokai could descend on him simultaneously. Holy sword or not, he would never survive.

Iren made a snap decision. Sprinting away from his opponent, he thrust his sword at one of the Yokai fighting Balear. Iren didn't even need to disarm this one. His unexpected attack sliced through the creature's neck, and it fell writhing to the floor. Iren stood in front of Balear, protecting him from further onslaught.

"What are you doing?" Balear cried. "Get out of my way!" The shout must have sapped the man's last reserves, because the next moment he dropped to his knees, heaving.

Sweat poured off Iren's body, despite the cave's cool temperature. Through his exhaustion, however, he noticed the Yokai tiring as well. Their whirling defenses, while initially effective, had a drawback over time. The constant motion drained their strength, and after the long fight, their swords moved far slower than they had previously. The Yokai must have hoped for a quick victory following their ambush, so the surprising strength of the defenders caught them unprepared.

The knowledge that these beasts also had a limit gave Iren courage and brought strength to his tired limbs. He kept pace with them better, slaying a third Yokai without much difficulty. Even so, every strike, every block, every tiny motion of his body now caused him pain. When his final opponent used his own strategy against him and aimed for his left hand, Iren barely managed to deflect the blow. Even so, one of the barbs on his enemy's sword cut a shallow but excruciating gash on his wrist, and he dropped the Muryozaki in surprise. His eyes went wide as he looked into the glowing face of the triumphant Yokai. The beast wasted no time in swinging its second blade to disembowel him.

A fervent roar issued from the far side of the room. Something whirled through the air and crashed into the Yokai's head, shattering its skull. Iren simply stared, dumbfounded. Then he saw what had struck the Yokai, and his amazement only deepened.

A miner's pick had embedded itself in the creature's temple. Iren traced the tool's path back and saw Dirio standing amid a pile of corpses, holding a hammer. He must have fought with the hammer in one hand and the pick in the other. Rondel stood beside him with her dagger dripping green ooze. The same substance covered the room, and Iren realized it was Yokai blood.

With the Yokai slain, Iren retrieved his sword, feeling the pain in his wrist fade as Divinion's healing power restored him. As he did so, Dirio lost consciousness, and for the first time, Iren noticed that the foreman bled profusely. Rondel wrapped the man's arm around her shoulders and carried him to where Iren and Balear rested, leaning him against a stalagmite. Iren couldn't pull his gaze from the foreman. Dirio's final act had saved Iren's life. Desperate, Iren placed the Muryozaki in the man's palm, holding sword and hand together the way he had the day before in the village square.

"Hey, stop!" Rondel shouted. "You're in no condition to do that!"

Iren didn't listen. He didn't care. He saw no one else, nothing else, except for Dirio. Healing light filled the room, and seconds later, the foreman coughed and opened his eyes. Iren's vision grayed, but at least he remained conscious this time. He stood and took a step back, silently thanking Divinion for his help.

As he did, Dirio's face filled with panic. He cried out, "What the... you...you're a Left!"

Iren scowled, noting the sword in his left hand. Before he could answer, though, Rondel said, "He's the person who saved your life yesterday, remember? That's all."

For a moment Dirio chewed his lip thoughtfully, eyeing Iren as though he didn't know what to make of him. Then the middle-aged miner surprised everyone by smiling, extending his hand, and saying, "Looks like I owe you my life again."

Iren returned the grin and took Dirio's hand, the first time in his life he had done so with anyone. Glancing at the miner's pick in the Yokai at his feet, he answered, "Let's call us even."

The young Maantec next offered to heal Balear's injuries, but Rondel blocked him. "Don't use any more magic," she said. "You'll pass out again, or worse. We can't afford that here, so just keep still. Balear's wounds won't kill him."

The team rested several minutes. Balear, Iren, and Dirio all sat on the cold earth of the cavern floor. Rondel paced the room, examining the damage. Alone of all of them, she looked completely hale, not even out of breath despite guarding Dirio against five Yokai at once. Iren felt terrible for doubting her. He'd questioned her character more than once since leaving Haldessa, but surely he'd misjudged her. Had she not fought alongside them just now, they all would have died.

"Something here doesn't add up," she growled, interrupting Iren's thoughts. "Amroth came this way, but we've seen no sign of him. These Yokai ambushed us. Why didn't they attack him?"

Balear gulped, white-faced as he offered, "Maybe they did."

"Then where's his corpse?" Rondel retorted. "If he died, we should see his body." She continued to pace a moment longer, but then she stopped and knelt, touching the ground and trembling. "Impossible."

Terror rose in Iren at the thought of something so awful it could make Rondel shake. The crone stood and leaned against the cavern's far wall, a hand on her head. With fear in her voice, she described her finding. Near the opposite end of the room from where they had entered, heavy, three-toed footprints dug deep into the soft gravel floor. The prints measured over twenty inches across.

"They look like Yokai footprints," she concluded, "but no Yokai has feet this size. No, this is an Oni."

Balear and Dirio both blanched, but Iren just stared blankly.

"Almost all Yokai look like the ones we just fought," Balear explained, "but once in a great while, a mutant Yokai is born that grows to extraordinary size. Those are the Oni. In shape they appear just like Yokai, but their immense bulk makes them terrifying foes. They can rip up trees with their bare hands, and their hides can deflect the sharpest blade. Even worse, they retain all the agility of their smaller kin. At least, so the legends say."

"In this case, the legends don't exaggerate," Rondel interjected. "I've had the misfortune to fight one or two Oni in my life. I don't consider it a pleasant experience." She paused, thinking. "Maybe the Yokai weren't lying in wait when Amroth came through here. Perhaps they took up their positions afterward. Yes, look here; the Oni's footprints turn around and lead deeper into the cavern. A bloodstained streak follows them: a red streak."

Balear's expression flared, and Iren and Dirio averted their faces. Yokai, and Iren guessed Oni as well, had green blood. This blood came from a human.

Rondel lowered her head. "Amroth most likely came charging in here after that Quodivar, and he met up instead with an Oni. Judging from the amount of blood, he didn't survive. The Quodivar man then informed the Oni that more enemies remained, so the Oni dragged Amroth's corpse away and ordered the Yokai we killed to set up an ambush."

Balear buried his head in his hands. He choked, "Of course. If they'd left Captain Angustion here, we would know to expect an attack. They had to remove him, dead or alive, in order to fool us into thinking the room was empty."

Iren swooned. Amroth was dead? He couldn't believe it. He wouldn't believe it. Lodia had no better soldier than Amroth. The captain had just become heir to the throne, and he would have made a far better king than Azuluu. This entire mission had been his idea. It wasn't fair for him to die now, not when they had come so close to victory.

"We have to press on," Balear said, clearly trying to sound stronger than he felt. "Even if he has fallen, we have to carry on Captain Angustion's orders. The Quodivar leader still lives, and we also have to rescue Dirio's fellow villagers."

Rondel gave him a skeptical look. "The three of you can barely move. Don't forget that in addition to that Quodivar leader, we also face an Oni and who knows what else. You think you can handle all that in your condition?"

"You said you've fought Oni before," Iren pointed out. "We'll have to rely on you."

Folding her arms, Rondel replied, "In case you haven't noticed, I'm not as spry as I used to be. Yes, I've fought Oni before, in my prime. Even then, I barely survived. If I need to fight one down here, on his terms, in his territory, with my movement confined by the narrow walls of the cavern, what chance do you think I have?"

Iren forced himself to his feet, wobbling on shaky knees. He steadied himself by sticking the Muryozaki's tip into the gravel floor and putting his weight on the blade. "If we retreat," he countered, "we'll never get this close again. They'll move their headquarters. We must keep going, for the sake of Veliaf as well as all of Lodia. The Quodivar are out there right now ruining lives, Rondel! They're ripping apart families and sowing chaos throughout this country! As long as I can still breathe, I won't let them do that!"

Rondel remained silent for a long time. Iren wondered if she was waiting to see if his resolve would falter. He knew it wouldn't. Even if he died in the process and no one ever knew he had gone to such lengths to help them, he would go on. He had seen Veliaf. He had seen all of the misery they had endured. His own paled in comparison.

At last the old woman nodded. "It is Okthora's Law. Evil must be annihilated."

Iren glanced at Balear and Dirio. "Can you two stand?"

Thanks to Iren's healing and their brief respite, Dirio rose to his feet. He grasped his pick and hammer tightly. With grim determination he replied, "I will go with you to the end. For Veliaf."

Balear, however, remained seated. "I'm sorry," he said. "My body has gone numb. I can't move at all. Go without me; I'll catch up with you later." He paused, then he hesitantly continued, "Oh, and Iren? Thanks for saving me."

Iren grinned sheepishly, but even as he did, Balear leaned back against a stalagmite, closed his eyes, and slipped into unconsciousness.

Leaving Balear, the three remaining fighters took off down the canyon. Iren brought up the rear, while Rondel lead the way. Once more they entered an unnatural-looking passage, perfectly straight and round.

"Obsidian," Rondel muttered as she rubbed a hand on the tunnel's smooth wall. "I wonder…"

Iren wanted to ask what she meant, but he could barely form words. Every step brought more pain. Despite his rest, his breathing remained heavy. More than once Rondel glared back at him, wordlessly begging for quiet, but Iren couldn't help it. He'd never felt so tired in all his life.

They traveled several minutes before the black tunnel ended. At that point, the passage widened into a gigantic domed space easily twice the size of Haldessa Castle's main hall. An underground lake took up most of the room's center, leaving a ring around the edge about twenty feet wide.

Iren gasped as he entered the chamber. More torches lined it than any other room they had yet encountered, but its enormity still made it hard to see all the way across the lake. Dozens of short wooden structures, perhaps six feet high at most, encircled the water. Heavy iron bars blocked their fronts. Dirio clenched his fists, and Iren understood why. He knew what those buildings were: cages.

Without a trace of caution, Dirio ran to the nearest enclosure, crying for Rondel and Iren to join him. Sure enough, though the cage could only comfortably hold two or three people, the Quodivar had shoved ten Veliaf citizens into it. Their bodies had bruises and whip marks all over them, and their dejected, empty stares told Iren more than any words could. They didn't give Iren, Rondel, or even Dirio a second glance. They had long ago accepted that the only people down here were those who wanted to hurt them.

Running his fingers over the bars and door of the cage's front, Iren despaired. There was no way to free the prisoners without a key. He couldn't cut the bars, and even if he could, he'd likely collapse the cage on the hapless prisoners. Dirio pounded a fist on the iron door, the harsh ring echoing through the round chamber.

Rondel's eyes sparked, and a moment later, she said, "There's a key on a nail by the entrance we just used."

Iren stared hard at the wall around the tunnel. He couldn't see anything. Throwing up her hands, Rondel stormed over to the passageway. She quickly returned with the key.

Dirio and Iren both shook their heads in amazement. At least fifty feet separated them from the wall, and the tiny key, no more than a few inches long and made of black iron, had rested squarely in a shadow where no torchlight reached. Rondel's Lightning Sight was not to be underestimated.

"Quickly," Rondel barked, "let's get them out before anyone else comes. We still have an Oni down here somewhere, remember?"

Fortunately, no Oni or anything else interrupted them as they moved from one cage to another. They worked around the circle, growing increasingly nervous. The room had another tunnel at the far end, this one leading up, and something about it made Iren jittery. Their journey through the mine and cavern had been too easy. Ten Yokai and a half-dozen Quodivar weren't nearly enough to guard all these slaves plus the treasure room earlier. Maybe the bandits had simply become so certain of victory that they no longer considered defense necessary. Enemies as capable as the Quodivar, though, didn't seem likely to make such a blatant mistake.

More than the lack of guards, the Oni's absence particularly bothered Iren. It must have come through this room; the tunnel had no other exits. It could easily have faced them here, preventing them from freeing the prisoners. Instead, it had retreated up the far passage.

The lack of enemies apparently didn't bother Dirio. With each cage he opened, his smile grew wider. He hugged each person tightly, telling them their slavery had ended. When he headed to the last cage, he practically danced with glee. As soon as he reached it, however, he stopped short and called to Rondel and Iren.

Unlike the previous cages, which had all held at least eight people, this cell contained only one. Amroth leaned against the cage wall, a streak of blood down his back. Dirio entered the cage and looked him over.

The captain was unconscious, and despite his best effort, Dirio couldn't rouse him. Still, Amroth looked remarkably unharmed, considering he had fought an Oni. The foreman determined that Amroth had no broken bones, though he did discover long furrows down the back of the captain's clothing. Heavy claws had left fortunately shallow wounds along either side of his spine. Iren started offering to heal him, but Rondel silenced the young Maantec with a slap to the back of the head.

When Dirio emerged from the cage, Rondel said to him, "Take the villagers and lead them back through the mines to Veliaf. Iren and I will go on ahead. Leave Amroth here. If he comes to, maybe he can help us."

The foreman opened his mouth to protest, but Rondel cut him off, "You'd only get in our way. Besides, someone who knows the path back should go with the villagers. They may know their way around the mine, but probably not through this cavern."

Nodding reluctantly, Dirio assembled his fellow residents by the tunnel they'd used to enter the room. With a final glance back, he and the rest of Veliaf's townsfolk disappeared.

With everyone else gone, Iren and Rondel stood side by side before the passage on the opposite end of the room, staring into its black abyss. Iren gulped. "What's waiting for us up there?"

Rondel palmed the obsidian wall. "Something I hoped I'd never see again."

"What are our odds?"

"Don't ask."

CHAPTER THIRTEEN
Change of Plans

The torch-lined tunnel led up, seemingly forever. Iren hadn't realized they'd traveled so deep underground. This path had no offshoots or large chambers like the others they'd passed through, though it did have occasional side rooms. They checked each one briefly for enemies, but all were deserted. One had a familiar-looking hand-and-a-half sword leaning against a desk piled high with sheets of parchment.

Each step made Iren more nervous, if only because of Rondel's anxious expression. After her display yesterday, he'd thought Rondel invincible. Apparently, she didn't see herself that way.

Finally the tunnel peeled away, returning Iren and Rondel to the surface. Instead of relief, however, Iren felt more claustrophobic now than at any point in the cavern. Densely crowded conifers towered over him. When he looked straight up, he could discern a miniscule patch of distant blue sky, but no more. His knees began wobbling uncontrollably. Although he'd never been here before, he'd heard enough from the others to know where he was: Akaku Forest.

The cavern passage had dumped Iren and Rondel into a courtyard hemmed in by a palisade of standing logs each wider than Iren and over forty feet high. Several structures made of crudely stacked logs and with spruce boughs for roofs dotted the area inside the wall. Most of the buildings were short, but two or three watchtowers rose above the stockade. None had windows, though Iren quickly noted the numerous arrow slits in all of them. Equally unsettling, the fort's builders had kept quite a few of the imposing Akaku spruces growing inside the stockade. Iren tried hard to convince himself that he only imagined the shifting shadows within their crowns.

"What is this—" he started to say, but Rondel covered his mouth. Apparently she wanted silence.

The old hag took a few steps forward, motioning for him to follow her. Slowly, she crossed the courtyard, stalking through it toward what looked like a stable built against one of the palisade walls. Her small frame generated no noise as it passed over the dense layer of spruce needles and icy slush covering the ground. Iren did his best to mimic her, though several times she glanced back at him with an exasperated look.

They should go back. He kept thinking that over and over again. They should go back, back into the cave, back to Veliaf, back to Haldessa. He didn't care about revenge. He didn't care if he lived the rest of his life alone in the Tower of Divinion. It was better than sneaking through this unnaturally silent fort, waiting for the inevitable ambush. He kept listening for the thrum of a bowstring, the whistle of a sword, or the swipe of a clawed hand from the shadows that would end his life.

Then he heard it. From inside the stable came a most un-horselike noise: the low moan of a person calling in pain.

Rondel unsheathed the Liryometa and entered the stable. Iren followed, his katana ready. He crossed the threshold and turned a corner, ready to fight for his life.

The stable itself was well stocked for a primitive wooden fort run by bandits in the middle of a forest. Well lit with candles, the stable housed extensive supplies of oats, straw, food, water, and riding gear. Over half a dozen fine war chargers, each putting to shame the horses Iren's group had ridden, whinnied and shook their heads in irritation at the newcomers. Despite their annoyed disposition, however, Iren had seen enough of horses in the past four days to know that each of these stood fully adorned and ready to ride at a moment's notice.

Other than the horses, the stables appeared uninhabited, at least until Rondel started inspecting the stalls. Inside one at the far end of the building was an unconscious woman, slightly taller than Iren and looking to be in her late twenties, with her arms and legs bound to the cross beams using heavy cord. She had several wounds that Iren could see, including a long gash down the right side of her face. Without thinking, he cupped the Muryozaki in her hand, letting Divinion's healing magic flow into her. He expected Rondel to yell at him, but she remained surprisingly quiet.

When he finished healing the woman, he sheathed his sword and stepped back. The warm glow of the candles accentuated her soft features, making her positively alluring. He knew he had never seen a more elegant woman in all his life. Haldessa had its share of beauties, but none of them could match this woman's grace. She had a rich tan complexion, darker than that typical of Lodians. Tight leather boots, leggings, and jerkin accentuated her slender yet muscular form. Adding a bit of color, an elaborately embroidered pattern of swirling vines with dark green leaves wound across her outfit.

More than any other part of her, though, the woman's hair caught Iren's attention. Rimming her face, her tousled locks reached midway down her back. Had that hair been brown, blonde, or any of the other colors common in Lodia, he still would have considered it beautiful, but nothing he'd witnessed at the castle could compare with this.

Her hair was the same shade of green as the leaves on her clothing.

Iren glanced at Rondel in search of direction, and for the first time, he saw her truly unnerved. He'd thought she had looked concerned on their journey through the tunnel, but she'd been stoic by comparison to how she acted now. Her eyes bulged, and her jaw hung wide open. Rondel's body trembled as though the young woman were, in fact, the most terrifying Oni she'd ever faced. Repeatedly, she tried to form words, but none came.

Sensing that Rondel had lost her wits, Iren asked, "What on Raa is she?"

* * *

Rondel ignored Iren utterly. In fact, she momentarily forgot he existed. She just stared blankly at the woman, refusing to believe the truth. She couldn't be here!

Her presence changed everything. All of Rondel's strategies and cunning deceptions had fallen flat upon beholding the unconscious woman.

She needed a new plan, and quickly. She felt Iren's skeptical eyes on her. The Rondel she had cultivated for him was always in control, but now she'd let that mask fall. Her true feelings were on full display, and even a social inept like Iren couldn't help but notice them. She had to get them under control, had to refocus, yet every time she looked at the woman's face, shock struck her anew.

She wanted to run, to take the woman and flee. She wanted to grab one of those fine horses and tear through Akaku, letting the hard spruce branches whip at her, ripping her clothes and slicing her skin. The pain would mean nothing. Every fiber in her body told her to take this woman and race all the way to Ziorsecth Forest. It was about the only way to make it in time.

She forced herself back, the effort more draining than any of the fighting on this mission. If she left now, all her efforts would be wasted. She was so close; it wouldn't take much longer. The treason that had buried itself for so long would soon emerge. Only then could her plan enter its final stage.

On top of that, there were the dreams, those dragon-cursed nightmares that kept her awake and filled her with a constant mix of regret and loathing. If she left now, they'd undoubtedly return, probably worse than ever. She managed a look at Iren and hoped that her malice didn't come through in her expression. It was all his fault. The dreams caused her enough problems when she'd lived just outside the castle walls, barely a mile from him. How bad would they become if the Oni killed him?

No, she couldn't leave this place just yet. Even so, she couldn't let this woman die.

She made her decision: gamble and hope for a good roll. Never in her life had she taken such a chance, but she didn't have much choice. She needed to remain here and see this to the end. There was only one way to do that and still get the woman to Ziorsecth in time. The dreams would return, but she wouldn't likely find time for sleep in the next few days anyway. With a great force of will, she faced Iren, adopted the fake innocent smile that served her so well and said, "You'll have to take her to Ziorsecth Forest."

Iren did a double take. "I have to do what?"

Her fragile grip on the false grin broke. She lashed out, "Know-nothing child! This woman is a Kodama, a guardian of Ziorsecth Forest. They're a cursed race; they die if they leave their forest home. I don't have a clue how she got here, but the only way to save this woman's life is to return her there as quickly as possible."

Furrowing his brow, Iren asked angrily, "Why should I have to go? Take her yourself, if you care so much about her. In case you forgot, we have an important job to do here! The Quodivar leader is here, and I won't leave until I have my revenge!"

Rondel couldn't contain herself anymore. She swung her wrinkled fist and struck Iren across the side of the face, sending the young Maantec sprawling. A brief pang of self-hatred and a flash of childhood memory long neglected hit her as she made contact. She repressed them both, concentrating on her anger. "Listen, idiot. Assuming Zuberi's even here in the first place, he has an Oni backing him up, as well as potentially more Quodivar and Yokai. You think you can handle all that without my help? You said yourself that you'd have to rely on me to complete this mission. If I go with her, how do you expect to defeat the Quodivar?"

Iren hauled himself back to his feet. "Fine, so let's deal with the Quodivar and come back for her afterward."

"We don't have time! Every second she stays outside Ziorsecth, she gets closer and closer to death. You need to take her immediately!"

Rondel still couldn't bring herself to look Iren in the face, but his unwavering posture showed his answer. The old Maantec fumed, her fists shaking. She needed a different tactic. With a great will, she softened her face and said, trying her best to sound genuinely pleading, "Please, Iren, do this for me. I told you of your past, of the Maantecs. I told you about the Muryozaki, Divinion, and the Dragon Knights. Please, save this woman for me. Only you can. Take one of these horses and ride hard. They're quality animals, and all of them are well-provisioned for a lengthy trip. Any one of them can get you across Lodia in a week. If you go due west, you'll hit Ziorsecth Forest, guaranteed. I'll open the fort's gate for you; it should be nearby."

Iren didn't reply initially. His body shifted slowly, turning from Rondel to the Kodama and back again. Just when Rondel felt he would refuse her, he said, "I wanted revenge with my own hands. I hope you know what I'm giving up here. I won't get another chance to avenge my parents."

Rondel couldn't help herself. She laughed and replied, "Karma isn't always so simple. Now move!"

Iren cut the cords lashing the Kodama to the stable wall. As he hefted her onto his shoulders, her scent, the fresh aroma of autumn leaves, wafted over Rondel. A deep, longing nostalgia struck her, but she pushed it back with a great effort.

Approaching the finest charger of the bunch, a sleek black stallion, Iren whispered in the horse's ear the words Rondel had used in Haldessa, "*Kuylet, trempiot.*" The majestic stallion nodded his head once in response to Iren's words, then allowed Iren to climb into the saddle with the Kodama seated in front of him. Despite herself, Rondel grinned slyly. The boy definitely needed to work on his listening skills, but on the rare occasions when he actually paid attention, he learned fast.

Just as they reached the stable door, however, the structure burst into flames. They had no warning; the whole building spontaneously combusted all at once. The horses reared and panicked in their stalls, and Iren's mighty warhorse shot through the open door, heedless of his rider's attempted commands.

As soon as Iren disappeared, Rondel's will hardened. Now came the critical moment. Clutching her dagger, she exited the collapsing building as calmly as though leaving her home in the morning. Her eyes sparked, and in the burning light she saw that the fires engulfed not only the stable but the entire fort. She couldn't locate Iren, but already large holes had appeared where portions of the stockade had burned. Maybe he had already escaped.

Or maybe he was already dead.

She had little time to dwell on it as the opponent she'd known was waiting for her stepped from the shadows. She cursed as she took him in. He looked just like the Yokai she'd faced earlier, but he stood well over three times their size. The Oni arched its back and issued a roar of challenge that echoed even over the howling flames. He wore no armor, and his only weapon was a short, fat, rectangular sword that glowed red, like it had freshly emerged from a forge.

Rondel steeled herself. Oni on their own made for dangerous opponents, but the cave had changed her mind about this monster. Lodia wasn't volcanic. No natural force carved those obsidian tubes or triggered the detonation that caused the cave-in. The fort's sudden combustion only provided more proof. Yokai possessed magic, but not at this level. Their casters traditionally focused on enchantments, carving spells into a weapon that could enhance its destructive power without requiring much magic to wield.

She shuddered, trying to remain calm and knowing she was failing. A thousand years had passed since she'd last seen it. Even then, in her prime, its strength had terrified her. The war should have destroyed it. The war did destroy it, or so she'd always believed. Yet here it was, right in front of her, in the hands of an Oni: the Fire Dragon Sword, Karyozaki.

CHAPTER FOURTEEN
Vengeance

"Whoa! Stop! Halt! Enough already!"

The panicked stallion couldn't care less about Iren's shouts as it raced through the forest. Only a few minutes had passed since fleeing the burning stable, and already numerous low-hanging spruce limbs had sliced up both Iren's and the Kodama's bodies. The horse broke the bigger ones, but the smaller, springier branches had an annoying habit of bending as the horse hit them and then whipping back at high speed.

Through the impacts, Iren struggled to keep hold of both the reins and the Kodama. He should have strapped her in, but it was far too late for that. Instead, he held the reins with one hand and kept her body pressed against his with the other. This close, her scent overwhelmed him. He didn't know what the smell compared to, yet it invigorated him and pressed him to continue.

"Ow!" he couldn't help but cry as a particularly nasty limb left a brutal welt on his arm. Even though it wasn't really the animal's fault, he still yelled, "Hey, watch it!"

His protestation went unheeded. The horse ran on and on, though Iren had the distinct impression the creature was running in circles. Despite the beast's impressive speed, the burning fort didn't look any further away.

"*Kuylet, trempiot!*" he roared in desperation.

The horse stopped so suddenly Iren was thrown forward, rolling over the Kodama's unconscious form. He fell hard on his face. Spitting out a mix of muddy slush and spruce needles, he heaved himself to his feet and glared at the stallion. "Perhaps a little gentler next time?" he asked.

The animal whickered and tossed his head noncommittally, his attention elsewhere. Iren crossed his arms, but the charger acted as though the boy didn't exist.

"Don't be so upset," a bass voice with a drawling accent said. Iren spun around to face it, and then he took an involuntary step backward. From the shadows of the forest emerged a giant man, over seven feet tall and so muscular he could probably snap an Oni's neck between his fingers. The fires from the fort lit up his countenance, revealing that he had dark brown skin and jet black hair, the look of a Tacumsah islander. Plate armor covered his chest and legs, and chain mail protected his arms and head. On the man's back hung a massive blade as long as the man was tall and over a foot wide at its base. It had to weigh an absurd amount. If all that armor and weaponry burdened the giant in the least, however, he didn't show it.

The islander smirked. "Nightraid never listens to anyone save the leader of the Quodivar."

Iren's eyes flicked to the horse. The stallion's focus had clearly shifted to the man. Both of his ears pointed directly at the giant, and it didn't react in the slightest to the sounds or sights of the fort burning in the distance.

Gulping, Iren returned his gaze to the armored man. "That means you're Zuberi." He spat the name, trying to keep his voice from quivering. It didn't help that he had to crane his neck upward to look at the Tacumsahen's face.

Zuberi nodded. "And you are Iren Saitosan, a Left."

Iren stopped dead. How could the Quodivar leader know his name?

An explosion from within the fort distracted them both. The dark-skinned man bellowed in a deep laugh, the forest quaking from the force of it. "Looks like Hezna is enjoying himself. He has all the fun." Zuberi paused a moment, then stretched out his right hand, offering it to Iren. "Well, shall we go?"

Iren feared for Rondel, but amid the flames he could see no sign of her. He put his left hand to the Muryozaki's hilt. "I won't go anywhere with you."

Zuberi maintained his arrogant sneer. "No doubt Rondel told you all about Maantecs. You know what Lodia has done to them."

The young man blinked twice. Something was very wrong here. He hadn't expected the Quodivar leader to know about him, much less the old hag and Maantecs.

"We can remake Lodia into a place of tolerance, where Maantecs need not live in fear," Zuberi continued, ignoring Iren's bewilderment. "Join me in overthrowing this miserable country. Maantec battle prowess is legendary. If you fight by my side, together with the Yokai, what enemy could stand against us?"

White rage welled in Iren. "Fight by your side?" he shouted. "How many Lodians lay dead because of you and your Quodivar?"

Zuberi brushed off Iren's question. "Their deaths are necessary. Besides, you have no reason to defend Lodia. Its people consider you a child of the devil! We of the Quodivar will not scorn you. Quite the contrary, we will celebrate and reward you for your abilities."

Acid filled Iren's reply, "I've heard enough." He didn't care how Zuberi knew about him, Rondel, or Maantecs. Only one thing mattered. The man he'd risked his life to meet, the reason he'd abandoned Haldessa Castle and left behind everything he'd ever known, stood before him.

The Muryozaki sang as Iren drew it from its sheath. "The first one is for Veliaf," he growled. "The last one is for my parents."

The giant seemed genuinely disappointed. "I feared you would answer that way. No matter, I'll take over this country regardless." Reaching behind him, he unclasped the gigantic sword and held it easily before him in one hand. Then he charged. Iren anticipated Zuberi's heavy armor and weapon slowing him, but that guess proved wrong. The Maantec barely had time to dodge as the first blow struck down, landing inches from Nightraid. The thick blade sent chunks of earth skyward, leaving a crater in the ground. The impact's force pushed the air away from it so that although Iren evaded the blade, the wind current caught him and tossed him into a tree trunk.

Zuberi raised his behemoth blade and grinned, utterly unfazed as he initiated a relentless assault. The Quodivar leader wielded his ridiculously heavy sword as though it were as dainty as Rondel's dagger. With each insane swing, he pushed Iren farther and farther back.

Even Akaku's mighty spruces didn't impede Zuberi. His slashes cut through their trunks in a single pass. Soon Iren not only had to dodge the blade, but the old growth timbers crashing to the ground all around him.

The young Maantec grimaced. Unlike the Yokai, Zuberi neither slowed nor tired. Adding to the problem, the Quodivar leader battled fully rested, while Iren had fought twice already this morning. His natural Maantec abilities did little to compensate.

His size disadvantage didn't help much either. With Zuberi's long arms and even longer sword, he could strike at Iren with impunity. More than once Iren tried getting in close, where the massive blade's size would work against his foe. That strategy failed, however, because Zuberi could swing so fast that Iren never had time between blows to maneuver for a counterattack.

As the fight went from bad to worse, Iren tripped over a fallen tree and fell on his back. Before he could stand again, the Quodivar leader's sword filled his vision. To Iren's surprise, instead of delivering the lethal blow, Zuberi said, "I offered you power. I offered you acceptance. No one has ever lasted this long against me. Why turn me down? Why die meaninglessly here?"

Even in defeat, Iren remained defiant. "Join you? You killed my parents!"

Zuberi let out his bellowing laugh again. "Afraid you'll have to be a little more specific. I've killed a lot of people's parents."

Iren gritted his teeth, trying to figure out how he could escape. He gripped the Muryozaki, intending to knock Zuberi's weapon aside. The Quodivar leader must have deciphered his plan, though, because with a swift kick, Zuberi knocked the katana out of Iren's hand.

The young Maantec panted frantically. He had no weapon, and without the Muryozaki, he couldn't access Divinion's magic. Not that healing would do much good against a direct hit from Zuberi. Stalling for time, he shouted, "Seventeen years ago, in Tropos Village, you slew my parents in the night! They were just simple farmers, yet you murdered them! What had they ever done to you? You claim you want acceptance for Maantecs, but you don't mean it. You killed them in cold blood!"

For the first time, Zuberi hesitated. Wrinkling his brow, he answered, "Well, if that's your reason, it's a poor one. Seventeen years ago in Tropos Village? At that time, I was no older than you are now. I was a brand new Tacumsahen pirate, as green as they get, setting sail to glory. I never even stepped foot on Lodian soil until ten years ago."

"You're lying!"

The giant shrugged. "Believe what you want. You won't live long enough to decide anyway." He raised his sword, but the death blow never came. A blue spark suddenly jumped across the blade, arcing up its length and striking Zuberi in the chest. The impact threw the Quodivar leader back thirty feet, rolling in the dirt.

Iren stumbled to his feet and glanced to his right. Rondel stood among the trees, her hair and outfit smoldering.

She didn't look at all like the Rondel he remembered. After the fights in the cave, she hadn't lost her breath or appeared tired in the slightest. Now she gasped for air, and her right hand braced against a nearby spruce for support. Even her Lightning Sight had faded.

"I told you to get moving, slacker," she wheezed. "What on Raa are you still doing here?"

Iren scowled and opened his mouth for a sarcastic comeback, but he didn't have time. Behind Rondel, a burst of flame erupted within the forest. From the center of the inferno, the Oni, Hezna as Iren recalled Zuberi calling him, emerged. The monster's yellow eyes and red hair danced in the foul light. His sword glowed like a poker.

Beside Hezna, Zuberi rose, using his sword to balance himself. The pair squared off against Rondel, who positioned herself between her foes and Iren.

"Hurry!" she called, not bothering to turn around. She held her tiny dagger aloft. It looked pathetic compared with Hezna's and Zuberi's weapons. "Get out of here!"

Iren's breathing halted as he realized what she was doing. In her condition, she couldn't defeat both enemies. He couldn't let her fight alone! He took a few steps toward the Muryozaki. Dizziness took him, and he dropped to his knees.

Rondel glanced over her shoulder. "What are you waiting for?"

The momentary distraction was enough. Zuberi and Hezna charged her. Rondel leapt aside, but just barely. She moved remarkably slower than when she'd fought the Quodivar in Veliaf. More unsettling, though, was how nothing of her former confident, smirking attitude remained. Instead, she looked haggard and worn.

The battle ended in an instant. A sideswipe from Zuberi's blade forced her to jump away, and as she landed, the Oni reached her. He struck her in the face with his elbow, and she collapsed. As she fell, her dagger dropped from her grip and rolled down a small incline, stopping at the Oni's feet. He picked it up, all but invisible in his clawed fist. Laughing cruelly, Zuberi walked over and gave her limp form a swift kick, sending her flying through the air and landing just a few yards from where Iren still knelt.

Iren stared in shock at Rondel's motionless body. He crawled to her, feeling for any sign of a pulse. He found none. Her eyes stared emptily into the canopy, unblinking.

No. No. No. The word repeated itself endlessly in his head. Soon he started saying it aloud, faster and faster, a constant chant of anguish and disbelief. Tears fell freely from his face. He'd never cried for another person in his whole life. Now he couldn't stop.

A pair of shadows enveloped him. Looking up, he saw Zuberi and Hezna silhouetted by the fire behind them. They looked at him with un-repentant glee, and then as one, their swords crashed down to end his life just as they had the old hag's.

A foot from his face, however, their weapons stopped short as a blind-ing light surrounded Iren. Barely conscious of what he was doing, Iren got to his feet, fists clenched, all hint of tiredness gone. His eyes burned bright white. With fear in their faces, the pair of murderers stumbled backwards.

Iren cocked his left arm as though about to punch, his hand glowing just like his eyes. As he threw his fist forward, a shining beam of white light lanced out of it. The attack struck Hezna a glancing blow, knocking the Oni sideways and into a tree. Zuberi wasn't as fortunate. The beam hit him at full force, and as it did, it took the form of a great reptilian mouth. It clamped down on Zuberi's body, crushing his armor, lifting him off the ground, and sending him rocketing through the forest, snapping tree trunks as easily as dried twigs. When the beam at last dissipated, the Quodivar leader crumpled to the ground and did not rise again.

Iren placed his hands on his knees, chest heaving. He had no idea what had just happened. Still, he knew one thing clearly. He'd gotten his revenge.

He had little time to celebrate as he fell forward next to Rondel, ut-terly spent. All feeling left his body. In a distant corner of his mind, he wondered about the beam. He didn't have the Muryozaki, and Rondel had said the sword connected him to Divinion. It was impossible to unleash the dragon's magic without holding the katana, yet he'd just done exactly that.

He would have to remember to ask her about it, when he saw her shortly in the next life.

As the seconds passed, though, he remained in the living world. A pressure rubbed against his face, and through the firelight he saw Night-raid's muzzle. He managed a faint smile. "What, now you feel like listen-ing?" The horse whinnied softly and nuzzled him harder. By a great force of will, Iren clasped a stirrup with his right hand.

"West," he murmured, but that single word sapped his last reserves. He closed his eyes and remembered no more.

* * *

Balear could finally move again, although he far preferred the numbness from earlier. At least then, he didn't need to deal with every muscle screaming at him. Despite it, he pushed through the pain, determined. Dirio had come by already, trailed by Veliaf's populace. They'd offered to carry him back to the village, but he'd declined. He couldn't go back yet, because the one person in all of Lodia that Balear wanted to walk by hadn't: Captain Angustion.

With extreme effort, Balear dragged himself down the tunnel and deeper into the cavern. On each step, he repeated the same word in his head, a mantra meant to force him onward when his body might otherwise fail him. Captain...

He stopped briefly when he reached the lake room, but finding the chamber devoid of life, Balear quickly pressed on. His vision grew hazy, and he needed to stop every hundred feet just to keep from passing out again. At one point, he reached a chamber that looked like a study, with a large wooden writing desk piled high with parchment. Candles lit the room, and to Balear's great satisfaction, a comfortable-looking chair sat next to the desk. Deciding the captain could wait a little longer, he fell into the seat.

He rested for several minutes, his strength slowly returning. His breathing calmed, and his vision sharpened. Absentmindedly, he picked up a few of the sheets on the desk and rifled through them, reading a few words here and there to test his eyesight. He'd skimmed several pages when his heart caught in his chest.

At first he doubted his own eyes, but when he flipped back to the top page of the stack, there it was. He would recognize that handwriting anywhere. The blocky script perfectly matched that on Rondel's waiver before they'd left Haldessa. He hastily shifted his gaze to the bottom of the page, where, sure enough, he found Rondel's signature.

He furrowed his brow, confused as to why the Quodivar would have writing of Rondel's. It looked recent, too. The date at the top matched the day they began this mission.

The fact that he sat alone and vulnerable in the heart of the enemy's base no longer bothered him. Even the need to find Captain Angustion vanished. All Balear's attention focused on the page before him. As he read it, his hands shook.

"Great Leaders of the Quodivar," he read, "I send humble greetings. It is time. Amroth, the fool, comes to kill you in stealth. In so doing, he leaves his beloved home without a captain to defend it. It is the chance we have long waited for, to strike Haldessa, obliterating it and its oafish king.

"Even with your combined strength, however, winning will be difficult. Neither of you has siege weapons capable of toppling Haldessa's walls, but fortunately, I know another method. Haldessa's baths are filled by a canal which connects to the nearby river. Each day, precisely at noon, the canal gates open to fill the baths. Strike then. Send an elite group through one of those tunnels, and they can open the castle gate, letting the rest of your army into the castle.

"I will force Amroth to bring me with him, to monitor his progress. I also plan to gain us a new recruit, a Maantec boy named Iren Saitosan, who Amroth selected for his team. Iren has suffered at the hands of Lodia, and once he knows his origins, he will surely support us in revenge.

"Already tasting success, Rondel Thara."

In a flash, events since their mission began snapped into focus. While Amroth delivered the waivers back at Haldessa, Rondel had disappeared, ostensibly to get more alcohol. In reality, the traitorous witch had secretly written this letter and added it to the morning's post. Mail carriers traveled fast, faster than their group had, so of course this letter arrived well in advance of them. She'd probably sent it to Veliaf, which was already under Quodivar control. She had convinced Captain Angustion to bring her along, even though he didn't want her. Even teaching Iren had served her own reasons. She'd wanted to gain his trust so she could convert the ignorant Left to the Quodivar. With the devil magic the pair of them possessed, Rondel and Iren's combined strength would make the Quodivar invincible.

Worst of all, this letter explained why the cavern had so few defenders. The Quodivar and Yokai were already marching to Haldessa. The city would be caught completely unprepared.

"So now you know," a grim voice said from behind him. Balear jumped so high he fell out of his chair and onto the rock floor. He drew his sword from the ground, expecting any second to die at Rondel's blade, but then he stopped short. Captain Angustion's pitying stare met his own.

"Sir!" Balear was so happy at seeing his commander alive that for a second he forgot the terrible letter.

The captain nodded. "I saw you coming from farther up the tunnel, but I wanted you to learn the truth for yourself. After they captured me, the Quodivar put my sword in here. When I stopped to recover it, I saw the letter. I've suspected Rondel for some time, but I could never prove anything. After all, she did kill quite a few Quodivar along the way. She clearly has no qualms about sacrificing her allies to achieve her ultimate goal. But then, why would a Left care about human lives?"

Balear gulped. "Where is she now?"

Amroth motioned up the tunnel. "You'd better see for yourself. Come, and bring that letter."

As they walked, Amroth said, "This passage leads to a fort inside Akaku. Rather, it used to. The fort's in ruins, and much of the forest around it is burning."

"What happened?"

"Treason. Rondel and Iren tried to kill the two Quodivar leaders."

Balear gave the captain a confused look. "That doesn't make sense. Why would Rondel kill the Quodivar leaders if she works for them?"

"To lead the Quodivar herself and to prevent them from exposing her. At least, so I guess. Her plan didn't work out the way she intended."

Balear cocked an eyebrow to prompt an explanation.

"Rondel counted, as I did, on Iren having enough strength to help defeat the Quodivar leaders," Amroth said. "He proved too weak, and Rondel couldn't match both Zuberi and an Oni at the same time. They killed her. I arrived at the end of the tunnel right as it happened."

"I suppose Iren died too, then," Balear said. A highly bizarre and unexpected pang of sadness struck him.

Surprisingly, the captain grinned. "Not quite. There's more to that boy than I ever imagined. When Rondel died, Iren lost control and fired off some kind of white beam that killed both Quodivar leaders in one shot. It had so much energy that even from where I stood, its shockwave knocked me flat. By the time I recovered, Iren had disappeared, taking one of the Quodivar's own horses and heading west."

When the pair exited the tunnel, Balear gasped at the ruin around him. The forest fire had mostly subsided, but everything within half a mile was scorched. A few of the larger trunks still burned, giving the scene a haunting glow. Three horses, the sole escapees of the Quodivar's stables, nursed their wounds as they wandered through the charred remains.

Though cowed by the devastation, Balear forced his thoughts back to the letter. "Sir, we should take those horses and ride to Haldessa! The Quodivar army is on its way there!"

Captain Angustion frowned. "Yes, but we have a second problem. When Iren left, I noticed someone else with him: a Kodama from Ziorsecth. I don't know if Rondel converted Iren or not, but based on that letter, we know she meant to. I fear we may have seen only a glimpse of Rondel's grand design."

"Grand design?"

"The Kodama provides the perfect cover for Iren to flee the country. Once he reaches Ziorsecth, Iren can convert the Kodamas and other nations to Rondel's cause. In the worst case scenario, we could face enemies on all sides. If Iren convinces our neighbors to attack us, Lodia will be overwhelmed."

Balear blanched. Even if they militarized the entire populace, they couldn't defeat a combined attack from the Quodivar, Yokai, Kodamas, and Tengu. "What can we do?" he cried. "We have to help Haldessa! We have no time to chase Iren!"

"Not necessarily. The crux of Rondel's plan for Haldessa revolves around the baths' canal. If I alert the king in time, he can order the canal gate shut. The Quodivar won't be able to infiltrate, and our archers will easily pick off their army from the safety of the castle walls. The king will follow my recommendations without question, so I'll go to Haldessa and try to prevent it from falling. You must ride west and find Iren. Bring him back to the castle, even if you have to kill him."

Balear nodded, tucking the incriminating letter from Rondel in his pocket. As he did, terrible worry swelled inside him. "Captain, what happens if you meet the Quodivar army along the way?"

A mad grin took the mighty soldier. "Then may the dragons protect me. But no more time! We must ride!"

With that, they each mounted a Quodivar horse and rode in opposite directions. Balear careened through Akaku, though each footfall of his steed nearly made him swoon. His body screamed at him to stop, to rest, perhaps even to curl up in a corner and die. Very soon, he would need to find a place to camp and recover, but not just yet. He couldn't let Captain Angustion down. He would locate Iren, and if the boy really had betrayed Lodia and chosen Rondel, the devil-child would die by Balear's hand.

CHAPTER FIFTEEN
Magic and Minawë

When Iren finally came to, at first he thought he hadn't. He opened and closed his eyes repeatedly, but he could tell no difference. His vision gradually adjusted, and the dim shapes of tall, spire-like conifers came into focus above him. He remained in Akaku Forest, probably surrounded by enemies. Through the dense trees, he spotted a couple stars. That meant he'd been unconscious at least half a day.

The smell of burning wood called him to attention. He forced himself into a crouch and reached for the Muryozaki, but its sheath lay empty on his hip.

"Still alive, huh?" a strong, feminine voice asked. He might have considered it melodious, if only it hadn't sounded so aggravated.

Turning to face the speaker, Iren saw the Kodaman woman sitting on a fallen log, tending a campfire with a stick. He stumbled over and took a seat next to the fire, opposite her. The soothing heat and crackling wood did wonders for his frayed nerves and exhausted body. "I'm glad you're awake," he began, but she cut him off.

"What brings you to this forest, Maantec?" She pronounced the last word like a curse.

Iren decided the best thing to do was not to get riled up. Instead, he grinned innocently and replied, "I rescued you from the Quodivar, and now I'm taking you back to Ziorsecth."

She folded her arms and scowled. "Moron."

His eyebrow twitched at the insult. This stupid Kodama was just like everyone else. He should ditch her in the woods. It would serve her right.

Rondel's final words, however, echoed in his head. She'd knowingly sacrificed herself so that he could escape and help this Kodama return home. He wondered if Rondel had known what a pain the woman was. Probably not. Then again, considering the Kodama's tone, the pair might have gotten along. Actually, the woman reminded him a little of Rondel. Aside from the prickly attitude, her deep green eyes were the same shade as the crone's.

"Sorry," he said, sarcasm involuntarily rising in his throat, "but I have instructions, and I don't plan on leaving your side. You're stuck with me until we get to Ziorsecth. Now where's my sword?"

She shrugged. "Not here."

Iren nearly fainted as the final moments of the battle replayed themselves in his memory. Zuberi had kicked away the Muryozaki. It probably still lay there, amid the charred remains of the forest. He swore. What was he supposed to do now, without Rondel, Amroth, or Divinion to guide him? He didn't even have a simple blade to defend himself! Worse, the stupid Kodama had set up camp smack in the middle of Akaku. If the Yokai attacked them now, they wouldn't stand a chance.

"You needn't worry," the woman said. "We're perfectly safe here. There aren't any Yokai near us."

He gave her a disbelieving look. "Oh, and how do you know that?"

She pointed at the trees. "The owls."

"Owls?"

"Of course. Can't you hear them hooting? They only do that when they feel calm and unthreatened. If Yokai were around, the owls would either fall silent or leave."

Iren shook his head. "We're totally unarmed and defenseless here, and you're telling me you've entrusted our safety to a bunch of dumb birds?"

She sighed. "Typical Maantec moron."

"Hey, I went to the trouble of rescuing you!" he replied. "Why do you keep calling me a moron?"

"Because you are. You have no idea what's going on, or what you're meddling in."

He growled with frustration. "I know exactly what I'm meddling in. I'm saving your life. You could at least tell me your name."

The Kodama said nothing for a moment. Finally, she answered curtly, "Minawë."

Iren extended his hand. "I'm Iren Saitosan, Minawë. Nice to meet you."

Minawë eyed Iren's palm like it bore some terrible disease. "Moron."

Exasperated, Iren threw up his hands. "What makes me a moron now?"

"Kodamas don't shake hands. When we greet a friend, we do this." She placed the index and middle fingers of her right hand vertically over her chest. When Iren smiled and imitated the gesture, she flushed angrily and turned away.

Several silent minutes passed. Iren knew he should rest, but he couldn't bring himself to. Perhaps he feared Minawë might run off if he took his eyes off her, but he also felt a mysterious draw toward her, even though she kept insulting him.

"So," he said, "how did you wind up imprisoned so far from home?"

Minawë glanced into the canopy, then said harshly, "I won't tell you. You bear both the name and weapon of our greatest enemy."

Iren was taken aback. "Your greatest enemy?"

"Moron, you don't even know your own history? A thousand years ago, the Maantecs started a war to subjugate the other species on Raa. Among those who still remember such things, that conflict is called the Kodama-Maantec War, although it involved all the races on Raa. After fifty years, we beat back the Maantecs until at last they retained only their original territory, Serona, west of Ziorsecth Forest. The Maantec emperor refused to surrender. As the Kodamas marched on the Maantec capital, he stood atop his tower at its center and uttered a foul curse."

Iren forced himself to ask the follow-up question, "What did the curse do?"

Minawë stared into the flames. "You know that Kodamas who leave Ziorsecth die, right? That wouldn't happen naturally. The Maantec emperor, with the aid of none other than Divinion himself, altered the structure of our bodies. He died in the process, but his spell nevertheless slaughtered every Kodama on the battlefield that day. It all but wiped out our species." She glared at him. "I awoke during your fight with the big human. I saw you use that beam against him. You consider yourself the Holy Dragon Knight? What nonsense! You're just like him, just like Iren Saito."

Shock ripped through Iren. "You bear both the name and weapon of our greatest enemy," she had said. Now he understood. He was named after the last emperor of the Maantecs, a Holy Dragon Knight who had perverted Divinion's magic for his own dream of conquest.

Iren clenched his teeth. Rondel had named him. Why would she name him after such a horrible person? An image of the old hag's lifeless body flashed before him. He'd never learn the answer now.

Still, he refused to accept that he could be like Iren Saito as Minawë had claimed. In frantic defense he cried, "You can't lump me in with some conqueror from a thousand years ago because of what I did at the fort. I don't even know what happened! I didn't have the Muryozaki, yet I still used Divinion's magic."

Minawë rolled her eyes. "Moron, that doesn't make it better. That beam didn't come from Divinion's magic. It came from yours."

Iren started, perplexed. "I don't have any magic," he countered. "The only magic I've ever used came from the Muryozaki."

"Naturally," she replied, as though his quandary made perfect sense. "You probably never received any training. Back at the fort, your body reacted instinctively, prompted by strong emotions and your life-threatening situation. It used your magic first to shield you, and then to slay your opponent."

"I told you, I don't have any magic!"

"Except for humans, every sentient species on Raa has magic. They draw it passively from the environment without even thinking. It's part of our biology. The way Mother explained it to me, our bodies have 'semi-permeable membranes.' Magic can flow in, but it can't escape. Unless, of course, the person forces it out in the form of a spell. Mother could tell you more, if we make it to Ziorsecth."

Although he couldn't decide whether he believed Minawë about him having magic or not, Iren smiled a little. Though only in passing, the Kodama for the first time sounded accepting of the idea that he would accompany her to Ziorsecth. Wanting to keep her in a good mood, he decided to at least act like he believed her. He said, "So our bodies absorb magic passively, and we use it in spells. But until the fort, I never cast a spell. Does that mean I have eighteen years worth of magic stored inside me?"

Minawë shook her head. "No, although you absorb magic at a constant rate, your body can only hold so much. Think of the magic as water and your body as a bucket. The water pours into the bucket, but at some point, if the bucket isn't emptied, the water simply spills out. Using magic can increase the amount your body can hold, but overusing it can deplete your biological magic."

Up until now, Iren had followed her well enough, but now he got thoroughly confused. "Biological magic?"

"Yes, the magic that sustains life. Biological magic allows us to grow, to survive, to exist. Like food and rest, biological magic preserves us. Its presence keeps us young and fit, and it's the reason for our immortality."

Iren put up a hand. "That's enough. I've played along to this point, but now I know you're just seeing how far you can take this. I know I'm not immortal. I'm eighteen, and I've grown up at the same rate as all the humans my age."

"Of course. Early in our lives, our bodies use some biological magic to develop into adulthood. Once we reach maturity, however, the magic shifts from growth to maintenance, keeping us at our strongest. We can stay that way forever, theoretically."

"In that case, how old are you?"

Minawë glared at him. "Whether among humans, Maantecs, or Kodamas, moron, it's rude to ask a woman her age."

Iren flushed. He never did do well with social graces.

For several minutes neither spoke. As Iren watched the fire and considered all Minawë had told him, an image of Rondel's decrepit form came unbidden to his mind. Hoping he'd waited long enough for the sting of Minawë's rebuke to fade, he cautiously asked, "I once met a Maantec who looked ancient. How do you explain her?"

A foreboding expression grew on Minawë's face. "That is the consequence of using biological magic. Understand that while your body can replace environmental magic easily, your biological magic is set at birth. Nothing can replace it. When you cast a spell, you use environmental magic first. Should you exhaust that supply, your biological magic can provide an emergency source of energy. Doing so gives you tremendous power. For example, Iren Saito used his to curse my race. But releasing your biological magic also ages you, hence why I said that we are 'theoretically' immortal. The number of years we have lived doesn't determine how old we look; the amount of biological magic we still possess does. Thus, an aged person can look youthful if they have wisely conserved their biological magic. Conversely, a young person can appear old if they've foolishly squandered it. Someone like your Maantec must have used nearly all her biological magic to become as you describe."

Iren wondered about Rondel. If Iren Saito's biological magic had enough potency to curse an entire species, it terrified him to think what spell she'd cast to age her so much.

"I mentioned earlier that using spells can increase the amount of environmental magic available to you," Minawë continued. "Using biological magic can counteract those gains. Our own magic attracts the world's magic. The more biological magic you have, the more environmental magic you can store, and the faster you recover from casting spells. To keep on using your old Maantec as an example, with so little biological magic remaining, she likely can wield only small amounts of environmental magic. Furthermore, she would require days or maybe weeks to recover from using a larger spell. By contrast, despite casting that massive beam just this morning, you've restored your magical reserves."

Iren stroked his chin. At first he'd doubted Minawë, but now he began to believe her. Her explanations revealed why Rondel relied on abilities like Lightning Sight that required little magic. They also accounted for why the lightning bolt she'd used against Zuberi had left her so drained. He picked up a pebble and tossed it into the fire, sending sparks hissing. She wouldn't have needed to cast that spell if he'd been strong enough to defeat Zuberi on his own. "I as good as killed her," he whispered. "Rondel."

Minawë's ears perked up. "Rondel? You know Rondel?" Her tone changed completely. She chirped like a small child.

Iren looked at his boots as he responded, "We traveled together for a while, before she…" he trailed off, unable to continue. Then his head snapped up. "Wait, how do you know Rondel?"

The Kodama leapt to her feet. "She's only one of the most famous Maantecs in history! I grew up hearing stories about her."

Iren was pretty sure he'd never heard any stories about Rondel as a child. Granted, no one ever told him any stories as a child, but he still doubted they existed.

Minawë must have seen the doubt on his face, because she said, "Humans probably don't know about her, but among my people, Rondel's considered a hero."

"A hero? I thought you hated Maantecs because of the Kodama-Maantec War."

"That's why she's a hero! You traveled with her, and you still don't know?"

Iren just furrowed his brow. "Know what?"

"You moron, Rondel's the most famous traitor in Raa's history! We won the Kodama-Maantec War because of her! A thousand years ago, thanks to her defection, we all but wiped out the Maantecs."

He couldn't believe his ears. Iren knew Rondel looked ancient, but he never would have guessed that she was a thousand years old. More disturbingly, she'd betrayed her own people, sentencing them to near extinction.

Iren shook his head, trying to clear his confusion by force. He'd thought he'd come to understand the old woman, at least a little bit. As Minawë spoke, however, he realized the truth. He didn't know a thing about Rondel.

What else about her had he gotten wrong?

He started to ask Minawë, since she apparently knew a lot more about the cryptic Maantec than he did. Before a word could exit him, however, she leapt across the space between them and clamped a hand over his mouth. Her eyes narrowed dangerously, and she whispered, "We have to go. I tied your horse up over there." She pointed, and he dimly made out Nightraid's muscular black form through the shadows.

Iren tensed. The Kodama's demeanor had shifted again. "What's going on?" he asked when she lowered her hand.

She shot him an angry look, then jerked her head upward and whispered, "The owls."

He looked into the canopy, listening hard. "I don't hear anything."

To his surprise, she nodded. "Exactly."

They'd just reached Nightraid when the first arrows started falling among them. From deeper within Akaku, shrill, maniacal cackling filled the air alongside the projectile rain. As he climbed into the saddle, Iren could see sulfurous eyes filling the trees.

Through the thick forest they raced, arrows coming from every direction. No matter how fast Nightraid galloped, they couldn't escape. The insane laughter grew constantly louder, until even the crashing of the stallion's hooves became all but lost in the din.

Minawë pointed up as an arrow whistled past. "They're in the trees, jumping from limb to limb!"

Iren took her word for it. He was too busy trying to keep Nightraid from panicking. Still, he remembered the Yokai in the cave and how they could jump extraordinarily high. Their short, reverse-jointed legs made them poor runners but, combined with their light frames, made them excellent leapers. That gave him an idea.

Pulling on the reins, he turned the horse hard to the left. The sudden change forced Nightraid to a momentary stop, and Iren felt a sharp pain in his right shoulder as an arrow grazed him. Then they flew again, heading off in a completely different direction.

"Where on Raa are you going?" Minawë cried. "Ziorsecth is west!"

Iren ignored her. He didn't know how far Ziorsecth was, but he doubted they could reach it without Nightraid resting. As long as they stayed in Akaku, the Yokai could keep pace with them, leaping from branch to branch with ease.

How long they galloped through the forest with death raining all about them, Iren didn't know. He'd long since lost track of time. More than a few well-placed shots gave both him and Minawë minor wounds, but fortunately Nightraid remained uninjured. With each impact, Iren missed the Muryozaki more. He hadn't realized how much he'd come to appreciate its healing power.

At last he saw his destination. In the distance, the trees thinned, and moonlight filtered through the branches. With a final burst of speed, they shot through the tree line and onto the open fields of Lodia.

He continued riding south hard for nearly ten minutes, not daring to glance back. The arrows quickly died away, and at last he chanced a look. The Yokai hadn't pursued him beyond the forest. Here in the open, they couldn't keep pace with the mighty warhorse. He stroked the stallion's neck in sincere gratitude, and Nightraid responded with a triumphant neigh.

Whooping as much from pent-up adrenaline as from happiness at their escape, he turned in the saddle to face Minawë. "How was that?" he exclaimed.

The green-haired woman made no answer. "Minawë?" Iren shook her lightly, but she didn't respond. He shook her harder. "Minawë!"

Her eyes were blank, her lips silent. As he released her, she lost her balance in the saddle, falling gracelessly from the horse and hitting the ground hard.

CHAPTER SIXTEEN
What Comes of Revenge

At twilight two days after escaping the Yokai, Iren sat on a moss-covered boulder in a small glade in northern Lodia, cold rain drenching him. Several yards away, tucked under an outcropping of rock barely large enough for one person, lay Minawë, still unconscious. She hadn't awoken since leaving Akaku.

At least she was still alive. From the moment they'd escaped the Yokai, Iren had pushed Nightraid almost constantly, pausing only to let the horse rest and to catch a few brief naps. Most of his sleeping he did in the saddle, though. He didn't really understand the situation, but he knew Minawë's survival depended on him getting her to Ziorsecth as quickly as possible.

Now, while it infuriated him, he once more had to stop and recover. Not that he could get any real rest, thanks to the rain. Even with his cloak wrapped tightly around him, he couldn't get comfortable enough to fall asleep. Instead, he munched distractedly on some salted meat he'd found in Nightraid's saddlebags. Nearby, the majestic stallion stood tied to a tree, snorting miserably.

When Iren finished his snack, he pulled out the small ocean rock from his pants pocket and cupped it in one hand, taking comfort in its smooth surface. He thought of the crashing waves of the sea, miles and miles away. Part of him wished he was back there. Life at the castle had been so easy. Sure, everyone despised him, but he'd come to terms with that. He didn't care that they stared emptily past him and called him horrible names. At least there, he'd never been in any real danger.

It had all sounded straightforward in the beginning. He would travel to Veliaf, kill the Quodivar leader, and avenge his parents. He'd done all that. He'd gotten his revenge. At least it appeared that way, but ever since that day at the fort, he couldn't get Zuberi's words out of his head. The Quodivar leader claimed he'd been a Tacumsah pirate seventeen years ago, far away from Lodia. At the time, Iren had convinced himself the giant was lying, but he didn't feel so certain anymore.

"Can't you sleep?"

Iren turned his head and saw Minawë inclined on her elbow, watching him. Her voice sounded gentle and full of concern.

"It isn't exactly a comfortable inn." He pointed with his thumb toward the treetops. "And the roof leaks."

Her expression didn't waver. "Somehow, I think it's more than the weather."

He sighed. It couldn't hurt to tell her, so he opened his heart, speaking first of his upbringing in Haldessa. He explained how the people there hated and feared him, even though they didn't know anything about him. He told her of Amroth and what he'd said about Iren's parents. He gave her all the details of the mission he'd been on, and how even though he'd gotten his revenge, he didn't feel satisfied. All the while she listened attentively, only interjecting briefly to ask an occasional question.

When he finished, Iren leaned back and, for the first time that he could recall, felt truly relaxed. He'd never talked to anyone like that before. Even though he knew it must bore her horribly to hear his life story, she never showed it.

As he thought about his words, however, he suddenly flushed, embarrassed. He shouldn't have said so much. This woman was a Kodama. She didn't care about him.

Seeking a distraction, he rose and walked over to Nightraid, who gave an annoyed whinny at the downpour. The horse swung his head back and forth, and despite numerous attempts, Iren couldn't calm the stallion. Finally, he said softly, "*Kuylet, trempiot.*" The horse settled, and Minawë raised her green eyebrows.

"You know Kodaman?" she asked.

Iren turned around. "Is that what it is? Rondel taught it to me, sort of."

"It means 'Horse, be at peace.' Kodamas have a strong connection with animals. All of them know our tongue. Of course they can't speak it, but they'll understand what you say."

Iren stroked Nightraid's mane. It made sense that Rondel would know Kodaman, since she'd betrayed the Maantecs to them.

"Tell me," Minawë said, an edge creeping into her otherwise kind voice, "How did you feel when you killed Zuberi? Did it make you happy?"

His hand stopped midway down Nightraid's neck. The horse nudged him with his muzzle, but he ignored the touch. "No, I guess not. I thought it would. Zuberi butchered many people to gain riches, and many more suffered because of the Quodivar he commanded. I'm sure that killing him made Lodia safer, but it's only left me confused. I don't even know if he murdered my parents."

"That's what comes of revenge." Minawë's voice no longer sounded gentle. It was cold.

Her change of tone shocked him. "What do you mean?"

"When I was a child, Mother told me that seeking revenge can't make you happy. If you fail, you'll either die or suffer for the rest of your life. If you succeed, you'll be left with nothing, a void in your soul that you can't fill."

Iren looked up through the trees to the gray clouds beyond, letting the rain pelt his face. As he stared upward, Minawë rose unsteadily and walked over to him, leaning against Nightraid's flank for support. Almost absent-mindedly, she reached into one of the stallion's saddlebags and pulled out a handful of dried apple slices. As she ate the first one, she said, "You know, for a Maantec, you're kind of weird."

Iren blinked twice. "What?"

"During the Kodama-Maantec War, your ancestors tried to conquer Raa. They considered everyone else beneath them, and they didn't care what anyone thought. You're different, though it took me a while to notice it. When you killed Zuberi, you looked just like the Maantecs from the war: arrogant and destructive. I hated you for it."

"Why did you bring me along, then?" he replied, a touch of resentment in his voice. "That fight knocked me out. You could easily have dumped me in Akaku somewhere and taken off on your own."

"True, but as you saw when we left Akaku, I can't travel outside the forest on my own."

Iren remembered how suddenly Minawë had passed out. "What happened to you that night?"

She grimaced. "Do you know why Iren Saito's curse kills Kodamas who leave Ziorsecth? It mutated our bodies. I mentioned back in Akaku that our bodies have a semi-permeable membrane that allows us to absorb magic. Saito's curse made Kodamas' membranes fully permeable, meaning magic can both enter and leave."

"What does that have to do with losing consciousness when we left Akaku?"

"Every species draws environmental magic from a different source. Maantecs pull from the air. Kodamas draw from other living things, plants in particular. In Akaku, surrounded by ancient spruces, my rate of magic coming in nearly equaled my rate of loss, but Lodia's open fields only have grasses. My body couldn't absorb enough magic, so it made me pass out in a desperate attempt to save energy. It happened when I first left Ziorsecth too. That's how the Quodivar captured me, and that's also why I needed your help. Akaku and Ziorsecth don't share a border. Even if I could have evaded the Yokai and ridden all the way to Akaku's western edge, I still would have faced a stretch of plains. I hated you, but you were my best hope for getting back to Ziorsecth alive."

Iren pouted. "I'm glad I'm so useful," he said, "even though I'm a moron."

Minawë winced. "Sorry about that. I misjudged you in Akaku. Now I see you differently. You care what others think of you. That's not a common Maantec trait."

He crossed his arms. "I don't care. What does it matter if they all hate me? What difference does it make if I live alone the rest of my life? As long as I get my revenge, that's what I care about. If Zuberi didn't murder my parents, then I'll find the true culprit and kill him. It's what I'm meant to do."

"You're lying. At least, if the story you told me about your past just now is true. Granted, you sought revenge. But you also agreed to bring me to Ziorsecth, and you did that before you saw Zuberi. If he hadn't appeared, you might never have gotten your chance to face him. You willingly gave up on revenge to get me to Ziorsecth. Even after I acted rudely, you still aided me. You said that I could have abandoned you in the woods if I'd wanted to. Well, you could have done the same to me when I lost consciousness outside Akaku. You could have left me and gone hunting for your parents' murderer. No one ever would have known. Instead, you rode all the way here, keeping me safe. You also fought to protect Dirio, Veliaf, and all of Lodia from the Quodivar. When Balear nearly died in the Yokai's ambush, you risked your life to save him. If you truly only care about your revenge, why did you do all those things?"

Iren stared intently at a thoroughly uninteresting fern. Minawë reached out and took his chin in her hands, forcing him to look in her deep green eyes. She held him there a moment before speaking, her voice soft yet full of conviction, "You believe you're an avenger, but I can tell you're nothing of the sort. Your heart doesn't seek vengeance; it seeks to protect others and fights only when it has no other choice."

Iren felt wetness on his cheeks. At first he blamed the rain, but no, he was crying. "I've been such a child," he whispered. Then, biting his lip, he said, "Minawë, thank you."

The Kodama smiled, and then to Iren's amazement, she leaned in and kissed him on the cheek. He raised his hand to his face, touching the spot with disbelief.

"Of course," she replied. "Let's get some sleep. You can take the dry spot under the rock; I don't mind the rain. Then tomorrow, we'll set out for Zior—"

She never finished what she was going to say, because at that moment, she passed out and fell headfirst into the mud. Iren cried out and bent over, pulling her up. He saw her hair. He hadn't noticed it while they were talking, but nearly a quarter of it had turned bone white. More disconcerting, shallow wrinkles crisscrossed the young woman's face. Already she looked fifteen years older than when they'd first spoken in Akaku.

He swore. Sleep would have to wait. Nightraid was doing most of the work anyway, and he'd at least gotten a few hours' break.

"Ready, Nightraid?" he asked the horse, loading Minawë into the saddle and then climbing up himself. "Ride with the speed of dragons!"

They tore through the woods, branches slicing into Iren's skin. He couldn't care less. Unless Nightraid absolutely needed a break, Iren wouldn't stop until they reached the border. He knew that saving Minawë's life would take everything he had left.

CHAPTER SEVENTEEN
To Protect Someone Precious!

Iren raced across the empty plains of western Lodia, the wet earth sending clumps of mud careening from under Nightraid's hooves. The weather from yesterday had not let up. As the dull gray of the afternoon darkened into night, Iren still couldn't see his destination. He hoped he'd nearly reached the forest, but in these conditions, it could be miles as easily as yards. He probably wouldn't see it until he smacked into a tree at full gallop.

Glancing at Minawë, Iren's concern grew. More than three quarters of her hair had turned white, and she looked over sixty years old. The pace of her aging had quickened, and she hadn't woken once since leaving the glade the previous afternoon.

"Nightraid!" he shouted. "I swear to you, if you make it to Ziorsecth in time, no one will ever force you to do anything again. You can live a free life; you'll have earned a fine retirement." He wished he knew Kodaman so that the horse could understand him. The stallion deserved something for his trouble.

Just then, over the wind, Iren heard an odd whistling behind him. He craned his head in time to see an arrow pierce the veil of evening and strike Nightraid in his right hind leg. Neighing in terror, the wounded horse lost control and stumbled. A second arrow screamed across the plain and struck the stallion once more, this time in the side, barely missing Iren's calf. In his panic, Nightraid's legs twisted among themselves, and he crashed to the ground. Reacting quickly, Iren gripped Minawë with both arms. Pushing off with his legs, he flung himself away from the horse to avoid getting pinned under Nightraid's bulk.

He hit the muddy plain at a jarring speed. The moment he landed, searing pain shot through his left arm as his wrist snapped. The shock forced him to release Minawë, sending her rolling along the ground.

Stumbling to his feet, Iren clenched his teeth, striving against a wave of nausea. After the frantic pace of the last few days, though, he found himself unable to cope. Limply, he fell to his knees. He longed for the Muryozaki's healing power, but his father's katana was gone forever.

As he knelt there, the sound of hooves reached him. Seconds later, a form emerged through the downpour. A mighty charger, nearly an equal to Nightraid, rode proudly forward. Pushing his long, soaked hair out of his face, Iren realized the horse bore a familiar person clutching a bow.

"Balear!" Iren cried. "What are you doing here, and why on Raa are you shooting at me? You could have killed us!"

Balear stared coldly at him as he dismounted. Walking up to Iren, he barked, "It took longer than I wanted, but I finally found you. I had to stop you from leaving the country by any means necessary. Iren, come with me. You're wanted for questioning."

This had to be a joke. "Wanted?"

The young soldier's expression didn't lighten. "Rondel betrayed us all. She gave away weaknesses in Haldessa Castle and convinced the Quodivar and Yokai to attack. Captain Angustion says you have information about her, so I need to take you to him."

Iren tried to get to his feet, but he could barely move at all. "You're insane!" he cried. "What proof do you have?"

Balear reached into his leather jacket, pulling out a piece of parchment. Handing it to Iren, he said, "Here's your proof. Rondel sent this just before we left on our mission."

Iren quickly read the letter, his fingers trembling. He couldn't believe the words. True, Rondel acted spiteful and annoying, and yes, she brutally slaughtered those Quodivar in Veliaf. Even so, she didn't seem like someone who would betray a city to thugs and monsters.

Then Minawë's words about Rondel came back to him. She absolutely could betray a city. She'd already done that, and more, to the Maantecs a thousand years ago.

"So let's go," Balear said. "I'm bringing you back to Haldessa."

"Why?" Iren shouted, anger and regret mingling in his voice. "What does it matter now, anyway? Rondel's dead."

Balear was adamant. "Dead or not, the letter implicates you. We can't take any chances. Look, don't make this hard. No one's officially charged you. You're not a criminal. Just come to Haldessa with me. Answer the captain's questions, and if you satisfy him that you aren't carrying out Rondel's agenda, he'll release you."

Iren considered for a moment, then shook his head. "I can't come with you."

Balear's expression flared, and he swung his bow. He snarled, "If you don't, it means throwing your life away. I said you aren't a criminal, but if you refuse to come, that makes you guilty of resisting arrest. Worse, I'll have to assume your refusal as an admission of aiding Rondel. That would make you guilty of treason against Lodia. Wanted posters will go up in every town and village in the country. Everyone will know your face and name. If anyone sees you, they'll execute you immediately. You won't be able to return to Lodia for the rest of your life."

Iren hesitated, uncertain what to do. He was only on this errand because Rondel had pushed him into it. If he defied Balear, he would be giving up everything he had ever known. He would be marking himself for death for the sake of a woman he'd only met a few days ago. It made absolutely no sense for him to resist.

And yet...

He glanced at Minawë, at her helpless form on the verge of death. Subconsciously, he reached up and touched the spot where her lips had brushed against him the night before, the first time anyone had ever kissed him. He made up his mind.

"I can't return to Haldessa with you."

Balear's hand reached for his sword. "Then you side with Rondel?"

"I don't know whether Rondel's guilty or not, but my choice has nothing to do with her." Iren's expression turned fierce, and he stared directly into Balear's eyes as he defiantly roared, "All that matters to me now is protecting the life of someone precious!"

Balear swore as he dropped his bow and drew his sword. "As you wish, traitor. Prepare yourself!"

Iren forced himself to his feet, facing Balear's blade with only his off hand and the Muryozaki's sheath. He should have felt terrified, but instead a serene calm filled him. His mind couldn't explain it, but his body knew what to do. "Balear," he whispered, "I'm sorry." He raised his right hand. Magic flowed into it, smoothly and easily, as though he'd done it a thousand times. White light engulfed his palm. The energy lanced out like a spear, striking Balear and knocking him on his back.

Turning to Minawë, Iren hefted her onto Balear's charger with his one good arm and began to climb in the saddle himself. An arrow grazed his cheek. It struck the horse just above the heart, killing the beast instantly. As the horse toppled, Minawë fell too. Her head struck the ground and bounced off the hard earth.

Iren whipped around and saw that Balear had retrieved his bow. With his last strength before passing out, the sergeant had attempted to shoot Iren from behind. The arrow might have missed its intended target, but in killing the horse, the damage done was just as great.

Rather than despairing, however, Iren's will steeled. Minawë needed to get to Ziorsecth. He couldn't surrender. With nothing left but a desire not to let down this woman who genuinely believed in him, Iren hauled the unconscious Kodama onto his back. He tried drawing on magic to restore some of his stamina, but he couldn't feel it at all.

The storm crashed with more intensive fervor, as though nature itself wanted to keep him from accomplishing his goal. Nevertheless he marched on a slow, inexorable trek west.

He didn't know if he was awake or dreaming. He wasn't even certain he was still alive. Minawë's body pressed against his, limp and breathless. With her on his back, her face rested on his shoulder. Even in this state, appearing as old as Rondel had, she still looked more beautiful than anyone he'd ever known. Though her eyes were shut, he recalled their emerald hue like two tiny forests, strong and frail at the same time.

He leaned his head against hers and rubbed her fine hair, undamaged despite her many ordeals. Its vibrant green, however, had vanished. All the hair he could see was white. Her lips, too, had lost their fullness and luster. Only now, staring at her lifeless visage, did he realize how much, in just a few days, he'd come to love her. He blamed himself for her misfortunes. If only he'd ridden faster, he might have saved her. If they could have stayed in Akaku just a few more hours, perhaps that would have given her the time she needed.

Her skin felt cold. It was over; he had failed. Reluctantly, he let her body fall.

As her face drifted from view, he started. He thought he'd seen a movement in her lips, or perhaps a shred of color in her cheeks. He pulled her tightly to him again, but she gave him no further sign, if indeed she'd given him one in the first place. Nevertheless, that wisp of life, real or imagined, motivated him. Despite the pouring rain, despite the dead weight of her body on his back, and despite his own exhaustion, he would continue until the end.

He tripped often, slipping in the ubiquitous mud of this vile place. Several times he stumbled not from the wet ground but from his own weakness. In desperation, he set down Minawë, then discarded his shirt, cloak, and even the sheath to the Muryozaki. His load that tiny bit lighter, he hefted Minawë onto his back and continued trudging.

As Iren became certain he could not take another step, he finally saw, at the limits of his vision, a line of trees. Hope came to him at last. It was the forest! It must be, for in a few more moments he would surely die. With the last of his strength he forced himself under the shield of its canopy. Beneath its boughs he gently set the lifeless woman he'd sacrificed himself for on the ground. His task completed, he collapsed amid the leaves and surrendered to the void.

Had he remained conscious a few more seconds, he might have seen the Kodama's hair shift ever so slightly as her body settled, revealing a single green thread that had previously been obscured.

CHAPTER EIGHTEEN
Haldessa Ablaze

Amroth charged across Lodia on his Quodivar warhorse, pushing the animal far beyond its limits. Foam flew from its mouth, and every footfall slammed with the ominous roar of gathering thunder. He had neither eaten nor slept since Veliaf, but he didn't care. Every second counted as he raced toward Haldessa.

He already knew the city would fall. The Quodivar and Yokai would reach the castle long before he could. Amroth hoped not to save the city, but to arrive before his enemies moved on to another target. He wanted them all in one place so that he could test the full range of power that now belonged to him.

At his hip, he felt the gratifying presence of his new sword, the Karyo-zaki. With unreserved glee he drew it, the blade glowing red like a beacon. The two concentric rings of symbols on its hilt shone a brilliant yellow.

He'd waited a long time to gain it. Amroth had seen its power the day Nadav died, and ever since, wielding it had become his all-consuming passion. It was strength absolute, and it was exactly what Lodia needed. That fool Hezna had wasted its magic. The Oni could have conquered Lodia with it, yet instead he'd hidden away in Akaku and let the Quodivar do the work. Now that Amroth owned the sword, though, he would make good use of it. He would carve out a new future for Lodia, one that would guarantee peace for his country.

He recalled with cold satisfaction the look on Hezna's face. While Iren's attack had slain Zuberi, it had only struck the Oni a glancing blow. He'd survived, but he couldn't move. When Amroth stood before him, the

Oni's eyes had grown huge in recognition. The captain had then plunged his sword up into the monster's jaw, one of the few weak points in the Oni's natural armor.

Once certain of Hezna's death, he'd plucked the Karyozaki from the Oni's own claws. Flames had risen around him, threatening to char him alive, but he'd paid them no heed. They'd licked his skin and left harsh burns, but he'd simply stared stoically ahead. Showing any weakness or fear would have caused the dragon to devour him. He knew as much from Nadav. Feng, greatest of the dragons, understood what truly mattered in this world: strength. If you had strength greater than anyone else, you could go unchallenged in all deeds. You could get what you wanted without hesitation.

At last the fires had reached their fever pitch, and then they'd crashed as one into the Karyozaki, so that the sword erupted in flame. From within the blade, Amroth had felt, rather than heard, a growling bass voice call to him, "Amroth Angustion, you have passed my test. You are the Fire Dragon Knight."

He hadn't smiled. He hadn't celebrated, even though it represented the pinnacle of years of preparation. He'd simply nodded, as though the dragon had told him nothing more exciting than the time of day, and replied, "Of course."

After passing Feng's test, Amroth had reentered the cavern and hidden the Karyozaki in an alcove off the main tunnel. He didn't want Balear to know about the sword, not yet. He'd seen how the sergeant reacted to Iren's magic, and Amroth didn't need his new weapon giving the soldier any doubts. Instead, he'd waited until the loyal fool tore off after Iren before retrieving the blade.

Now, as the sun rose two days after leaving Akaku Forest, Amroth crested a small hill and arrived just outside Haldessa. Even though he expected it, the sight still gave him pause. Flames dotted the city, their smoke rising above the castle battlements. The stench of blood and ash reached him, but he didn't retch. It only reinforced what he knew he had to do. The Yokai and Quodivar had triumphed, using the baths to breach the castle just as the letter had instructed. Amroth wondered if any of the Castle Guard remained alive, valiantly yet futilely attempting to repel the invaders.

He dismounted, and for the first time since gaining the Karyozaki, doubt entered his thoughts. On his ride here, he'd felt so confident, but now he realized the immensity of his task. Hundreds, perhaps thousands, of enemies awaited him within the city and the castle.

Inside his head, Feng growled, "You have no choice! Set the entire city ablaze! Consume your enemies with their own fires!"

Amroth wavered. He'd known from the beginning it would probably come to this, but here, at the end, he hesitated. "Feng, how can I? There may still be citizens inside!"

"The Quodivar and Yokai will kill everyone anyway," the Fire Dragon replied matter-of-factly. "Whether they die by your hand or your enemies', they will still perish. You might as well take your foes with them."

The captain clutched his open hand to his head. "I can't!"

Sharp, hot pain wracked his chest, like someone driving a superheated spear through him. He fell to his knees, crying in agony. Feng roared at him, "Weakling! How could I ever have accepted you? You're nothing like Nadav!"

Through the torment, Amroth forced himself to his feet. The face of his old commander reappeared before him. "What would Nadav do," he murmured, "if he stood here instead of me?" In an instant, the captain had his answer.

He would cleanse the city with dragonfire!

Raising his arms, Amroth reached out with Feng's power to the flames already burning throughout Haldessa. He swung the Karyozaki, letting the full force of his magic fuel them. At once they accelerated and spread, igniting all in their path. Amroth watched callously as they engulfed the city.

Within minutes, the previous battle sounds ceased. The captain then stretched out his hand, calling to the fires like a god. All the flames died at the same time, but their thick, black smoke lingered.

Amroth stood transfixed by the damage from his spell. Where Haldessa had once stood, only ashes and the castle walls remained. He'd razed the city to the ground.

Inside his head, Feng asked him, "Are you crying? Nadav would laugh at you. I suppose I shouldn't be surprised. The castle's thick walls preserved its structure, but you destroyed all its finery. Its grand paintings and tapestries, centuries of labor, annihilated in seconds. Even a few you made yourself, correct? And of course, the king and everyone else inside have most assuredly died. You slew them all with your own hand."

For a moment Amroth didn't reply. He took a deep breath and closed his eyes. When next he opened them, they were dry and glared unfeelingly ahead. "I don't care." His voice rang brusquely against the hillside. "Art won't make Lodia stronger. Neither will feasts or lazy oafs who claim kingship yet sit hidden behind walls counting gold. I haven't destroyed anything today. I have purified. You and I have cleansed this den of soft luxuriousness. You say I killed Azuluu? Well, what of it? That's cause for celebration, not mourning. His death means the death of Lodia's weakness, and the birth of its true greatness. After all, he did name me his heir."

Amroth raised his weapon before him, its red body shining at his words. He grinned savagely. "Karyozaki, the Fire Dragon Sword," he said. "A fitting weapon for the new king of a better, stronger Lodia."

CHAPTER NINETEEN
Home in the Trees

Iren had no doubt; he was in Hell.

He overlooked an expansive plain choked by smoke and war cries. White flames burst from the ground and spurted high into the air. In their midst, thousands upon thousands of shapes clashed, the screams of the dying reaching him even at this distance.

The situation was hopeless. Those fires didn't care who lived or died. If they could wipe out everyone and everything on the plain, they would. He had no choice. This fighting had to stop. Raising his arms and summoning the full draw of his power, he prepared to cast his spell.

With a scream, Iren Saitosan awoke and shot into a seated position. He didn't stay there long, though, as a torturous jolt ripped through him and sent him back to the floor, gasping.

While his pain subsided, Iren took stock of his location. He was lying in a tiny enclosure not tall enough to stand up in. The structure was earthen, save one wall made of thick wooden poles spaced a handbreadth apart. He winced. Someone had captured him.

More than his imprisonment, the mere fact that he was still alive surprised him. He'd expected to die after carrying Minawë into the woods.

Forcing himself to sit up, slowly this time, he groaned and looked through the wooden bars. His cage sat on the ground in a quiet forest. As far as he could see, gigantic trees, some with trunks thirty or forty feet in diameter, dominated. Their thick canopies blocked out nearly all the sunlight, darkening the wood into subdued twilight. He could spot no evidence of inhabitation: no buildings, no farm fields, nothing but his cramped prison.

He couldn't see anyone around, either. His captors had apparently left him unguarded. He didn't have a weapon to cut the wooden poles, but maybe he could still escape. The puny prison surely couldn't withstand the kind of beam he'd used against Zuberi. He focused, but he couldn't draw on any energy. That confused him. He'd used magic against both Zuberi and Balear. Minawë had said the magic resided inside him. His body was like a bucket, with magic constantly refilling it. If that were true, he should be able to feel it now, yet he felt nothing. Frustrated, he leaned against the back wall of the prison and crossed his arms.

Rather, he tried to cross them. His right arm shifted just fine, but his left one was immovable. For the first time, he realized a splint held it tightly to his chest beneath his shirt.

His shirt! It was different, far different from the one Amroth had given him back in Haldessa. Whoever had captured him must have not only set his broken arm but dressed him as well. He still had on his old pants, but they looked miserable compared with the glowing shirt, pure white and crafted of what felt like fine silk. Even the best noblemen in Lodia would only have one or two garments of such quality. In all his life, Iren had never expected to find himself wearing clothing as fine as this.

As he contemplated his new attire, he heard a strange voice. It came from behind him, calling in a singsong tone with a high pitch. A few seconds later, a young boy carrying a wooden plate and cup and dressed in white clothes that looked like miniature versions of Iren's rounded the cage. The child grinned as he sang to himself. Iren noticed the boy's short green hair and at last knew for certain that he was in Ziorsecth Forest. Forgetting the cage's height, he tried to stand and smacked his head hard on the ceiling. That, combined with the strain on his sore muscles, dropped him back into a prone position. He moaned.

The Kodaman boy just laughed, saying mockingly, "You would do better not to cry so much, sir. It doesn't suit you."

The child spoke so fast and with such a squeaky voice that Iren had trouble comprehending him. He understood enough to catch the insult, though. He glared at the boy.

"Oh, don't look at me like that, sir," the Kodama said with false injury. "Without our help you surely would have died, and being hurt is better than being dead!"

Admitting the wisdom in the young guard's words, Iren obliged himself a thin smirk. Returning the expression, the boy set down his cup and plate, loaded with food, in front of the cage. Immediately ravenous, Iren reached through the bars and pulled chunks of the meal back, devouring them. The meat looked like smoked fish, but it didn't taste at all like the saltwater varieties common in Haldessa. An assortment of berries and dark, robustly flavored mushrooms three times the size of any Iren had ever stolen from the castle's kitchens rounded out the dinner.

When he'd finished everything, Iren asked his guard, only mildly sarcastically, "So who do I have to thank for my accommodations?"

"You're here at the request of Queen Aletas. She asked me to take care of you, although you haven't been much for conversation until today." The boy laughed at his own wit. "I've had to watch you sleep for a whole week. You're quite a lazy fellow!"

"Enough, Ulto," an authoritative female voice sounded from behind the cage. "Leave him alone." The boy chortled and trotted off. A moment later, a female Kodama, this one fully grown, appeared before him.

She looked about the same age as Minawë when they'd first met, but Iren knew he couldn't trust appearances. This woman could be twenty, two hundred, or two thousand and still look the same. Still, something about her made him think that she was very old. Unlike the boy guard or Minawë, this Kodama exuded formality. In contrast to Minawë's loose tousled hair, this woman tied hers in a tight bun atop her head. Her dress, made of intricately interwoven silks and dyed a brilliant green that matched her hair, made Lodia's most ornate clothing look plain. On the whole, the woman transfixed Iren. He found her at once beautiful yet, in a way he couldn't place, terrifying.

With a sweep of her hand, the wooden poles of his prison fell aside. The Kodama gestured for Iren to emerge. He stretched his three unbroken limbs, ignoring his sore muscles as he reveled in his ability to stand. Recalling an earlier conversation with Minawë, he took the index and middle fingers of his right hand and placed them vertically over his chest in the Kodaman sign of friendship.

The woman looked surprised that Iren knew their custom, and she only haltingly returned the gesture. At length she spoke, every word calm and regal, "I apologize for the prison, but we take no chances here. We have not welcomed outsiders into Ziorsecth in a thousand years, and we have not welcomed Maantecs for far longer. My name is Aletas, Queen of the Kodamas."

Iren told Aletas his name, and when she winced, he quickly added,

"I'm sorry. I know about Iren Saito, the man who cursed you, and I have no connection to him. Minawë told me about his horrible deeds." Shock struck. "Wait! Minawë! What happened to her? Did she…"

The Kodaman queen adopted an inscrutable expression. "You should see for yourself. Come with me." She walked to the base of a huge maple some hundred feet away. Gingerly, Iren tried a few steps, and when he found his legs could support him, he followed after her.

"Minawë's in my house at the moment." She gestured at the tree's enormous trunk, which easily measured thirty feet across.

Iren cocked an eyebrow. "Queen Aletas," he said, "forgive me, but what do you mean 'your house?' That's just a tree, albeit a big one."

The Kodama shook her head. "You Maantecs never did understand how we live. Let me show you." She waved her hand again, and to Iren's amazement, a line appeared in the trunk. It arched from the ground, up seven feet high, and then came back down. Giving it a light push, Aletas forced the wooden plug inward. It rotated on hidden joints, and Iren gaped as it swung aside.

The interior of the tree had been hollowed into a grand living space, leaving the outer two feet of wood to form thick walls. "Most of the inside of a tree is dead," Aletas explained as they stepped through the threshold. "All the vessels that transport water and nutrients are along the outer edge, just below the bark. Leaving this outer ring provides both structural support and allows the tree to continue growing. Our homes are truly one with the forest. We have no buildings, which makes for perfect camouflage. No one can find our villages unless, like us, they already know where they are. Your prison sat in the middle of Yuushingaral, our capital. You couldn't see us, but everyone in the village could see you."

Iren walked around the carved-out room with an expression of amazement. Even though the tree had no windows, the chamber was well lit, thanks to a round, white orb floating near the ceiling. "We light our homes with magic," Aletas answered when she caught him staring at the strange glowing ball. "It produces neither flame nor smoke, so it does not betray our presence. From the outside, you would never know this tree made such a comfortable home."

The room's all-wooden furniture impressed Iren as much as the magical lighting. Rather than separate pieces, all the décor, including a long sofa, six chairs, and two low-slung tables, melded into the wooden floor. Combined with their elegant, curved lines, the pieces looked truly organ-

ic, almost still growing. Aletas said, "We carve everything at the same time
we hollow the tree, shaping it into whatever pattern suits us. This way."
The queen motioned to the back end of the room, and Iren noticed a set of
narrow wooden stairs winding their way up and around the trunk.

Following the queen, he asked, "How many floors are in this place?"

"We use as much of the tree as possible. My home has four floors,
each narrower than the previous, until the trunk diverges into its canopy.
Traditionally, we use the first floor for gathering, hence all the seating. The
second floor is primarily for cooking and eating, and we devote the higher
floors to sleeping areas. Ah, here we are." She left the stairs at the third
floor. Unlike the open floor plan of the entry room, this level had walls in
it to create separate rooms. Peering into them, Iren saw more organically
carved wooden furniture, this time beds and dressers.

"In here," Aletas motioned.

Iren had barely taken a step inside the room when he was suddenly
ambushed. A pair of slender arms wrapped themselves around his neck
so hard he could barely breathe. Minawë's face, even younger and more
vibrant than the day he'd met her in Akaku, appeared in front of him. In
an exasperated tone she cried, "You moron, what took you so long? I got
tired of waiting!"

For several seconds Iren struggled to form words. At last he stammered, "How? Last time I saw you, you looked as old as Rondel! How did
you survive? How did you regain your youth, when biological magic can't
be replaced?"

Minawë smiled and released him. "Kodaman sentinels found us on
Ziorsecth's border a week ago and brought us here to Yuushingaral. As for
how I recovered, I just used this." She patted the wall of her room.

"The tree?" Iren looked doubtful.

"Unique among all species, Kodamas can restore their biological magic," Aletas interjected. "It comes at a terrible cost, though. The environmental magic we regularly absorb from plants doesn't harm them. But in
desperate need, we can restore our biological magic by directly siphoning
it from another life form. Doing this nearly always kills whatever we use,
but Ziorsecth has so much magic, we can draw from it with impunity."

"Mother gave me enough of her biological magic to bring me back to
consciousness," Minawë motioned at the queen. "Then we both used the
tree to restore our younger forms."

Iren was still digesting that Minawë had survived, but her statement sent his head whipping to Aletas. "You two are mother and daughter?"

The queen nodded, and Minawë blushed, apparently embarrassed that she had identified her royal heritage. Iren, however, only felt new respect for her. He had no idea she was a princess, yet somehow, it felt appropriate. She had such strength, such willpower, and such courage. She'd risked her life to enter Lodia, though he had no idea why.

Now seemed as good a time as any to ask, so he said, "Minawë, there's something I've wanted to know ever since I first met you. Why did you come to Lodia, when you knew it would probably kill you?"

Now mother and daughter both looked embarrassed, and neither answered for almost a minute. Finally, Aletas, gripping herself tightly, murmured, "I made her go."

Anger flew into Iren's eyes. He roared, "You? Her own mother? Why?"

Minawë put a soothing hand on his shoulder, but he shrugged her off, waiting for Aletas's reply.

The queen's voice remained subdued. "For information."

"Information?" Iren shouted as loud as he could. "You Kodamas haven't left your forest in a thousand years! What information could matter so much now?"

The queen sighed and sat on the bed. Minawë joined her, putting an arm around her for support. They looked odd together, their similar apparent ages making them seem more like sisters than mother and daughter.

"Several weeks ago," Aletas began, "the Heart of Ziorsecth gave me a vision. It showed me our forest, our beautiful home, burning. A giant firebird descended from the eastern sky and set it ablaze. The inferno consumed even the Heart itself in an explosion that shook Raa to its core. Something foul dwells in Lodia. I had to know what it was so we could prepare. Whoever I sent would almost surely die. I could command no one to do it, but Minawë volunteered."

"Why?" Iren turned to Minawë. "Why would you do that? Why would you sacrifice yourself for someone else?"

Minawë shrugged. "Why did you?"

Iren stopped short.

"Ziorsecth is my home," Minawë explained. "My only family dwells here. If I lost them, where else could I go? I would gladly die if the information I gathered helped them live. I learned little, though. Originally, I'd planned to go from Ziorsecth to Akaku, passing through Caardit along the way. The distance between the two forests is small in that region, and I thought I could make it before the curse attacked me. Unfortunately, I lost consciousness almost immediately after leaving Ziorsecth. A group of Quodivar must have found me and taken me to their base in Akaku. When I awoke there, Zuberi tortured me for information. When it became clear I would reveal nothing about my home, he grew frustrated and knocked me out. That's when you found me. In the end, I made a worthless journey. I know I didn't see any giant firebirds." She crossed her arms and glared at the floor.

Iren looked at Minawë as though seeing her for the first time. She'd wanted so desperately to get back to Ziorsecth, and at last he understood why. He'd thought she simply wanted to live, but she didn't care about that at all. All she wanted was the chance to pass on the little she had learned in Lodia to her fellow Kodamas. Still, it was hard not to see her mission as a failure.

But maybe it didn't have to be. Minawë might not know much about Lodia, but Iren did. At least, he knew more than any Kodama. "Queen Aletas," he said, "I can tell you what's going on in Lodia."

The queen rose from the bed, regal even in that simple gesture. "Actually, Maantec child, you can't."

He snorted indignantly, mostly because she called him "Maantec child." Sharply, he asked her, "Oh, and why not?"

She swept gracefully past him to the bedroom door, her silk dress flowing behind her. "Because you don't understand a thing about what's happening in Lodia."

"And you do, I suppose?"

"Well, better than you, anyway. Follow me; I'll show you my source. Minawë, you should come too."

Iren thought the queen would lead them back downstairs to the foyer, but Aletas went up instead, leading them to the top floor.

"I have only one chamber on this level, the guest room," she explained as she pushed open the door a crack. "I suppose I should offer it to you while you stay in Yuushingaral, but regrettably, it's already occupied."

Aletas opened the door the rest of the way and walked in. Curious who could give the Kodamas information, Iren hurried up the last couple steps and entered. As he did, a sarcastic voice said, "Hey, long time."

Iren's jaw dropped. Sitting in a carved wooden chair, wearing Kodaman robes, calmly reading a book, and sipping a drink, was Rondel.

CHAPTER TWENTY
Evil Unveiled

Iren stood frozen in the doorway, fists clenched, face livid, caught somewhere between relief that the double-crossing witch was alive and fury at the depth of her betrayal.

In absolutely no hurry whatsoever, Rondel set down her book on the end table beside her and rose. "Care for a drink?" she offered, holding out her wooden cup. "Kodaman brandy, made from distilled maple sugar."

"I'm not thirsty," Iren growled.

"No? A shame. The taste is distinctive, though admittedly it always reminds me a bit too much of breakfast. Well, if you change your mind, I'm sure Aletas must have a bottle or two still hidden somewhere in this tree, the squirrel."

Aletas folded her arms but said nothing.

"Can't you look a little more excited, Iren?" Rondel prattled on, her familiar dumb smirk filling her face. "I did come all the way from Haldessa just to see you."

Iren flared and lunged forward. With his unbroken arm he grabbed the diminutive Rondel by the lapels of her robe, bodily lifting the old woman and driving her against the far wall. He pinned her there with her feet dangling. Her cup crashed to the floor, spilling its contents. The pungent maple smell hit Iren's nostrils, but he ignored it as he yelled, "How dare you talk about Haldessa! Let me guess; you left it burning in ruins?"

If Iren's reaction took Minawë, Aletas, or even Rondel aback, they didn't show it. The two Kodamas simply watched passively, silent observers leaning against the wall by the room's entrance. Rondel maintained her grin, apparently unthreatened.

The traitorous hag's smile only incensed Iren further. "Stop that ridiculous look! I know it's false! You can't fool me anymore, Rondel. I know the truth now. Balear found your letter and showed it to me. I still have it, too, right here in my shirt pocket." He glanced down, but then his expression flattened. In his anger, he had forgotten. He'd cast away his shirt, and the letter implicating the crone, during his flight with Minawë. The only evidence of Rondel's guilt must surely be shredded beyond recognition on the Lodian plain.

Rondel cocked a mischievous eyebrow. "What's the matter? Lose something?"

Growling, Iren smashed her against the wall again.

The old woman didn't seem concerned. "Really, Iren, this is unnecessary."

"Like hell it is!" He prepared to slam her into the wall a third time, but Minawë intervened, rushing across the room and grabbing his arm in midair.

"Stop!" she cried. "Enough! Calm down and let Rondel explain."

Iren screamed in her face, "I won't listen to anything she has to say!"

From the other side of the room, Aletas said matter-of-factly, "Why not? What can it hurt? You can't go back to Lodia. They'd kill you."

Iren halted, mouth open, as his confrontation with Balear came back to him. In the eyes of Lodia, he'd thrown in his lot with Rondel. He'd become a traitor, marked for life. "Fine," he spat, releasing Rondel roughly before plopping himself on the bed, his right arm folded over his splint. "But if I don't like what I hear," he glowered at Rondel, "I'll kill you."

The diminutive Maantec chuckled. "You can try."

Aletas groaned. "Rondel, you're not really helping."

"No, I suppose not," Rondel conceded, though she sounded far from sincere. "You never did know how to have fun, Aletas. Fine, fine, might as well get down to business. Let's start with the simplest matter: why I'm still alive."

Despite Iren's best attempts to maintain his fury with her, he had to admit that particular subject made him curious. After all, he'd checked her pulse himself.

She explained, "You know that I manipulate the lightning in my body. By increasing its flow, I make myself faster and stronger. What would happen if I decreased it?"

"You'd get weaker," Iren guessed.

Rondel half-smiled. "And suppose I stopped it entirely?"

Iren froze on the bed. "Impossible."

"The brain regulates all the body's functions, even involuntary ones, by electric signals. Turn off those signals, and the body stops breathing, stops blinking, even stops its own heart. For all intents and purposes, it dies."

"Except," Iren found himself muttering, "the brain itself remains alive."

"Correct," Rondel said, "and critically important, otherwise I couldn't start my signals up again. I'd really die then. Of course, the brain can't live without air or blood for very long. A high-risk technique to be sure, and I can only maintain it for a few minutes. In this case, though, it lasted long enough. My senses continued functioning throughout my death state. I saw you unleash your beam. I heard you fall and get dragged away by your horse. And I saw Amroth finally reveal himself."

Iren frowned, confused.

"I told you before," Rondel went on, deducing Iren's expression. "I've suspected Amroth had an ulterior motive from the beginning, but I couldn't prove anything. I played along with his scheme, hoping he would eventually reveal his treachery. After you left, he did. He came out of the tunnel, fully armed, and marched right up to Hezna. He drew his blade and cut the monster's throat."

"What's your point? That's why we went on that mission in the first place."

"Only in the most basic sense. Amroth didn't just want to kill Hezna. He wanted what Hezna had. The moment the Oni died, Amroth took the monster's sword. You couldn't have recognized it, but I did. It was the Fire Dragon Sword, the Karyozaki."

Iren's pulse quickened. That Oni had been a Dragon Knight! "What happened to Amroth? Wouldn't the dragon have tested him?"

Rondel nodded, her expression ominous. "He did, and Feng accepted him. I don't have all the details, but I do know this much. Amroth didn't become the Fire Dragon Knight by accident. He knew what he was doing."

Iren sat pensively for a minute before bursting into loud, wide-mouthed laughter. "You're insane!" he replied. "Absolutely crazy. You don't honestly expect me to believe this nonsense, do you? You betrayed Lodia to the Quodivar and Yokai, and you think you can cover it up with this ridiculous story? Look, even if I don't have the letter, I still read it. I know what it said, and I know who signed the bottom of it." He stood. "I've heard enough. Amroth befriended me when no one else would. He rescued me as an infant, and he gave me a chance to avenge my parents. I won't let you make up lies about him! I'll kill you, Rondel, and when I carry your corpse back to Lodia, they'll know I'm not a traitor."

Rondel didn't react. Aletas, however, piped up, "You think that will solve anything? Amroth will still put you to death. He's planned to from the beginning."

Iren rounded on her. "How would you know? This is Lodian business, anyway, and none of your concern!"

Aletas was unflappable. "It concerns us now, foolish Maantec child, because the two of you came here. Traitors or not, Lodia will see Ziorsecth as harboring you. Besides, I've read the letter. It doesn't implicate Rondel. Quite the contrary, it proves her innocent."

"You've read the letter?" Iren shook his head in disbelief. "How?"

Rondel's grin returned, wider than ever. "Because I brought it here!" With a relaxed stretch, she stood, strode across the room to the bed, and hauled out a traveling pack that had been sitting beside it. Opening the flap, she reached in and removed the letter Balear had shown him, as well as the tattered shirt and cloak he'd cast away.

"Take a closer look at that note," Rondel said, handing it to Iren, "and the truth will come to you."

Iren read through the letter, but if there was something there other than Rondel's obvious betrayal of Haldessa, he missed it. "It has your signature, and I recognize your handwriting," he pointed out. "Remember, I saw you write out that waiver for Amroth at the castle."

To Iren's surprise, Rondel nodded. "Impressive, you picked up on it faster than I did. You're correct. That handwriting perfectly matches what I used on the waiver. Find anything strange about that?"

Iren stared at the letter, thinking back. He recalled how Rondel had completed the waiver with exactly these letters. She wrote slowly, painstakingly, her right hand shaking with effort. Realization struck. "You wrote the waiver with your right hand, so as not to reveal your Left identity. Amroth, Balear, and I were all watching you. To write to the Quodivar, though, you'd obviously do that in secret."

Rondel smirked. "And if I were writing in secret, why use my off hand? Would I not write with my left hand? It would give me both better penmanship and an alibi should someone discover the letter and ask me to provide a writing sample."

With new interest, Iren looked over the note, wondering if it could really be a forgery. He didn't see how that was possible. Even with Rondel's blocky characters, no one could perfectly duplicate her handwriting.

"Do you recall Amroth's speech the night before we set off on our mission?" Rondel asked. "He mentioned the many great artworks in the hall, and how he'd painted some of them himself. A little thing, but in this case, it explains much. Beyond superb combat skills, Amroth also possesses masterful artistic talents. He can do almost anything with his hands, including copy someone's handwriting."

"To do that, though," Iren pointed out, "he'd need a sample of your writing."

"Ah, but he did have a sample: the waiver. Do you honestly think that bunch of nonsense was a legal document? I've traveled Raa for over a thousand years. Lodia has never demanded such a waiver from anyone. Amroth made it up for the purpose of obtaining a complete sample of our handwriting." She reached into the pack again and pulled out a second sheet of parchment, which she passed to Iren. "The original waivers have conveniently vanished, but guessing that Amroth had some agenda, I memorized what he had us write. Take a look."

Iren read through the waiver text. "I, Rondel Thara, do here absolve Amroth Angustion, my Great King and Leader Azuluu, and all agents of the government of the Nation of Lodia and City of Haldessa of any responsibility should I perish on this dangerous mission. I recognize the task's extreme peril and small window for success, but my desire to bring justice to the Sneaky and Monstrous Enemy of Lodia, the Quodivar, is unquestionable." Rondel had also copied the date and her signature at the bottom.

"Incredible," Iren said after he'd finished. The old Maantec was right; the document contained every letter of the Lodian alphabet. In addition, when he compared it to the letter to Zuberi, he found that the note only used capital letters also found in the waiver.

"Amroth said he delivered the waivers to Azuluu's legal assistant, but he lied. Instead, when he left us, he ran back to his own room and copied my writing to create the letter to the Quodivar. I followed him at a distance, pretending to seek more alcohol, which, by the way, I also found time to get. Once he'd written the letter supposedly from me, he simply placed it with the castle post, more than likely bound for an accomplice in Veliaf."

Iren couldn't believe it. He fell back on the bed. The whole thing - the speech, Amroth telling him about his parents, the mission to stop the Quodivar leadership - was all a sham, all designed to gain Amroth the Karyozaki.

It all seemed unnecessary though. If Amroth only wanted the sword, there was no need for such deception. He didn't have to frame Rondel, and he certainly didn't have to send the Quodivar and Yokai to Haldessa.

That thought made him bolt into a seated position. "Rondel, what happened to the castle?" he asked. "If the Quodivar received the letter, they would know how to attack it!"

Rondel silently retrieved her fallen cup, staring into the empty mug as though searching for answers in its depths. "Iren, you guessed correctly that I left Haldessa in ruins. The city has burned to the ground."

Iren felt grateful he sat on the bed, because he swooned. Nearly all his memories were of Haldessa Castle. Up until the past month or so, he'd never gone anywhere else. He knew every passage by heart. He remembered the city lying just outside the castle walls, always bustling with excitement. How he'd longed to take part in that! He tried unsuccessfully not to think about the city's populace. The Quodivar must have caught them totally off guard.

"This news would be bad enough on its own," Rondel said, "but I'm afraid it gets much worse. You see, neither the Quodivar, nor even the Yokai, put Haldessa to the torch." She paused. Peering over her cup's rim at him, she continued in a deadly whisper, "Amroth did."

Stunned, Iren barely managed to meet Rondel's gaze.

"I arrived just in time to witness it," she said. "The Quodivar and Yokai had breached the city and the castle. Amroth used the Karyozaki's magic and set everything on fire. The castle is nothing but an empty shell now. It was horrifying. I've seen neither such magic nor such cruelty in the thousand years since the Kodama-Maantec War ended. Many innocent victims still lived when Amroth unleashed his attack. He killed them all. Amroth wiped out the civilian population, including the king."

Iren's head snapped up. It had to be a lie. It had to be. He only survived today because Amroth had protected him from execution. They'd fought side by side against the Quodivar. They were friends. Surely, the captain wouldn't betray Iren. Surely, he wouldn't betray Lodia.

His mind wanted so badly to deny it, yet the forged letter stared mockingly back at him, its letters spelling out their cold truth. Amroth had used him, hoping he would help kill Zuberi and Hezna. Once Iren had accomplished that mission, Amroth had always intended to get rid of him. The captain had even gone so far as to specifically include Iren's name in the letter to the Quodivar, guaranteeing that Iren would be cited as a potential traitor.

Numbly, Iren got to his feet. "It can't be. It can't be." He kept repeating the sentence, as if saying it enough times would make it true. Rondel and Aletas just watched, letting him work through the struggle on his own. Minawë stepped forward and started to put an arm around him, but the physical contact was too much. He bristled and shouted, "It can't be!"

Before anyone could stop him, he rushed out the door, down the steps, and was gone.

* * *

Iren had no idea why he was running, let alone where he was going.

Still, it felt good to run. The pounding of his boots on the thick mat of fallen leaves, the shouting of his muscles as they begged for air, and the rapid breathing trying to meet that demand all called for concentration. While he ran, he didn't have to think. While he ran, he didn't have to see Amroth's face bubbling up in his consciousness.

He couldn't trust anyone. He'd put his confidence in Amroth, and the captain had slaughtered an entire city. He'd considered Balear a comrade, yet the soldier had tried to kill him. He was better off on his own, the way he'd lived in Haldessa all those years.

For what felt like hours, he continued running. He had no idea how far he went. It didn't really matter, as long as he put distance between himself and everyone else.

Perhaps if he'd paid slightly more attention, he would have noticed the cliff. As such, he didn't even slow down as the forest abruptly ended, and he found himself no longer running but falling.

He had just enough time to curse before he hit the water. Pain shot through his broken left wrist as the impact ripped away its sling. The smell of saltwater filled his nostrils, a scent he'd always found pleasing. Now it terrified him. Desperately, he tried to swim, but he had no clue how. He'd never been in water deeper than the bath in Haldessa. With each second, his head dipped lower. Soon he started gulping mouthfuls of liquid. The harsh water burned his throat and lungs. His vision faded, and he realized he would drown. He didn't care. No one could betray him after he died.

Just before he blacked out, a strong, lithe arm wrapped itself around his middle. Vaguely, as though in a dream, he felt the sensation of movement, of someone or something tugging on him.

When he awoke sputtering, he lay face up on a sandy beach, staring at a bright, sunny sky. The smell of the ocean overwhelmed him, and he heard the familiar calls of the gulls and gentle crashing of the surf. It was impossible, yet it seemed he had returned to Haldessa, back to the coast of his childhood. Shielding his eyes from the harsh glare, he struggled to sit up, fighting nausea. He was soaked, and sand caked his clothes and skin.

"You all right?" a concerned voice said from behind him. He craned his neck around and saw Minawë, herself thoroughly drenched.

"I guess so," he lied. His broken left wrist ached horribly. "Did you pull me from the water?"

She nodded.

Iren eyed her suspiciously. He didn't know if he could trust her. Amroth and Balear had both betrayed him; Minawë could do the same at any time.

Unable to face her any longer, he turned his gaze to the ocean. The surf roiled. It was high tide, and even from here, Iren could tell the water had a strong current. It could have easily washed them both out to sea. Nevertheless, she'd braved it, risking her own life to save his. He doubted Amroth or Balear would have done that for him.

"By the way, moron," Minawë said, "if you ever do something that stupid again, don't worry about drowning. I'll kill you myself."

Something about the way she said that made it hard for him to know if she was joking or not. He decided it best not to push the issue. Instead, he asked, "What is this place? Surely I didn't run all the way to Lodia, yet this beach looks just like it."

Minawë laughed, clear and mirthful. Iren couldn't imagine a sweeter sound, and it made him happier just to have it cross his ears. "No," she replied, "you're still in Ziorsecth, or at least on its edge. The forest surrounds this inland ocean on three sides, and the Eregos Mountains form its southern edge. This is the Yuushin Sea, and we named our capital after it. You only ran a few miles. Actually, you have pretty poor aim." She pointed to the right. The coast rose rapidly from the gentle sandy beach where they rested to a tall bluff, not half a mile distant.

She knelt down and smiled in his face. "You jumped off near the top. A thousand feet closer in this direction, and you'd just have run into the surf instead of off a cliff."

Iren nearly fainted again. From here, the bluff looked quite imposing. The fall alone should have killed him. If Minawë hadn't come for him, he would not have survived.

Not that he was much better off. He winced as a fresh wave of pain jolted his broken arm. Minawë's playful grin vanished. "Let's get you back to the village. A dunking in the Yuushin Sea is bad enough on its own. I won't have you getting an infected arm on my watch."

She helped him to his feet, and they had just about left the beach when Rondel burst through the tree line. The Maantec woman took one look at Iren and shook her head. "I swear I can't leave you alone for five minutes without you getting into some kind of trouble. You really are an idiotic student."

Iren frowned at the old hag. "I think I preferred it when it was just Minawë on the beach. And since when am I a 'student' anyway?"

Rondel smiled. "How else will you become skilled enough to stop Amroth?"

He blanched. "Stop Amroth? He wiped out a city!"

"Which is precisely why he must be stopped. You think Haldessa will satisfy Feng? No, his fires will spread, and they'll do so all the faster now that Amroth has become king of Lodia."

The words took a few moments to register. Iren recalled how Azuluu had made the captain his chief advisor, and therefore heir to the throne, during the feast before their mission. With Azuluu dead, Amroth had full command of the country.

"So let's go," Rondel barked. "We don't have time to waste on you resting. Hurry up, slacker!"

Iren took a step backward, protesting, "Forget it! In case you didn't notice, I have a broken wrist. Besides, what about you? If you went to Haldessa and saw Amroth torch the city, why didn't you stop him? What happened to 'evil must be annihilated?'"

Sparks flashed in Rondel's eyes as Lightning Sight activated. "You think I didn't want to? Between his kingship and his possession of the Karyozaki, Amroth has become the greatest threat to Raa since the Kodama-Maantec War ended. If I could have killed him, I would have." She sighed. "At the moment, though, I can't. When Hezna beat me, he took the Liryometa. Amroth grabbed it along with Feng's sword. Without Okthora's magic bolstering my own, I don't stand a chance against him. Remember that bolt of lightning I used against Zuberi to save you? That took nearly all the magic I had. I can't compete with Amroth as I am now."

Iren shuffled his feet in the sand. If he could have defeated Zuberi on his own, if Rondel hadn't needed to rescue him, maybe none of this would have happened. Haldessa might still stand. All those people might still be alive.

Rondel ignored his self-pity. "Now you understand why I came to find you. You're going to stop Amroth and get the Liryometa back for me."

"Be serious!" Iren felt himself sweating. "If you can't fight him, how can I? If you're counting on Divinion's help, give up. I lost the Muryozaki in Akaku."

Rondel deactivated Lightning Sight. "Are you that dense?" She pointed back in the forest. Aletas stood just inside the tree line, watching them. In her arms she held a long bundle wrapped in silk. Rondel retrieved it. "Amroth took my weapon, but in his excitement over obtaining the Karyozaki, he forgot all about yours." She unwrapped the cloth and revealed Iren's katana, shimmering white in its sheath. "You and this sword may be our only hopes for stopping Amroth."

Iren reached out with his right hand and grasped the blade's hilt. He felt an odd tingling in his left arm, and seconds later, it healed. He then took the Muryozaki from Rondel and drew it with his restored arm. It was like reuniting with an old friend.

The crone turned and left the beach. At the forest's edge, she said over her shoulder, "Follow me."

"Where?" Iren asked.

"It's time you understood the full secrets of that sword. It's time you became a real Dragon Knight."

CHAPTER TWENTY-ONE
Crown of Flames

In a posh mansion by the Bay of Ceere, King Amroth Angustion sat in an ornately carved high-backed chair, watching the sun rise over the water and grinning to himself. Behind him, he could hear the servants running pell-mell trying to please him, rearranging the furniture to his exact tastes.

A week had passed since his coronation. With Haldessa in ruins, Amroth had designated nearby Ceere as his temporary capital, commandeering the largest house for his residence.

Looking out the window, he could just barely make out Haldessa's remains atop the bluff that formed the northern end of the bay. He'd conscripted half of Ceere's populace to restore the castle. He couldn't wait to return there. It was his destiny, after all. The Azuluu line had been one of worthless kings, grown fat on peace and oblivious to the dangers of this world. Peace only came through power. Nadav understood that. Amroth understood it too.

Very soon, the rest of Lodia would as well. Right now, the country was but a speck on the continent of Raa. Amroth would change that. Under his leadership, Lodia would cover the world.

He'd taken a desperate gamble from the beginning, but it had worked out in the end. He'd achieved it all: his revenge, the throne, and the best prize of all, the Karyozaki. Hezna never deserved it. From the moment the Oni became the Fire Dragon Knight, Amroth had plotted, trying to figure out a way to kill the monster. All those years living as a simple farmer in Caardit, he'd wrestled with the problem. No matter how he tried, he couldn't come up with a way. He couldn't do it, not without being a Dragon Knight himself.

It was thanks to Iren that he had succeeded. Rather, it was thanks to Amroth's own foresight in perceiving Iren's usefulness seventeen years ago. When Amroth and Captain Ortromp had gone to investigate the presence of a Left farmer, Amroth had seized on that mission as a way to become Captain of the Guard. He'd told Iren that he regretted Ortromp's death, but he'd always intended to kill the useless captain and take his place. The Left provided the perfect cover. Amroth could blame Ortromp's death on the Left, and no one would question it. He'd thought a promotion was all that mission would yield him, until he'd seen the Muryozaki.

Nadav had told him about the Ryokaiten, so he'd recognized Divinion's blade immediately. At first he'd considered killing the infant boy resting against it and becoming the Holy Dragon Knight himself. Had he done that, however, he would never have passed Divinion's test of purity of heart. Besides, he didn't want Divinion. He wanted Feng.

Then the helpless baby Iren Saitosan had given him an idea. He couldn't defeat Hezna, but if he had his own Dragon Knight, someone he could mold and shape into the perfect weapon, then perhaps he could. Iren would become his pawn, left alone to grow up despised by everyone. Amroth had known what would come of doing that. Iren would learn to hate. All Amroth needed to do was channel that hatred by presenting the boy an opportunity for revenge and pointing him in the right direction.

Once Iren had slain Hezna and obtained the Karyozaki for Amroth, he would have outlived his usefulness. To prevent him from ever becoming a threat, Amroth would arrest him for treason and have him executed. Here the destruction of Haldessa came into play. Once the Lodian people saw the fake letter from Rondel, they would blame her and Iren for the city's demise. They wouldn't bother searching for other evidence. Lefts were children of the devil, after all.

Of course, Haldessa's annihilation had been about so much more than framing Rondel and Iren. It had provided a vital diversion too. Even with a Dragon Knight supporting him, Amroth had known that he couldn't reach Hezna if all the Yokai remained in Akaku Forest. Opening Haldessa to attack would empty the forest and expose the Oni. The city had needed to die so that Amroth, and ultimately Lodia, could triumph.

Besides, Haldessa's destruction wasn't in vain. Its vulnerability had baited the Yokai and Quodivar into concentrating in one location. In wiping out Haldessa, Amroth had eliminated Lodia's two greatest threats in a single glorious onslaught.

Only Rondel could have disrupted his scheme. She always got in the way. Without her, Nadav would still be alive. The night she'd helped him in Haldessa with the infant Iren, he'd needed to stomach his hate and put on a front of decency. All the while, he'd wanted to kill her, but she could have carved him into pieces before he'd finished drawing his blade. She could have wrecked his plan at any time, had the senile Maantec ever guessed his intentions.

Even the most dangerous of foes, however, had their uses. Holy Dragon Knight or not, Iren lacked experience and might lose against Hezna. Rondel, though, could almost certainly slay the Oni. Amroth merely had to convince her to do it.

In that regard, Iren had proven doubly useful. The night Amroth first showed Rondel the baby boy, the old woman had acted stunned, even terrified. Over the next several years, though, Amroth had noticed something odd about Rondel. Occasionally, he would catch glimpses of her spying on Iren. For whatever reason, she was drawn to the boy. Amroth had therefore crafted his speech the night of the feast to publicly announce his intent to bring Iren on his impossibly dangerous mission. Rondel would never allow Amroth to take Iren out of her sight, not into such certain death. She cared too much for that little wretch.

The old fool might think herself clever, but she'd fallen for Amroth's wiles as easily as Iren had. Not only would her presence on the mission guarantee that Hezna would die, but in so doing, she would also allow Amroth to gain the Karyozaki. Once he had it, he could use its power to finally get revenge on her. By implicating her in the same treason as Iren, he could slay them both with the full blessing of the Lodian people.

At least, so he'd intended. One element in the sequence had gone awry. Iren had escaped. Amroth hoped Balear could remedy that situation, but even if he failed, it made little difference. Iren didn't understand magic or the dragons. With Rondel dead and the Liryometa in Amroth's possession, the boy posed no real threat.

The new king of Lodia laughed as he held up the dagger, causing the servants to eye him curiously. The weapon was undeniable proof that he had avenged Nadav. Those final hours in the cave, when all his deceptions had come to a head, he would forever consider his proudest moments.

After killing the Quodivar guards in the treasure room, Amroth had

chased the fleeing thief alone. Ostensibly, he had done that to prevent
the bandit from raising the alarm. In reality, though, Amroth had merely
wanted to buy time and put space between himself and the others. He'd
just reached the next room when he'd heard the gurgling sound of a stran-
gled and bleeding man. Stopping short, he'd found Zuberi and Hezna
waiting for him, the thief butchered by the Oni's claws.

Amroth had bowed low to both of them, hiding his distaste. "The
others will arrive soon. We must act quickly."

Zuberi had grinned. "Lord Hezna, if you would?"

The Oni had snapped his fingers, and a violent explosion rocked the
cavern. "'The others' are now buried in stone," he'd growled. "Amazing
what Feng's magic can do when channeled properly. But then, you'd know
all about that, wouldn't you, Amroth?"

Hezna's arrogance had only made Amroth want to tear the Oni's
throat out more, but it had been too soon. "Don't get overconfident," he'd
said instead. "Rondel is with them."

Zuberi had shrugged. "No matter. We'll wear her down. Lord Hezna,
let us put that vermin you've caught to good use. Use his blood and make
it look like we've captured our dear friend Amroth. Then when his comrades come to rescue him, your Yokai can ambush them."

They'd all had a good laugh, including Amroth, although he'd doubted
the Yokai could win. "It won't be enough," he had dared to counter. "You
both know Rondel's legend, and the boy I mentioned in the letter, Iren
Saitosan, wields the Muryozaki. You'll have to kill them yourselves."

"Ah, yes, the Lefts," Zuberi had scratched his chin. "Direct them to
the fort. There's no room to swing here." He'd tapped the handle of his
massive sword, then disappeared deeper into the cavern.

Hezna had then smeared the dead bandit's blood on Amroth's back
and left the room, dragging the corpse along the floor. Amroth had joined
him, walking in front so the Oni's giant footprints would disguise the captain's. At the room with the lake, Hezna had run his claws shallowly along
Amroth's back to give the illusion of combat. The captain had feigned
unconsciousness in one of the cages while waiting for the others to arrive.

Amroth had expected Rondel to win against Hezna easily, but Iren's
stupidity and weakness turned out to be the new king's greatest unexpected boons. When Rondel's desperate attempt to save Iren had drained her
of her magic, Amroth had watched gleefully as Hezna finished her. He'd
never heard sweeter music than Iren's anguished screams after checking

Rondel's pulse.

The Lodian king laughed again, standing from his chair and brandishing the Karyozaki and Liryometa together. Flames danced around him with each swing. Soon fires swirled around his head, a far more appropriate crown, he thought, than Azuluu's useless trinket. Elation filled him. Rondel and Hezna were dead. The Yokai and Quodivar were finished. He possessed the Karyozaki and Lodia's throne. He'd achieved complete victory.

"Not quite," a growling voice said.

The king glanced around the room, frantically eyeing the servants, but none of them reacted. Only he could hear the words. He motioned for his staff to exit. Although he knew the voice's source, he didn't want to speak to it while others were around. They would think him crazy, talking to a sword.

"Feng," he barked when everyone else had left the room, "what do you mean? No one can challenge us."

The raspy voice of the dragon laughed, a cruel, harsh cry that made the sword itself vibrate. "Fool, you're either blind or stupid."

Amroth started to rebuke the dragon when Balear burst into the room, red-faced and sweaty. The king tempered his rage at the disturbance. Right now, he needed Balear's information above all else.

The young soldier approached Amroth gingerly, eyes wide in terror. The king frowned, confused by his subordinate's reaction, but then he realized he still had fires surrounding him. He doused them with a gesture.

"Captain Angustion!" Balear cried. "What happened? Haldessa is leveled, ashen, the castle in shambles! Did you arrive too late to stop the Quodivar? And what was all that fire just now? Has devil magic possessed you like it did Iren?"

Amroth simply smiled and stood motionless for a moment. Then he let fire issue forth in a circle around his feet. It whipped about, encircling him and rising until it encased him like a small typhoon. All the while, he maintained his supremely confident smile. Portions of the room ignited. After fifteen seconds, he released the magic, and the inferno ceased.

"My reward," he said, "for stopping the Quodivar." He held up the Karyozaki. "Remember Iren's sword, with the power to heal? I now have one too, but with a rather more useful ability." He glared at the young man. "By the way, Balear, you'll address me as 'King Angustion' or 'my liege' from now on. Azuluu has died. I am king now."

Balear looked at once both shocked and conflicted. "Congratulations, my liege," he managed. "I grieve for King Azuluu's passing, and I hope we'll have peaceful and prosperous times under your leadership."

"I intend nothing less," the king asserted. He stepped past Balear and strode across the room. He entered the long central hallway of the mansion, moving so quickly the young officer needed to run to keep up with him. Amroth asked tersely, "Now tell me what has happened! I assume you brought Iren with you."

Balear didn't answer right away, which annoyed Amroth. He wheeled around, leaning domineeringly over the young soldier. Fire leapt around his head.

"I'm sorry, my liege," Balear stammered. "I did as you ordered me to. I caught up to Iren Saitosan just outside Ziorsecth, but he used some kind of devil magic on me. He knocked me out. When I came to, he'd disappeared without a trace. I assume he went into the forest."

Amroth clenched his fists, fires igniting in them as he did so. He forced his voice to remain calm. "Well then, give me Rondel's letter and go on your way."

Balear gulped. "I allowed Iren to read it in order to convince him of Rondel's treachery. I thought that he would then return, but he still refused. We fought after that, and I never got the letter back. I believe Iren has it now."

The dragon's cruel laugh filled Amroth's mind. "So much for your flawless plan. Nadav would be disappointed."

Amroth resisted the temptation to cry out. It didn't matter anyway. With Rondel dead, Iren was irrelevant. If he had gone to the Kodamas and left Lodia forever, so much the better.

"Are you so certain he went alone?" Feng crooned inside his mind. The dragon's sense of superiority was starting to wear thin.

"What do you mean?" he asked belligerently, not caring that Balear could hear him.

Balear, apparently thinking the king was talking to him, started to speak, but Amroth silenced him with his palm. The dragon replied, "If you have any doubts, why not give Balear the Liryometa?"

"What good will that—" Amroth stopped. He knew what good that would do.

"Balear," the king said, "you have come through many dangers, and I feel you've earned a reward. Please take this dagger, the weapon of the traitor Rondel, as a gift from me. May it always remind you of the rewards of loyalty and the penalties of treason."

Timidly, like the dagger might stab him of its own accord, Balear accepted the prize. "It's too short for me," he mumbled, clearly embarrassed.

The king barely heard him. His breath caught as he noted the disturbing lack of change in the young soldier. "Balear, do you feel any different?" he asked.

Balear's confused expression provided all the confirmation Amroth needed. If Rondel had truly perished, the dagger would have tested Balear. The sergeant would either have become the Storm Dragon Knight or died. The fact that neither had happened meant that Rondel must still be alive.

Feng mocked the king, "Still so convinced of your invincibility? All your grand designs, and the woman you most wanted dead has eluded you. If you have no greater ability than this, you'll wind up a more miserable king than Azuluu. Lodia will crumble in a month."

"Stop talking!" Amroth roared, forgetting Balear and the numerous servants farther down the hall. He swung his fist, and a plume of flame shot forth, igniting a tapestry. The elegant fabric went up as easily as an oil-soaked rag, obliterating years of painstaking work in seconds.

Balear and all the servants looked at their new king with astonishment. Amroth glared at each of them, daring them to question him. Finally, he turned on his heel and stormed back to the room he had vacated, slamming the door behind him.

CHAPTER TWENTY-TWO
The Kanji Circles

Rondel and Aletas stared at each other, their expressions frosty. Several feet away, Iren and Minawë watched the spectacle without comment, fearing to incense the two elders further.

"We need a place to train," Rondel pointed out.

"Train in Lodia," Aletas retorted. "I won't have you blowing up my forest."

Rondel rolled her eyes. "You know we can't go there."

"Well, you can't stay here!"

Iren shifted his gaze between the two, confused by the change in their demeanors. They'd seemed fine back in the house when Rondel was explaining about Amroth. Now Iren wondered which of them would throw the first punch.

Minawë didn't share his disbelief. She whispered in his ear, "Didn't you notice before? Mother and Rondel didn't make the friend sign when we entered the guest room. Also, when you attacked Rondel, Mother didn't intervene."

"What do you suggest, then?" Rondel continued, oblivious to the pair whispering next to her.

"Go to Serona. He should see it anyway. He needs to know the danger he poses."

Iren's ears perked up at that. Minawë had mentioned Serona during their journey. It was the homeland of the Maantecs, and the place where they met their demise a thousand years ago. She'd told him that it lay west of Ziorsecth.

Rondel whined about the distance, complaining that she would likely break a hip along the way, but she finally acquiesced, "Very well, but we can't wait that long to start his training. We'll begin on the way there." Aletas shot her a contemptuous look. Rondel raised both hands innocently. "Just the basics!"

The queen didn't look happy about the situation, but she turned away and left them without further argument.

"Guess we're done here," Rondel said. She glanced at Iren, her stupid grin rising to the surface. "Look lively! We're bound for Serona!" She started walking west through the forest, not bothering to wait for a response.

"When did she get so enthusiastic?" Iren grumbled. He didn't dare ask how far Serona was. He was sure he'd rather not know.

Iren and Minawë now stood alone in the woods. Suddenly, Iren felt uncomfortable. He couldn't meet the Kodama's eye. Instead, he dug the toe of his boot into the soft forest earth.

"I guess I won't see you for a while," Minawë said at length. Her voice trembled.

"Yeah," Iren managed. The word was flat and woefully inadequate, but he couldn't think of anything to say.

"I never got to thank you before," the princess said. "If it weren't for you, I'd be dead now."

A lump formed in Iren's throat. "You don't have to thank me. Anyway, I could say the same thing to you. I'd be at the bottom of the Yuushin Sea if you hadn't dived in after me."

"That's true," she admitted, "but all the same, I wanted to thank you." She wrapped him in a tight embrace. Unused to such close contact, his first instinct was to recoil, but slowly he relaxed and let her hug him. Her hold was soft, yet strong as well. He smiled. It made him feel secure in a way he'd never experienced before.

They stayed like that a few moments before off to the west a high-pitched, sarcastic voice called, "Pick up the pace, slacker! Serona won't come to us!"

The pair separated, and Iren felt his face redden. Nervously, he asked, "Will I ever see you again?"

Minawë smiled, but Iren thought he saw sadness underneath the expression. "I'm sure," she said, but the waver in her voice told him more than the words.

Then she was gone, leaving Iren alone in the woods. He sighed. He had no idea what kind of training Rondel planned for him, but he knew he wasn't going to like it. Still, he supposed he shouldn't keep the impatient hag waiting. Following Rondel's voice, Iren raced to catch up to her.

"About time," Rondel spat, glaring up at him.

"Just because I had someone to say goodbye to," Iren retorted. "I wasn't really expecting to get kicked out of Yuushingaral. What was all that with Aletas, anyway? Something happen between you two?"

Rondel shrugged. "Nothing in particular. Aletas lost her husband to Iren Saito's curse a thousand years ago, and she still bears a deep grudge against Maantecs because of that."

"So then, she didn't fight that day?"

"No. In Kodaman culture, the king leads the army, but the queen truly rules the race. She oversees all non-military affairs. Even before the curse, Aletas almost never left Ziorsecth. She never fought in the Kodama-Maantec War, as far as I know. However, her husband, Otunë, did. He wielded the Chloryoblaka, the bow of the Forest Dragon, Dendryl. He also fathered Minawë."

Iren's thoughts drifted back to the Kodaman princess. If Otunë had fathered her, yet died during the Kodama-Maantec War, then that meant Minawë had to be nearly a thousand years old. He swallowed hard. No wonder she'd gotten upset when he'd asked about her age.

"Anyway," Rondel continued, going back to her original topic, "while Aletas directed the brunt of her anger at me, she was equally incensed with both of us. She hid her ill will toward you, since you rescued Minawë. Truthfully, though, she abhors our presence here."

"Why?"

"Ever since the Kodama-Maantec War ended and her husband died, Aletas started fearing the dragons and, by extension, Dragon Knights as well. You carry the Muryozaki. That alone makes her despise you."

"That's crazy," Iren said. "Divinion is the Holy Dragon, right? That makes him good. Aletas shouldn't fear him or me."

"You don't understand," Rondel replied, shaking her head. "None of the dragons, not even Divinion, are inherently good or evil. They just are. After all, when Iren Saito cast his curse on the Kodamas, which dragon lent him power?"

Iren didn't have to answer. He knew it well enough: Divinion.

"The Ryokaiten only create a conduit between dragon and knight," Rondel explained. "The wills of both parties determine the nature of that bond. Draw your sword, and I'll show you what I mean."

Iren pulled out the Muryozaki, and Rondel pointed to the three concentric rings of Maantec writing that emanated from the dragon's heart on the blade's hilt. "I told you before that the kanji enchantment allows for a connection between you and Divinion, but there's a lot more to it. Actually, only the innermost ring allows a knight to draw on the dragon's power. The second ring permits the dragon to test would-be knights. Most important by far, though, is the outermost ring."

"What does it mean?" Iren asked, rubbing his thumb over the strange characters.

"That circle keeps the dragon's will in check. It prevents the dragon's spirit from leaving its gem except when the knight calls upon its magic."

"Why is that so important?"

"Use your head! Back in Veliaf, I explained how using the dragon's magic is a contest of wills between the two of you. The more magic you draw, the more of the dragon's will enters your body. If you only use a little magic, the dragon's will can't affect you. But if you draw too much, the dragon can enter your mind. In the extreme case, it overwhelms you and transforms you into a dragon, as I previously explained. Do you understand? The third kanji circle is the reason why you could communicate with Divinion after you healed Dirio, but normally you can neither see nor hear him. Without that ring, Divinion's will could enter you regardless of any spells used."

Iren shrugged. "That doesn't sound like a bad thing. I mean, I'd probably understand a lot more about being a Dragon Knight if I could talk to Divinion all the time."

Rondel threw her arms in the air. "Fool, letting your dragon inside your mind is the last thing you should ever want! Once there, he can manipulate you, using your insecurities to gradually take over your mind. Over an extended period, your personality would change until you literally became the dragon."

"Why would the dragons do something like that?"

"For the most part, the dragons despise mortals. In their eyes, not only did we eternally imprison them in gems, but then by making the Ryokaiten, we tried to tame them. When a dragon wrests control from its knight, it takes advantage of the situation to get revenge on the mortals who dared to contain them. They transform the knight's body to match their own dragon form, and then they rampage and slay all in their path."

Iren thought back on his experience with Divinion. Granted, he'd only met the dragon once, after healing Dirio. Still, Iren didn't consider Divinion evil. At the very least, he didn't seem like someone who would commit genocide. Confused, Iren asked, "Rondel, does any of this really apply to me? Divinion's the Holy Dragon, after all. Even if I lost control and set him loose, surely he would do nothing but good for Raa."

The old woman replied without hesitation, "Are you willing to take that chance?"

Rondel let her question hang. When Iren didn't answer, she turned away and resumed walking. Iren followed her silently for over an hour before Rondel called them to a halt. "This looks like a good spot," she said. "We can train here a while before continuing westward."

Iren glanced around, unimpressed. This patch of woods didn't seem any different from the others they'd walked through. "What kind of training?" he asked. "What do I have to do?"

Rondel gave him a mischievous grin that made him gulp. "Simple," she said, "hit me."

CHAPTER TWENTY-THREE
Loyalty's Reward

Balear walked through the world yet felt as though he had departed reality. He'd left Captain, no, King Angustion's temporary lodgings and made his way to Haldessa Castle, wandering its vacant halls like a ghost. The cold, charred stone bore testament to the battles fought here, the opulence ruined, and the voices silenced. Each step rang, echoing hollowly through the ruin.

Ever since he'd caught up to Iren outside Ziorsecth, everything Balear had thought he'd known had upended itself. He'd found Iren's healing abilities bizarre, but that white light from his palm had been more than Balear could handle. Balear wanted just to dismiss it as devil magic, but Iren's words kept coming back to him: "All that matters to me now is protecting the life of someone precious!"

Balear kicked a piece of rubble. Iren's changes were unsettling enough, yet they paled in comparison to what had happened to Haldessa and, more disturbingly, King Angustion. As Balear meandered through Haldessa's vacant halls, dark premonitions gathered around him. If enemies could bring down this great castle, then truly nothing on Raa was secure.

King Angustion, however, hardly looked affected by the tragedy. He was more interested in trinkets like Rondel's dagger. Balear held the traitor's tiny weapon in his hand, doubt gnawing at him. What kind of leader would the new king be? The mere fact that Balear asked himself that question mortified him. He'd always believed in his superior officer. A truly gifted man, the king saw events ten steps in advance and reacted accordingly. Moreover, he never lost his temper. Even when his subordinates failed, he forgave them and motivated them to try harder next time.

Balear wondered what could have caused such a dramatic change in King Angustion's behavior. He'd never seen the man react as violently as he had that morning. Doubtlessly, devil magic had something to do with it. From the second Balear had laid eyes on the king's new sword, glowing red like some demon's blade, he'd been convinced. That weapon was evil.

Still, the king had confronted countless challenges in his life. The crown, the sword, and the magic had all only recently come to him. With time he would adapt. Until then, Balear would simply have to accept the king's temperament and support him faithfully.

Balear spent most of the afternoon wandering the castle, absorbed in old memories and fighting back tears. By dinnertime, his whole body ached both physically and emotionally, and all he really wanted was a hot meal and a long, long rest.

He received neither. The castle's kitchens were just as obliterated as the rest of the place. In one of the pantries he came across some not completely charred bread, salted pork, and ale so old he determined no one should ever drink it. He was so famished he consumed it anyway.

As for sleep, he'd nearly returned to Ceere to find a room for the night when a young man ran up, a servant in Amroth's new residence by the look of him. The man bowed deeply to Balear, saying, "King Angustion sent me to find you. He commands all Castle Guard members to meet with him immediately."

The order unsettled Balear. After the display that morning, he had no desire to see the king just now. Then again, that outburst was probably all the more reason not to keep him waiting.

The servant led the way back to the house and ushered Balear into one of King Angustion's chambers. With the sun fully set, the room had a morbid feel to it, lit only with candles on tall, narrow sconces. Balear gulped, not just at the setting but at the small number of those gathered. Including himself, not even a dozen Castle Guard members stood before the king.

The moment Balear arrived, King Angustion began, his tone grave, "Look around, all of you. This is all that remains of the Castle Guard. This is all that remains of Lodia's strength. Only you few, who were not at the castle when the Quodivar attacked, escaped with your lives."

Balear glanced at the other men assembled, realizing that they all came from the same company, a group regularly detached to Ceere to monitor the docks. He wondered what each of those men felt at this moment, to have survived when so many others had fallen. He knew how he felt about it. If not for his loyalty to Lodia, he would have killed himself the moment he'd heard.

"Haldessa's fall taught me a critical lesson." The king met the eyes of everyone in the room, his words boring into them with cold intensity. "Lodia is weak. It has been weak for centuries. We pretended the Castle Guard was an army, but they never amounted to anything more than a minor militia barely able to defend itself. To be sure, we defeated the Quodivar and Yokai, but it cost us nearly all our strength. Our neighbors will not sit idly with us in such dire straits. They will attack unless we rebuild quickly!"

Balear frowned, not sure how to take King Angustion's speech. He agreed that rebuilding the Castle Guard and Haldessa was a good idea, but he didn't follow the king's logic about the neighboring countries. Lodia had solid relations with all of them aside from the Kodamas, and they never left their forest anyway. Even in Lodia's weakened state, it was hard to see any of the surrounding nations as dangers.

"But we must do more than rebuild," King Angustion continued. "We must make ourselves stronger than ever before. Therefore, these are my orders. Travel throughout Lodia and spread my edict that all young, able-bodied men are hereby immediately drafted into Lodian military service. They shall come to Haldessa, where I will personally train them. We will have a grand army of Lodia! No one will stand against us, because our numbers and skill will make any potential adversary quiver in fear!"

Glancing around, Balear could see the other Castle Guard members looked as uneasy about the king's decision as he was. None of the history books recalled a time when Lodia possessed such an army, nor had any king instituted a draft in the country's written history.

"My liege," the head of the Ceere detachment spoke up, his voice trembling, "what is the purpose of this army? Do you intend to attack another nation?"

King Angustion gave the man a look of such withering contempt that Balear flinched, remembering the fireball from earlier that day. "Its purpose does not matter. I am the king, and you shall obey or be found guilty of treason! You do not understand the peril surrounding us. Thanks to Balear's failure," he turned his harsh gaze to the sergeant, "both Rondel Thara and Iren Saitosan remain at large. These traitors seek to poison our neighbors against us."

Though he looked like he might wet himself, the Ceere company leader dared to open his mouth once more, "Great king, do you really believe these criminals pose such a danger? After all, they are just two people and—"

He never got to finish his sentence, because in that moment, King Angustion flicked his hand at the man. A jet of flame shot forth, igniting the soldier's clothes. The poor man screamed and fell to the floor, writhing as he tried to douse the flames. No matter how he rolled, however, they would not abate. The fires burned until his flesh caught as well. Balear turned away, unable to watch as the soldier's cries gradually faded. When he dared look again, he immediately wished he hadn't. Where the man had stood less than a minute ago, only ash remained. The other Castle Guard members stared in horror at their king. Balear felt the urge to vomit on the spot, the spoiled ale in his stomach not helping matters.

"Let those who would resist the draft know that this is the penalty of disobedience. I will not suffer any insubordination." King Angustion let his words hover in the air alongside the acrid smell of burnt flesh. He then took a seat on his high-backed chair and gave a dismissive wave of his hand. The meeting was over.

The remaining soldiers tripped over themselves getting to the door, all but one. Balear hung back, some strange force holding him in place. He longed to question his new king, to demand why the man he loved and admired would do such a vile thing, yet he dared not. To question the king was, as his liege had made quite plain, equivalent to treason and punishable by death. Besides, although the king might use brutal tactics, Balear reminded himself that Azuluu's luxuriant ways hadn't made Lodia secure. On the contrary, they had led to its near destruction. Perhaps this new approach, violent though it may be, was the right way to protect Lodia.

He'd just made up his mind to leave when King Angustion barked, "Wait, Balear."

Balear knelt before the king, his head bowed and eyes downcast. "How may I serve?"

"You will not leave with the other Castle Guard members. I want you to remain in Ceere with me." Balear dared a glance up, and for a moment he saw a shred of his former commander, a reassuring smile on his battle-weary countenance. "You are, without a doubt, the most skilled and devoted soldier I have. I need valuable men like you for the battles to come. When Rondel and Iren attack us, we must be prepared."

Balear couldn't say for sure about Rondel, but he had his doubts about Iren. He still couldn't get Iren's last words to him out of his head. All the same, he had no intention of voicing those concerns. He enjoyed breathing too much. Instead, he said, "You honor me, King Angustion. I look forward to protecting Lodia alongside you."

The king nodded, apparently pleased. "When the new recruits arrive, they'll be green and vulnerable. They won't last five minutes against Kodamas or Tengu, or even the hardened seafaring humans of Tacumsah. They can become an invincible force, but to do so, they will need extensive training. Such an undertaking is too much even for me. I need a second-in-command. This person must possess absolute loyalty. He must inspire the troops and carry out my orders unquestioningly to lead us to victory. Balear, I would like that person to be you. As a reward for your loyalty, I hereby name you General Balear Platarch, head of the First Army of Lodia."

The new general prostrated himself, murmuring his humble acceptance. When it became clear the king had nothing more to say, Balear begged permission to leave. He received only a curt nod in reply, but he considered that more than enough. He rose and departed as quickly as he dared.

As he trudged through Ceere's streets in search of the nearest inn, Balear turned the conversation over in his head. General of the First Army of Lodia? He couldn't decide whether he felt honored or disgusted.

CHAPTER TWENTY-FOUR
Kindred Spirits

Iren howled as he hit the ground hard. Ten feet away, Rondel stood, arms crossed.

"We won't stop this until you land a blow!" she roared. "Now hurry up and attack!"

Cursing, Iren struggled to his feet, massaging the new burn on his right arm. "Hit me," Rondel had said. Since she'd said those two words yesterday afternoon, he'd lost count of how many injuries he'd sustained. This one would heal just as all the others had, thanks to the Muryozaki in his left hand, but that didn't make it hurt any less.

It also didn't help that he was starving. The last time he'd eaten was the plate of food his miniature Kodaman jailor had brought him.

Finally, to make the situation just that much more intolerable, Rondel hadn't budged an inch since they'd started. She simply stood there, as immovable as any of Ziorsecth's trees. Anytime Iren got close to her, she sent out a jolt of electricity from the end of her right index finger. It wasn't enough to kill, but each one knocked Iren flat and left him writhing for a few seconds.

Gritting his teeth, Iren looked around for anything that could give him an advantage, but he'd long since tried everything he could think of. He'd attempted feinting, weaving, even climbing one of the nearby tree trunks and trying to surprise Rondel from above. Every time, the decrepit buzzard used the same counter, and every time, it worked.

Next, Iren attempted to sneak up on her from behind. Just as he raised his arm to strike, the finger appeared from over Rondel's shoulder. The blue bolt landed with perfect accuracy.

"Get up, slacker!" Rondel taunted. "This is no time for a nap!"

Iren tasted blood; he'd bitten his lip on his way down. "I'm really questioning your teaching style."

"Do something about it then."

Gritting his teeth, Iren muttered, "Fine." Short-range attacks weren't working. To hit Rondel, he needed a long-distance strike. Since he didn't have a bow, that left him one option: magic. He focused, trying to remember how he'd felt when he'd used it previously. Against Zuberi and Balear, the magic had come instinctively. Both times, he'd done it without the Muryozaki. Now though, just like in the cage in Yuushingaral, he couldn't feel it at all.

His frustration deepened. Rondel wielded her magic easily enough. Why on Raa couldn't he do the same? Incensed, he stomped his foot against the ground.

A glow, ever so tiny, appeared in his right hand. He stopped, wondering if it could really be that simple. Now that he thought about it, it made sense. Fighting Zuberi, he'd felt furious at Rondel's apparent death. Against Balear, he'd gotten angry over the delay in getting Minawë to Ziorsecth.

He focused again, this time concentrating on all of Rondel's insults. He thought about his childhood, and the way people treated him like a demon. Finally, he let Amroth's face appear in his mind's eye, the arrogant face that lied and said it cared before bathing Haldessa in flame.

The white beam erupted with a deafening bang, the tip forming the head of a dragon as it engulfed the spot where Rondel stood. Iren panicked, certain that he had not only landed a hit but slain the old woman as well. A second later, however, a slight breeze wafted behind him, and a single finger pressed into the back of his neck.

The jolt ripped through his body, and he crumpled to the ground. Rondel walked into his field of vision and sat cross-legged in front of him, annoyance on her wrinkled face. "You used that spell to kill Zuberi." It was not a question. "It would probably kill me, too, if you could actually hit me with it."

Iren tried to reply, but he couldn't make his mouth move. In fact, none of his muscles would respond, no matter how much he struggled.

"Don't bother," Rondel said, like she could read Iren's mind. "I gave a sharp burst of lightning magic directly to your spine. It overloaded your nervous system. You can breathe, and your heart will keep beating. Any voluntary motion, however, is impossible for at least the next fifteen minutes. All the better, since I want you to shut up and listen."

If Iren could have changed his expression to glare at the sadistic bat, he would have.

"You've used magic before, but that attack proves you don't know anything about it," Rondel criticized. "That beam had great power, but it was also slow, predictable, and used an incredible amount of energy. You only have so much environmental magic at any given moment, and Divinion's power is also limited for reasons we previously discussed. You have to use spells strategically. What would have happened if we'd been fighting for real just now? You'd have exhausted your energy in that one blow, leaving you powerless. By contrast, consider me. I've used magic to hit you constantly for the last day, yet I could still deliver a blow that, in an actual battle, would have killed you. I'd have plenty of time to finish you while you lay there helpless."

Iren half-listened to Rondel's words, more focused on the mistake the old hag had just made. She considered her technique so perfect that she hadn't bothered disarming him. The Muryozaki still sat in Iren's grip, and Divinion's magic was already healing the damage from Rondel's blow.

He had plenty of rage to channel into the magic this time. As it built up, unable to release thanks to his paralysis, he began to sense its flow. It pulsed through his body like blood. Concentrating on it, he found he could direct it wherever he wanted it to go. That gave him an idea. The large beam moved slowly, but if he gave the magic a smaller outlet, maybe he could increase its speed. Instead of his whole fist, he would channel the magic into a single finger on his right hand.

Without warning, he fired. Instead of a broad beam, however, the attack was thin and focused. Its smaller size reduced its power, but when it struck Rondel in the gut, it still launched her backward twenty feet. Iren leapt up, fully healed, and raced toward Rondel with a smile on his face. "How about that?" he cried.

The old woman dusted herself off. "Not bad," she replied, nodding. "Now we move on."

"Move on to what?"

Rondel closed her eyes. "To this." She opened them again, and Iren blanched at the sparks flashing in them.

"I went easy on you before," she said. "This time, the exercise is the same, but I won't hold back. You'll face Lightning Sight and the same speed I used to kill those Quodivar in Veliaf."

Iren shuddered. He could already feel the lightning bolts striking him. Rondel didn't attack, however. Instead she abruptly vanished. A second later, she reappeared over fifty yards away, waving animatedly.

Iren's jaw dropped in dismay. Even running flat out through the underbrush, it would take him over ten seconds to cover the distance Rondel had covered in just one. By the time he reached her, Rondel could easily run off in some other direction.

"Long range then," he muttered. He channeled magic into his right index finger. His new tight beam was exactly what he needed. It traveled faster than his eye could track. Surely at this range, even Rondel couldn't avoid it. He raised his finger and pointed it at the crone.

The shot never fired. Just before Iren released the magic, Rondel disappeared again. A second later, she reappeared behind him, kicking him in the back and sending him sprawling. His concentration lost, the energy he had gathered dissipated back into his body.

"Lightning Sight let me read your lips," Rondel said with a mix of amusement and confusion. "Why do you do that?"

Iren rolled onto his back, coughing in the dirt. "Do what?"

"Talk to yourself. You used to do it at Haldessa too."

Iren's brow furrowed. He'd never noticed before. He thought for a moment, and then he said, "Nobody in the castle would talk to me. I guess I just needed some conversation." He paused. "Hang on. How do you know I talked to myself at Haldessa?"

Rondel deactivated Lightning Sight and sat on the ground beside him. "Iren, I'm sorry."

"For what?"

"I've known of your Maantec heritage from the day Amroth brought you to the castle. I could have taken care of you, raised you, protected you. I did none of those things. Instead, I let my hatred of you cloud my judgment."

Iren shoved himself to his feet. "What do you mean 'your hatred of me?' What did I ever do to you?"

Narrowing her eyes, Rondel murmured, "You were born."

Iren threw an arm out to his side and roared, "What is this? Everyone in Haldessa hated me because I was a Left. How can you, a fellow Maantec and Dragon Knight, feel the same way? I didn't choose this life! I didn't ask to be a Maantec!"

"Do you want to know the truth, Iren? I hate Maantecs. I hate every single one of them. That's why I betrayed them a thousand years ago."

Iren's mind flashed back to Minawë in Akaku, telling him how Rondel was the most famous traitor in Raa's history.

Rondel continued, "During the Kodama-Maantec War, both sides fought to a standstill. The Maantecs couldn't penetrate Ziorsecth, and the Kodamas couldn't make any progress in Serona. The stalemate lasted years. Thousands died on both sides. Finally, I couldn't take it anymore. I'd had enough of taking orders and killing because someone else said so. I decided to start a new life, one independent of everyone else. I dedicated that life solely to Okthora's Law: evil must be annihilated."

The crone's wrinkled face became cold and determined. "I started with the Maantecs, a race of fools willing to sacrifice Raa for the sake of conquest. I offered the Kodaman king, Otunë, my support. With my knowledge of Maantec defenses and my power as a Dragon Knight added to his army, we crushed all resistance. We stormed through Serona, wiping out Maantecs until we reached the capital. It should have ended there, but Iren Saito cast his curse and slew the Kodaman battalions."

She raised her open palms before her face, and they shook horribly. "For a thousand years after that terrible day, I avoided my own species, perfectly content to shun and be shunned in return. That is, until that interfering Amroth had to go and bring you and the Muryozaki into my life."

"You could have killed him," Iren pointed out, "or me, for that matter."

Rondel shook her head. "Evil must be annihilated. You were just an innocent infant. I couldn't kill you. And while I didn't trust Amroth, I had no proof against him. Truthfully, what I really wanted to do the moment I laid eyes on you was to flee Haldessa and never return."

"Why didn't you?"

She laughed a harsh, self-deprecating bark. "You think I didn't try? As soon as Amroth left my home, I ran. Then the dreams started. The farther I got from Haldessa, the more I had them. They were all the same. I saw you in some pain or danger. In a few you died. They became so bad I couldn't sleep. Only in Haldessa could I get any rest. Even there, you were always on my mind. The only way to relieve the dreams completely was to see you. I've watched you from the shadows nearly all your life. It made me hate you all the more, because you kept dragging me back to a past I desperately wanted to forget. I dared not let you notice me. If you did, I feared you would seek me out yourself. Then I would never be rid of you."

Iren stared at the old woman, dumbfounded. He'd never caught her observing him, yet somehow, he knew she spoke the truth. Numerous times, he'd sensed that he wasn't as alone as he appeared. Most recently, he recalled the shadows moving oddly in the baths before Amroth's feast. Now he understood. Rondel had been watching him, even there.

"What changed your mind?" he asked. "You revealed yourself to me at the stables."

"Not by choice." Rondel scowled. "Amroth forced my hand. I believed that he wanted to use you, that he sought your death. The dreams were bad enough when only the castle wall separated us. If you died, I feared I wouldn't survive them. I hated you, yet my life was bound to yours. So while my whole being seethed at the thought, I had no choice but to make myself known to you."

Iren thought back on those early days with Rondel. She'd avoided looking him in the eye, and she'd always had a bottle of some vile alcohol in her hand. A thought occurred to him. "That's why you drank so heavily. It let you overcome your aversion to me."

Rondel stared at the ground. "Yes. Sober, I couldn't bring myself to face you, let alone talk to you. And I had to talk to you. I had to train and protect you so that you stayed alive, not for your sake, understand, but for mine."

Iren looked at the old Dragon Knight, his head a jumble of emotions. Part of him felt pleased. What Rondel said meant that even though it was in a perverse, self-serving way, she cared about him. Still, a greater part of him felt furious, and that portion ultimately won. With a growl he shouted at her, "I didn't ask for this! Why me? Thousands of Maantecs died because of you! You went a thousand years without caring for a single one, and then suddenly, you just became obsessed with me? What makes me so special?"

She tried to meet his gaze but couldn't. Wet spots formed under her eyes. "You and I are more alike than you realize. Do you know why I want the Liryometa back so badly?"

Iren folded his arms. What did that have to do with anything? He said, "You miss Okthora's lightning magic, the way I missed Division's healing power."

Rondel shook her head and replied, "Selfish and arrogant, just like him. No, slacker, Okthora has nothing to do with it. I'd want that weapon back regardless, not for what it is, but for who it belonged to." She paused and took a deep breath, letting it out slowly before saying, "It was my father's. He used it to protect my family the day they were butchered right in front of me."

The young Maantec's anger vanished at once, replaced by horror at Rondel's revelation. "What happened to them?"

"I lived in Serona at the time, only five years old. My parents farmed rice, a poor life, but we managed. One day, as I played in the fields with my brother, we heard our mother calling for us. My brother went ahead, but I slipped and fell. I cried, hoping he'd come back and carry me. He didn't. Finally, I picked myself up and ran home. When I got there, the house was burning, and a dozen men surrounded my family. My father defended them with his only weapon. He managed to slay three of the attackers, but in the end he died, along with Mother and my brother. I screamed, but that only made the thugs aware of my presence."

She halted in her story, choked up. At last she pressed on, "I knew they would kill me. I panicked and ran to my fallen father, begging for him to help me. In desperation, I grabbed his dagger and raised it, but the thugs just laughed at my vain attempt. They struck as one. In that moment, I felt a surge of energy flow through me, like a thunderstorm trapped inside my body was trying to rip itself loose. I still don't know exactly what happened, because I passed out. When I woke up, though, all the thugs lay dead around me, scorched."

Iren knew enough about magic to understand. "You used lightning magic without intending to."

Rondel nodded. "Yes, so I believe, especially because shortly thereafter, who should arrive at the burned wreckage of my home but the Storm Dragon Knight herself? She took me in, raised me, and gave me a new name."

"A new name?"

"She said that my old name no longer mattered, because that part of me had gone away forever. She asked me what I wanted to be called."

Rondel smiled sadly, her eyes welling with tears. "Do you know what the Liryometa is? It's a dagger, sure, but that term can apply to any number of similar weapons. Its round pommel, hilt, and crossguard, however, give it a second, more specific name. It's called a rondel."

Iren's eyes went wide. "You named yourself after your father's weapon?"

"He protected my family with it, and I swore I'd use it the same way. In time, I even transferred the Storm Amethyst to it, turning it into the Liryometa. I have nothing else of my family."

She sighed and stretched. "When Amroth told me how he found you, I knew you had suffered the same tragedy I went through, and I knew all too keenly the pain you would feel when you grew old enough to know what you had lost. That was why I couldn't abandon you, even though I hated you. You see, as much as I hated you, I loved you even more."

For what seemed an eternity afterward, the pair stood silently, the only sound the soft rustle of wind through the late spring leaves.

CHAPTER TWENTY-FIVE
The First Army of Lodia

General Balear Platarch of the First Army of Lodia sat alone atop the Tower of Divinion on a hard bed that a few months ago would have disgusted him to touch. Now Iren Saitosan's abandoned chamber was Balear's only spot of respite in a world he no longer recognized. Miraculously, it had survived the flames that devoured Haldessa unscathed. It comforted Balear that a tiny shred of the castle he remembered endured.

Even here, though, he couldn't escape the shouting of the drill sergeants, the snapping of whips, and the incessant crackling of fires. Something was always burning these days. The king delighted in igniting whatever happened to annoy him at any given moment.

With a great effort, Balear heaved himself off the bed and walked to the room's window. Looking south, he saw a landscape transformed by fire, sweat, and blood. King Angustion had conscripted over half the town of Ceere, including some women and children, to repair the castle. Four months had passed since Balear's promotion to general, and the citizens had admittedly made impressive progress. They'd completed most of the restoration, more out of fear than loyalty, but it didn't come close to resembling its former splendor. It had no beauty in it anymore. It simply existed, a disgusting edifice of cold stone atop an empty bluff.

Beyond the castle, the city of Haldessa was even worse. The king showed no interest whatsoever in its reconstruction. A few Ceere residents had started a collection to rebuild, but King Angustion had forced them to stop upon pain of death. Any spare money, he'd explained, needed to go to the country's new army. They required armor, weapons, places to sleep, and food, an absolutely ridiculous amount of food. The wreckage of Haldessa had thus become a tent city where the conscripts slept, four on top of each other. More than one outbreak of disease had already swept through the camp and wiped out nearly five hundred soldiers before it could be contained.

Despite the setbacks, the king drove them ever harder. Like the residents of Ceere, fear made them obey. Everyone had seen the corpses. The king burned alive anyone who questioned him and mounted their charred remains on pikes. Balear could see them from here. They numbered over one hundred, and at least one a day got added to the tally.

It made him want to vomit.

He knew he should be out there now. He should be training the men, convincing them of the king's masterful strategic vision for Lodia, but he couldn't. He couldn't fake it anymore. Every time he walked among them, he saw their hollow eyes, their frightened stares, and their barely veiled frustration and anxiety. King Angustion had assembled the largest fighting force in Lodia's history, over five thousand, yet Balear had serious doubts about their capabilities. These were not soldiers. They were farmers, traders, and even boys not yet fully grown to manhood. They hadn't chosen this life.

As Balear gazed out the window, he realized, for the first time, he hadn't chosen it either. The man he'd admired since childhood no longer existed. Each time he talked to King Angustion, his liege was increasingly agitated. The king muttered to himself almost constantly and spoke to the flames that followed him. Balear remembered labeling Iren's abilities "devil magic," but his former idol's newfound skills deserved that title far more.

Despite that magic, however, the king bordered on paranoid. Approaching him from behind usually proved fatal, as he had a tendency to whip around and launch a scorching wave of heat before he'd even seen what he had attacked. Balear gingerly stroked his singed left arm, a memento of the first and only time he'd made the mistake of surprising the king.

A knock at the door startled him. Turning around, he started to say, "Come in," but the door had already opened. King Angustion stood before him, wreathed in flame.

Balear gulped. As general, he was supposed to be among the men. If the king had decided that his underling was disobeying orders, Balear knew he wouldn't leave this room alive.

"How may I serve?" Balear asked meekly, his head bowed, not daring to look his king in the eye.

"Ready the men to move out," the king barked. "We head west. I want us on the march by nightfall."

Balear started. He knew he risked death, but he couldn't stop himself from saying, "My liege, with all respect, it is already three hours past midday. Mobilizing the army will take days. The logistics involved in such an operation—"

Fwoosh. A searing jet of heat lanced past his left cheek, scorching a round hole one foot in diameter through the wall behind him. "Logistics do not concern me, General. Get them moving; I don't care how."

"Of course, King Angustion." Balear bowed low, his body trembling. He had no idea how he would get five thousand men on the road before sunset. He doubted all of them would even know they were leaving by then. "My liege, if I may, where shall I tell the men we are headed, and on what mission? Has a city come under attack?"

"No," the king replied gruffly, "but they could fall at any moment. Ziorsecth threatens our western border. While our army trains here, we've left Orcsthia and Caardit exposed. The Kodamas could conquer them easily. For Lodia's safety, we will crush the Kodamas utterly."

Balear couldn't believe what he was hearing. Even schoolchildren knew the Kodamas never left their forest. "Please, sire, why the Kodamas? They hide within their forest and have had no dealings with the outside world in—"

Fwoosh. A second jet shot past his right cheek, burning a second hole in the wall identical to the first.

Balear prostrated himself. "Of course, King Angustion. I live only to serve."

"Of course you do," the king said. He spun on his heel and strode from the room, leaving Balear lying face down on the cold stone. When at last the young general worked up the nerve to stand, he clutched his head with his hands in despair. Numbly, he walked to the window, horrified by his former role model's decision. Balear wondered how many Lodians would die in this battle. How could he lead them to their deaths, when he himself did not agree with this course of action? Yet if he disobeyed, King Angustion would surely kill him and then march on Ziorsecth anyway.

Abandoning hope, he started to leave Iren's room. As he did, the painting of the serpentine white dragon caught his attention. He'd never paid it any mind before, but now he felt drawn to it. He approached it uncertainly, his hand outstretched. Despite the dragon's roaring expression, its blue eyes did not appear angry. Quite the contrary, they were filled with understanding. They looked at Balear, and he had the oddest sensation that they not only looked at him, but through him. Those eyes held him spellbound for a moment, and then, as though a thick curtain fell away from his mind, he knew what he needed to do.

Racing down the tower steps, he ran at full speed to the stables. "Where's my charger?" he cried to the stable boy. The child gasped, no doubt shocked by his general's wild expression. Nevertheless, he pointed Balear in the right direction.

Balear stroked the horse's neck a moment before hoisting a saddle onto him and mounting. With a furious crack of the reins, the warhorse shot from the stable. The general rode through the camp at full gallop, and though many stared at him with wonder, no one dared try to stop or question him. When he reached the encampment's edge, he turned his horse west and bore forward, heedless of the sun in his eyes. He knew, with a certainty he couldn't explain, that only one person could end King Angustion's…no, Amroth's madness.

Iren Saitosan.

CHAPTER TWENTY-SIX
What's Most Important?

Iren made up his mind: leaves and dirt tasted really, really bad.

He'd long since lost track of the weeks. Even with nothing else to focus on, Ziorsecth's thick canopy made telling time difficult. And Iren had plenty else to focus on, what with all the bruises, scrapes, and occasional broken bones he received thanks to Rondel's harsh training methods. Her earlier softness hadn't lasted long. If anything, admitting that she cared about him had only bolstered her resolve to toughen him. Without the Muryozaki, he probably would have keeled over long before now.

Granted, he'd improved his control of Divinion's magic. Beyond just firing it in a beam, he could channel the light's energy into his muscles, giving them speed and stamina far beyond normal. When Rondel dodged and ran away, although Iren still couldn't keep up with her, she no longer completely left him behind either.

Heaving himself onto his hands and knees, he coughed on a mouthful of detritus from his most recent landing. Despite his progress, he'd come no closer to striking Rondel a second time. Even unarmed and without Okthora, she evaded every beam, every sword stroke, every single cursed thing he tried to do.

Picking maple leaves out of his sweat-soaked hair, he surveyed his tattered clothes with disdain. Divinion might heal wounds easily enough, but the dragon couldn't sew.

It didn't help that they'd brought no supplies with them, instead relying on the forest. Rondel considered it more training. Iren was supposed to find all the food and water they needed. Water posed no problems; they constantly came across small springs and streams while traveling. Food had given him trouble initially. He couldn't identify any of the plants that were safe to eat, and all the animals scattered at the noise of the battling Maantecs. Lately, though, it had gotten easier. He'd refined his control of his ranged magical attacks to the point where he could reliably strike even small animals from far away.

Iren collapsed backward. "This is impossible!" he shouted. "How do you expect me to defeat you? You've done this a thousand years longer than I have."

"Which is why we call it 'training,'" Rondel said. "How else will you get the experience to match me?"

"I'll never match you. Look, this is clearly wasting both our times. Let's go back to Yuushingaral. We'll figure out another way to stop Amroth."

"Go back?" she roared. "No, we will stay. We will stay until I say you are strong enough. Of course that may take a while, given how pathetic you currently are."

Iren pouted. "You make it sound like I'm not trying."

"Because you aren't! Do you honestly expect to defeat me with the amount of effort you're putting forth?"

"I'm working as hard as I can!"

Rondel hauled Iren to his feet, then slapped him hard, knocking him back to the dirt. A jolt of electricity went along with the strike. The crone asked, "Painful, slacker?"

Iren gritted his teeth and glared at the sadistic bat.

"You've always taken the easy road!" Rondel yelled. "No one respected you in Haldessa, but instead of trying to earn it by acting decently, you turned into a hooligan just to get attention. All your ridiculous outfits, and your even more ridiculous hair," she pointed at his shoulder-length tan locks, "just prove my point. You wasted your potential every minute you lived in that castle. You could have become the finest soldier in the Castle Guard, but did you even try to train with them? No, when they said you couldn't participate, you retreated to your tower. You learned the basics by watching them, but you never had a real teacher who would correct you. Now, with each move, your flaws are pitifully obvious. You have a weak stance, and you give away every attack you make."

"I survived those fights against the Quodivar and Yokai," Iren countered, his temper and voice rising as he regained his feet. "I even killed

Zuberi."

Rondel's harsh tone did not abate. "You would have died your first night out of the castle without the Muryozaki to heal you, and only Dirio's last-second toss of his miner's pick spared you from the Yokai. Zuberi would have killed you if I hadn't intervened. Even with my help, you still would have died, except your magic reacted instinctively. You've only survived this long thanks to outside help and incredible luck. Those things are useless! You didn't earn them, and you can't depend on them against Amroth. If you want to defeat him, then stop slacking off and put forth some real effort!"

In a flash, white light engulfed Iren. He wouldn't listen to this stupid old hag badger him any longer! The light spiraled outward, swirling around him. Leaves and twigs snapped and split, tossed about as though a hurricane were ripping through the forest. His eyes glowed white, and the Muryozaki gave off the same gleam. "Shut your mouth, Rondel!" he cried. "You don't know anything about me!"

The old woman stood firm, even as the air whipped around her and threatened to send her airborne. Ignoring Iren's outburst, she spat, "You can't win if you constantly hold yourself back and give up when you find a problem difficult!"

The light around Iren condensed so that his entire body shone. The trees stopped moving. Iren pointed the Muryozaki's tip straight at Rondel.

The crone cocked an eyebrow and flashed her signature sarcastic grin. She probably threw him some snarky comment, but Iren couldn't hear anymore. The light had all but consumed him. It operated of its own accord, independent of his will. Focusing on the Muryozaki's tip, it grew brighter until all else in the area looked like blackest midnight and it shone like the lighthouse at Ceere.

Then it fired.

The beam measured over thirty feet across, obliterating all in its path as it rocketed through the forest. The katana itself must have absorbed the recoil; otherwise, the spell's force would have thrown Iren off his feet. For nearly ten seconds the energy erupted from the Muryozaki, until Rondel crashed into Iren at full speed, knocking the sword from his hands. As the connection between Iren and Divinion broke, the beam abruptly ceased.

The young Dragon Knight shook his head, dazed. He looked upon the aftermath of his attack, his whole body numb with horror. Everything in the beam's path had simply vanished. The magic must have annihilated the air itself, for as soon as the beam disappeared, a harsh sucking noise followed as the atmosphere rushed to fill the vacuum. The swath of destruction proceeded over five miles.

Rondel stoically beheld the devastation, her back to Iren. "See how much magic you still have?" she berated. "That proves you're training the way you've lived your whole life: halfway."

Iren wanted to argue, but he couldn't form words. The beam had drained him completely. He felt lightheaded, and then the edges of his vision blurred. He hit the ground.

Instantly his head felt better. He pushed himself to his knees, then halted, confused. Hard, flat stone had replaced the soil and leaves of the forest floor. He stood and looked around. It was nighttime, or at least dark enough to be. He gulped. He'd been here once before.

Barely a minute passed before the majestic form of Divinion appeared on the horizon. Iren waited timidly for the serpentine beast to approach.

The massive creature landed before him, but Iren could tell nothing of the dragon's mood. Divinion's body shook, light streaming from him as he transformed into an old man.

The Holy Dragon smiled as he approached Iren. "So, we meet again. I wondered when our next chat would happen."

Though the dragon didn't show any outward sign of disapproval, Iren nevertheless cast his eyes away from Divinion, hot with embarrassment. All he could think of was his violent loss of control, and he knew that Divinion had witnessed it. Worse, he'd used Divinion's own strength to cause the destruction to happen.

"Divinion," Iren began, struggling to find words, "why did you choose me? I couldn't even control my emotions just now, and I caused a tragedy because of it."

The old man put an arm around him. "Do you know what allows you to access your magic? Why you could use it at some times but not others?"

"Anger drives it," Iren replied. "When I get angry, it forces the magic to the surface."

Divinion sighed. "No, that isn't true. What about when you healed Dirio? Were you angry then?"

Iren's head snapped up. He met Divinion's gaze. "No, I felt terrible for him. I desperately wanted him to survive."

"You cared for him. That emotion brought forth magic. It happened with Minawë, too. I wasn't with you at the time, but I can see it in your memory. When you learned that Amroth had betrayed you, you fled the queen's home. In the process, you fell into the Yuushin Sea and would have drowned had Minawë not rescued you. Why could she pull you from the ocean, leaving Ziorsecth in the process, when Aletas could not?"

Iren shrugged. He hadn't thought about it before. Minawë had told him that when she'd first entered Lodia, she'd lost consciousness almost immediately. She shouldn't have been able to rescue him from the Yuushin, yet she had.

"The reason," Divinion answered for him, "is that Minawë no longer suffers from Iren Saito's curse. You cured her of it outside Ziorsecth. You could not have known, but you never would have gotten her back to the forest in time. She would have died before you knocked Balear unconscious. But in that moment when you decided to help her, when you told Balear all you cared about was protecting her, you cast a spell without realizing it. You broke the curse on her, saving her life. That's why your attack was so weak when you hit Balear. You had almost no magic left after curing Minawë."

Iren's whole body trembled. "Where, then, does the magic come from, if not from anger? Rondel controls hers so flawlessly!"

Divinion replied, "Something you must understand is that our magic fundamentally differs from Rondel's and Okthora's. Their abilities stem from a substance of the physical world: lightning. Your magic comes not from anything external, but from within yourself. Your untamed heart is its source. Whatever color your emotions take, so too will your magic. When you love, you heal. When you care, you protect. When you hate, you destroy."

Iren cried, "Then I must never use magic again! I can't control what I feel! Look what I did in Ziorsecth just now! What if I did that in Yuushingaral, or in a Lodian city?"

"No one can control their emotions completely," Divinion said, "nor should they. Your feelings, by their nature, are wild and beautiful. As long as you hold true to them, they and you will be worthy enough for me."

"Then...do you forgive me for what happened today?"

To Iren's astonishment, the old man chuckled. "As Rondel said, you lack experience. With time and teaching, you will better understand your emotions. You will learn how to express all of them in the right ways at the right times." He paused a moment, apparently distracted, and a sad smile appeared on his face. "Once again our time together draws to a close."

Divinion took a few steps back, and in a flourish transformed into a dragon. As he took flight, Iren shouted in alarm, "But how can I know which emotions are the right ones? How do I stop myself from causing another disaster?"

With a voice that shook the universe, Divinion replied as he faded away and all light vanished, "Commit to what's most important."

Confused by the dragon's words, Iren cried, "Wait, Divinion!" He scanned the void, searching in vain for any sign of the Holy Dragon. "What's most important?"

His only answer was silence.

CHAPTER TWENTY-SEVEN
Saito and Saitosan

Light returned to the world, and Iren lay on his back looking up at the dense Ziorsecth canopy. Somewhere nearby, a fire crackled. Heaving himself to a sitting position, he saw Rondel tending a campfire with a stick.

"I met Divinion again," he told her reluctantly.

Rondel stared into the tiny blaze. "I'm afraid I must apologize to you again, Iren. I meant to provoke you today. I needed you to understand the danger inherent in Divinion's power. I never expected that level of damage, though. Had I known that would happen, I would have stopped you sooner."

For a long time they both just sat, the snaps of the flames and the occasional call of a bird the only sounds. At last Rondel stood, dusted herself off, and said, "Well, now's as good a time as any, I guess. I intended to wait until later in your training, but given the events of today, you should see it. Come with me." She doused the fire and began walking west.

Iren hauled himself off the ground and followed her, wondering where she was dragging him off to now.

They walked for hours, never speaking. Initially, every patch of forest looked the same as the next, but eventually, Iren started noticing changes. The trees became shorter, thinner, and packed more closely together. Iren felt heat in front of him, like sitting next to a bonfire, though he could see no flame. The sky, which finally became visible, looked ominous and filled with black clouds. Iren had long anticipated exiting the forest and getting reacquainted with the open air, but now he had a strong urge to flee back into the woods.

When the plants peeled away, Iren stopped dead, his jaw slack at the scene before him. He and Rondel stood on the edge of a vast, almost perfectly flat plain. With nothing to block his line of sight, Iren could see for miles with ease, though it brought him no comfort to do so. He couldn't spot a single living thing: no animals, no trees, not a single blade of grass. It wasn't hard to understand why. Large fissures crisscrossed the plain in a twisted, seething lattice of destruction. White-hot flames spurted from these crevasses, shooting hundreds of feet into the air, baking everything around them. Iren felt like he had walked into a kiln, even though the nearest crevasse was nearly half a mile away.

Just standing on the plain's edge, Iren's mouth grew parched. The landscape offered no relief; not a drop of water flowed through it. Here and there, channels ran which might once have contained rivers, but they had long since dried up. Even the parts of the soil untouched by the fissures cracked from lack of moisture.

To worsen matters, the plain was no desert. Thick, moisture-laden clouds filled the sky, stretching over the expanse all the way to the horizon. Lightning arced from sky to ground and cloud to cloud dozens of times each second. The storm gushed with rain, the greatest downpour Iren had ever witnessed. Even so, the ground remained baked. The heat of the flames evaporated any precipitation long before it hit the ground. Combined with the fires, the storm bathed the field in an unearthly glow.

Iren fell to his knees before the terrible landscape. Juxtaposed with the natural splendor of Ziorsecth, he could hardly believe such polar opposites could stand one another's presence.

"Welcome to Serona, Iren," Rondel said. "Welcome to the home of the Maantecs."

Iren whipped his head to face her. He couldn't believe this was Serona, home of the greatest civilization in the history of Raa.

Rondel clutched her arms to her chest. "It didn't always look this way. For thousands of years, Serona was lush and green. The final battle of the Kodama-Maantec War turned it into what you see."

Iren struggled to find his voice, finally saying dubiously, "That happened a thousand years ago."

"The dragons don't think about time the way we do. When we cause disasters like this, the repercussions must linger. That way, future generations will understand the consequences of wielding weapons they cannot control." Rondel pointed at the nearest crevasse as its flame rent the air asunder. "See those fires? Underneath Serona sits a gigantic lake of lava. Prior to the Kodama-Maantec War, it provided us with hot springs and majestic geysers. On the day of the final battle, though, it became Serona's undoing. When the Kodamas invaded, the Fire Dragon Knight, a Maantec named Nadav, used his biological magic to call the fires from the depths. He died in the process. The very fires he summoned enveloped and consumed him."

Iren gave her an odd look. "Did you say Nadav?"

"Yes, what of it?"

He shook his head. "I don't know. I have the feeling I've heard that name before."

Rolling her eyes, Rondel replied, "You interrupted me just for that? Honestly, do you have any attention span whatsoever? Anyway, after Nadav died, neither the Kodamas nor the Maantecs could rescind the fires. Working with the Water Dragon Knight, a Kodama, I used nearly all my magic to create a massive storm, the clouds you see overhead. The Water Dragon Knight perished, and I became the withered crone before you. Despite our sacrifice, though, the fires surpassed us. Their heat simply energized the storm, ensuring that it would never abate. I tried to improve the situation, but in the end, I only made it worse."

Iren stared across the desolate landscape. All this destruction had happened because of Iren Saito and his war. Iren gulped. Although he didn't want to, he knew he needed to ask. "Rondel, why did you name me after Iren Saito, someone who brought so much pain into the world? Was it because you hated Maantecs? You wanted me to suffer, so you gave me his name as a punishment?"

Rondel's focus shifted out over Serona. Her mouth worked slowly, chewing on the words she planned to say. At length she answered, "Despite what you may think, I am not that vindictive. Amroth merely caught me by surprise when he revealed you. When I first saw you, I couldn't help but think of Saito. Even as an infant, you bore an uncanny resemblance to him. I wish now that I had named you differently, but I must admit, it fits you well. You still look like him, and the two of you have a lot in common, more than you realize."

"How can you compare me to him?" Iren protested. "Iren Saito was a monster!"

She shook her head, a nostalgic smile on her face. "In the end, yes, but when I first met him, I had never encountered a gentler person. After my parents died, other than the Storm Dragon Knight, no one cared about or even noticed me. Iren Saito did. He healed me from my sorrow. I don't think I ever laughed as much as when I spent time with him. The day he asked me to marry him was the happiest of my life."

Iren's jaw dropped. "Iren Saito was your husband?"

Rondel flushed. "When he and I wed, I thought of nothing but the bliss of our immortality together." Her expression soured. "How dreams fade."

"What happened?"

Serona's flames reflected in the old Maantec's emerald eyes. "He became the Holy Dragon Knight and Emperor of the Maantecs along with it. Over time, his status changed him. He became convinced of Maantec superiority. He said the other races needed our guidance to survive and that Raa could only have peace if Maantecs ruled it. I went along with him at first. He still captivated me, and when he spoke, I couldn't help but melt before him. Eventually, though, I could no longer support him. I know I made the right choice when I marched against him in the final battle, but that doesn't mean I don't have any regrets. To this day, when I think of him, I still see the young man who rescued me from despair and taught me how to love."

Rondel gazed at Iren with longing. "Remember how I told you I drank so that I could approach you? I did that not just because of your Maantec heritage, but because you reminded me of Saito. Though he died a thousand years ago, you and he share a lot in common. Iren Saito was selfish and arrogant, but he also had a kindness and nobility that few Maantecs possess. He had a strong desire to protect others, no matter the cost to himself." She laughed a little. "He also had a tendency to be headstrong and not to listen to his elders. Sound familiar?"

Iren gestured harshly at the burning plain. "Now I understand why you and Aletas wanted me brought here. By showing me the disaster Iren Saito created, you thought you would provide such a searing image that I wouldn't repeat his mistake. You believed that since I share so much in common with Saito, I would turn out just like him."

Rondel shrugged. "Aletas might think that, but I don't. At least, not anymore. Admittedly, that's why I didn't tell you everything about magic when we first met in Lodia. I feared teaching you more than absolutely necessary, in case you did wind up like him. However, I no longer have that fear."

Desperate hope filled Iren's heart. "Why not?"

"When we first encountered Minawë, in Akaku, you could have left her and pursued your revenge. Instead, you helped her. Iren Saito would not have made that choice. He may have started the Kodama-Maantec War with intentions of protecting others, but he became so obsessed with victory that he lost sight of that goal. When I reunited with you in Yuushingaral and saw Minawë still alive, I knew I could put my faith in you. Tell me; after all the alcohol you saw me drink in Lodia, how much have I had since we met in Aletas's tree?"

Iren thought back. "Aside from the glass you were drinking when we first reconnected, not a drop. You didn't bring any with you on this trip."

"Correct. I no longer need it. When you threw away your desire for revenge in order to help Minawë, I realized that while you and my husband are similar, you're also very different. Back when we were traveling in Lodia with Amroth and Balear, I couldn't bring myself to look at your face. Every time I tried, I saw Saito staring back at me. But now I don't have any difficulty looking you in the eye, because when I look at you now, I no longer see Iren Saito." She smiled genuinely. "I see Iren Saitosan."

Iren beamed at the compliment, but then a new confusion came to him. "Wait. If you didn't bring me here because you feared I would become another Iren Saito, why did we have to trudge all the way out here in the first place?"

Rondel folded her arms. "I say all these kind things to you, and that's how you respond? If you must know, I wanted to motivate you, slacker. See those fires out there? The Karyozaki created them. I brought you here not because of Iren Saito, but because of the Fire Dragon, Feng. That monster enjoys destruction, and he chooses his Dragon Knights well. Nadav believed in strength and nothing else. He believed that the strong deserved to live, and the weak deserved to die. A thousand years later, Amroth seems almost like Nadav reincarnated. I brought you here to understand the consequences of failure. Should Amroth triumph, the fires of Serona will no doubt spread and engulf the world."

Iren's throat felt dry, and not just because of Serona's heat. Horrid visions danced through his mind: Lodia's fertile fields naked and withered, and Ziorsecth and Akaku Forests without a single tree.

"Come," Rondel interjected on his reverie. "We must not linger. No living creature can survive Serona, and even to dwell on its edge invites death. We'll find a place to rest and then resume your training."

The old Maantec turned to reenter the woods, but Iren suddenly reached out and grabbed her wrist. "Rondel, I just remembered."

She looked curiously back at him, then started at his ashen face. "What is it?"

"That name...Nadav. I knew I'd heard it before, but I couldn't place it. What you said just now, though, triggered my memory. Amroth mentioned it to me, the first night we left Haldessa. He said Nadav was his commander in Caardit."

Now Rondel's turn to tremble and sweat had come. "Nadav?" she repeated, panic in her voice. "You're certain?"

The moment Iren nodded, all the color drained from her face as well. "We must return to Yuushingaral immediately!" she cried. "Even now, we may be too late!"

CHAPTER TWENTY-EIGHT
Reunions

Rondel shot back into the forest, her speed enhanced by magic. Iren kept pace with her, and she loosed a grim smile at his progress. In four short months of training, he had come far. As he sped through Ziorsecth, his body blurring alongside Rondel's, she wondered if he finally comprehended her tough teaching strategy. By pushing Iren to the brink of what his body could do, Rondel had forced the young Maantec to greatly increase the amount of environmental magic he could use. That magic now carried him as swift as any eagle. Still, she knew he hadn't progressed enough, not considering what Iren had just told her.

She finally understood Amroth. All of his plans, all of his deceptions, the true purposes behind them made perfect sense to her. It made her furious, the way the man had fooled her. In spite of her Lightning Sight, he had totally blinded her to his true identity.

"Rondel," Iren shouted, "what's happened? What does some militia leader in Caardit have to do with the Fire Dragon Knight of a thousand years ago?"

"Everything," she replied, Lightning Sight activating as her rage took her, "they're one and the same."

"What? How is that possible?"

She gritted her teeth. "Nadav isn't a Lodian name. It's Maantec, and in the last thousand years, I've known of only one."

"You said Nadav died in the Kodama-Maantec War!" Iren countered. "How could Amroth know about him?"

"Because Amroth is a Maantec."

"Impossible! You're joking!"

"I wish. He must have hidden his left-handedness all the time he lived in Lodia. He probably even strategically used some of his biological magic in Haldessa to gradually age himself, all to reduce any suspicion of his Maantec heritage."

"Maantec or not," Iren asked, "what connects Amroth to Nadav?"

"Amroth must have served under Nadav in the Kodama-Maantec War. During the war, Nadav campaigned in Lodia, trying to bring the humans under Maantec control to fight the Kodamas. However, a force of humans, Tengu, and Kodamas rose in union against him and all but wiped out his army outside Caardit. With no other options for retreat, Nadav took his few survivors north into the frozen wastes of Charda, where the other races dared not follow. According to the report he later gave Iren Saito, Nadav relied on his fire magic to keep his men alive. He even risked excursions into Ziorsecth to bring the men food, since almost none exists in Charda. Eventually, Nadav got the entire group back to Serona, thin and weary but alive. From that moment on, Nadav's companies showed absolute loyalty to their commander, and they always fought harder than any other unit. Any one of them would gladly have died to support the man who success-fully brought them through that icy nightmare."

"That means Amroth fought in the Kodama-Maantec War," Iren said. "He's one of the few Maantecs who survived the final battle."

Rondel nodded. "During that battle, all Nadav's men rallied around him. When Nadav unleashed the fires beneath Serona, the flames swal-lowed up him and his companions. They even destroyed the Karyozaki."

"If the fires destroyed the sword," Iren asked, "how did that Oni back in Akaku get it?"

"That had me puzzled from the moment I first laid eyes on Hezna, but I think I can finally guess at least some of what happened. Amroth, perhaps alone of Nadav's men, escaped the fires and found Feng's gem, the Burning Ruby. The stones containing the dragons are indestructible, so even Serona's flames couldn't melt it. Amroth must have spent the last thousand years trying to reforge the Karyozaki."

"He obviously succeeded."

"Yes," Rondel admitted, "which begs the question, how did Hezna acquire it and not Amroth? I suppose at this point it has little relevance. The more immediate problem is that Amroth can finally achieve his ulti-mate objective."

"Which is?"

Lightning Sight flared. "Isn't it obvious? Total revenge against the Kodamas, the species he considers responsible for Nadav's death."

Iren looked shocked, but Rondel shook her head, knowing she'd only told him half the story. Amroth sought revenge against more than the Kodamas. He had another, far more personal vendetta in mind. He wanted vengeance against the person whose treason brought about the final battle and, in so doing, had forced Nadav to unleash the spell that killed him and his subordinates: Rondel herself.

With their enhanced speed the journey to Yuushingaral, a distance of over a hundred and fifty miles, took less than three hours. Rondel expected to find the Kodaman capital exactly as they'd left it, but instead they entered a village in total disarray. Whereas before it looked just like any other patch of forest, now dozens of Kodamas ran frantically from tree to tree, delivering messages, supply crates, and weapons. Rondel frowned, fearing they had arrived too late.

Stone-faced sentinels greeted Iren and Rondel and ushered them immediately to Aletas's tree. Every Kodama they encountered bore arms. Even the small boy Rondel had seen guarding Iren during his imprisonment bore a short bow and quiver. Rondel doubted the boy would serve as more than a target in battle, but she respected the child's apparent lack of fear.

Her own trepidation had to be more on display. Iren Saito's curse had nearly wiped out the Kodaman population a thousand years ago, and the species had never recovered. With their long lives, the Kodamas, like the other immortal races, had always been slow to reproduce. Before the curse, they could resist any force bearing down on them, but no longer.

Iren's somber expression indicated he felt the same way. Both Maantecs knew, with a certainty they dared not set in words, the outcome of this battle.

Every last Kodama was going to die.

The pair entered the queen's tree, and the door sealed itself behind them. Taking seats in the tree's entry room, they waited a moment as three figures walked down the stairs to join them. First came Aletas, her normally deep tan complexion gone thoroughly pale. Though she looked as youthful as ever, her gait shuffled like a cripple's. She carried a tray of teacups, but with each step they rattled, threatening to spill with her unsteady walk. The second person was Minawë, doing her best to say reassuring words to Aletas.

As the third figure came into view, Iren suddenly leapt to his feet, his body taut. Despite the grave situation, Rondel couldn't help but grin. The boy must have thought he'd never see this man again.

Balear Platarch looked uncomfortable in his Lodian military uniform, and his face contorted in a mix of happiness and guilt as he recognized Rondel and Iren. They all exchanged greetings, then sat down together. Aletas sighed as she set her tray on the table between them all, visibly relieved when everyone had taken a cup without any spills.

Iren fidgeted in his seat, and Rondel laughed inwardly. The poor child surely felt out of place. After all, Aletas had more or less kicked them out of Yuushingaral just a few months ago, and the last time he'd seen Balear, the Lodian had tried to kill him.

"Well now," Rondel began, when it became obvious that everyone else was just as ill at ease as Iren about the situation, "what brings you to Ziorsecth, Balear?"

She asked her question calmly, as though posing it to a casual tourist. When Balear remained silent, both hands gripping his mug, however, Rondel's expression turned grave. When she spoke again, she made her voice lower in tone and deadly serious, "Could it have anything to do with Lodia's new king and Fire Dragon Knight, Amroth Angustion?"

Balear's head snapped up. Rondel smirked and explained what she'd seen after the battle in Akaku and the connection between Amroth and Nadav. At first Balear expressed disbelief, but then Minawë pulled out the forged letter Amroth had written along with the waiver text Rondel had copied.

The young soldier sat back and rubbed his temple. "I've been a fool," he moaned. "All this time I believed I was helping Lodia, when in reality I was only serving King Angustion's…no, Amroth's desire for power."

"We all fell for Amroth's lies," Iren said. "Even Rondel didn't suspect his Maantec origins."

Rondel nodded. "The past is the past; let's deal with the present. Why did you flee Lodia? What does Amroth intend to do?"

Shuddering, Balear told his sad tale. He spoke of Amroth's edict to raise an army, the horrible conditions the soldiers had to endure, and the absolute loyalty, upon pain of death, the king demanded of them.

Sparks flickered in Rondel's eyes, even though she didn't intend it. Lightning Sight had a way of activating itself whenever she lost control of her emotions. Right now, she couldn't tell at whom she felt angrier: Amroth for causing such evil, or herself for not realizing his plan and stopping him sooner.

Balear then turned to Rondel, looking her over as though judging her. Trying to force herself into calmness, she resorted to her faithful standby of a fake smile and sarcastic retort. "How long it's been since a handsome young man has deigned to glance at me! To what do I owe the pleasure?"

The human said nothing for a moment. Finally, resolving some inner struggle, he stood and produced from behind his back a dagger, one with a perfectly round hilt and pommel.

Rondel's sarcasm died in her throat, and her false grin vanished. She stared dumbstruck at the blade in his hand. It was her rondel, the Liryometa.

Turning it around, he offered it to her, "Amroth made perhaps his sole mistake with this blade. He gave it to me, although I don't know why. I think it's about time it returned to its owner."

Rondel gingerly took the weapon, relief washing over her as thoughts of her father filled her. She held the rondel as she would a child, delicately stroking its fine features. After nearly a minute, Iren coughed, pulling Rondel from her memories. Standing, she thanked Balear solemnly, meaning it more than any words she'd said in centuries. Then, reluctantly, she returned the blade to its sheath on her belt, feeling complete for the first time since Akaku.

As she sat back in her chair, she did so with newfound respect for Balear. He had clearly risked his life to defy Amroth and ride to Ziorsecth. More than that, he had done so knowing he was betraying his own species to another. She knew that feeling all too well.

She also understood why Amroth had given the young man the Liryometa, and the knowledge incensed her. Fearing Rondel had lived, Amroth had used Balear as nothing more than a test subject to be sacrificed. Even Nadav, uncivilized brute though he'd been, always cared for his subordinates. Amroth had truly descended into madness.

Aletas set down her cup. She hadn't consumed a drop in all the time they'd been talking, even though she hadn't said a word up until now. "You two have good timing returning here. Balear arrived in Yuushingaral this morning and told me what he just told you. I believe him, if only because he must know he has no way of returning to Lodia alive after entering this forest."

The discussion next turned to logistics for the coming battle, and Rondel noticed Iren's eyes glazing over. Holy Dragon Knight he might be, but he was still only eighteen years old. No doubt he must have found the details horribly dull and overwhelmingly depressing. Even for Rondel, the numbers made grim news. By Balear's estimates, the Lodian army had nearly five thousand soldiers, though they lacked siege weapons, cavalry, and fighting experience. That might give the Kodamas an edge, except that even if they marshaled their populace from every corner of Ziorsecth, they could field barely a thousand defenders.

Adding to the problem, Amroth's army had already set forth. Although they would move slowly across Lodia, Rondel doubted half the Kodaman force could reach the forest's eastern edge by the time the enemy arrived. Worse, nearly every Kodama skilled in magic had served in the Kodama-Maantec War and therefore died in the final battle. The remaining ones could perform basic spells, like opening the doors of their tree homes and creating the orbs that lit them, but such minor abilities would not turn back an army.

An urgent knock on the tree caused everyone to jump. Minawë ran and created an opening, revealing the sweaty face of a Kodaman man. He surveyed the room, his eyes falling on Iren.

Silently, Rondel swore, knowing what news the man brought. She rose to stop him from speaking, how she had not yet decided, but before she'd reached her feet he blurted out, "Queen Aletas, our scouts report an enormous detonation in western Ziorsecth. A miles-long swath of forest has vanished!"

The queen flared. She reached across the table and wrapped her hands around Iren's throat. "You!" she cried. "Left-handed demon! What do you think you're doing? How dare you show your face here! Get out of Ziorsecth at once!"

Rondel got behind the queen and tugged at her arms. "It wasn't his fault!" she cried, but Aletas would not be dissuaded. Her grip tightened.

"Minawë!" Rondel called in desperation, but the Kodaman princess, for the first time since Rondel had met her, stood frozen with indecision. Her eyes flicked from Aletas to Iren, unable to decide who to support.

Aletas whipped her elbow around and struck Rondel in the jaw, sending her sprawling. "Don't you dare speak her name! You're as bad as him!" She lifted Iren by the throat and tossed him across the room, her strength incredible even by Rondel's standards. "Get out of my sight, before I kill you both myself!" She collapsed back into her chair, moaning, "Why? Why did this have to happen? We've left the world alone for a thousand years. Why, Rondel? Why did you have to go and involve us in your Maantec squabbles? Haven't the Kodamas suffered enough because of you?"

Rondel hauled herself to her feet, for once in her life at a loss for words, sarcastic or otherwise. Aletas was right; she couldn't involve the Kodamas in this anymore. They had just one option.

"Iren," she called, "let's go. We'll go to Lodia and fight Amroth alone. That way, his army will never reach the forest."

There was no response. "Iren?" Rondel turned a circle in the room, dread taking her. She put a hand to her head. "Not again."

The fool had already left.

CHAPTER TWENTY-NINE
The Sea Stone

As bright stars and the first full moon of autumn filled the night sky, Iren Saitosan sat on a sandy beach overlooking the Yuushin Sea. Four months ago, Minawë had rescued him from the water here. The waves lapped gently, soothingly, against the shore. Their sound and salty aroma reminded him of Haldessa, and of how it was no more.

In his left hand he fingered the black sea stone he'd brought from Lodia, the sole memento of his childhood. He smiled a little despite himself. After all his journeying, after all the fights and training with Rondel, he still carried it with him.

"How long do you plan on staying out here?"

Iren turned in the direction of the melodious voice. "As long as I have to, Minawë. Maybe forever."

The lithe Kodama stepped onto the beach, the moonlight reflecting perfectly on her white silken robe. Sitting beside Iren, she wrapped her arms around her folded legs, her head resting on her knees. For a moment she said nothing, simply watching the waves on their endless cycle. Finally, without taking her eyes from the ocean, she said, "After you left, Rondel told us what happened during your training. Mother's furious, of course."

Iren leaned back so he was lying in the sand, hands behind his head and gazing into the heavens. "So you know, then?"

She nodded.

"When Rondel told me she didn't see Iren Saito in me, I felt overjoyed," Iren said. "Both she and Divinion accepted what I did in the forest.

Terrible as it was, they made it sound like it was something that needed to happen. I almost believed them, but now I don't know. I wonder if, despite their kind words, I really am becoming another Iren Saito." He grimaced and looked at her. "How can you stand sitting out here and talking to me, knowing all Saito did to your people and that I could wind up the same way?"

Shrugging, Minawë replied, "You aren't Iren Saito."

Iren grasped a pile of sand in his right fist. "Close enough."

"But not the same," Minawë insisted. "You may have similar names, but a name doesn't mean anything. It doesn't mean you'll become like him."

"I have many of his traits; even Rondel admitted that. I have the Holy Dragon too, just like him."

"I suppose, but those similarities don't just describe you and Saito. They match someone else, too."

He looked at her curiously. "Who?"

She smiled. "Your father."

"What would you know about my father?"

"I know that he was a Holy Dragon Knight, even if he didn't realize it. I know that he cared for others, and I know that he died fighting with every last shred of his strength to protect his wife and son. If he had found me in Akaku, he would have done exactly what you did. Even if you do resemble Saito, I would say you resemble your father, the humble yet brave farmer, far more so."

Iren paused, reflecting. Ever since he had learned of Saito, he had compared himself, and been compared by others, to the ancient tyrant. For the first time, someone had compared him to his father. He liked that connection a whole lot more.

"So you don't have to wind up like Iren Saito," Minawë concluded. "If anything, I'd say you'll surpass him."

Iren threw up his hands. "I've already done that," he said. "Iren Saito wanted to conquer the Kodamas. Thanks to me, he'll finally accomplish his mission. When Amroth gets here, it will mean the end of Ziorsecth."

Minawë folded her arms. "What on Raa are you talking about? Didn't you spend all this time training so you could stop Amroth?"

"Yes, but he's only coming here in the first place because of me. Don't you see, Minawë? Everything that's happened has been my fault. Because of me, Amroth obtained the Karyozaki. Because of me, Haldessa burned to the ground, and Amroth became king of Lodia. And now, because I came here, Amroth will chase me and wipe out you, the Kodamas, and this entire forest." He sighed and whispered, "I should have jumped out that window in Haldessa. Then none of this ever would have happened."

Minawë stood and glared at him. "How did Divinion pick such a moron to be Holy Dragon Knight?"

He leapt to his feet. Rounding on her, he shouted, "How dare you!"

The Kodaman princess didn't flinch. Instead, she replied, "What if you had killed yourself in Haldessa? Then you never would have rescued me from the Quodivar. I'd be dead too."

Iren took a step back. He stared at her, wide-eyed.

"Amroth would have come for the Kodamas eventually anyway," she pointed out. "You might have given him the excuse he needed, but he always belonged to Nadav. He would pursue our extinction until his last breath. We could not avoid this confrontation. Even if it is our destiny to lose this fight, though," she smiled warmly, "I'm glad you didn't kill yourself, so that at least I got to meet you."

"Minawë," he said her name with some surprise, but then he closed his eyes and returned her expression. "I'm glad I didn't kill myself either, so that I got to meet you too."

"Besides," the Kodama continued, adopting a wry look, "we're not as doomed as you think. We still have the Heart of Ziorsecth."

"The Heart of Ziorsecth?" Iren remembered Aletas mentioning it before, and how it had given her a vision. "What is it?"

"You walked through this forest. What did you see?"

Iren blinked a couple times. He was pretty sure this was a trick question. "Trees?" he asked.

"No, moron, you didn't see trees. You saw a tree. One. All of Ziorsecth has but one tree."

He scoffed. "I may have grown up in a castle, but I know enough about trees to know that I saw a lot more than one of them while that senile slave-driver was hauling me all over the place."

"And had you paid the slightest attention in those wanderings," Minawë chastised, "you might have noticed that every tree belonged to the same species, the Ziorsecth Maple. West of here, along the coast of the Yuushin Sea, sits the Heart of Ziorsecth, the largest tree in the world. Our sacred place and the burial ground of our people, we've never allowed a non-Kodama to visit it, not even Rondel. Its stems fill Ziorsecth, almost twenty thousand square miles. You see, unlike other maples, the Ziorsecth Maple can produce root suckers, new stems that sprout from its root system. Because of that feature, every tree in Ziorsecth is connected. They all share the same roots, and they grow so closely together that a nimble Kodama can cross from one end of the forest to the other without touching the ground."

Iren had to admit that the Heart sounded impressive, but he still didn't understand how some overgrown weed could help them defeat Amroth.

Just then, shouting from the forest reached their ears. Minawë scowled. She stormed off the beach toward the ruckus, with Iren rushing to follow her.

As he reached the tree line, Iren beheld Rondel, a longbow strapped to her back, swinging her arms and screaming. Beside her, Aletas acted in much the same manner. Iren sighed, wondering if they were still arguing about his loss of control.

"Absolutely not!" Aletas yelled.

"You know you have no choice!" Rondel responded. "Do you want Lodia to butcher your people?"

The queen's face strongly resembled an over-ripened tomato. "Whose fault is that in the first place?"

Rondel looked like she might burst a blood vessel. "Coward!"

"Interloper!"

"Children!" Minawë suddenly roared, her voice shearing the cool night air and cowing the two elder women into silence.

"What's going on here?" Iren asked, not sure he wanted to know the answer.

Aletas gave a haughty flick of her hair but otherwise refused to acknowledge Iren's presence. With an exasperated groan, Rondel said, "We cannot defeat Amroth and his army as we are. At first I thought we could avoid getting the Kodamas involved if Iren and I went to Lodia alone, but now I realize that's impossible. The two of us can't overcome five thousand soldiers, let alone them plus the Fire Dragon Knight. They would kill us and continue their march, wiping out Ziorsecth. If we fight separately, we'll all die. However, even together, we still can't overcome the odds. We have but one chance of victory."

Iren and Minawë both looked at her hopefully. Meanwhile, Aletas stared at a nearby rock as, with utter seriousness, Rondel said, "We need a third Dragon Knight."

"Brilliant!" Iren shouted, throwing up his hands. "Except we don't have another Ryokaiten. Even if we did, how would you train its knight in time?"

He thought he'd deflated the old hag for once, but she grinned and replied, "Actually, we have both a third Ryokaiten and Dragon Knight standing right here with us." She gestured at Aletas. "My dear queen, may I show them?"

The normally regal Aletas had veins popping out of her forehead. "You dare…"

Rondel simply stared innocently back, saying nothing. At last the queen pressed her fingers into the bridge of her nose and said, "So be it. You'll do it regardless. You never would listen to me."

The diminutive Maantec reached behind her and pulled out the bow she carried. It was unlike any Iren had ever seen. Though made of wood, it didn't look brown but rather yellow-green, like a recently cut branch. Living vines laced around the center, forming a grip both firm and comfortable. They raced out to either end of the bow, and near the handhold they twisted together to form three concentric circles of Maantec kanji identical to that on Iren's sword.

"Behold the Forest Dragon Bow, the Chloryoblaka," Rondel said. "A thousand years ago, I recovered it from the battlefield on Serona after King Otunë's death. I returned it to the Kodamas and gave it to Aletas. She's left it unused ever since."

Minawë's eyes widened. "Then Mother, that means you control Dendryl! You're the Forest Dragon Knight!"

Aletas folded her arms. "No. At least, not anymore. That weapon belongs to a former life. I'll have nothing to do with it."

Minawë looked on the verge of tears as her mother spoke. "Why?" she cried. "Facing the might of Lodia, why would you deny the magic of Dendryl? Why would you deny the magic of…of…" she barely managed to mumble, "of Father?"

The queen flared, "Have none of you seen Serona? Have none of you gazed upon its fires that still scar the earth a thousand years after their summoning? That is what the dragons bring to Raa. I watched everyone I cared about march off to war a thousand years ago, and not one of them returned. Why did they die? Because of a dragon, and not just any dragon," she jabbed a finger at Iren, "because of the Holy Dragon!" Aletas was screaming now. "The being that supposedly embodies all that is good in this world slaughtered my husband and nearly extinguished my entire species! Now, another Dragon Knight comes to complete the task. Heaven may have created the dragons, but they are no blessing. They are a curse, a plague that will ruin us all!"

Iren listened to the queen's tirade with pity. In many ways, she was right. She was wrong on one critical point, however. Unsure where his courage came from, he said, "Queen Aletas, you cannot fault the dragons for the Kodamas' suffering. The blame lies with people, like Iren Saito and Amroth, who let their desire for power consume them. But that has nothing to do with dragons or Heaven. Heavenly hands don't shape this world; people's hands, our hands, do. Our hands can heal others or wound them. Our hands can pick up the outcasts and help them live better lives, or they can swing swords and cast deadly spells. We, not dragons, make these choices. The dragons are neither curses nor plagues; they are gifts. How we use such gifts, though, isn't fixed. We decide. We decide whether to use Heaven's gifts for salvation or destruction. Amroth chose the latter, but I for one will choose salvation!"

As Iren spoke, he became more and more passionate, his voice rising and his excitement growing until he shouted as loud as he could. When he finished, he blinked several times. He felt like he had momentarily departed reality. Immediately, he realized how rude he must have sounded, criticizing this queen who had lived far longer and seen much more of life than he had. Still, he knew in his heart he'd spoken the truth.

For a long time nobody moved, tensely awaiting Aletas's reaction to Iren's outburst. She worked her lips, biting her lower one nervously. Finally, the queen said, "Evil will triumph if we do nothing." She sighed, gazed up at the forest canopy, and, after a pause, smiled broadly as she whispered, "Yes, I too will choose salvation."

Rondel gave Iren a knowing smirk. "Take your bow, Queen Aletas, and may it defend your people as it did in ancient times."

The Kodaman queen wrapped her hand around the Chloryoblaka and lifted it. She drew a long breath, and then slowly exhaled through her teeth. "We have much to prepare and little time to do so. Rondel, I will gather the Kodamas and head for the forest edge. Meet us there in five days. Minawë, let's go."

Minawë joined the queen, and the pair began to leave. As they stepped away, Aletas turned to Iren and said, "For the moment, Maantec, it seems I need you. I won't force you out of Ziorsecth. Can you keep your emotions in check and avoid another disaster?"

Iren gave her the same wry expression Minawë had used on him ear-lier that evening when describing the Heart of Ziorsecth. "I guess you'll have to wait and see."

Aletas didn't look at all thrilled with his answer, but Minawë laughed and nodded approvingly. The two Kodamas departed, leaving Iren and Rondel alone on the beach's edge.

Rondel clapped the young man on the back. "You know, slacker, you give quite a speech when you have to."

Iren chortled. "I wish I knew where it came from. I think Divinion gave me a helping hand."

"Did he now?" She didn't seem convinced.

They stood together quietly for a few seconds, but then Rondel asked, "By the way, what's that rock you're carrying?"

Iren glanced down. His left hand still clutched his sea stone. He tossed it gently a few times, considering. Finally, he shrugged and replied, "What, this? I don't think it matters anymore."

With a mighty throw, he hurled it across the beach and into the sea, forever lost amid the endless waves.

CHAPTER THIRTY
The Meaning of Strength

A week later at sunset, Iren stood on the eastern edge of Ziorsecth, beholding the land he once cast aside. Shadows fell thick on Lodia as the sun dipped below the tree line. Balear, Minawë, and Rondel rested beside him, preparing, each in his or her own way, to face the unthinkable.

Balear looked worst off of all of them. He trembled constantly, and he kept fingering his blade, then looking at it with disgust. Iren could guess what was going through the man's mind. He had betrayed Amroth, a man he'd admired more than any other. He had betrayed Lodia, the country he'd devoted his life to protecting. How many men would die because of him? How many would he himself have to strike down?

Only Rondel seemed calm. Seated on a rock, she stared at the empty expanse of Lodia, waiting for fires on the horizon that would herald the enemy's arrival. Alone of all of them, she knew about war. She had witnessed Serona. She had seen the land rent asunder and the Kodamas slaughtered. Tonight, that history that might well repeat itself.

Iren rolled his shoulders, trying to make his wooden armor more comfortable. He wore a breastplate, bracers, greaves, a helmet, and a round shield large enough to protect him but small enough to leave him room to swing the Muryozaki with one hand. Minawë had given him the armor, and both she and Balear also wore sets of it. She'd offered Rondel some as well, but the old Maantec had declined, preferring not to inhibit her movement.

Though made of light tan wood, the armor was no thicker than normal plate. When Minawë had first shown it to him, Iren had possessed little confidence in it until she'd explained, "Our smiths use spells to condense the wood. Pound for pound, wood is stronger than steel. This armor will match any in Lodia, yet it weighs much less."

It was indeed lightweight, but Iren did find it itchy. Then again, it might just be nerves. At last report, a mere six hundred Kodamas had reached the forest's edge. Lodia's army outnumbered theirs nearly ten to one.

From atop her rock, Rondel shifted to look probingly at Balear. "Describe Amroth's sword for me. I only saw it briefly during my fight with Hezna."

The former general jumped when Rondel spoke to him, but he stumbled through his depiction. When he finished, the crone frowned and said, "Iren, show Balear your sword."

Iren did so, and as Balear looked at it, Rondel said, "Balear, I need you to remember. Do you see the symbols on Iren's blade? Did Amroth's sword have the same writing?"

Immediately, Balear responded, "Yes, exactly."

Rondel heaved a sigh of relief, but then the Lodian began again, "Wait. Wait a second." The old Maantec tensed. Balear said, "This sword has three circles. Amroth's only had two."

Swearing, Rondel got up and began storming around the woods. Iren said nothing, but he understood. That third circle kept the dragon's will in check. Without it, the dragon's and knight's psyches could merge. Whoever had reforged the Karyozaki had, whether by accident or design, done so incorrectly. They'd only engraved the first two circles. It explained why Amroth's behavior had changed so drastically since becoming the Fire Dragon Knight. He wasn't Amroth anymore; Feng had manipulated his thoughts and twisted his mind.

More than the number of soldiers they faced, that fact worried Iren most of all. Judging by Rondel's reaction, she felt the same way. After all, as little experience as Iren had as a Dragon Knight, Amroth had even less. Had Amroth's sword been forged correctly, Iren might have stood a chance against him. Feng's dominance, however, made such victory unlikely.

Iren opened his mouth to ask Rondel how to deal with Feng, but as he did, Minawë leapt to her feet and shouted, "I see them!"

Everyone rushed to her side. Balear's trembling got so bad Iren feared the poor man might faint. Iren felt much the same way as he noticed, on the horizon, flickering torches pierce the night. Their line stretched for miles. Iren couldn't feel his individual heartbeats. They came so fast that they all blurred together.

Not long after the torches appeared, faint, rhythmic impacts reached his ears: drums, pounding out the unceasing march of the Lodian army. Rondel's face hardened further, if that were even possible. "Minawë, I trust all the Kodamas have taken their positions?"

She nodded, but Iren was skeptical. Despite Minawë's assurances that six hundred Kodamas had gathered, Iren had seen barely a dozen, and then only on the way here days ago. He hoped Aletas hadn't decided to have her people retreat and make Iren and Rondel fight alone.

If Rondel shared that concern, she didn't voice it. Instead, she said, "Good, then listen carefully. When the enemy gets here, Iren, I want you to help the Kodamas battle the Lodian soldiers." She clenched her fists and teeth. "I will fight Amroth alone."

Iren leapt forward in protest. "You can't! You told me yourself you couldn't match him!"

Balear nodded his agreement. "The Lodian army only has conscripts. If the king falls, they'll likely flee. We should target him first."

Rondel replied, "True, but five thousand soldiers can still do a great deal of damage before Amroth dies. We must keep them away from the forest as much as possible. Iren, I intended to train you for at least several more months, maybe years, before we faced this foe. Even then, I planned to confront him together. We no longer have that luxury. The Kodamas need help against the Lodian soldiers, which means we can only field one Dragon Knight against Amroth. I'll have a better chance against him than you would. Besides," she flashed him a fierce expression, "Amroth wants me in this fight. This is my fate. I will follow Okthora's Law."

"Evil must be annihilated." Iren and Rondel said it at the same time. The young Maantec choked back tears. Rondel was throwing her life away, yet he could do nothing to stop her.

"Rondel, what should I do?" Minawë asked.

"Take Balear and rendezvous with the other Kodamas. Make sure Balear gets a bow. He'll need one."

The Kodaman princess protested, "I want to stay and fight with you and Iren!"

To Iren's amazement, Rondel reached up and placed a gentle hand on Minawë's shoulder. "You really are your parents' daughter. I know you want to help, and that's why I'm asking you to go to the other Kodamas.

Get into the trees; we'll need all the support we can get."

Minawë looked like she might argue, but then Iren stepped forward. "I'll be counting on you," he said. "You and I fought hard to cross Lodia and get here safely. During that journey you showed a resolve unmatched by anyone I've ever met. If we battle this night with half of your courage, I know we'll triumph."

Despite herself, she smiled, eyes shimmering as she replied, "You moron." Then she motioned to Balear and said, "Let's go."

The group separated, Iren and Rondel stepping just beyond the forest. As Iren crossed the tree line, he heard Minawë call out, "Hey, Iren!"

He turned, and despite the gloom, he could see that her face glowed with confidence. "When we win this battle," she shouted, "let's go home to Yuushingaral together!"

Nodding slightly, he answered, "You got it."

With that, Minawë and Balear departed, leaving Iren and Rondel alone on the forest's edge. Lodia's army was now only a few miles away. As they approached, a torch at the front of the column erupted into a vast pillar of fire. Iren spat. Amroth obviously cared little about surprise or conserving his magic. He walked boldly, his flame creation twisting and licking the sky as though longing to consume the heavens themselves.

Rondel unsheathed the Liryometa. "I'll draw Amroth away from the main force. Wait here and let Lodia's army come to you."

"Why? They'll overwhelm me and charge into the forest. I can fight more freely on the plain."

"All this time, and you still talk back," Rondel retorted. "Just do as your teacher instructs. The Kodamas will trim their numbers for you."

Iren cocked an eyebrow. "What Kodamas? I still have yet to see this mythical force."

Rondel smirked. "That's the point, slacker. You can't see them," she pointed at Lodia's army, "and neither can they."

"You know, you're supposed to keep secrets from your enemies, not your allies."

"Sometimes it's strategic to do both."

Iren pouted. "That's a bunch of nonsense, and you know it. Stubborn old hag."

"Petulant child."

"Withered bird!"

"Numbskull!"

The pair glared at each other several more seconds. Then, on the verge of battle, with death steadily approaching, they both laughed. Rondel walked a few paces toward the advancing Lodian force and, without looking back, said, "Whatever happens, I want you to know I've never had a better student."

Crossing his arms, Iren said doubtfully, "Oh? I suppose that's because you've never had another student?"

The old woman craned her head around and shot Iren an impish smile. Then, activating Lightning Sight, she launched into the night.

* * *

Rondel bounded across the plain, the Liryometa gripped in her left hand. It took all she had not to look back at Iren. She wondered if she'd prepared him for what he would soon face and whether or not he would survive the night.

It was all the more reason for her not to delay. At top speed she flashed toward the Lodian army, even knowing that such a direct approach made her vulnerable to arrow fire. She doubted Amroth would have his archers shoot at her, though, for two reasons. First, he'd seen her easily dodge arrows back in Veliaf. Second, and of far greater importance, she was certain that Amroth would want to kill her personally.

As Rondel approached, the pillar of fire guiding the Lodians vanished, and Amroth stepped forward. Rondel could barely tell that he was the man she remembered from Haldessa. His eyes gleamed sulfurous yellow like a Yokai's, and a burning crown adorned his head. Even his skin had changed. Gray and cracked, it looked like freshly cooled lava.

When Amroth spoke, Rondel grimaced. His tone was hard and gravelly, not at all like the charismatic voice he'd once possessed. "Rondel, how good of you to save me the trouble of burning down the forest to find you." He grinned. "I see you have the Liryometa again. That means Balear betrayed me after all. Where is the fool? I'll kill him second, after you of course."

Ignoring him, Rondel pointed at the Karyozaki, glowing red in his right hand. "For shame, Amroth! Still hiding after all this time? Why don't you put that silly sword in the hand it was meant for?"

The king cackled maniacally. "So that's your plan! Rondel, for someone so ancient, you certainly lack wisdom. Do you honestly think this army will desert me if it learns I'm a Maantec? Fear makes them follow me. Tell them I'm a Maantec! Tell them I'm a Left! Their fear will increase that much more, and they'll fight all the harder to save themselves from my wrath!"

Rondel scowled. "Nadav would weep if he saw how far his beloved Feng's standards have fallen."

Amroth's laughter turned to fury in an instant. "How dare you speak his name, murderous wench! I'll have my revenge, and all the world will know Nadav's rightness, his absolute truth that strength alone brings about peace."

Lightning Sight's sparks cascaded across Rondel's eyes. "You have no clue," she said, her voice venomous, "about the meaning of strength."

Craning his neck, Amroth called over his shoulder, "Captain!" A young man stepped nervously forward wearing hastily and poorly crafted leather armor. Rondel felt heartened. Amroth's army might have size, but it had no fight in it.

"Send all troops into the forest," the king ordered. "Kill everyone you encounter, man, woman, or child."

The soldier gulped, clearly unenthused by the order, but he saluted and departed rapidly. Amroth then turned back to Rondel, leering down at her. "You say I don't know about strength? Why don't you teach me, then?"

Rondel allowed the faintest of smiles to cross her face. She'd hoped for this reaction. With her enhanced speed, she dashed to her left and called out, "Come on!"

Flames engulfed the king, and he rocketed after her. His captain gave the signal, and the army resumed its march.

Rondel zigzagged away from the main force, always keeping Amroth out of reach. When half a mile separated her from the army's nearest flank, she stopped and caught her breath for a few precious seconds while Amroth shot toward her. The speed the fire granted the king astounded her. Although it didn't match her own, the difference was less than she'd anticipated.

Amroth stopped twenty feet from Rondel, flames licking around his feet. He held the Karyozaki aloft, now in his left hand.

"One question," Rondel said.

"Of course," he answered, dripping with false sincerity, "I'd hate for you to die unfulfilled."

"That Karyozaki isn't Nadav's. Where did you get it?"

He clenched the sword. "I suppose you should know," he replied in his harsh voice, "considering that everything I've done for the last thousand years has been because of you. That day in Serona, Nadav, the greatest Maantec in history, perished because of your treachery. I vowed then to get revenge on you and the cursed Kodamas who caused our Maantec Empire to fall. I retrieved Nadav's Burning Ruby, but without its Ryokaiten, it had no power. For centuries afterward I traveled Raa, searching for anyone who knew the secrets of creating Ryokaiten. Desperate, I sought out the Yokai. Their magic can't compare with ours, but they do have great skill in enchanting weapons. Their leader, the Oni Hezna, agreed to help me reforge the sword." He snarled, "That beast betrayed me, though, and when we finally completed the Karyozaki, he took it and became the Dragon Knight instead of me!"

"And a much finer knight he made," Rondel sneered. "Unlike you, he had the sense not to trust Feng and only sparingly used the dragon's magic. Amroth, do yourself and Lodia a favor. Throw away that sword! Neither you nor Hezna had a complete picture of what the Karyozaki was or how to forge it. Without the third kanji circle, Feng will consume you! It's already begun; I see it in your face and hear it in your voice. I know you desire revenge against me, but I also know that, deep down, you truly want peace for Lodia. You'll have neither if Feng takes over your body!"

Amroth didn't answer immediately, and Rondel began to hope that he would listen to her. The ploy was desperate, but if she could separate Amroth from Feng's influence, maybe, just maybe, she could avert the coming tragedy.

The king closed his eyes and chuckled lightly. "I couldn't throw away this sword even if I wanted to. Feng would never allow it."

With a curse, Rondel raised her blade. As feared, nothing remained of Amroth's former self. She had no choice. Evil must be annihilated.

The pair squared off across the expanse of field, but neither moved. After several minutes of the stalemate, Amroth resumed his earlier cackling. "I knew you wouldn't!" he mocked. "Thanks to the Kodama-Maantec War and Feng, I know your fighting style. You rely on those eyes, because they let you react to any attack by the enemy. Therefore, you'll never make the first attack. You'll wait to see how I move."

Rondel flinched but said nothing.

"Normally, that's a solid plan," the king continued, "but not against me. You can respond to my movements, but what if I don't move at all?" The flames licking Amroth's feet accelerated, rising around his body and engulfing him in a fireball. The king's feet lifted off the ground.

Without warning, the burning sphere leapt forward, Amroth at its center. Rondel's eyes widened in shock. The king hadn't moved a muscle to launch his attack, so Lightning Sight provided no warning whatsoever.

Still, just enough distance separated them that she avoided Amroth and got behind him. The Liryometa hurtled toward Amroth's neck. When it impacted the flames, however, an unexpected resistance stopped it. As though they had become solid, the fires repelled Rondel's strike and knocked her off-guard.

Lightning Sight gave her only a split second of notice as Amroth's left arm swung around and the Karyozaki's tip emerged from the flames. Rondel leapt backward, but her off-balance posture made her slow. Searing pain ripped through her as the blade slashed a long line across her cheek. She fell to her knees, grasping at her face. It felt like Amroth had poured magma into the open wound. Through the agony, the wound made her realize why the Karyozaki gave off its distinctive red glow. Feng's magic superheated it.

Amroth laughed. "Not bad! That swing was meant to behead you."

Rondel snarled in frustration. She'd known Amroth would be unlike any opponent she'd faced. Every other Dragon Knight fought alone, simply drawing on the dragon's magic for additional strength. The Karyozaki's botched reforging, however, meant that in Amroth's case, Feng could actively intervene. They might occupy one body, but she battled two opponents all the same. The fire shield's repulsion of her thrust convinced Rondel of that. Amroth couldn't have followed her movements, nor could he have tracked the Liryometa well enough to time the block. Feng could.

The realization that she fought both Amroth and Feng filled her with dread, but it also gave her a sliver of optimism. If she could hold out long enough, maybe she could win. Her plan was risky and far too slow considering the dangers her friends faced, but it was the only chance she had.

Steeling herself, Rondel rose and charged the king at full speed, her body flickering as she raced over the plain. She ducked and dodged, weaved in and out, striking quick blows with her rondel. The fire stopped every attack, and each time Amroth countered with his sword. All the while, Rondel kept Lightning Sight focused on him, never wavering, barely blinking.

As she frantically maneuvered, her enhanced senses noticed Amroth start breathing heavily. Maintaining the fireball evidently required considerable magic. Feng could control the sphere, but the dragon could only use magic he channeled through Amroth.

After what felt like an endless procession of blows, counterblows, blocks, and narrow escapes, the fire's intensity changed. It pushed less strongly against her attacks. Sensing victory, she leapt forward, thrusting the Liryometa to direct all her energy at a single point. The rondel easily pierced the outer layer of Amroth's shield, but then the fire changed shape. It had formerly engulfed the king, but now it focused only on the point Rondel had struck. For a moment the two techniques clashed, sparks and flames erupting from the impact in a blinding shower. Then, with a blast of heat, Amroth's magic shot around the Liryometa. The flame impacted Rondel like a battering ram, knocking her back fifty feet, sprawling in the dirt. Amroth collapsed on his hands and knees, sweat pouring from his body. The fires around him vanished, leaving the pair in black night.

Rondel groaned and tried to move, then yelped as agony filled her left arm. The landing had broken it just below the elbow. The Liryometa lay a few feet away, torn free of her grip. Groping, she recovered it with her right hand and struggled to her feet. The pulsing in her arm made her dizzy, but she knew her strategy had worked. She walked over to where the king still knelt. He'd begun coughing up blood.

"It's over, Amroth." Rondel tried to make her voice firm, but it quivered slightly from the pain. "As I said, you don't understand strength. That flame shield may have protected you, but no one can maintain a spell like that for long. I knew you didn't have the control necessary for an extended battle. Actually, I had to teach Iren the same lesson. You've exhausted your magic. Please, preserve your sanity. Toss aside that flawed sword and accept death gracefully. Do it for Lodia, for peace."

The king looked at Rondel, and to the old Maantec's amazement, tears and a wild, terrified expression covered Amroth's face. "Rondel!" he wailed, and his voice now sounded the way it had the day they'd departed Haldessa, "Kill me! Kill me before he comes back! Feng, he's insane! He's planning to—"

Amroth never finished, because at that moment, violent, wrenching laughter exited his lips, and then Rondel's whole world exploded.

CHAPTER THIRTY-ONE
Ziorsecth Rises

On the edge of Ziorsecth Forest, Iren Saitosan waited with held breath as the Lodian army closed for the slaughter. Seconds earlier, he'd seen the pillar of flame disappear and a huge fireball he assumed was Amroth fly away from the army. He couldn't spot Rondel, but he could picture her drawing the king away from the main battle. It was a smart tactic. According to Balear, they faced a large but unmotivated army. Keep Amroth away from the forest, and the Kodamas might just win.

That is, if any of them showed up. Iren kept glancing behind him, but he couldn't spot a single Kodama inside the tree line. Part of him feared they'd simply given up and fled. Aletas could just be using him and Rondel, putting them in front to kill as many as possible before dying.

Another part, the larger part, felt differently. The queen had said she'd chosen salvation, and Iren believed her. Aletas trusted him to fight alongside the Kodamas. He would trust the Kodamas to fight alongside him.

The Lodians' torches provided Iren his first hint that something had changed. All at once, a dozen or so of the lights at the head of the approaching column faltered. A second later, the humans' screams reached him. Then, all around him, he noticed a shift in the forest. The night birds and insects stopped calling. The owls, as he remembered Minawë pointing out to him in Akaku, ceased hooting. In their place was a low thrum that seemed to come from everywhere.

With each passing second, the screams of the dying humans grew louder. Their lines broke down as the undisciplined conscripts panicked. Rondel's words came to Iren: "That's the point, slacker. You can't see them, and neither can they."

Now he understood. The reason he hadn't spotted any Kodamas on the battlefield was because they weren't on it. They were above it, in the treetops, firing their bows as fast as they could manage. The narrow openings between the upper branches functioned like arrow slits, and with their green hair and brown wooden armor, no one could see them. By contrast, the Lodians' torches and exposed position on the plain made the humans easy targets.

Iren wished the Lodian soldiers would save themselves and withdraw, but whether through a few skilled leaders or their deep-seated fear of Amroth, they gradually regrouped. He couldn't tell their losses, but Iren knew the arrow barrage must have been devastating. Even so, the tactic had run its course. The Lodians now realized they couldn't remain on the forest outskirts. Worse, they had figured out their torches simply made them more obvious targets. Dousing their lights, the Lodian army fell into blackness. The arrows continued, but the screams came less often.

Then a new, far more terrible sound joined the din: thundering feet. The enemy soldiers charged for the forest as quickly as possible. No doubt they hoped that once inside, they would be less exposed to the withering projectile rain.

As the Lodians ran, Iren heard the first Kodaman cries from behind and above him in the trees. The attackers had figured out where their enemies were, and while the humans could both run and shoot over the darkened plain, the Kodamas were essentially trapped. They needed to stay close to the tree line in order to fire.

Iren raised his shield, guarding himself in case a stray arrow tried to find him. This point in the battle was why Rondel had wanted him to hold his position. The crafty bat knew the Lodians would make a break for the forest. Once they reached the trees, firing from the canopy would become all but impossible, thanks to the tight interlocking branches of Ziorsecth's joined trunks. If Iren could dam even a small portion of the enemy army outside the forest, though, he would give the Kodamas time to trim their numbers that much more. Drawing the Muryozaki, he steadied himself to fight for his life.

The first wave of soldiers hit him less than a minute later. For a long time after that, he couldn't remember what happened. He saw only flashes as his world dissolved into a never-ending series of attacks, blocks, and screams. More than one glancing blow landed on him, but the Muryozaki healed his injuries. After the first couple enemy strikes hit him, he used magic to increase his speed and strength so that the Lodians couldn't keep pace. The ground near him became slick with blood. Caught in a nightmare, the ever-rising pile of corpses made maneuvering ever more difficult. Soon his boosted speed gave him little advantage, because he simply had nowhere to go.

Just as Iren became convinced he would drown in the death he was creating, the enemy onslaught abruptly ceased. Glancing about, he realized he stood alone on the plain. He had cut through those rushing his position, but many more had gone right past him.

The thrum of bowstrings fell silent, and an eerie calm settled over Lodia and Ziorsecth alike. Iren took a moment to collect himself. He wondered how many he'd slain, and how many still remained. He had no idea, but he doubted the Kodamas held the advantage.

In any case, standing around granted him little. Charging into the forest, he readied his sword but saw nothing. He heard nothing. The sounds of battle had vanished, despite the hundreds, perhaps thousands, of remaining foes.

As he stumbled through Ziorsecth, searching in vain for someone, friend or foe, the leaves on a nearby blackberry bush suddenly stirred. Not the faintest breeze passed through the forest understory; something had made the plant move. An enemy must have hidden himself in the shrub. Iren leapt forward, slashing the Muryozaki. It passed easily through the briars, carving away branches but nothing more. Frowning, Iren examined the bush closer. It was empty.

"Stupid squirrels," he muttered. He was on edge enough without the wildlife adding to his stress.

He'd just resumed his search when a second bush stirred. This time, instead of attacking, he held his position, waiting to see what would happen. As he watched in nervous anticipation, the bush moved again. This time, he noticed other shrubs dancing as well, and something else. From deeper in the forest came a low, slithering sound. Iren panicked, fearing the approach of some monster. The terrifying noise grew in intensity, increasing in volume until it came from all directions. It sounded like a giant serpent winding its way between the trees.

Iren's breathing came in ragged gasps, and sweat dripped from his body. He hadn't counted on this. Amroth must have kept some dark magic beast in reserve, waiting for the right moment to attack.

Frantic shouts and crashing feet rushed toward him. Iren raised his sword, determined to fight Amroth's monster. A shape flailed in the dark in front of him, but ally or enemy he couldn't tell. Holding his attack, Iren watched the person approach and then flee straight past him as though he didn't exist.

Then Iren saw, not ten feet away, a pair of eyes gleaming in the dark. Dropping his shield, Iren focused magic into his right palm. Whatever this demon was, if it wanted to eat him, he'd make it suffer first. As he raised his hand to fire, however, a familiar voice issued from the direction of the eyes, "Hold, Maantec. I'm not your enemy."

Iren hesitated, but then he halted his spell. "My queen?"

Aletas walked up to him, the Chloryoblaka gripped in her right hand. "What do you think?" she asked, a smirk reminiscent of Rondel on her face.

"Think of what?" Iren asked. "What's going on here?"

The queen's grin did not relent. "Don't you know? Maantecs never were bright. Come with me; I'll show you."

The queen led Iren through the woods back toward Lodia. The moment he reached the tree line, he gasped. All along the forest edge, he could see humans fleeing the forest. On their heels stampeded a horde of plants. Vines raced across the ground, whipping up and entangling foes. Briar bushes followed, slicing their enemies apart with spines. No matter how fast the men ran, the plants overtook them. Iren shuddered.

"Behold the power of Dendryl, the Forest Dragon. Ziorsecth will rise and defend itself when enemies threaten it," Aletas said. Her earlier smile had disappeared, and now not a flicker of enjoyment crossed her face. "This was my husband's favorite spell, and it's the reason the Maantecs couldn't invade Ziorsecth. I never thought I would use it."

Iren's jaw dropped. "You did this?"

Aletas looked ill. "Yes, and it's taken its toll. The Lodians are retreating not a second too soon. I can't control the plants any longer."

The queen dropped to one knee, panting, and Iren rushed to her side. At first she recoiled, but then her exhaustion caught up with her. She leaned heavily against him, permitting him to support her weight.

When the Kodama's breathing calmed a little, Iren glanced north toward Rondel and Amroth's location. The fires had disappeared, which he took as a good sign.

Aletas must have made the same determination, because she said, "I believe the battle is over." Relief poured from her voice. "If the fires are extinguished, Rondel must have won. I didn't expect her to prevail."

"That's proof you don't understand Rondel at all," Iren replied, though in truth he hadn't anticipated Rondel's victory either.

To his surprise, Aletas gave him a warmhearted smile. "Perhaps. Perhaps I misjudged both of you. You are like Iren Saito in many ways, but not in those that matter most. You fought valiantly to defend Ziorsecth, despite having nothing to gain by doing so."

Iren's cheeks reddened from a mixture of embarrassment and elation not just of victory, but of having Aletas accept him. Mostly so the queen wouldn't see him in such a state, he pointed his face away from her and toward the Lodian plain. A few enemy troops had escaped, but Iren doubted they'd attack again. Amroth himself couldn't make them reenter Ziorsecth, not after they'd witnessed ordinary weeds butcher their countrymen.

The ease of the Kodamas' victory amazed Iren. Just a few short hours ago, he'd huddled with his companions around a campfire, certain of failure. Now they'd achieved a miracle, and he barely felt tired. He'd hardly used any magic at all.

At that moment, without warning, a red glow bathed the landscape. Iren and Aletas turned to the north, the source of the radiance, and their jaws dropped. A mushroom cloud expanded from the field, rising over a mile into the air. Even from so far away, the heat striking the pair was so intense they both shielded their faces. Through his fingers, Iren saw the detonation's flames coalesce into a sight even more horrible. The base formed two legs with long, clutching talons. A pair of wings sprouted from the fire's midsection, stretching for hundreds of feet. Finally, at the top, a long, slender neck emerged, and atop it rested a head that narrowed to a single point, giving the entity the look of a giant, burning bird.

Aletas collapsed, her hands gripping the soil. She gasped, "Feng!"

Iren stared at the dragon too, a single word filling his brain. Ignoring Aletas, ignoring the promise of death that confronting such a foe represented, he shot toward Feng, that word howling from his lips.

"Rondel!"

CHAPTER THIRTY-TWO
Sacrifice

Pain.

That was Rondel's world. Burns covered her, and try as she might, she couldn't move. She lay face down, just inside the forest. When the explosion struck, the shockwave sent her flying through the air until she collided with a tree. Bones in her back shattered under the force of the impact, and she knew the blow had paralyzed her.

Just as bad, when she opened her eyes, she couldn't see. Even with Lightning Sight, her vision returned only white. The detonation's intense light had burned her retinas. Dimly, she could feel trickles of blood running from both ears down the sides of her face. Amroth's explosion must have deafened her as well.

No, she realized as fear took hold, not Amroth's. Feng's.

A slow sigh escaped Rondel as she resigned herself to death. No technique she possessed, magical or otherwise, could help her. Already she could sense Feng approaching, the withering heat of his flames increasing by the second. The temperature around her became unbearable, and she knew the Fire Dragon readied his deathblow.

It never came. The agony wracking her body proved that well enough. Instead, a soothing sensation ran through her head. A familiar voice whispered, "Don't try to move. I'm healing your wounds."

Her blind eyes futilely tried to catch a glimpse of her rescuer, the one who had restored her hearing. "Hey, slacker," she managed.

"Stay quiet, you stupid old hag; talking makes you die." The young man's tone was insistent but not panicked.

Rondel had no intention of obeying. With all her remaining strength she said, "Iren, listen to me! Your foe isn't Amroth anymore. I thought I could defeat him by making him exhaust his magic, but I fell right into Feng's trap. Without the third kanji circle to restrain him, he took advantage of Amroth's weakness to conquer the king's mind and force the transformation. Now Amroth is gone, and Feng has taken his place. We do not face a Dragon Knight, but a dragon! Feng must have planned this from the moment he tested Amroth. Hezna had the mental strength to resist wielding the Karyozaki unless absolutely necessary, but Amroth lacked the Oni's willpower. Feng knew he could take advantage of Amroth's desire for strength and control him. Now that he's free, the dragon will rampage until he destroys Raa. Do you understand? Don't waste your magic on me! You've got to save what energy you have to fight that thing."

A brief silence followed before Iren replied, "If you speak the truth, then all the more reason to heal you. I'd much prefer attacking him as a team."

Rondel felt tears on her cheeks, and she reached a hand up instinctively to wipe at them. She stopped short. A few seconds ago she couldn't move at all. Blinking several times, Iren's shape came into focus, and beyond him, a white, shimmering light.

The Storm Dragon Knight stood, fully healed. She marveled at her restored body, but Iren amazed her even more. Back in Veliaf, the child had passed out for hours after healing Dirio. Rondel's injuries made the foreman's seem minor by comparison, yet Iren remained on his feet, awake and unaffected by his use of magic.

In addition to healing her, the boy had also constructed a barrier of light that encircled them. Rondel reached out and touched it. It felt as solid as the firmest stone wall, yet it was barely an inch thick and easy to see through.

"I never taught you to create a shield," Rondel pointed out, stroking the barrier in awe.

Iren looked sheepish. "I didn't know I could do that until just now. Feng lunged for you, and I knew I had to stop him somehow. The light shot from the Muryozaki and surrounded us. Feng's been pounding on it ever since, but he can't get at us. I don't understand it, but I'm certain of that much."

The mention of Feng pulled Rondel from her fascination with Iren's new ability. Looking past the light, Rondel saw the Fire Dragon's birdlike form. The monster stretched high into the sky, a beast of flame. Jets of fire spurted from him at random, and he directed more than a few right at them. Each time, the shield's smooth contours easily deflected the flames.

"So, how do you want to fight this thing?" Iren asked.

Activating Lightning Sight, Rondel observed Feng's every detail. Dismay filled her, and she returned her vision to normal. "It's worse than I thought," she sighed. "On the rare occasions when a Dragon Knight has lost control in the past, the dragon transforms their body. We see that here with Feng. However, in every other case, the physical body has remained, so stopping the dragon simply requires knocking the body unconscious. That allows time for the dragon's will to recede into its Ryokaiten as the third kanji circle's spell takes effect. Unfortunately, the Karyozaki has no third circle to pull Feng's will back into the sword. To make matters more hopeless, the transformation completely obliterated Amroth's body. This monster is pure flame, so we can't hurt it. The only way to defeat it is to put it out."

Iren gulped, and Rondel understood why. They couldn't possibly extinguish such a massive inferno.

"Fires need three things to burn," Rondel continued, thinking out loud in hopes that a plan would come to her, "fuel, heat, and air. Remove any one, and the fire dies. In this case, the sky provides plenty of air, so that option's out."

"Then remove the heat!" Iren shouted. "Create a storm, just as you did in Serona! The rain will drench even that mighty flame."

She rolled her eyes. The boy may have come far, but he still had a lot to learn about listening. "Don't you pay the slightest attention? That spell nearly killed me, and I was in my prime then. I also had the Water Dragon Knight to help, and the spell did kill him. Alone, on a clear night like this, I couldn't make it storm enough to fill a bucket, much less drown that thing."

"Then how do we defeat it?"

Rondel grinned. An idea, a risky, desperate, totally absurd idea had finally occurred to her. "We remove its fuel."

Iren swept his gaze across the burning Lodian fields, his expression one of incredulity. The fires had already spread into the outer reaches of the forest as well. Between the dry plains grasses and the nearly infinite expanse of Ziorsecth, plenty of tinder existed.

In this case, however, that vegetation mattered little. "The fuel for that beast doesn't come from the plants," Rondel explained. "Look up there, at the place where the bird's heart would be. Can you see it?"

Iren strained his eyes, shielding them as he attempted to look into the core of the terrible flame hundreds of feet in the air. After a moment he shook his head and turned away.

Rondel activated Lightning Sight. "I feared as much. Unaided eyes can't pierce such distance, but mine can. At the creature's heart, the Karyozaki pulses. The portion of Feng that escaped into this world remains linked to the sword. That blade provides the true fuel, magical energy, needed to maintain the firebird. Separate the two, and the beast will lose its sustenance. It will burn through its magic in a second and destroy itself."

Iren gritted his teeth, apparently trying to think of some plan. "I know what to do," he said at last. "I'll use the same light beam I used when I lost control in the forest. If it could make miles of trees vanish, then it easily has the strength to dislodge that sword."

The boy had hit upon the same idea she'd come up with, albeit with one minor difference. "You could do that," she contended, "if you could see the Karyozaki. It will take precise aim to hit the sword from so great a distance. No, only someone with enhanced vision can see the blade and strike it reliably." She loosed a wild smile, more because she couldn't believe what she was about to say. "I'll do it. I might just have enough magic left for one full-sized lightning bolt. I'll need time to focus that much energy though, and Feng must not suspect our plan. He could easily dodge or block the attack if he anticipates it. Can you distract him long enough?"

Her request made Iren white-faced. She didn't blame him. Outside, the seemingly invincible Feng still pounded mercilessly upon Iren's barrier. Unlike before, however, the shield now flickered with each blow. Despite the child's progress, Rondel knew the shield's change indicated he couldn't maintain it much longer. "How much time do you need?" Iren asked faintly.

Her expression turned dour. "As much as you can give me."

Iren looked through the shield at the firebird towering thousands of feet above them. Rondel was thoroughly impressed when he replied with only the slightest waver in his voice, "You got it."

* * *

A final blast from Feng shattered Iren's barrier into a thousand shards of light. In that instant, the young Maantec leapt into action. Meanwhile, Rondel crept deeper into the forest and, Iren hoped, out of Feng's sight.

Stuffing his fear, Iren rushed headlong into battle. He charged across the plain, his Muryozaki awash with white light. Though he came barely past Feng's toes, he attacked with reckless abandon, slashing repeatedly at the flames. He thought he would cut right through them, but instead they resisted his presence. In response to each sword stroke, a blaze erupted from the impact site and chased after him. Soon his shirt smoldered. The Muryozaki kept him healed, but his strikes proved useless. He stood more chance of harming the ground.

His efforts did succeed in one way, however, and the one that Rondel had intended. Feng craned his head down and looked at the bug at his feet called Iren Saitosan. The monster crowed with laughter and then boomed in a crackling voice, "What is this? A second Dragon Knight comes to die?" He raised his enormous foot and stomped down on Iren, who just barely dodged out of the way. Even so, the waves of heat emanating from the firebird as his claws impacted the dirt sent the Maantec sprawling.

Feng laughed. "Not bad! How about this?" The dragon reared up, and from his chest two lanky arms sprouted, each tipped with giant hands and long, grasping fingers. The arms reached to the ground, and soon the battle devolved into a desperate struggle just to avoid getting crushed by Feng's feet or clenched in his fists.

Iren's movements gradually slowed. His arms and legs felt as though he'd chained one of Ziorsecth's trees to each limb. He couldn't last much longer. If Rondel didn't attack soon, they'd lose their chance. Feng would kill him, and then the beast would wipe out the forest.

In his exhaustion Iren tripped, and Feng seized the opportunity. Wrapping him in one hand, the creature lifted him into the air, cackling all the while. Even though Feng had no physical form, the fire exuded tremendous pressure, keeping Iren pinned. Burns covered him, and the intense heat quickly incinerated his clothing and wooden armor, leaving him naked. The Muryozaki tried to heal him, but it couldn't keep pace with Feng's magic.

Feng stared at him with hollow eyes on his birdlike head. "Iren Saito-san, how worthless your life has been."

Despite his pain, Iren glared at the beast, not wanting to give Feng satisfaction. His defiance only made the dragon angrier. "That won't do!" Feng cried, squeezing Iren until his ribs snapped. Iren howled, and the corners of his vision grayed as he flirted with unconsciousness.

"Better," the dragon said, his cruel beak twisting into a smile. "In return, let me tell you something as you die. Do you remember the night before your mission with Amroth, how he told you of your parents' murders? He hinted that the Quodivar leader killed them. You know better, though, don't you? You killed Zuberi, but he sated neither your bloodlust nor your desire for vengeance. Isn't that correct?"

Through the torture of his injuries, Iren spat, "What do you know? You weren't even there!"

The horrid smile filled with savage glee. "Amroth was my Dragon Knight, as was Hezna before him. I know what they knew. I know Zuberi was not the murderer, and I know that Amroth lied to you. He said he rescued you, but he did no such thing. He only decided to spare you at the last second because he realized he could use you to get revenge on Hezna. Do you understand now? Zuberi didn't kill your parents; Amroth did. He slew them both alongside Ortromp so he could get the credit for killing the Left and take over leadership in the Castle Guard."

"You're lying!"

Feng crowed. "It's why I accepted Amroth as my Dragon Knight! I looked into his heart and saw his hunger for power. He willingly killed others and tormented a member of his own species, you, for years just to increase his dominance. I could hardly ask for a finer knight."

Iren sobbed as Feng's words burned him harsher than any flame, but his tears evaporated as soon as they formed. Even after learning that Amroth had used him, Iren had still acknowledged him as the man who had saved him as an infant. That wasn't the case at all though. Instead, Amroth had manipulated him from the beginning, convincing him of a false revenge so that he would become the captain's weapon. Iren had accepted Amroth's lie wholeheartedly, even killing for the sake of it. The faces of those he'd slain floated past Iren's vision. All those battles, all those dead, had gained him nothing. At long last he knew his parents' killer, but he couldn't get revenge. Feng had already taken care of that.

The dragon tossed him down hard, and Iren smashed into the ground, bones breaking on impact. The landing jarred the Muryozaki from his hand, and it skidded several feet away. Iren tried to reach for it, but his limbs wouldn't respond. Desperately, he tried to think of a plan, but he came up with nothing. He could only watch as Feng's giant foot approached, ready to squash the last vestiges of life from him.

"Keep away from him!"

The female voice roared from just inside the forest, and suddenly a barrage of arrows pelted Feng's chest. Most fell uselessly to the ground or ignited the instant they touched him, but the distraction changed the beast's attention. Feng sent a jet of flame to halt the attack. The projectiles ceased for a moment, but then resumed from another part of the forest.

At the edges of his vision, Iren saw two people kneeling next to him. "Rest easy, Iren," one said, the familiar voice gentle like one of Ziorsecth's streams. "We'll take it from here."

"Minawë," he managed, but he could say no more.

She smiled, raised her bow, and began firing rapidly, running to make herself harder to hit.

The other person, Balear, knelt and wrapped Iren's charred form in a green cloak. "Your clothes got burned by that monster," the man explained. "The Kodamas gave me that cloak while we hid in the trees, but I think you've more use for it than I do. No offense, but your charred posterior won't make a great impression on your girlfriend. Oh, and by the way, you did great, Iren. I'm proud to call you a friend."

With that, the Lodian stood and fired on his former king.

The arrows continued to fly for nearly thirty seconds longer before Feng shouted, "Enough!" so loudly the tree leaves shook. Blazes erupted from him in every direction, and the screams of dying Kodamas reached Iren's ears.

Iren feared for Minawë and Balear, but he had little time to dwell on them. The red light from Feng's body suddenly vanished, replaced by a blue-purple flash that changed the landscape momentarily into brightest day. Iren smiled. Minawë's distraction had given Rondel enough time.

With a sharp crack that echoed across both field and forest, a bolt of lightning arced from just inside the woods and hit Feng. Iren knew right away that it had struck its target, because Feng roared a genuine cry of pain. The bolt knocked the glowing Karyozaki free from the dragon, casting it into the open air with a thin trail of flame following it. Joy filled Iren's heart as he waited for the fire to die.

As the seconds passed, however, Feng remained. Iren cursed silently. Even as Rondel's strike knocked the sword loose, the dragon had sent out a tiny burning tendril to follow it, maintaining the connection between the sword and his body.

Iren despaired as Feng simultaneously extended two great hands, the first to retrieve the fallen Karyozaki, and the second to annihilate the person who had dared to harm him. Iren's only relief was that he couldn't see

Feng strike his teacher dead.

"Now," the Fire Dragon growled as flames licked Iren's body, "for you." With each word, the earth vibrated.

Iren closed his eyes, accepting his fate, but then something odd happened. Feng had stopped speaking, yet the land beneath Iren continued to tremble. Deep booms echoed across the forest. Confused, he looked around as best he could. The trees themselves were moving. Their leaves shook as if in a storm, despite the windless night. The ground's tremors grew more intense, and Iren sensed that they came not from Feng, but from within Ziorsecth.

With a harsh grinding sound, the trees just north of Iren gave a great heave and pulled free of their roots, rising and moving of their own accord. Aletas, Queen of the Kodamas and Forest Dragon Knight, stepped into view. "Didn't I tell you, Iren?" she asked, though she kept her gaze fixed on Feng. "Ziorsecth will defend itself when threatened. While I draw breath, Feng will not step foot inside this land!"

The queen's level of magic amazed Iren. She'd looked exhausted after controlling the vines and shrubs to attack Lodia's army, yet she could still control these mighty trees as well. At first he couldn't explain it, but then he noticed how the queen stood. She held the Chloryoblaka in her right hand and had her left palm pressed against one of the nearby trees. At last, Iren understood. Back in Yuushingaral, Aletas had explained that Kodamas could replenish their biological magic by siphoning off other life forms. The queen wasn't using her own magic. Instead, she was channeling the tree's energy, and thanks to its shared root system, all of Ziorsecth's as well. In spite of his throbbing body, Iren felt relief. Feng couldn't defeat an entire forest.

Four broad maples charged the dragon, each over a hundred feet tall. Feng still dwarfed them, although they at least came farther up on him than Iren had. They struck at his legs, battering him with thick limbs like clubs.

Feng's new foes didn't bother him. "Wood?" he mocked, his voice reeking of contempt. "You send wood against the Fire Dragon?" With a casual raise of one arm, he set the four trees alight. They continued to smash at him valiantly as they dissolved into ashes.

More maples attacked the dragon, but his flames destroyed each one. Aletas next sent vines tunneling through the ground, having them rise up and wrap around Feng's legs in an attempt to immobilize him. The plants withered and died the moment they touched his scalding surface.

Still Aletas did not relent, and Iren began to question the queen's strategy. She had to know those plants stood no chance against Feng, yet she persisted anyway.

A few minutes later, Iren got his answer. The booming and tremors from earlier grew greater and greater, and they came far more rapidly. A strange sloughing sound joined them as well, and Iren had the impression that something enormous approached them. Aletas smiled mirthlessly. "You lose, Feng."

With a final wrenching screech, the monstrosity within the forest burst onto the plain. Iren gaped. Standing toe to toe with Feng was the largest tree he'd ever seen. It stood at least as tall as the monstrous dragon, and its limbs stretched farther than Feng's wings. Iren couldn't believe a plant could grow so large, but then he remembered Minawë telling him of Ziorsecth and how it was really a single tree with many trunks. The Heart of Ziorsecth, the central pillar from which the forest originated, was the greatest tree ever to sprout.

Looking at it standing firm against Feng, Iren believed it.

The Heart of Ziorsecth swung one mighty limb and smashed Feng in the head. For the first time, Iren saw the dragon stumble. Flames licked at the Heart's branches, but their thick bark refused to burn.

"Aim for the sword!" Iren choked out. "That's his power source!"

Aletas nodded her affirmation, and the Heart focused all its effort on Feng's chest. It bashed and battered, and finally the dragon fell. The tree swung its largest branch straight down on the Karyozaki, but at the last moment, Feng twisted away. The monster screamed his aggravation. Apparently, he hadn't expected a plant to outclass him. He closed his wings around himself and tucked his head in, seemingly trying to protect his sole vulnerable spot.

All at once, Feng erupted in a giant mushroom cloud. The explosion knocked Aletas, standing over a mile from its epicenter, to the ground. The Heart of Ziorsecth evaporated.

Iren had a recollection of Minawë's room. Aletas had spoken of her vision about a firebird and the Heart of Ziorsecth engulfed in flames. It had come to pass.

Before Aletas could rise again, the dragon lunged forward and seized her, lifting her high into the air and beyond the forest. Removed from her source of power and overcome by the exhaustion of using so much magic, Saito's curse afflicted her in seconds. Through Feng's grim red light, Iren saw the queen's hair turn from green to shining white. When the last hair changed, Feng casually tossed her limp body back beside Iren. She fell to the ground without the slightest resistance, her face so withered she made Rondel look youthful. Emptiness and terror filled Aletas's unblinking eyes. Iren had no doubt.

The queen was dead.

Feng had defeated them. The Kodamas' bows no longer fired, and first Iren, then Rondel, and even Aletas, with all the might of Ziorsecth behind her, had fallen.

He wanted revenge. He wanted to make Feng suffer. Try as he might, though, Iren couldn't make his body move. His vision faltered, and he slipped into unconsciousness.

From somewhere in the shadows, he heard a voice call, "Slacker!" He groaned. Rondel had decided to haunt him from beyond the grave. Wonderful.

"If you want to defeat him," she cried, her words echoing from the past, "then put forth some real effort! You can't win if you constantly hold yourself back and give up when you find a problem difficult!"

"What do you expect me to do, you brainless old hag?" Iren cried inside his mind. "I can't move!"

"Remember!" Divinion's voice, gentle yet with a force to shake all of Raa, boomed from the darkness. "Commit to what's most important. You did it for Minawë when you brought her to Ziorsecth. You can do it here, too."

Iren's anger swelled. "But what's most important? What good would knowing that even do? I'm about to die, and so are my friends. I can't do anything—"

He stopped. His friends? Throughout his eighteen-year life, he'd never befriended anyone. He'd lived alone in the Tower of Divinion. People had called him a monster, a Left, and he'd taken out his frustration and sorrow on them until he became the very devil the bigoted Lodians claimed he was.

Divinion, though, had looked at Iren and not seen a monster. He'd seen the lonely boy Iren himself refused to recognize. He'd rescued Iren from the depths of his self-made prison, and thanks to Divinion's help, Iren had found friends. Flashes of faces came to him. Dirio. Balear. Aletas.

Rondel.

Minawë.

"What's most important?" he'd asked the Holy Dragon.

Now he knew.

His eyes snapped open, and with a surge of effort, he reached out his hand and clasped the Muryozaki. Its healing power washed over him, and he stood and marched onto the plain.

Feng beheld his final enemy and chuckled. "Not dead yet, Iren Saitosan? I'm impressed you can still move. You've come for revenge, no doubt."

Iren met the abomination's gaze without a trace of fear. "No," he replied calmly. Though he did not speak loudly, his voice carried across the landscape so that all heard it. The forest itself shook under the weight of his words as he said, "I don't care if Amroth used me, or if he killed my parents. I don't care about revenge. Right now, I only care that I have friends depending on me. I swear that I'll protect them!"

All at once, blinding light erupted from him in a great tempest, engulfing him. It condensed around his body, solidifying into a gleaming full suit of armor, white with blue streaks and made of the same material as the Muryozaki. The brightness then focused on his back, and as Iren yelled defiantly, two radiant wings of light sprouted from either side of his spine.

CHAPTER THIRTY-THREE
The Wings of Dragons

Rondel tried to stand, but even breathing hurt. She supposed she should feel grateful she could breathe at all. Her three cracked ribs and shattered right arm and leg, however, made it hard to see the bright side of her situation.

She sat with her back against a tree, panting as she frantically tried not to black out. She'd put everything short of her biological magic into that lightning bolt, leaving her helpless against a retaliatory strike. Had she possessed any sense at all, she would have let Feng kill her. Instead, survival had intervened. Instinctively, she'd drawn a miniscule amount more of Okthora's magic, just enough to grant her a little extra speed.

Using that magic, though, had been more damaging than anything Feng could throw at her. Already she could feel Okthora's will brushing against her own. If she lapsed, even for a second, he would rip control from her.

"Come now, Rondel," a tantalizing male voice whispered inside her mind. "Would I really do something like that to you?"

She spat blood. "Yes, you absolutely would, Okthora."

The dragon's smooth voice became affronted. "Really, Rondel, you should think better of me. I merely wish to talk. I so long for conversation. After all, the last time we spoke was the Battle of Serona, correct? It's been a thousand years."

"Another thousand would have been too soon," she growled.

A burst of white light filled the plain, interrupting their conversation. Rondel beheld Iren shining with two brilliant wings on his back. Though initially gratified to see the boy alive, her expression quickly darkened.

"No!" she cried. "Iren, you fool!" The boy had used too much of Divinion's magic. Even if Okthora didn't take over her body, Raa would soon have two unstoppable monsters to deal with anyway. Their inevitable duel could level the continent.

Inside her mind, Okthora chuckled. "It isn't quite that bad, you know."

"What are you talking about? Iren's turning into a dragon!"

"Actually, the opposite is happening," the Storm Dragon replied. "Iren isn't turning into Divinion. Divinion is turning into Iren."

Rondel scoffed. "Impossible."

"You know that using my magic requires a contest of wills between us. Draw a small amount, and you easily win. Draw more than you possess, and my will breaks yours and takes over your body. That happened to Amroth, unleashing Feng. But what would happen if you had a will so resolute, so unyielding, that I couldn't break it, even if you drew more magic than your body could handle?"

Rondel's breath caught. "The Dragoon…no, that's just a theory. Every Dragon Knight arrogant enough to attempt that transformation failed. Besides, I never spoke of it to Iren; I didn't want to tempt him. How could he succeed where so many others failed without knowing what he was doing?"

"That I cannot answer," Okthora conceded. "I can say this much, though. Whatever Iren is fighting for must be very important to him."

As Okthora spoke, Rondel gazed in wonderment at Iren. Despite the absurdly bright light emanating from him, she didn't need to shield her eyes. Rather, a great sense of calm flowed from the glow. Iren stood there, toe to toe with Feng, and Rondel knew the young man felt no apprehension. She couldn't believe it. "Okthora," she asked, "just what is happening to Iren? What does it mean to become the Dragoon? If he isn't transforming into a dragon, why did his body change at all?"

The Storm Dragon laughed. "No one can channel that much magic without changing. When a knight becomes the Dragoon, their mind remains in control, but they acquire wings, as well as armor forged from the dragon's scales. The Dragoon is the Dragon Knight perfected. It has all of the dragon's power without any loss of control."

At these words, Rondel grew puzzled. "Why are you telling me all this? Had you kept it secret, I might have despaired to the point that you could wrest control from me."

"I considered that," the dragon admitted, "but you know my law. Evil must be annihilated. I dislike Kodamas and Maantecs, but I hate Feng. He is a perversion of what the dragons are supposed to be, and he must be punished. The Dragoon is our best chance of stopping him. The boy doesn't need any distractions from me. Besides, I can already feel the Storm Amethyst tugging at my will. I probably couldn't overcome you now if I tried. Next time, though, I won't go so easy."

Gradually, Okthora's presence faded from Rondel's mind. When she was certain he couldn't take over her body, she turned her full attention to Iren. With the smallest of motions of his right hand, the Dragoon sent a wave of light rippling behind him into the forest. It filled the woods, briefly brightening Ziorsecth's understory to the level of a desert at noon. It collected on Rondel, and a brief tingling sensation swept her body as her shattered bones knit themselves together.

The young man next stretched his wings to the sky and, with a glance toward the heavens, took flight, shooting into the air at such a pace Rondel could barely track him.

Rondel heaved herself to her feet. As Iren climbed ever higher, she couldn't help taking a step forward and saying, "That's the way, Iren. Go; fly on the wings of dragons!"

* * *

Iren didn't have a clue what had happened to him, but that fact didn't bother him. Every movement felt natural, no more unusual than walking or speaking. He didn't concern himself with the knowledge that he could fly, or that he had healed, in an instant, the wounds of every living thing in Ziorsecth within ten miles of his location. All he knew was that he had to protect those important to him, and that meant stopping Feng.

For his part, Feng expressed no concern at Iren's transformation. No doubt the dragon believed that since he'd swatted this insect once, he'd easily do so again. Without any effort, Feng sent a jet of flame at Iren, engulfing the Maantec. The dragon sneered, "Perfect shot!"

When the smoke cleared, however, Iren remained unfazed, not a scratch or burn on him. His armor absorbed the heat without difficulty, and inside Iren felt perfectly comfortable.

Focusing magic on the Muryozaki, Iren launched himself at Feng. With a single swing he slashed through the dragon's left shoulder, his magic forming a blade that extended beyond the sword's tip. Feng's arm separated from his body and fell, extinguishing itself before it reached the ground.

Iren comprehended in a flash. Without its connection to the Karyozaki, the fire couldn't survive. He readied for a second strike, but without warning the dragon regrew his lost arm. Grabbing Iren's leg, Feng swung him in a broad arc and then hurled him through the air. He struck the plain at immense speed, leaving a crater where he landed. Even so, he got back on his feet in seconds, uninjured.

"Divinion," he shouted, "I thought that would work! I severed his arm; how could he make a new one?"

"Arms and legs belong to the flesh," Divinion explained. "Feng is pure flame. He only has arms and legs because he chooses to have them. As long as the fire exists, he can change its shape however he wishes. Moreover, he can move the Karyozaki to any point on his body."

The dragon's voice echoed inside Iren's brain. Ever since the Dragoon transformation, as Divinion had called it, the two of them had become partner minds. Iren gritted his teeth. "So the only way to stop him is to put out the entire flame all at once?"

"So it would seem."

"How do we do that?"

The dragon thought for a moment, then replied, "I have a plan."

Divinion relayed his idea, but Iren shook his head. "He'll never fall for that."

"You survived two of his strongest attacks, and you're the only obstacle left in his path," Divinion pointed out. "He won't let you escape."

"I hope so." Iren fired a tight beam of white light at Feng's left leg, just like what he'd used to strike Rondel during their training in Ziorsecth. The attack cut through the limb, severing it as the beam pushed the air away. The dragon toppled precariously, but then he just created a new leg and regained his footing. Iren surrounded himself with a shield of light and took flight once more, this time heading not only up but also north, away from the battlefield.

"Coward!" Feng bellowed, but Iren didn't change course. In response, Feng spread his wings and shot into the air, chasing Iren at full speed.

Glancing behind him, Iren yelled, "Well, we got his attention!"

Divinion's voice stayed calm, "Keep on this route, and don't let him fall too far behind."

Higher and higher Iren climbed, until the trees of Ziorsecth looked like blades of grass. All the while flames scorched past him. The better-aimed bursts hit his shield and deflected, but each impact jarred the barrier. As Feng's rage grew, so did his power.

After a few minutes, the flames striking the shield abruptly stopped, and Iren halted his flight. A moment later, Feng loosed a terrible cry. Iren whipped around. To his amazement, the Fire Dragon was shrinking. Already the head and upper torso had vanished. Iren smiled. Divinion's plan had worked.

At this altitude, the Holy Dragon had explained, there was no air. While Iren's bubble of energy contained enough for him to breathe, Feng had no such protection. Without air, the Fire Dragon's flaming shape couldn't burn.

As the fire shrunk, the Karyozaki responded, sinking lower in Feng's body. At last it rested at the bottom of the infernal monster's toe, and Iren knew it was over.

The last flames, however, did not extinguish. Inside his mind, Iren felt Divinion's annoyance. "The toe must be just low enough that is has enough air to continue burning. Quickly, fire a beam and destroy it!"

Iren never got the chance. Its tiny flame keeping it alive, the Karyozaki abandoned its quarry and plummeted to the ground. As it fell, the fire rekindled, and from that remnant, the firebird returned.

"I'm sorry, Iren," Divinion said.

"He won't make the same mistake again," Iren pointed out. "Now that he knows the limits of his flame, he'll stop before he gets this high. He's also likely realized that he doesn't have to come get us, either. We'll have to descend soon, or I'll suffocate."

"What do you propose, then?"

Iren had no answer for the dragon. Still, he couldn't abandon his friends. As long as he continued living, he would never stop fighting this beast. He must come up with something. He had to win! If only he could force Feng back to this altitude! He wracked his brain but couldn't think of a way to do it. Despite the immense magic the Dragoon form gave him, creating and sustaining a bubble large enough to trap Feng was beyond him. He felt certain he could make one, but extending his energy out that far would weaken it tremendously. Feng could easily breach it.

Seeking inspiration, he surveyed the world far below him. From this height, he could see nearly all of northern Raa. To his horror, as he beheld Lodia, he noticed dots of flames in a rough line running east to west across the landscape. Amroth's army must have pillaged their way across the country in order to maintain their supplies. The demented king had come to Ziorsecth to incite a tragedy, but he had done that in his own lands long before reaching the forest.

At the limits of his vision, Iren spotted the eastern ocean that bordered Lodia. He fantasized that he could see the Tower of Divinion, his residence for so many years. He wondered if the Holy Dragon's painting still remained after Haldessa's destruction, and whether he would ever see it again. His whole life, he'd tried to get away from that place. Now, he had an odd feeling of nostalgia. For all its prejudices against him as a Left, Lodia still deserved protection. It deserved better than Feng.

As he floated there at the edge between air and space, the first stretches of dawn appeared far to the east over the ocean. The sun cast forth its tendrils over the darkened world. Iren marveled at the way the light spread, pushing away the darkness and replacing it with the hope of a new day.

Immediately, he knew what to do.

"Iren, you must descend," Divinion warned. "Your air supply has nearly gone."

He had already begun to drop. As he plummeted, he released his shield and took a deep breath, savoring the crisp autumn air. Feng sent a torrent of fire blazing at him, but Iren dodged it nimbly. He careened around the monster, flying at a dizzying speed. Undeterred, Feng shot wave after wave of flames, filling the sky with their blistering heat, crimson glow, and choking smoke. Two miles above the ground, the fires detonated all around Iren, but he didn't retaliate. Instead, he merely spun in ever tighter circles, the Fire Dragon at their center. All the while he kept his attention focused solidly on Feng, his expression locked in concentration.

After several minutes, Iren's speed dropped. The Dragoon armor, which previously had felt all but weightless, grew heavier with each passing second. The wings on his back flickered; even the legendary Dragoon's magic had limits. He was almost out of time, yet he couldn't quit, not yet.

His wings flashed once more, then vanished, sending Iren hurtling toward the plain. His armor remained intact, but he knew it had only a few moments left. Seeing Iren fall, Feng crowed in victory and sent one of his arms surging forward, snatching Iren from midair around the chest. The dragon pulled Iren to his mouth, the flames adopting a smug expression.

"All that effort, all in vain," Feng laughed. "You never attacked me once!"

Iren didn't look upset that Feng had captured him. He stared passively at the monster poised to end his life. Then, he flashed his own rendition of Rondel's signature grin. "Naturally," he replied. "Did you think I performed all those aerial acrobatics for nothing? I needed time to create this." He opened his clenched right fist, and from it floated a tiny, glowing white orb, no larger than a cherry.

Feng sneered, "What do you plan to do with that, poke out my eye?"

The Dragoon kept his smirk but didn't respond. Sure, it looked tiny, but that was only because he had it under extreme pressure. All the time he'd spent spiraling around Feng, he'd fed both his own and Divinion's magic into it. Now all his energy was in there, and he was using only Divinion's power to contain it. If his link to the Holy Dragon broke, he'd have nothing left to hold the ball together.

Iren closed his eyes, remembering when he'd lost control in Ziorsecth. He recalled the sucking sound as air rushed to fill the vacuum the blast had created. At the time, he'd hated himself for causing such destruction. Tonight, though, he'd make good use of that experience.

His eyes snapped open, and he stared without fear at his enemy. "Feng, you made one critical error tonight."

"Oh? What's that?"

"When you grabbed me, you didn't trap my hands." With that, Iren opened his left hand, and the Muryozaki, his sole connection to Divinion, dropped into open space.

As soon as sword and hand separated, the tiny orb, freed of its magical constraints, erupted. The detonation happened in an instant, stretching out a mile in all directions. It exploded high enough that it didn't reach the ground, but its shockwave snapped tree limbs and knocked everyone below off their feet. The discharge engulfed Feng's body. As the air around him vaporized, his inferno fizzled out in a puff of smoke.

Iren's vision briefly glowed white as the blast ignited. "For you, Minawë," he whispered. Then all went dark.

CHAPTER THIRTY-FOUR
A New Heart

Rondel had decided. No music on Raa could match the beauty, or the sadness, of Kodaman funeral hymns. Their melodies, played on simple wooden flutes, wound their way through the forest, and the plants and animals all vibrated in sync with their lilting tunes.

A month had passed since the battle, and the leaves of Ziorsecth's maple forest gleamed yellow and vibrant red. On this breezy afternoon, they cascaded like rain. As they landed, they filled the ground with their soft touch and brilliant color that contrasted perfectly with the gray-stemmed trees that created them. Truly, even the finest gold and jewels could not equal their splendor, much less their sorrow. For with each leaf that descended, Rondel felt the forest crying as it buried its dead.

Despite the grim circumstances that brought her here day after day since returning to Yuushingaral, Rondel never ceased marveling at the location: a gaping hole in the earth five hundred feet wide and over two hundred deep on the edge of the Yuushin Sea. Scattered maples dotted the crater's edge, and swaying grass and wildflowers filled the space between them. Simple wooden markers, thousands of them, covered the grove.

This was the Heart of Ziorsecth, the sacred place of the Kodamas.

Rondel stood behind Minawë, who knelt on the ground, openly weeping before a pair of graves. To honor Rondel's valor in both the Kodama-Maantec War and the battle against Amroth and Feng, Minawë had granted the old Maantec a unique privilege. She was the first non-Kodama to behold this place. Rondel understood why the Kodamas shunned outsiders from it. She could feel the weight of the lives of every fallen Kodama here, and she found their legacies heavy indeed. This race had suffered more than any other on Raa, and they deserved it least of all. They could live perfectly content passing a quiet existence beneath the trees.

Four hundred of the wooden markers bore green vines adorned with white and purple flowers, indicating those who had fallen in the recent battle. Rondel had attended every burial. These dead represented over two thirds of the Kodaman force gathered and just under half the entire population. Though Rondel took pride in shielding herself behind a mask of sarcasm and laughter, even she couldn't help but mourn at the sight.

Saddest of all was the new Kodaman queen crouched before her. Minawë stroked the board in front of her with her long, gentle fingers, tracing the carved letters that bore the fallen's name. Opening her mouth as if to speak, she could not form words, and her hand dropped from the marker amid fresh sobs.

Uncharacteristically, Rondel hesitated. She and Minawë had spent the past month here, never once returning to Yuushingaral. Minawë came to these two graves every day before dawn, and she never left them until well after sunset. Each day Rondel tried to comfort her, to say something to her, but she never could find the words. At last, this day, she forced herself to speak, "They both fought to protect you, to the very end."

Minawë craned her neck around, revealing her tear-stained face. Rondel placed a wrinkled hand on the Kodama's shoulder. The gesture felt forced, but she couldn't think of anything else. In many ways, despite Minawë's age, she was still a child. Aletas had raised her sheltered beneath Ziorsecth's canopy, oblivious of the outside world. The Kodama-Maantec War had ended before she was born, so she'd never experienced real danger or grief until recently. The last six months, Rondel knew, had shaped this Kodama more than all the rest of her thousand years combined.

The two women remained in that position for a few seconds before Minawë rose to her feet and resumed staring hard at the graves before her. They continued standing in silence for several more minutes before they heard a voice call from behind them, "Hey, did you miss me?"

The pair faced the newcomer, and in an instant Minawë's grieving face blossomed into a mix of joy and astonishment. Balear emerged through the trees, flanked by two Kodamas, but none of them had spoken. The voice belonged to the fourth among them - weak, shaky, and leaning on Balear's shoulder.

It was Iren Saitosan.

With a knowing expression, Rondel watched as Minawë ran across the open space, wrapping her arms around Iren in a tight hug. The old Maantec followed at a methodical pace.

"Moron, you had us worried!" Minawë exclaimed, and she gave him a playful flick to the forehead.

"I told you he was lazy," Rondel chimed in. "Look at him, first time out of bed in a month! Hey, slacker, did you even bother to wash before coming here?"

Iren flushed. "You should all act a bit nicer to me, you know. I didn't plan on waking up at all. I still don't know what happened, or how I survived. I couldn't get out of bed in Yuushingaral until this morning. Do you know I've had to spend the past month with only Balear for company? He wouldn't tell me a thing about the way the battle ended, the tight-lipped jerk. Also, you should taste his cooking. Disgusting!"

Balear made an indignant noise and faced Iren, their noses almost touching. "Hey, I'm the one who dragged your sorry backside all the way here to see these two. Show a little appreciation! Besides, you can't blame me for not telling you what happened. I don't understand it myself. I told you what I do know already. I saw the explosion, with you at its center. Feng disappeared, and I thought for sure you had died."

"I think I can answer some of your questions," Rondel interjected. "What you unleashed surpassed any spell I've seen, even at the height of the Kodama-Maantec War. In fact, it not only defeated Feng, it destroyed the Karyozaki." She reached into the pocket of her shirt and pulled out a large, bright red jewel. "This is all that remains: the Burning Ruby, the gem that imprisons Feng. As for how you lived when even the Karyozaki met its end," her tone became grave, "you should find the nearest clear pool of water and examine your reflection."

Iren reached a hand up and felt his face. The moment he did, he recoiled. "What happened to me?"

"You're still eighteen years old, but you look in your late twenties. In those final moments after the explosion, you used some of your biological magic, or rather, Divinion used it for you. It saved your life, but it also aged you ten years."

"How could Divinion do that?" Iren asked. "I released the Muryozaki."

"Yes," Rondel agreed, "but part of his will temporarily remained inside you. With no other magic to draw on, he used your life's energy to maintain the Dragoon armor both during the blast and afterward, when you fell. The Dragoon armor is made of dragonscale, Divinion's in your case. Prior to his imprisonment, the Holy Dragon's hide was impervious to all forms of magic, so his armor protected you from the blast. It also absorbed the impact when you hit the ground, which would have killed you as easily as the explosion. You should see the crater you made sometime. It's quite impressive."

Iren felt his face again, this time holding his hand there as he stroked his month's growth of beard and more refined jaw. He ran his fingers through his hair, noting how short it had become.

"The first time Feng captured you, he burned your hair off and left you bald," Minawë explained. "Actually, I think you look a lot better now without that raggedy mop on your head." She smiled and winked at him.

Iren flushed. Clearly anxious to change the subject, he turned to Rondel and asked, "What happened to the Muryozaki? It could have healed me immediately, yet here, a month later, I can barely get out of bed." He gestured at the Burning Ruby in Rondel's palm, abject grief on his face. "Based on that, I suppose I already know."

Rondel threw her arms in the air. "I swear, will you ever get better at listening? Honestly, students today! Pay attention!" She lifted back her cloak. To Iren's obvious bewilderment, she revealed the katana, fully intact, sheathed at her hip. "Didn't you ever wonder what the white metal the Muryozaki is made from is?" She paused for effect. "It's dragonscale. This sword predates the dragons' imprisonment. Thousands of years ago, Maantec smiths crafted it from one of Divinion's scales. The Holy Dragon provided the flames for the forging process. Just like your Dragoon armor, magic has no effect on it. According to Maantec history, it took nothing less than the Holy Diamond itself to engrave the kanji circles in the blade's hilt. Once that was done, the sword absorbed the diamond of its own accord, as though desiring to reunite the dragon's flesh and soul."

She removed the sheathed Muryozaki from her belt and offered the blade to Iren, who took it and held it close. He gripped the hilt, waiting for its healing power to take effect. As time passed, however, his expression grew unsettled. He shouted, "It's not working! What's wrong?"

"I'm sorry, Iren," Rondel said, "but that's why I kept that sword with me instead of letting you have it back right away. I feared this might happen. The amount of magic that the Dragoon form channels is extreme. Maantec bodies, indeed the bodies of any race save the dragons themselves, aren't designed to handle that much magic flowing through them all at once. It could have killed you. To protect your life, once the Dragoon form ended, your body severed its connection to all exterior magic. Without that link, you can't use magic, even from the Muryozaki. It could take years to heal, if it ever can."

Though she had not intended to do so, Rondel realized she had struck the man a hammerblow. Iren cradled the Muryozaki like a dead infant. "I can't believe I'll never see Divinion or hear his voice again, and that I've aged ten years overnight." He stroked his new, unkempt beard. "I've never had facial hair before. This will take some getting used to."

Minawë laughed clearly, the first time Rondel had heard her do so since the battle. "You should feel lucky that's all that changed about you, moron. You could have ended up as withered as Rondel!"

The playful taunt broke Iren's somber mood. Everyone laughed except Rondel, who gave a loud, resentful snort. "How ungrateful!" she cried, acting deeply offended for a few seconds before chuckling despite herself.

As the group's fit subsided, Balear took a few steps back. "Well," he said, a definite note of hesitation in his voice, "now that Iren's doing better, I should get on my way."

They all stared at him. "On your way?" Iren asked. "To where?"

"Where else? Back to Lodia."

Rondel grew stern. "Balear, I'm certain Amroth made news of your betrayal public. Wanted posters of you probably hang all over Lodia. If you return there, don't expect a warm welcome. At the very least, they'll shun you. More than likely, they'll try to execute you."

Balear set his jaw. "Lodia is my home. I can't abandon it."

Minawë spoke up, "You defended my people in battle. You've beheld the Heart of Ziorsecth. By the customs of the Kodamas, you are one of us. You'll always have a home here, if you want it."

Rondel nodded her affirmation. "Take some advice from an old woman who knows. At the end of the war, the traitor is the only person left without a home to call her own. You won't get many invitations like Minawë's. Don't pass it up lightly."

"I do not," Balear replied, unwavering, "but I must see this through. Thousands of my fellow Lodians have died, and many of our villages lie in ruin thanks to Amroth's brief yet all too lengthy reign. The country will no doubt enter a period of weakness and turmoil. Maybe you're right, and they will kill me for returning. Even so, I'm a knight of Lodia, first and foremost."

The former general turned to Iren. "I think I understand you a little better. Now I know what you suffered, abhorred by the very people you wanted to recognize you. I fear my reception in Lodia, but what I learned from you gives me hope. This world has things worth risking your life for."

Iren put out his hand and said, "Commit to what's most important."

Balear smiled and took Iren's hand. "I promise I'll do just that. I'll bring peace to Lodia, and not the 'peace' Amroth sought, using force to crush all resistance. I'll bring a genuine peace, where Lodia and its neighbors forge new alliances better than our old ones, and where we replace mistrust and ignorance with knowledge and understanding."

Minawë beamed. "I see that Amroth's crimes do not represent Lodia's true character. For centuries, my people have avoided humanity, but who knows? Perhaps you shall lead our nations, Balear, on the path to mutual understanding between Kodamas and humans. Please return and visit us."

"When I restore peace in Lodia, you may count on it."

The new queen turned to the two Kodamas who had escorted Iren and Balear and asked them to lead the Lodian back to his country. The trio departed eastward.

When they fell from sight, Rondel gave a little cough. "I guess that means I'd better head off too."

Iren turned in shock to face her. "What do you mean? You're not staying in Ziorsecth either?"

Rondel grunted. "Do you have any idea how much of a pain you've made my life these past six months? You know, I led a pretty leisurely existence for many years before you and Amroth arrived on my doorstep. Then I had to go and decide to teach you. Pretty soon, I'm fighting for my life against bandits, Yokai, Oni, and even a dragon. And what reward do I get out of it? I have to deal with some slacker with an attitude!"

Scowling, Iren replied, "I see you're still the same stupid old hag you were when I first met you stumbling out of a horse stall."

"Respect your elders!"

"Be kind to your student!"

"Brat!"

"Fogey!"

The pair gave a loud "Humph!" and then refused to look at each other. After several seconds, though, teacher and apprentice simultaneously began cackling so hard tears formed in their eyes.

Minawë turned her head back and forth, alternately focusing on Rondel and Iren, clearly confused.

As their laughter ended, Rondel walked over to the pair of graves she and Minawë had visited every day since the battle. She raised her right hand and formed the Kodaman friendship gesture, saying seriously, "Aletas, in the end, you lived up to Otunë's legacy as Forest Dragon Knight. I'm glad you two can rest together in this place. You have much to be proud of. You defended the Kodamas, and you raised a fine daughter." She cast her eyes at Minawë, who, along with Iren, had come to the graves as well. "Make sure you take care of this boy, Minawë," she gestured at Iren. "He's utterly incapable, you know."

The Kodama nodded sadly but didn't respond.

Suppressing tears, Rondel left the graves and took a few steps into the forest. Over her shoulder, she waved. "Take care, slacker," she said.

"See you, old hag," Iren replied. Rondel could hear his voice catch.

When she'd just about reached the limits of where she knew the others could see her, Iren suddenly called to her, "What about your nightmares? If you leave me, won't they make you unable to sleep?"

She craned her head around to face him, answering confidently, "I'm not concerned. I think they just wanted to tell me something. It took me longer than it should have, but I finally heard the message." She gazed through the canopy at the patches of sunny sky beyond, and then, without another glance back, disappeared into the forest.

* * *

For a few minutes Iren stood there, unable to tear his eyes from the spot where Rondel had vanished. Finally, Minawë shook her head. "She might be crazy, but I'll miss having her around."

For the first time since Rondel announced her departure, Iren remembered that Minawë stood right next to him. He gave her an odd look, but she dismissed it with a wave.

"Never mind," she said in answer to his expression, chuckling.

Iren looked over the graves before them to the gargantuan crater that dominated the scene. "What will happen to Ziorsecth?" he asked. "You told me the forest is a single tree, originating with the Heart. With the Heart gone, will Ziorsecth die too?"

Minawë replied, "Without Ziorsecth, the Kodamas would all perish.

But Ziorsecth will outlive us all. True, the forest is one plant, but plants and animals are different. If you remove a limb from a tree, that tree will still grow. The same holds true for Ziorsecth. It will draw from its countless stems, and that energy will birth a new Heart of Ziorsecth." She pointed to the crater's center. "Look down there, if you doubt me."

Iren stared hard. At first he saw only brown earth, but then, at the center of the crater, he noticed a flash of green. A foot-tall seedling had sprouted from the soil.

"Ziorsecth's Heart is already reborn," Minawë said, "and aided by the forest, it will grow rapidly. One day, this harsh scene will again become the glorious sacred grove of my people. Besides, it has more than just the forest to help it. Come with me, and I'll show you."

Together the pair made their way into the crater until they stood beside the new Heart of Ziorsecth. Iren gasped. Next to the seedling lay the Chloryoblaka.

"After the battle, Rondel wanted me to take Dendryl's bow and become the Forest Dragon Knight. I refused. Mother didn't want that power; she took it because she had no other choice. I want to honor her decision. Besides, with Feng defeated, the Kodamas don't need a Forest Dragon Knight. Here, perhaps its magic will flow into the earth and aid the Heart of Ziorsecth's growth. I hope it can remain here until the Heart's trunk buries it, and it forever becomes part of the forest itself."

Iren knelt before the Chloryoblaka, honoring the sacrifices of those who had carried it into battle. After a moment, an idea came to him. Standing, he pulled the Muryozaki from his belt and laid it alongside the bow.

"What are you doing?" Minawë asked.

"You heard what Rondel said. This sword is useless to me now. Let it stay here too, and maybe it can also aid the Heart's recovery."

Minawë hugged him. "Thank you, Iren."

The pair lingered beside the Heart for a few more minutes before making their way up the far side of the crater, Minawë helping Iren negotiate the steep slope. When they reached the top, they both collapsed from exhaustion on the rim, overlooking the Yuushin Sea.

When they'd caught their breath, Minawë put her hands under her chin and said, "You know, my people call this place sacred, but I don't see it that way. I feel no joy here, only sorrow and loneliness."

She peered over her shoulder at her parents' graves in the distance.

"We Kodamas have never been numerous, and Ziorsecth is vast. Defending its borders spreads us thin. Rarely do we gather, and when we do, it's more often for grieving than for celebration. I never knew my father; he died in battle before I can remember. Mother, though, was always there for me. I never felt alone as long as I knew she was nearby. Now she's dead, along with so many others, and you and everyone else are leaving too. I can't bear the solitude."

With a long sigh, Iren asked, "What are you talking about, moron?"

Minawë crossed her arms. "Who are you calling a moron, moron?"

Iren rolled his eyes. "Who said I'm going anywhere?"

She looked shocked. "Aren't you going back to Lodia? To your home?"

He shrugged. "I don't have a home in Lodia. The only place I ever lived was the Tower of Divinion, and I don't know if that still stands. Even if it does, I can't call it a home. I hated every minute there. Frankly, nothing remains in Lodia for me. I'm not like Balear. I made no oaths to king and country." He gave her a wry look. "Besides, I have a far more important promise to keep."

Minawë raised an incredulous eyebrow.

"Don't you remember?" he asked. "Just before the fight against Amroth, you called to me, 'When we win this battle, let's go home to Yuushingaral together!'"

A wide grin filled her face, and joy enveloped her until her radiance surpassed any light Iren had created as the Holy Dragon Knight. Excitedly, she leapt to her feet, saying, "Iren, ever since you came here today, I've wanted to tell you something." She held out her hand.

"Welcome home, Iren Saitosan."

For a long time he couldn't answer. His heart thudded as it never had before, even in the deepest, most desperate throes of battle. He breathed deeply, his lungs filling with the satisfying combination of loamy scent from the woods behind him and the salty air of the ocean waves breaking below him. At the last, he took Minawë's hand, pulled himself to his feet, and kissed her softly. As they separated, he gazed deep into her emerald eyes and replied, "Yes, I am home."

ABOUT THE AUTHOR

Josh VanBrakle is an unrepentant lefty who is overjoyed to live in an age when authors can type their stories instead of handwriting them. His love of fantasy and science fiction, kindled by *The Lord of the Rings* and *Star Wars*, led to a dream of publishing a novel that refused to let itself get pushed aside. A late-bloomer to writing professionally, Josh first trained in forestry and economics. In his day job, Josh works for an environmental non-profit promoting rural land conservation. Originally from Hershey, Chocolatetown USA, Josh now lives in the Catskills region of upstate New York with his wife Christine and their two ill-behaved cats.

The Wings of Dragons is Josh's first novel, so if you enjoyed reading this book, please visit its page on Amazon.com and leave a review! Share what you loved as well as what can be improved. Josh reads every review and strives to incorporate those comments to help him grow as an author and make his future books better.

To stay up to date with the latest news about Josh's upcoming titles in *The Dragoon Saga*, please visit www.joshvanbrakle.com.

www.ingramcontent.com/pod-product-compliance
Lightning Source LLC
Chambersburg PA
CBHW022201170626
46807CB00005B/2304